Portia Da Costa is one of the most internationally renowned authors of erotica.

She is the author of seventeen *Black Lace* books, as well as being a contributing author to a number of short story collections.

D1637890

Also by Portia Da Costa

The Accidental Series:
The Accidental Call Girl
The Accidental Mistress
The Accidental Bride

Gothic Series:
Gothic Blue
Gemini Heat
Gothic Heat

Novels:
Hotbed
Shadowplay
The Tutor
Entertaining Mr Stone
Continuum
Suite Seventeen
Hotbed
The Stranger
In Too Deep
The Gift

Short Stories:
The Red Collection

Entertaining
Mr Stone

PORTIA DA COSTA

BLACK
LACE

1 3 5 7 9 10 8 6 4 2

First published in 2006 by Black Lace, an imprint of Virgin Publishing
This edition published in 2014 by Black Lace,
an imprint of Ebury Publishing
A Random House Group Company

The Random House Group Limited Reg. No. 954009

Addresses for companies within the Random House Group can be found at:
www.randomhouse.co.uk

A CIP catalogue record for this book is available from the British Library

The Random House Group Limited supports The Forest Stewardship
Council® (FSC®), the leading international forest-certification organisation.
Our books carrying the FSC label are printed on FSC® -certified paper.
FSC is the only forest-certification scheme supported by the leading
environmental organisations, including Greenpeace.
Our paper procurement policy can be found at:
www.randomhouse.co.uk/environment

Printed and bound by CPI Group (UK) Ltd, Croydon, CR0 4YY

ISBN 9780352340290

To buy books by your favourite authors and register for offers visit:
www.randomhouse.co.uk
www.blacklace.co.uk

This one's for the two Vs.
Valerie, critique partner extraordinaire,
and the magnificent Vincent, who
breathes life into Clever Bobby Stone.

Contents

Prologue — 1

1 **The Borough of the Damned** — 9

2 **Collision Course** — 22

3 **It's true! It's really true!** — 39

4 **Summoned to the Presence** — 53

5 **The Director's Preference?** — 68

6 **Taken for a Ride** — 78

7 **Right Here, Right Now** — 99

8 **Show and Tell** — 113

9 **Out to Lunch** — 130

10 **Crush** — 142

11 **Wuff! Wuff!** — 157

12 **Uh oh! Busted!** — 173

13 **A Cunning Plan** — 187

14 **Payback's a Bitch** — 200

15 **Mentor** — 218

Epilogue — 234

Prologue

I'm staring at the door again. That big old looming great door that leads to his office.

It's huge and there must be half an oak tree there, with all sorts of knots and whorls in it, all polished to within an inch of someone's life. Two of the knots look exactly like a pair of eyes, and they're watching me. Staring me down, the way he does.

Somewhere in my innards I start to quiver. Oh, hurry up, you bastard! I can't wait any longer. Buzz me in!

As if he's read my mind with his voodoo mentalist powers or something, there's a sound like the squawk of a giant mechanical bird, and Mrs Sheldon, his PA, says, 'You can go in now, Miss Lewis.'

She gives me a kindly, clear-eyed smile, the old dear, and nods.

She hasn't the faintest idea what's going on, bless.

Now the moment's come, I'm both terrified and so excited I've almost forgotten how to put one foot in front of the other. It seems to take about a year actually to get to the door, and when I get there, my feet glue themselves to the carpet for a while.

Robert Stone, CPFA, Director of Finance.

I have a mad urge to kiss the nameplate, but I resist. Mrs Sheldon might start to suspect something at last if I start doing weird and worshipful things in the outer office. Better save those sorts of activities for the inner sanctum.

A firm, resonant voice calls out 'Come!' from beyond the whorly wood.

Oh shit! I've kept him waiting. I'm in for it now. Or at least I hope I am.

With a moist shaking palm – and some moist shaking in other bits of my anatomy – I twist the big brass door handle, push open the door and sidle inside.

He's on his feet, which throws me. And I stand there like a twit, just gaping at him, while he turns away from the window that looks down over the courtyard. I wonder who he's been watching. He likes to watch, and in this mad place there's often something going on that's worthy of his special and unusual attention.

But I'm woolgathering. I should be concentrating. He's looking at me. Waiting for me to say something. But unfortunately I'm gob-smacked. As usual.

The Director of Finance. Stone. *Mr* Stone. Clever Bobby. Whatever.

Well, he's a tall man, and imposing. Not fat exactly, but no Greek god either. Just an average-looking, middle-aged, slightly greying, five o'clock shadowy (he says he has Italian ancestry), suit-wearing local government bigwig.

Theoretically, he's the sort of bloke you wouldn't look twice at in a crowd, especially if there was plenty of younger talent around. But in practice, well, he makes my knees disintegrate and this yearning, gnawing sensation start up somewhere around where I think my heart is.

I'm just about to topple over when, thank Christ, he says, 'Take a seat, Maria.'

I take one. It's the very plain hard chair, a few feet from the front of his desk. I don't feel any better at all because I know this chair of old.

'So!' he says, sounding quite bright and perky as he leans forward, his palms on his desk for a moment, supposedly studying some papers spread out over his blotter. The sudden movement stirs a whiff of Mr Stone smell – a mix of Dior and just a hint of not unpleasant late afternoon sweatiness – and I have to concentrate really hard not either to topple off the chair or crawl across the room on my hands and knees and press my face against his nether regions.

'Your latest performance review,' he continues, giving me a look like the devil. He's really trying not to laugh, because basically this is all bullshit. The person who's supposed to do reviews is Mr I'm-so-trendy, designer-wearing, one-time arch nemesis, full-time bisexual William Youngblood, the Human Resources supremo. And, what's more, Stone put me through one of these same 'reviews' only four days ago.

'Leaves a lot to be desired, doesn't it, Maria?' he says, as if I've any idea what's written on the paper in front of him. Raising his eyebrows, he pushes himself upright again quite quickly, snatches his stainless-steel rollerball from the desk and twirls it in his fingers. He has this way of being both nervy and totally relaxed and in control all at the same time and it's bloody disconcerting. He comes across like some naughty, overgrown imp about to play a trick on me.

I swallow. Oh, the tricks.

'Nothing to say?'

My mouth is dry. I'm suddenly impatient with all this poncing about. I wish he'd get on with it.

'I—'

Voodoo ray style, he reads me.

'Are you wearing knickers today?' he asks in the same tone of voice he'd use if he was asking me to get on the Intranet and call up some council house income stats for him. He flings down his pen again and moves quickly round to my side of the desk – light on his feet for a big man – to stand before me, reaching down to lay his hand lightly against my cheek. His skin isn't soft like a pen-pusher's. He's a man of action, although he doesn't do sport. He just plays games.

Still, I've lost my tongue somewhere.

'Knickers, Miss Lewis?' he prompts, fingertips still against my face. They're only blood heat, naturally, but it feels as if he's branding me.

'Um ... yes.'

'Yes what?'

'Yes, Mr Stone, I'm wearing knickers.'

His fingers slide delicately across my face, and for a moment his thumb settles on my lower lip. When he withdraws it, he studies the trace of clear lipgloss that clings to his skin, then seems to zone out for a moment. Maybe it's a make-up ad fantasy? Kate Moss pouting for Britain. I don't know.

Then, 'Details, Miss Lewis, details!' He's brisk as he whirls away again and goes back to the window.

'They're pink ... er ... cotton and Lycra. They're a thong, actually.'

I stutter and choke on the words as if he's asked me to reel off a whole string of the foulest, most depraved obscenities. Which he has, as good as, for the purposes of this entertainment.

'A thong, eh?' He leans against the window jamb, looking out again, bracing himself with one arm raised, elbow crooked, cradling his head.

He's having the time of his life, as he always does.

'Not really appropriate for work, that, is it?' he queries, not looking at me. He doesn't need to. He's seen every inch of me in Technicolor close-up, plenty of times. He could probably draw a picture of my sexual topography if he wanted to. And he might actually want to, one of these days.

'I don't suppose so,' I mutter. The garment in question is rapidly becoming pretty sticky, and I'm filled with a sick, almost head-spinning urge to show him. I want to feel ashamed and grovelling. I want to crawl on my belly for him. Do anything. Expose anything. Endure anything.

'Better take it off then, hadn't you?'

Yes!

I start to wriggle on my seat and fish around under my skirt but, before I've made any headway, he's watching me again, bitter-chocolate eyes intent and rather bright. He's smiling with them, even though his stubbly face is perfectly straight.

'Not like that, Miss Lewis. Stand up. Lift your skirt.'

I obey, hauling up the cotton fabric, although to be honest I don't have far to haul it as it's rather short. Something else that's inappropriate for work, even if it's entirely appropriate for entertaining Mr Stone.

I'm not very graceful when I'm nervous, and I scuttle and hop as I step out of my thong. I'm probably getting a black mark for that too. With no instructions as to what to do with the thing once I'm out of it, I just stand there, thong in hand, still holding up my minuscule skirt and blushing furiously. I daren't look at my prize, but know they're moist, to put it mildly. I can smell myself (and I'm pretty ripe because it's been a long day waiting for this) and I'm sure he can too.

He nods towards his desk, but I play dumb. He raises his eyebrows like some playful demon and my sex clenches.

'On the desk, please, Miss Lewis,' he directs as if it's a folder full of fiscal projections.

Both my ears and my clit are pounding by now. Semi-manufactured embarrassment and total horniness in equal measures. I spread my little thong out neatly in the middle of his blotter, just the way he prefers, sticky side up.

He folds his arms.

He unfolds them and then rubs his bristly chin.

He paces up and down behind his desk, head cocked, perusing my offering.

He pauses, taps his pursed lips with his knuckle, nodding.

Boy, is he making a meal of it today!

He crosses his arms around his body, looks first at the crotch of my knickers, then at my face, and goes, 'Hmm...'

Not once yet has he looked at my bush, which is still in plain sight beneath the hiked-up hem of my skirt.

'Pretty conclusive evidence,' he observes, in a passable impression of my favourite television detective, who I've told him more than once he resembles.

For several minutes, he just stares at the manifestation of what he so effortlessly does to me, as if seeking the meaning of life in that dark pink diamond shape.

Just when I think I might pass out, he moves towards me. The smell of Dior and the wolfish tang of perspiration grows stronger, and without thinking I breathe in deep. He watches the lift of my breasts beneath my top as he stops, just inches from me, but doesn't yet touch me.

'So,' he murmurs again, head tilted to one side, all nervy again, yet somehow also less fazed by the situation than I could imagine any other man in the world would be.

I'm still holding up my skirt with one hand, but the other just hangs down at my side as if I have no bone, no muscle tone to support it. It stays there when he reaches down summarily between my legs and begins to manipulate me.

Touchdown, the crowd goes wild! Or at least all the nerve-endings down there do. The ones that have been screaming for just this delicious bit of business since before I even arrived in the outer office. I start to make little gasping, grunting noises, and to wiggle my hips to his rhythm, but he shakes his head slightly, and goes 'Uh oh!' beneath his breath.

I bite my lip, and his eyes narrow and go all sultry and heavy-lidded, the skin at the corners of them crinkling in a way that's both boyish and indicative of the grip of middle age. My arousal ramps up another notch just from that one single thing.

It's hard to stand up and it's hard to stand still. I feel as if I'm in some weird place that's a million miles away from the Director of Finance's Office in Borough Hall. I'm in some parallel universe with new rules and new people. I'm fighting to control every muscle in my body, and there's a little wetness slipping down the inside of one of my legs.

And still he fingers me.

'I think I might fall over,' I gasp, in an odd, light, high-pitched voice that doesn't sound a bit like me.

'Well, hold on to the chair, you silly girl,' he chides, increasing his rhythm, getting a little bit rough.

My clit sings, gathers itself. I grab on to the chair back with my free hand. He continues to rub, his own free hand hanging loosely at his side, quite relaxed, as if unconnected with what's going on down below.

And then I come. Come in massive wrenching waves, and his free hand isn't unconnected any more because it's around me, cradling and supporting me when I can no longer support myself.

'Oh, Bobby,' I whisper, completely out of it, but he doesn't chide me for my impertinence. He just holds me for a little while longer while I descend again.

But he's hard. Very hard. I can feel it jabbing into my bare thigh, through the cloth of his trousers. And a moment later he hustles me towards his desk and drapes me over it face down.

There's a rustle, and the familiar music of a very

smooth-running, expensive zip whooshing down. A hand presses on my back, flattening me against the blotter, and against my own fragrant, incriminating knickers, then the same hand manhandles my thighs apart and prises open my sex.

'Oof!'

The air rushes out of me as his cock rushes in, and as he begins to thrust, hard, he mashes my clit against the desk.

I come again, and I'm seeing stars.

Oh, Clever Bobby!

1 **The Borough of the Damned**

Another day working in the Borough of the Damned. I've only been here an hour and I'm bored out of my mind.

I glance up at the clock and it's like we're in one of those Fifties psychological B-movies, and the second hand is crawling at quarter speed. I look around the room and we're still in the 50s. Massive old desks, a great big marble fireplace, discoloured magnolia wash on the walls – where you can see it for project planners and dog-eared information posters – even potted plants on the window-sill. It's as if someone had to sell off their unwanted mansion or something, and a whole bunch of us local-government office drones, complete with our various accoutrements, have been beamed in to take up the space. The only signs of twenty-first-century progress are the VDUs with their floating, bobbing Borough-coat-of-arms screensavers, and their keyboards and assorted peripherals and other gubbins. And the cabling that Health and Safety have supposedly checked and approved, but which isn't safe at all. The prospect of seeing somebody I don't particularly like trip and go arse over tit is one of the few bright moments in my day.

Sigh.

This is a crap job, but I suppose I should be grateful. With a CV like mine – questionable to the point of non-existence – I'm lucky to be working at all. I still can't believe they offered me a post, but against the odds and all the laws of reason they did, and I accepted. And now I'm here.

But I'm bored, bored, bored.

Suppressing the urge to lay my head down on the desk amongst the assorted paperwork and have a snooze, I apply myself to filling in codes on forms for Small Business Loans. I really have no interest in what I'm doing, and I'd far rather speculate about the lives of my work colleagues. Or at least I would if the ones in my immediate vicinity were even the slightest bit interesting. Unluckily for me, they're all depressingly diligent and into their work. But still, the evil sex pixies of my imagination can't help extemporising.

I wonder if Sandy's getting any? And if so, how much? Her boyfriend Nigel, who works in another section of this godforsaken department, looks as if he might be a bit of a cocksman, but she's too prissy looking and self-consciously nice for me to imagine them getting up to anything exciting. He probably has to fill in a form in triplicate if he wants to get his leg over. She looks up and gives me a puzzled smile, because I'm staring at her, and I try to picture her on her hands and knees while Nigel gives it to her, doggie style. Interestingly, she's still wearing her prim white shirt and her grey pencil skirt, pushed up to her waist to reveal a pair of slutty red split-crotch panties.

Wild!

'Are you okay, Maria?' Sandy asks, looking a bit spooked, as if she's seen what I'm seeing.

'Yeah, fine, thanks,' I answer, plastering on a bright team-player smile and putting my head down again.

But the damage is done now. Those pixies are really on the case and I can't seem to resist the erotic thoughts. Damn! It's bad enough working here in the desert of not getting any, without my overactive imagination tormenting me about it. I haven't had a boyfriend since I left London and, because I'm supposed to be economising to pay off my debts, I've actively resisted going out anywhere to look for another one.

Consequently, no sex. Which I didn't think was bothering me. Well, not any more than my trusty Magic Rabbit can accommodate. But now it seems that it is. Worse luck.

Unable to summon any enthusiasm for loan forms, I gaze upwards. If only I could see what was happening in the offices across the central courtyard. There might be all manner of funky stuff going down. I've been told that despite its stuffy, dusty, thoroughly repressed facade, Borough Hall is a actually steaming hotbed of horny licentiousness, but I can't say I've seen the evidence of it with my own eyes yet. Unfortunately the windows in these ground-floor offices are high, and I can only see obliquely into offices on the second and third floors across the way. A couple would have to be bonking on the actual windowsill for me to see them from this angle.

Fifteen minutes pass. I drift into a coma. And then Sandy says, 'Fancy a walk? These timesheets need taking to admin.'

It's minion work, but I smile and leap up cheerfully. Anything to break the tedium.

Outside, clutching the timesheets, I opt for the scenic route, which means promenading all the way round the four sides of this humungous old warren of a building instead going directly to an office which is only actually a few doors away. I can always say I called for a pee.

There's not much to see, though. The wood panelling, though surprisingly well polished, isn't particularly interesting to look at, and the paintwork above it is the same uniform shade of grimy dun as the offices. The whole place needs jazzing up a bit. Or burning down.

Maybe I should suggest a makeover to my new boss, Mr Stone, the Director of Finance? Not that a lowly cockroach like me gets to speak to 'the exalted ones' all that often. Frankly I'm amazed that he interviewed me in person in an establishment that's as hung up on hierarchies and pecking orders as this one.

But he did. And it was weird. Him and the Human Resources guy, William Youngblood, the head honchos of their departments, conducting the interview of a temporary, supernumerary Clerical Assistant, Grade 2. I would've thought that they'd have plenty of mid-range bods to do a job like that. Let's face it, I'm only one of the department's bottom feeders.

When I've dumped my timesheets in an office that's no more exciting than my own, apart from a few people standing round swearing at a Xerox machine that's spewing paper out as if it's possessed by the devil, I decide to treat myself to an extended side trip.

I'll go and see Mel.

Mel's an acquaintance. Well, more like a friend. I think. I don't know. I haven't actually known her that long and I'm not quite sure what to make of her yet. But suddenly I think it would be nice to see her.

You could say that she and I live together, although that's not exactly true. We actually have flats in the same house, but I didn't realise that until I met her, quite by accident, elsewhere. I was browsing in the market round the corner, looking for some sensible work clothes on a factory seconds stall, when I stepped back into the light to see whether a basic black skirt I wanted to buy was in fact basic black, and not cheap, institutional navy. There was a bump of bodies and I knocked into her and the carton of coffee I was carrying in my free hand went all over her jacket.

Auspicious meeting or what? If the roles had been reversed, I might have flipped, and got cross and told her to bloody well be careful, but she just said 'No problem. Let me buy you another coffee. I know a place just around the corner.' As if it were her fault. Which it wasn't.

What I didn't realise at the time was that she was trying to pick me up.

Luckily, when I reach the main entrance foyer, Mel is in her little security cubby-hole, just where I've been hoping she'd be.

'Hiya, soldier, how's it hanging?' I greet her, feeling a little bit nervous, and she turns from hanging keys on a pegboard to give me a sexy once-over. I can see she appreciates my shortish skirt and my tight little embroidered cardi and camisole. (I never actually bought those sensible work clothes after all, and until somebody calls me on it, I'll take my chances with what I've got!)

Mel looks pretty hot too. Boy, does she love that uniform! Dark blue shirt (with epaulettes, no less), tie, crisply pressed pants, Doc Martens polished like mirrors. It plays right into her army bitch/policewoman fetish. All she needs now is handcuffs, a long-handled night-stick and a piece!

She's a dyke, of course.

'It's hanging okay, babe,' she answers with a wink, stepping out into the foyer. 'How about you?'

Mel works shifts, and has an active social life as far as I can tell, so I don't really run into her that much around the house. This is the first time I've seen her in several days. She's at Borough Hall for seven, on her Kawasaki, while I've started getting lifts in with Greg, a guy who also has a flat in the house with us.

'I'm bored out of my mind, Mel. When's all this hot action you keep telling me about going to start?' I joke, referring to her own joke, when she originally told me that this job was about to come up. It was that first day when we were chatting in the café and, for no apparent reason, I'd just spilled my life story in addition to my cappuccino. 'I haven't seen anything juicy at all yet. And it's not for want of looking!'

I pout a little. It's fun to flirt, even if I'm not sure whether I'll be able to follow through on it. For a moment, I remember the sudden realisation – which came not long after the job news – that Mel was a girl who liked girls. I thought (and almost said!) 'Wow! A lesbian, that's interesting.' I'd never had any openly gay friends before, not even at Uni, but I'd always wondered if I could fancy a woman.

I can tell she likes me. She makes no secret of it. And, to be honest, I *am* tempted. Quite a bit, in fact. I've never been with a woman, but there's a first time for everything. And Mel is desperately cute in that outfit with her short-cropped blond hair and her fresh rosy complexion.

'Be patient, love. You'll happen on something when you least expect it,' she says sagely, all the time looking as if she'd like to make some of that action happen right now, there in the cubby-hole behind us. I feel a twitch of reaction, a definite frisson, and I'm almost on the point of opening my mouth again and saying something really stupid, when we hear the sound of raised voices coming to us from down the long diagonal corridor to our left.

Two men are approaching, deep in conversation, and even from a distance it's obvious they don't like each other very much. They're not shouting, they're not gesticulating, but there's antipathy coming off them in waves and crashing right over me and Mel.

The shorter guy is William Youngblood, the Borough's Human Resources Manager, who is seriously cute. Lean, blond, very groomed and urban in a dark suit, dark shirt and tone-on-tone dark tie. My totty detector goes 'Ping! Ping! Ping!' like active sonar.

But the other man. Oh, the other man! With him it's 'Battle stations!' and the siren's whooping. 'Dive! Dive! Dive! ARROOOBAH!!!!'

Mr Robert Stone. Director of Finance. The top of my particular food chain in Borough Hall.

By the book, Youngblood should be the more fanciable. He's younger, prettier and cooler. But Mr Stone beats him hands down in the expert opinion of my hormones.

Yet I can't explain why.

He's middle-aged, actually quite grey at the temples, big and kind of stocky. His complexion is a tad on the swarthy side, and he almost always looks as if he needs a shave, even at 9 a.m., when he sweeps in, his long dark overcoat flying, while I'm loitering around the time-clock, just hoping to catch a glimpse of him passing by.

My daily fix.

Compared to smooth, sleek Youngblood, Stone is Mr Average, just a chunky managerial bloke in a suit. But every time I look at him both my autonomic nervous system *and* my nether regions go on red alert.

To put not too fine a point on it, I'd give him one!

Though they're actually barrelling quite smartly along the corridor, we're back in the B-movie slo-mo phenomenon from the office again. I've no idea what they're at odds about, but Youngblood looks mad as hell. And even madder for the fact that Stone isn't showing *his* annoyance at all, even though I can somehow sense he's just as pissed with Youngblood as Youngblood is with him.

Stone's only give-away is that he's tapping his fingers on the edge of the leather document folder he's carrying. And yet my Scooby sense where he's concerned tells me that this particular bit of nonsense is more about winding Youngblood up than an expression of his own nervousness or stress.

As the two bear down on us like a pair of municipal Reservoir Dogs, I realise that I'm standing around in the foyer, just doing nothing and making the place look untidy. At least Mel is actually supposed to be here, on duty.

I babble something like 'Thanks for letting me know about that. I'll pass the message on.'

Mel says, 'No problem' in an official-sounding voice, even though she's actually grinning at me out of the eye-line of the two big chiefs.

Now, to speak or not to speak? That is the question. Theoretically the Borough is a progressive, open-door-policy, equal-opportunities kind of employer, not a feudal demesne. But some of the youngest school leavers daren't even utter a syllable in the presence of the head honchos, and try their best to blend into the panelling whenever the likes of Stone and Youngblood pass by.

Me, well, I'm a bit older and I've been around men a bit more, so I smile brightly and say, 'Good morning!' in their general direction, as they draw alongside us.

Youngblood gives me a grudging nod and doesn't break his stride.

Mr Stone, however, stops, right in front of me, and favours me with a slight smile, followed by an unashamedly quantifying look. The whole sequence lasts less than a second, and I might even be imagining it, because his expression barely alters from sober and serious. But somewhere in the back of his eyes there's a twinkle, a kind of spark that says, 'Watch out, little girly, you don't know the half of it!'

It's like being thumped in the solar plexus. That, and feeling as if his hand has just slipped inside my knickers!

My mouth drops open but, before I can say something irredeemably imbecilic, he answers, 'Good morning, Maria. Settling in OK?' His head cocks to one side in a birdlike expression of genuine or cleverly bluffed interest. His fingers are still tap, tap, tapping against his document case, but now it's me he's playing games with because I'm drowning deep in my masturbation fantasy and that long forefinger of his is the one that's doing the business.

'Yes, fine, thank you.'

I sound like a robot, but there's nothing robotic about my eyes, which defy all logical control and drift downwards towards the crotch area of his charcoal-grey suit trousers.

Moron! How could I possibly have imagined that a hawk-eyed guy like Mr Stone wouldn't notice that unsubtle manoeuvre? And he most certainly has, because the slight smile is a good deal less slight now, and he shakes his great head infinitesimally and almost but not quite laughs.

'Excellent!' he says roundly. 'Well, must be off. No peace for the wicked. Nice to know you're happy here.'

With that he turns quickly and with an elegance you wouldn't expect in a big, beefy guy, and strides off toward Youngblood, who I come out of my stupor to realise is standing a few yards away, looking impatient and even more miffed than ever. Then he too shoots me a look, antagonistic but in a strange way also quite sexy, and the two of them waltz off, resuming whatever the highpowered squabble was that they'd been embroiled in when I first set eyes on them.

It's all over in about half a minute but, as the two men disappear around the corner, Mel laughs softly and observes, 'Uh oh, it looks like Clever Bobby likes you.'

She's right. I think. Unless my finely honed instincts are deceiving me. I've always been able to tell pretty accurately when a bloke fancies me and, at the risk of sounding clichéd, there's definitely 'chemistry' between me and Mr Stone. Not that there's much chance of being able to do anything about it. He's my head of department, and I'm the newest and lowliest of his many employees. The sediment in his pond.

But that doesn't stop me fantasising.

I've never been with a guy that big. He's both tall and stocky with it. Is his dick in proportion? I muse. I imagine him on top of me, inside me, overwhelming me with his flesh while his bright, clever eyes bore into my soul.

Snap!

I jump when Mel clicks her fingers next to my ear.

'Hey! Where were you?' She grins at me as I transition back to reality. 'Away with the fairies? Or was it with our esteemed Director?'

'How did you guess?'

'You've got that starving-castaway-eyeing-up-a-fish-and-chip-supper look,' she says sagely, as usual summing things up more tellingly than I ever could.

'Yeah, he's quite something, isn't he?'

It's a surprise when she agrees.

'But he's not your type, obviously.' I narrow my eyes, studying her. Is there something I've missed? Have I read her wrong?

'No, but I can still see the attraction on a purely scientific basis. He's big, powerful, impressive, and he's got status.'

But it's more than that. She knows it. I know it. I'm just about to launch into a debate about the real reasons why a woman might want to shag the Director of Finance when the Borough Hall clock boings out the hour and I realise just how long I've been out of the office.

'I'd better be on my way or Sandy will send out a search party,' I say, rifling through a sheaf of pathetic and implausible excuses for my long absence. 'See you ... er ... sometime.' It's a bit awkward, living near to someone yet in some ways inhabiting an entirely different planet.

As I flip my fingers at her, Mel darts forward, and right out of the blue, plants a quick kiss on my cheek. I'm so flabbergasted for a moment that I completely forget to look around and see if anybody's watching us. Fortunately, there's no one else in the entrance hall, but immediately my mind throws out Mr Stone, complete with that flare of secret amusement in his eyes.

You'd love that, wouldn't you? I say to him in absentia.

I bet you like to watch. I bet it really gets your rocks off.

So I have two things to obsess about and speculate on for the rest of the day.

1. Having sex with Director of Finance Stone.
2. Having sex with a woman, i.e. Mel.

Great! Either way I'm in trouble. If I attempt to make a move on Mr Stone, there's massive potential for screwing up a job that I really need, and I might not easily get another. If I make a move on Mel, I might end up in a hugely embarrassing and stupid situation if I don't actually like girl-on-girl action when it comes down to it. It wouldn't be the first time I'd thought I fancied something, or somebody, only to realise I was so, so wrong.

It's a lose-lose, lose-lose situation. Because, basically, I *do* want them both.

Needless to say I'm making plenty of mistakes on the loan application forms, and if I don't shape up I'll probably get the sack anyway. It's a merciful release when Allsopp, the 'grey man' who's in charge of our section, tells me I'd better take an early lunch, then maybe come back with a sharper, clearer mind?

Not much chance of that, but it's such a relief to get out of the office again that I favour him with my best smile and assure him that he's 'so right' and I'm sure I can do better this afternoon. Not too sure I like his slightly over-enthusiastic reaction to this (not *more* complications!) but, what the hell, I'm out of jail, if only for an hour.

It's raining outside, and the streets are slippery and even greyer than usual. Not for the first time, I wonder what I'm doing back in this town, but then I remind myself that I'm skint, and it's a lot cheaper to live here than a big city. And somehow 'grey' here seems welcoming and familiar and rootsy, whereas in the metropolis it's just cold and rather frightening on your own.

Still, it's actually quite cold here today, and the chill and the wetness quickly seep through a mac that's designed more to be looked at than to serve any practical purpose. I scuttle into the Cathedral Shopping Centre and promise myself that there'll be no actual shopping, just looking.

The shops are tempting though. M&S, BHS, Body Shop, Miss Selfridge. But, in my new spirit of sensible spending only, I resist the expensive designer sandwiches in Marks and settle for a cheese-and-pickle from The Butty Bar, and, as a special treat for my frugality, I allow myself a celeb mag in W.H. Smith.

I take a quick scan of this as I hover just inside the Centre's automatic doors, hoping the rain will abate. It's all the usual stuff, mindless really, but I can't stop being fascinated in a watching-a-car-wreck way. Here they all are, the usual mix of pop stars, footballers, footballers' wives and people who are famous only for being famous, like reality-show contestants. I remember my own brief and equally meaningless fifteen minutes of fame when I appeared in mags like this for a week or two while I was dating a man who had a bit of a profile.

But nobody would remember me now, I decide, grimacing at my reflection in the glass, especially the image of my soggy mac and my bedraggled hair. I'm just a moderately pretty blonde with a half-way decent figure, and a smile that was always nervous for the camera. A common phenomenon in mags like these, and as instantly forgettable and throwaway as they are.

Uh oh! Potentially gloomy thoughts! I banish them and smile at my own reflection. Not nervously, because despite the rain, the greyness and the less than stellar job, I'm glad to be back. Home.

And there are other compensations, I think, my mind

flicking back to the images of Stone, and of Mel, and suddenly seeing them both as delicious challenges to be relished, not possible problems.

Go girl!

I stride out into the rain.

2 **Collision Course**

Another day in paradise? I think not.

But today I do have a certain special little something to brighten the boredom. I found it yesterday afternoon, while rummaging around in the office when all the others were out. It's the most unlikely masturbation aid you could imagine, but here it is.

A tiny photograph. Clipped from the Staff Association magazine. It's only black and white, but it's enough. It's an image of our esteemed Director of Finance, Robert Stone.

I smooth my finger across it, trying to iron out the crinkles I made in it while stuffing it in my pocket when Sandy came back from wherever she'd been. It's just paper, but I get this weird, weird frisson as if I'm touching the man himself, slowly caressing that rounded, dark-stubbled jaw. He's actually smiling in the photo, and it's a warm, natural, unaffected smile as if someone's just said, 'Hey, Bobby! Smile for the camera!' and he's turned around, caught unawares, yet untroubled by being photographed. His eyes are a bit scrunched up, because it must have been sunny, but it shows his teeth, which are scarily white and even in an almost Hollywood way.

Bobby.

Clever Bobby.

I like that nickname, because he *is* clever. Obviously blindingly intelligent to have got where he is and be in a position of authority, but also clever in a quite different way. A way that I don't quite understand on one level, but which I know in my gut on another. It was shining in his eyes yesterday, in the entrance hall, and I fancy I've seen it every time we've ever run into each other, starting at that brief but unexpectedly successful interview that he and Youngblood conducted.

He does fancy me. Mel's right. He fancied me right out of the gate.

Hah, getting ideas above your station, Maria Lewis, I chide myself. But I can't stop gazing at the little picture and trying to fathom what's going on behind that deceptively sunny smile.

I'm still worshipping my icon when Sandy dashes in and I secrete Mr Clever Bobby Stone under yet another depressingly thick pile of Small Business Loan applications that I'm supposed to be processing. How many of these poxy little companies is the Borough dishing out the Council taxpayers' money to, I wonder. Then instantly lose interest again as I've far more compelling topics to ponder upon.

I don't know whether it's because I've been fantasising about Stone, or just because I'm so desperately waiting to sniff out some of those secret sexual shenanigans that Mel told me about when she first gave me the nod about this job, but on a closer look at Sandy I think she looks decidedly furtive. And excited. And sexy.

Sexy?

As a rule, Sandy's anally tidy, but right now her hair is sticking up slightly at the back, and there's a definite pink flush to her pale cheeks. She's biting her lips too, and keeps touching her fingertips to the corners of her mouth as if she's been eating something and she's worried about crumbs or residue of some kind.

Maybe she has been 'eating' something?

Suddenly I'm grinning like the Cheshire Cat.

Oh my God, has Sandy just nipped away to give Nigel a blowjob?

Surely not? She's so prim, so law-abiding, the very last person you'd imagine as a secret fellatio slut!

But still, her eyes are bright, and she keeps looking around, as if she's terrified somebody will spot something untoward about her appearance. I catch her eye, and as if to confirm my suspicions, she blushes even more wildly.

Bingo! I'm right! She *has* been up to something and, even if it's not giving Nigel a blowjob, it's certainly something she shouldn't have been doing in work time. Something very, very naughty.

'Any chance of a coffee, Maria?' she says in a rather sharp voice, obviously trying to put me back in my lowly place as well as distract me.

'Yes, of course,' I say. Then the very devil gets into me. 'Would you like cream with that?'

Her painstakingly plucked eyebrows fly up, and I know we're communicating. 'We haven't got any cream. What on earth are you talking about, Maria?'

So flustered.

'No, of course we haven't. Forget it. *I* don't know what I'm talking about either.' I grin, apparently backtracking, but not really giving any ground at all. Her face is crimson now. 'I won't be two ticks,' I murmur, crossing to the table in the corner where the kettle is, and smirking broadly now she can no longer see my face.

The rest of the morning is much more fun, and I divide my time between actual work, baiting Sandy with searching looks and slight grins which I smother before she has chance to call me on them, and long, detailed bouts of fantasising about blowjobs. In most cases it's my secret picture of Mr Stone that inspires them, but sometimes it's Sandy and her bloke Nigel. And I'm watching.

By mid-morning I'm totally losing my grip on reality and I can't bear to be cooped up in here any longer. I need some air! Or something.

I request a brief cigarette break.

'But I didn't know you smoked,' Sandy mutters, eyes narrowing suspiciously.

I feel like saying 'I don't' because I really don't, but I just give her a challenging look and, in the absence of Allsopp, who's off somewhere, she says it's OK.

Snatching up my bag, I speed-walk to the nearest exit leading to the central courtyard and almost fall out on to the lichen-fringed cobbles in my haste to taste some slightly fresher air. A few people are out there, really smoking, and I make a show of fumbling in my bag, then muttering, 'Oh, bollocks!'

'Want one of mine?'

The voice is familiar and quite welcome, and I turn to face my housemate Greg, who's holding out a tin containing several rather crumbly-looking rollups. Dope? I wonder, then catch the smell of the one he's smoking, which proves to be some infinitely smellier but quite innocuous herbal concoction.

'Thanks, but no thanks. I've given up really. I just wanted to get out of the office for five minutes, that's all.'

For a moment he looks crushed that I've rejected his love token, a forlorn look in his rather delicious puppy-dog eyes, then he shrugs and says, 'I know what you mean. And I should do the same.' He wrinkles his nose in distaste and chucks his barely smoked fag down on the cobbles, stubbing it out vigorously.

I like Greg. He's sweet, and also extremely cute in a classic techno-geek sort of way. Not much taller than me, he doesn't look as if he's started shaving regularly yet, and he has brushy, sticky-up brown hair that he does a real number on with Surf Hair Gum every morning before he sets out for work. He's young, but he's also freakishly intelligent and a true technical genius, which, in a bizarre way, I find irresistibly sexy. Obviously I'm getting into bright, clever men since I got back up here.

Without his knowledge, I slot Greg into the pantheon of my fantasies *du jour*, alongside Clever Bobby.

Now here's a lad who really would appreciate a blow-job, I think, as I watch him kicking aimlessly at the corner of a loose cobble. I get the distinct feeling that he's really not had all that many.

We chat for a minute, mainly about what was on the telly last night and boring work stuff, but, just when I'm about to take my leave and head back to the office and my Sandy-baiting, I experience a peculiar, shuddering, crawling sensation somewhere in my midsection. It actually makes me sway slightly for a moment. Greg asks what's wrong, and I mutter something about blood sugar and getting a biscuit when I get back to the office.

But inside I'm still shaking. It's like every clichéd 'cold shiver down the spine', 'someone walking over my grave', 'psycho prowler watching me' sensation rolled into one, and irresistibly my eyes are drawn upwards to a window on the first floor. For just a moment, there's an intimation of movement there, the tail end of a figure stepping back out of view. It's frustratingly indistinct, but every instinct and mental synapse just yells out 'Stone!'

'What's up there? Whose are those offices?' I ask. My knowledge of the geography of Borough Hall is still quite sketchy, but my interview was up there somewhere, and my internal radar concurs that up there must be where Stone is.

'Oh, that's the Eagle's Nest, so to speak,' says Greg, still eyeing me worriedly as if he's waiting for me to keel over and wondering if he'll be able to catch me if I do. 'Where the bigwigs live in the rarefied atmosphere that's too luxurious for us mere mortals.'

'Bigwigs like Robert Stone, you mean?'

'Ah yes, our esteemed D of F. Yes, he dwells up there,' intones Greg, voice suddenly cold. 'Why, are you thinking of paying him a visit?'

'I might drop in,' I reply airily.

'Yeah, right.' Greg laughs, but again it sounds bitter.

'Why not? He's just a man, Greg. He's not actually a god, even if the top brass in these sorts of places like to think they are!'

I'm protesting, because both the feminist and the peon in me tell me that I should. But that other bit of me, the bit that did all the shuddering and shaking just now, is turning over the idea that Robert Stone might just be a god after all. In some weird, indefinable way that I've not yet got the measure of.

'I might drop in then too,' says Greg almost slyly. 'They're all pretty useless with the technology up there. Some of them actually think I'm a bit of god in my own way.' He smirks and puffs up a little, cheered up again and righteously proud of his own talents. 'Although naturally not a single one of them will admit it.'

I look at him more closely and realise that I'm missing something. There's a strange, smug, almost creepily knowing expression on Greg's face that's totally at odds with the general bashful admiration he usually exhibits around me.

What does he know? Is it more of that stuff that Mel was hinting about? Was Sandy really out of the office this morning fellating her boyfriend? Is everybody at it in this godforsaken place? Except me?

I'm right on the point of asking Greg a pertinent question that I know will embarrass him, when the cold shudder sensation flutters inside me again, and I'm irresistibly drawn to looking upwards.

And this time I'm rewarded. A familiar, looming, stocky figure seems to fill the entire middle window of a row of three, clearly and breath-catchingly visible behind the lattice-work of ornamental leading and the pollution-smeared glass.

Robert Stone.

I feel my arm lifting of its own volition, to wave to him, and I have to grab one hand with the other to stop me making a complete fool of myself. A smile, too, fights to manifest itself on my face. And, even though I win the battle against it, I feel as if every visible part of me has given away the turbulence of my reactions to him.

He, in turn, does not give even the slightest inkling of a response. I can't see his face too clearly, but there's no smile, no gesture, no twitch of recognition, even though his gaze is locked unwaveringly upon me. And remains that way for what seems like several minutes. In fact, it's no more than a couple of seconds before I have to look away, blushing as fierily as Sandy did earlier, and feeling as if I've walked out into the courtyard without my skirt and my knickers and nobody out here smoking has bothered to tell me.

When I look back up again towards the first floor, the frame of the window is empty again. And I feel as if I've just gone backwards through a wind tunnel.

'Are you sure you're all right?'

Greg's voice seems to be coming from the other end of that wind tunnel, and it sounds faint beneath the roaring of blood in my ears. I turn to him and he's watching me with obvious concern.

'Yes! I'm fine! Don't fuss!' I snap, then feel like a bitch when his pretty face falls. 'Sorry,' I add, 'it's been a bit of a weird day so far.'

And the last few seconds have been the weirdest ones of all.

After leaving Greg with repeated assurances that I am in fact OK, I come inside. Suddenly, I don't like the courtyard much any more. I feel as if I was an animal in a pen just now, and Robert Stone was the stock-master, judging and assessing me. And on the basis of his complete lack of reaction, finding me wanting.

Despite the fact that I've been out of the office twice as long as I said I would be, I slip into the cloakroom and lock myself in a cubicle. I wasn't aware that I wanted to pee but, when I settle down on the discoloured wooden seat, I realise that I'm bursting to go. And yet I can't. Everything down there feels odd. Tight. Tense. I try to think of thundering waterfalls and the local river rushing over the weir.

But all I see is Robert Stone's oval, impassive face and the faint hint of stubble around his chin that I find so sexy.

'Oh, please let me pee!' I whisper. And I'm imploring him, not my own recalcitrant body.

I wriggle on the seat. I try to brace myself, tugging on the toilet-roll holder until I almost wrench it off the wall. And suddenly I see again the slow, faint, wry smile that he gave me at the end of my interview. The 'well, I know what the outcome is but you'll have to wait' expression.

The floodgates open and I'm peeing and peeing and peeing as if it's never going to stop. The relief is so euphoric that I zone out and almost completely forget about Stone.

But not quite.

When the flow is over, he's there again, and still with that oblique smile.

Oh God, I want him!

Reaching down, heedless of my own water still clinging to me, I touch myself, and find a different moisture.

I close my eyes to shut out the peeling paint, the dust bunnies in the corner of the cubicle where the cleaners haven't quite probed thoroughly enough, the faint indentations of painted-over graffiti on the back of the loo door. I close my eyes and there's just me and Stone, in an anonymous room somewhere, and it's his hand upon me, intimately, not my own.

The contact is so light, but that's all that's needed. His

index finger is big and square-tipped, the way the rest of him is big and vaguely square-shaped, but it dances like thistledown upon my flesh, right at the perfect, most sensitive, most responsive hot zone.

He teases. He smiles in my mind. I moan, the sound broken and falling from my lips. It's a loud sound too, and, even as I utter it, I hear someone else enter the cloakroom, but my mouth won't obey me and I go on moaning.

Oh, Mr Stone, I think, surprised by the formality, yet knowing it's right for the moment. Please let it be you, I plead, knowing it's absurd that he should enter the women's lavatory, but hoping all the same. Tears spring from my eyes as the distinct sound of women's footwear clatters across the tiling, and another cubicle door opens and closes.

'Mr Stone' places the fingertip that's touched me against his lips in a 'shushing' gesture, and I have to bite my own lips as my body convulses and orgasm descends through my senses in a huge, lowering rush.

Minutes pass and I'm still on the bowl, slumped backwards, the pipe to the high old cistern digging into my spine. I feel as if I've run a race, or climbed a hill. I have no air in me at all, and I keep gasping in great, gusty inhalations.

Stone's gone now. At least that awful, scary, wonderful manifestation of him that took control of me a short while ago and became part of my masturbation. And I feel bereft without him, almost tearful.

Post-coital *tristesse* without the coitus.

I pee again, tidy myself and creep out of the cubicle. Whoever came in and did what they had to do has done it and gone again now, and I've no way of knowing who was here and if they wondered what I was up to making all that noise.

Maybe women playing with themselves in the lavatory are commonplace here, I think as I stare into the mirror. I'm determined not to return to the office with any kind of telltale on me. I don't want Sandy looking at me and knowing my dirty secrets, even if I have been away for about four times as long as I said I would be. Meticulously, imagining I'm a surgeon about to perform an open-heart procedure, I scrub and scrub at my hands with the cheap and nasty soap in the dish. It's grotty stuff, but no trace of my odour must remain on my fingers. Not even a hint of it. I wish I had a deodorant stick with me, and a change of knickers, but I have to make do with a spurt from the can of inexpensive body spray I have tucked in my bag.

With that, and a dab or two of cream-to-powder wonder foundation, I'm as ready as I'll ever be to face my public. A good job, as the big clock suddenly boings the quarter hour, and it dawns on me that my five-minute cigarette break has actually lasted three-quarters of an hour.

Oh shit!

Genuinely worried, I fly out of the Ladies and not looking where I'm going, I slam straight into a tall, broad, dark-clad figure moving quickly along the corridor in the opposite direction.

Oh God, it's *him*!

I feel myself starting to go over like a bowling pin, both from the physical impact and the collision of fantasy with reality. But, before I can topple, two hands clap hard around my upper arms, take my entire weight and hold me upright without the slightest show of effort. Dimly I hear the slap of leather against marble as his zippered document case hits the ground, dropped and forgotten.

Robbed of all sense and co-ordination, I seem to hang there, in his grip. Staring. His eyes scan me, cruising over my face, then downwards, and his expression is amused, certainly, but also disturbingly analytical. After what I did, and what I felt, back there in the cloakroom, I feel intimately connected to him but clearly all he feels for me is mild interest and curiosity.

Or is it?

Light shifts somewhere in those densely brown eyes of his and his lips – curiously soft-looking in close-up – twist just a little.

Blinking stupidly, I wonder how long he's been holding me. It seems like several hours now, but can only really have been a couple of seconds.

'Maria ... Maria ... Maria ...' he murmurs, releasing me, his fingertips still hovering close to my upper arms for a moment in case I'm still floppy. 'What on earth are you up to? Don't you know it's dangerous to run in the corridors, on these tiles?'

Like a great dark bird of some kind, he suddenly swoops down and catches up his case. I flinch, because he's such a large man and his movements are large in scope too.

But when he straightens again, he seems to hesitate, and his broad brow furrows slightly. And his nostrils flare.

Oh. Dear. God.

He can smell me!

I can't smell it myself, but I suddenly realise he *can*. And it's the odour of sex. The scent, the pheromones or whatever, that have been generated by what I just did in the toilet cubicle. He glances downwards at my hands, and the curve of his lips increases a little. Even though I scrubbed them several times, it's as if he can see the spoor of my masturbation shining there like a fluorescent tell-tale.

The hours of our extended moment stretch into millennia and some kind of conversation that I'm barely aware of on a conscious level bounces to and fro between us.

He knows.

I know he knows.

He knows I know he knows.

When he speaks again, though, his voice is perfectly normal. And solicitous in a way that's almost insulting after all that deep, perfect communication. He talks to me as if I'm just anybody.

'Are you all right, Maria? You look a little shaken. You'd best get back to your office and sit quietly for a while. Have a cup of tea, perhaps?'

'OK. Right. I will. Thanks.' I sound like a robot but he seems not to notice. He just dips again, and retrieves my bag, which I'd been completely unaware of dropping until now, then hands it to me.

'OK then. Take care,' he says briskly, and for just a moment, his hand settles on my arm again and it's like an electric shock. His eyes narrow infinitesimally. 'Are you sure you're not coming down with something? You look rather warm, Maria. Are you running a temperature?'

Yes, I bloody well am! I want to shout at him. Can't you see the steam coming out of my ears?

What's more, I feel like a dog that's suddenly hearing things on a different frequency. I could almost swear that he just emphasised the word 'coming'. There's nothing in his face that gives him away. No smirk. No wink. Nothing. But there in his eyes again that imp of mirth is capering.

'No, I'm fine. Thanks. Honestly,' I mutter, lying through my teeth.

He shrugs his solid shoulders. 'If you say so.'

Then he's moving away, striding with purpose towards one of the main exits, and I feel as if my heart's been ripped out, the sense of loss is so enormous.

But just as he reaches the door, and while I'm *still* standing there like a ninny, he turns and calls out, 'If you still feel shaken up, Maria, take the afternoon off and go home for a lie down. And if Allsopp says anything, just refer him to me.'

And then he's gone, sunlight silhouetting him briefly as I murmur 'thanks' again.

I *am* shaken. More than I care to admit. And there's nothing I'd like better than to go home for that euphemistic 'lie down' Stone suggested. But instead I go back to the office and try and carry on with my day, as normal.

Or as normal as can be when I suspect my life has suddenly changed completely.

I work on my assigned tasks. I chat casually with colleagues, no longer bothering even to bait Sandy now that her potential naughtiness has faded and become almost insignificant. My mind is like a hard drive that's been split into two (or partitioned, as Greg would no doubt say). One part is performing routine operations, while the other part is processing and reprocessing every bit of information I know about Robert Stone, and every bit of footage of the interior movie of our interactions so far.

He wants me, I'm convinced of it. And I want him with an intensity I've never felt before. I imagine what it would be like to fuck him – and I think it would be very good indeed! – but I find my thoughts meandering off down other paths. Not exactly about fucking at all.

I think about certain movies I've seen. About documentaries on the telly. Advertisements. Images in fashion layouts in glossy magazines.

I think about what I know, which is precious little in terms of personal experience, about S/M and what the men and women in those earnest documentaries describe as 'power exchange'. It's never touched me before. Never come on to the radar of things I want to do.

But now, with Stone, I think it could do.

Or could it?

I'm a novice. I'm Alice in Wonderland. I'm probably totally imagining things and he thinks I'm just another new employee. A moderately pretty one, but nothing particularly special.

When it's finally time to go home, my head is spinning and I've a slight headache, and I'm almost wishing I'd never come back here and had just stayed in London and tried to tough things out there.

'Are you OK?' says Greg when we meet again at the time clock. He looks genuinely concerned, and it alarms me that I might look so rough, what with one thing or another, that even a man would notice it.

'Yes, thanks. I'm fine. Why do you ask?'

He looks at me sharply as we make our way to the car park.

'I had a call from the D of F a short while ago. Asking me to keep an eye on you. He said he'd seen you earlier and you looked a bit out of sorts.'

What?

'Did he indeed?' I feel a prickle of alarm crawl across my skin. What's going on?

'How does he know that I ride home with you?'

'Oh, Clever Bobby knows all sorts of things,' Greg says, that odd note in his voice again. 'But so does Clever Greg.' He gives me a wink.

I let that one ride, but I can't help thinking of that peculiar moment I had with him out in the courtyard, when he seemed to be hinting at some secret knowledge that he was privy to. He unlocks the door, opens it for me, then, to my astonishment, puts his hand under my elbow, helping me into the car as if I'm a geriatric duchess who needs lifting in and out of conveyances.

What the hell has Robert Stone said to him?

Once we're under way, Greg fusses with the heater, then even bothers to ask before tuning the radio to his favourite local station, an 80s retro channel, which always seems an off-the-wall choice for a supposedly hip young man like him, but there's no accounting for taste.

I keep thinking about Stone, though. Who else?

'Is Robert Stone married?'

It's apropos of nothing Greg and I have touched upon so far in our chatter, but, when I glance sideways at him, he doesn't look surprised.

'No. Not now. He's a widower, actually. His wife died three years ago.'

A very different emotion rushes in on hearing that. I forget the strangeness and the sense of being in some kind of very real but delicious danger when I'm around the man. A plain, simple sympathy and sadness on his behalf engulfs me.

Poor man. I imagine circling my arms around his large, solid body and embracing him. I imagine the feel of his crisp, grey-frosted hair against my fingers as he lays his head on my shoulder while he sobs.

The sensation is so real, I almost feel teary. But then, inevitably, I'm imagining another kind of comfort. And I'm lifting a sheet and welcoming that stocky form, naked, into my bed.

We kiss, and he's leisurely, circumspect, not wild and impatient and anxious to impress, like most of the men I've been with. I imagine a long, slow exploration by a man who's very clever with his hands, just as he is in every other way.

'Are you sure you're all right?' Greg inquires, and I suddenly realise that I'm in a Renault, with him, and not a wide, white-sheeted bed with Robert Stone. It's quite a disappointment.

Ungrateful cow, I chide myself, and give Greg a warm smile as he turns very briefly towards me.

'I'm fine, thanks, Greg. I was just thinking about Stone. Does he have a girlfriend or anything?'

Greg has a nice mouth, but it thins as he frowns and changes gear rather jerkily. I've upset him somehow, and I guess that it's because he likes me, and I keep yammering on about Stone every time I see him. But I can't help myself, the man is on my mind.

'Nobody steady,' Greg answers, and he no longer sounds particularly cross, as if he's got over his jealous moment. In fact he's smiling again, in that same sly way I keep noticing. As if he's privy to some juicy secret that he's determined to keep to himself. At least for the moment.

'There's been talk, of course,' he goes on, as he swings the car into our road, 'about several different women. Well, I mean, he's in a position of power. Girls are bound to find him attractive.' He shoots me a sly glance as we pull up in front of the shabby grey stone house, split into flats, which is where we live. 'But he's got a reputation for being a bit kinky. You know?'

Kinky? Oh God, yes! Suddenly I can completely believe that. It's as if my imagination has been reading some kind of secret information that's floating in the air at Borough Hall. The idea that Robert Stone might have 'kinky' interests just about confirms everything that my secret radar has been sensing.

It's an intense moment. It's pivotal, somehow. But I keep things light. It's probably not a good idea to intimate to Greg that I think *I* might be kinky too. He might get ideas.

'How can anybody possibly know that? How could they? Has somebody caught him spanking his PA or something?' The vision of Stone punishing the woman, who must be in her sixties, is truly bizarre. 'He's an intelligent and powerful man. Surely he wouldn't do anything so silly and leave himself open to blackmail. Would he?'

Greg just shrugs, and waggles his eyebrows.

'Greg! Tell me! If there's some dirt on Robert Stone, I'd really love to know it!'

'Maybe another time,' he answers, suddenly sounding far more confident and in control than I've so far thought him to be. 'But it'll cost you.'

As we let ourselves into the house, I pester him a little more, but he remains adamantly close-mouthed, and I rather admire that. Young Greg is actually far more grown up and emotionally savvy than I would ever have given him credit for.

Perhaps Bobby Stone isn't the only one who's clever?

3 It's true! It's really true!

The next few days are fiendishly frustrating.

In every sense of the word.

Greg remains like a brick wall against which my questions and wheedling are totally ineffectual, and in the end I just give up rather than continue pathetically to beg for information. I'd rather give him the impression that I don't care. Even if I do.

But the worst thing is that each day, after we've arrived, no amount of lurking around the time clock and darting in and out of the adjacent cloakroom, just checking, gets me even the slightest sniff of a glimpse of Robert Stone.

In the end, I ask Sandy, as casually as I can, why Mr Stone isn't to be seen around the building.

She gives me a look as if to say, 'What business is it of yours, peasant?'

'Oh, there's a big CIPFA conference in Bournemouth, didn't you know? He's giving the keynote address. Pretty crucial stuff, you know.'

Oh. Right.

Immediately I'm whisked away into some kind of huge auditorium, and Stone stands before the assembled masses supreme, like an emperor. They're all cheering, and he acknowledges their worship, and I have to pull myself up sharply before it all becomes dangerously evangelical. Clever Bobby preaching the new religion of perv!

After this news, though, I have even less interest in my tasks than usual. In fact Borough Hall suddenly seems a bleak and almost desolate place. As I trudge along the corridors, ferrying post to and fro, collecting photocopies and generally doing all the grunt work that my lowly position entails, it seems as if a certain discreet lustre has been leached out of the atmosphere. I realise that, without consciously being aware of the fact, I always feel a sense of expectation, of possibility, of suppressed excitement when Stone's in the building. And when he's not there it's just a sink of dullness, a kind of deadpool.

The weekend following seems to pass in a kind of stupor, even though I finally make time to visit my sister and her family, who still live here in some kind of desperate suburban perfection, and who all, without exception, consider me a weirdo and a waster.

But on Monday I enter the Hall with Greg, and suddenly my heart gives a single, hard thud. I haven't seen him, and I've no way of knowing how I know, but I would stake my life on Stone being back in the building. I don't even bother to patrol the entrance. I just know he's around – and that it's only a matter of time before I see him.

And, with the Return of the King, Borough Hall seems to shake off its dormancy.

Sandy in particular seems distracted. Edgy. Bursting with an excitement that seems strangely akin to my own, although I don't think she gives two pins about our esteemed Director of Finance, other than any prospects for professional advancement that he might be able to confer on her.

She keeps making cups of coffee and not drinking them. She looks at her watch every five minutes. She even seems to be wearing a new shade of lipstick, one that's a hotter pink and much sexier-looking than her usual neutral rose.

She's up to something, and my mind turns to blowjobs again.

I've been thinking quite a bit about Sandy, in between my long meditations on Robert Stone.

I can't see why she would nip out in office time to get up to anything naughty with Nigel – mainly because they live together. Unless, of course, it's the thrill of the forbidden? Which I can perfectly understand, but which I just can't associate with a – let's face it – rather stodgy couple like Sandy and Nigel.

So it must be someone else.

As soon as that dawns on me, something else does. A horrible, horrible thought.

What if it's Stone? And maybe her feigned lack of interest in our boss is just a cover?

And yet somehow, almost immediately, I sense it's not him. I'd know. I don't know how, but I'd know.

The day passes in a state of high but unacknowledged tension. Sandy's wired. I'm wired. Everyone else in the office is snappish and wary, as if they sense something but don't know what it is. Needless to say, all this leads to another display of shining clerical efficiency from me, and I blot my copybook by putting calls through to the wrong people and accidentally shredding an active application form, which has to be reissued. Bollocks!

And every time I look at Sandy I *still* think about blowjobs!

First I imagine her on her knees sucking fervently at the flesh of some faceless man. They're in this building somewhere, I sense, and I wonder what possible locations would lend themselves to illicit nookie.

The basement, probably, which is a warren of corridors and small rooms that parallels the layout of the upper world we work in. Plenty of tucked-away niches to get wild in down there.

But, inevitably, I soon lose interest in Sandy's cock-sucking prowess and begin to obsess about my own, and about the penis I long to fall down and worship.

Will Stone's sex be as big as the rest of him?

I'm not especially fixated on large penises, but I find myself hoping the man is in proportion, as long and as tall as he is. I imagine it lewdly poking out of his immaculate suiting, raw and feral against the civilised elegance of his clothing. As I make myself some coffee, and pour in milk, I see the white fluid and think immediately of semen. His semen. And the taste of it.

Oh that's gross, Maria, I tell myself, shaking my head to dispel the images, if even for a moment.

Afternoon arrives, and hello, hello, Sandy disappears!

And it's nothing official. She hasn't gone out meeting a client, and she leaves no word as to where she's going. She just creeps out when she thinks nobody's looking. I'm looking, of course, and I have to smother a grin, because she's so furtive that she might as well be in some kind of comedy murder mystery. She glances around just like a classic sneaky miscreant. I've got my head down, with my hair a bit round my face, so I'm able to observe her at an angle as she slips away.

I grit my teeth. What excuse can I come up with to follow her? I've just been to the Ladies. I went to collect post ten minutes ago. We have plenty of milk, timesheets, rubber bands, blank CDs, everything we need.

I'm dying of frustration, desperate to get out of the office, and the minutes tick, tick, tick by.

Where is she? Has she indeed snuck away to a tryst? Is she in the basement? Where, where, where?

After a lifetime of around fifteen to twenty minutes, the gods suddenly smile on me. A porter comes with an armful of files and says that Mr Stone wonders whether I'd be kind enough to help him out with a little job. The files need returning to the basement document store and, as Mr Stone's PA's chest is bad and would be irritated by the dust, could I possibly put the files away instead? He's even brought the key to the relevant rooms.

Stone, I love you! I think as I jump straight to my task, and for a moment I'm shaken by the thought that it might not be just a figure of speech. I'm certainly obsessed with the man, at least. And by some mental telepathy he's just handed me the very escape I'd been pleading for.

So off I go, my mind already bouncing around between Sandy, her unknown lover and the Director of Finance, before I've even got to one of the narrow, tucked-away staircases that leads to the cellars.

Christ, it's grotty down here! And it's a labyrinth too. I swear this place must have been designed by Escher, honestly. Or maybe Doctor Who? I should be putting down a trail of breadcrumbs so I can find my way out again.

And, within moments of descending, I feel as if I'm being coated with a layer of the ancient dust that lies over everything. I can smell it. It invades my nostrils, pervasively dry and peppery and gritty. And the weak emergency-style lighting makes things worse. If I were of a nervous disposition, I'd be imagining serial killers or zombie brain-eaters lurking around every corner of the maze of mildewed corridors and poky little rooms down here. Fortunately, though, I'm too caught up with my personal fantasies to let my mind go all haunted-house-horror on me.

Sandy. Stone. Mystery blowjob guy. Me giving Stone a blowjob. Round and round and round and round and round.

But finally I realise I'm going to have to concentrate on the task in hand. Or, firstly, I'll never find the shelving areas that I'm supposed to be looking for, and, secondly and worse, I'll get completely lost and never find my way back to the surface.

Eventually I find the section I need in a long, partitioned cellar that's both document store and depository of antediluvian furniture. Lord knows where it all came from and who used to use it, but it's certainly a perfect venue for secret illicit sex.

And suddenly thought gives life to reality.

I stop in my tracks, a box of files clutched against my cardigan, arrested by the distinct sound of a sharp, female cry echoing from beyond the door that connects the next cellar to this one.

And it's not Jack the Ripper hacking up a victim through there. It's the sort of cry I make myself when I'm with a man and it's hot and heavy.

Irresistibly drawn, I slip off my shoes so I won't betray my presence, pop them on top of my files and then pad towards the door. Beyond, there are more tall metal racks holding files, and beyond them more mouldering furniture.

Oh God! It's true! It's really true!

On a battered and saggy couch upholstered in maroon moquette lies Sandy, Miss Prim from my office. And between her widely spread legs, with his face firmly planted in her pussy, is a man I really didn't expect to be there.

It isn't her boyfriend Nigel, and isn't – thank God – Robert Stone. No, instantly recognisable by the shining, almost unnatural gold-blond of his hair, it's the Borough's Human Resources Manager who's giving Sandy head as if his life depends on it.

Bloody hell, William Youngblood! Who'd have thought it? He's the very last person I could have imagined shagging a popsy down here in the basement. He's so fastidious, so groomed, so self-assured. And here he is on his knees, grovelling around like a rutting hog amongst the drifts of dust, the spiders and the silverfish, performing cunnilingus!

My eyes feel as if they've popped out on stalks like a cartoon character's and I'm so surprised that I nearly drop my files and my shoes all over the stone floor. But in a moment of uncharacteristic self-possession, I manage to hang on to them, then I creep forward and slide into a conveniently roomy niche shaped from filing shelves, piled-up chairs and a couple of bookcases. There's a gap in the shelving that makes for a perfect hidden viewing slot for someone sitting on the floor, and as I hunker down it occurs to me that this set-up looks a little *too* convenient. Like someone's fashioned it especially for spying on illicit liaisons acted out on that couch. But I decide to wonder just who might have built this little hide later. Because the floorshow in front of me is far too delicious.

Sandy promptly goes up about a zillion notches in my estimation.

Not only is she slapper enough to be down here in work time, shagging someone who isn't her boyfriend, but she's really entered into the spirit of things in the skanky whore department. Her neat white blouse is open down the front, and her demure-looking *broderie anglaise* bra is pushed up haphazardly to reveal her breasts. And not only is her grey skirt rucked up around her waist, her knickers and tights are still entangled around one of her ankles as she wiggles and lifts her bottom off the couch to encourage Youngblood's keen attention between her thighs.

You go, girl! I think, all solidarity with her as she grabs his perfectly gelled hair and makes a complete mess of it while she yanks him even closer to the heart of the action.

Youngblood is semi-stripped for action too. His jacket and trousers are on the floor close by – neatly folded, I notice – and his designer boxer shorts are round his knees. From this awkward angle, I can't quite see it –

curses! – but he's obviously busy wanking himself as he works.

Youngblood! I marvel again. Fancy meeting you here!

At my interview, in the presence of Stone, I admit that I didn't really take a whole lot of notice of our Human Resources Manager. But, if anyone had asked me, I'd have tagged him as a smooth and very sophisticated seducer. Mr Silk Sheets, Champagne, Mood Music. The whole package. But here he is, wallowing like a pretty blond piggy at the trough of easy sex, his bare shins resting on the grimy stone floor and his tongue lapping nineteen to the dozen.

This is all too much for me. The frustrations of the weekend, my hot speculative thoughts about Stone, the strange, latently sexual atmosphere that seems to pervade the entire Hall, it all gets the better of me. Carefully setting down the files and my shoes, I adjust my position, reflecting that this is definitely a bona fide peeping 'hide', because there's even a piece of old carpet on the floor here to make things more comfortable. My eyes are still focused totally on Sandy and on William Youngblood's shining head jammed up against her pussy, but I slip my hand inside my knickers and go straight for my clit.

Come to mama!

I'm wet down there, even more so than I expected, and I start to rub in a quick, steady rhythm as if my subconscious director of operations is aware, in spite of everything, that it's not a good idea to be away from the office for too long.

Sandy is biting her lip, trying to hold in her cries now, and I'm very jealous. It's far too long since I got some of that. Some blindingly good head from a guy with a long, flexible tongue who knows how to use it. My mind instantly flips me back to my job interview, and Mr Stone flicking his tongue-tip fleetingly along the edge of his lower lip as he reads my application. Our eyes met then, in the knowledge that my credentials for the post were an absolute joke, but still he championed me in the face of Youngblood's justified opposition.

My finger's moving at a fair lick, and it's hard not to gasp and wriggle. But nobody's going to hear me when Sandy is grunting and sighing and shuffling about far more athletically than I am.

Wrong!

Suddenly I'm in a major *Jaws* forward-tracking-zoom-out-shot moment, and everything around me recedes at light speed. I don't know how it's happened, or why there wasn't even the slightest hint of warning, but I'm no longer alone in the confines of my little den.

Beside me, hunkered down on his heels, is Robert Stone, completely owning our claustrophobic little space.

I'm frozen – apart, astonishingly, from my finger, which continues to circle inside my knickers. I can't seem to stop. My eyes are locked with Stone's and it's as if he's doing some kind of Derren Brown psychic mind-warp thing and compelling me to continue my masturbation.

My jaw drops, and he taps one long forefinger to his lips in a silent shushing gesture, then nods towards the scene on the couch and mimes the word 'continue'.

Continue what? Watching? Playing with myself? Both?

I try to obey.

The playing with myself is easy. I've never wanted or needed to do it more than at this moment. But it's difficult to sustain any interest in Sandy and Youngblood when my eyes only want to look at the man beside me.

With no apparent discomfort, he adjusts his position. The guy must be at least six foot four, but he folds his bulky body neatly and sits on the carpet, just inches from me (in fact, our feet are touching), oblivious to the fact that his undoubtedly high-end suit must be getting plastered with dust from the aged carpet. He wraps an arm across his chest, and presses the knuckle of his free hand against his chin as he watches me. As I continue to watch him back, he nods again to the couple on the couch.

I turn my attention back to Sandy and William Youngblood but, overlaid across the image of them, I see a pair of heavy-lidded, dark yet brilliant eyes, just the colour of expensive high-octane bitter chocolate. I know he's not watching them. He's watching *me*. And as my cunt is covered, it's my face that he's scrutinising.

Things have moved on outside in the slightly less hot zone.

Youngblood's face is out from between Sandy's legs and he's about to mount her. She's so enthusiastic for this that she's actually tugging him towards her by his dick, which is OK but not particularly impressive.

Immediately, Youngblood phases out of existence and it's Stone – *Mr* Stone, I suddenly correct myself, for no apparent reason – there in front of me, and his dick *is* impressive. Perfectly in proportion to his imposing height and girth. A bit of a monster, just like he is, sticking out from the fly of his perfectly tailored suit. Against his wishes, I sneak a quick glance at his *real* crotch, but in the relative gloom there's nothing to see, and he's not touching himself or anything. He's just as he was before, his chin on his fist, an amused, pensive expression on his swarthy, shadowed face.

He mimes 'tut tut' and I shoot my eyes back to the creaking couch.

Sandy and Youngblood are really going at it now, like the proverbial bunnies. And it's not an elegant sight, more a kind of badly syncopated locomotion. Youngblood's bum is bouncing and Sandy's hitching herself about, trying to get a rhythm. Judging by his strangely tentative performance, it's no wonder she makes him eat her first. I certainly would.

And if it wasn't for Mr Stone watching me, I'd probably be trying to stop myself laughing at the sight of them now, rather than trying to stop myself groaning and grunting and writhing about as I climb inexorably towards orgasm.

Fuck it! I don't want to look at them. I want to look at *him*! And as I shuffle round and meet his gaze, he does a thing with his right eyebrow that makes me almost boil over.

I'm so close. I'm biting my lip. I'm drowning, drowning, drowning in that wry, amused expression of his. My hips lift and work and I press hard where it matters. And as I do, Mr Stone does the strangest thing. He reaches over and passes his fingertips over my eyelids, gently pressing them closed the way a medical examiner does for a corpse in a cop show.

It's a delicate action, bizarrely tender, and it tips me over. My cunt clenches again and again, tugging at my gut, my heart, my soul. I taste blood in my mouth from all the lip biting and I subside backwards, aware that strong hands are preventing me from falling and then settling me carefully on the carpet.

From a great distance, I hear more grunting and scuffling and a gasped 'Oh God!'

Sounds like Sandy is getting off too.

It takes a minute or two, or three, for me to get my breath back. But as I slowly return to the land of the living, I realise that it's in my interest to get my act together, and for me and Mr Stone to get the hell out of Dodge before the lovebirds get their act together. If Youngblood and Sandy walk past here, they'll be able to see into this nook, especially if it's got two occupants rather than one.

But as I drag my hand out of my knickers and open my eyes, I find I'm alone. Completely alone. And there's no indication that I was anything *but* alone here, except for a faint heel scuff on the carpet. And even that could be from me, not him.

Leaving my files but grabbing up my shoes, I tiptoe away towards the exit, my heart still racing. I hope to find Stone, even though I haven't the slightest idea what I'm going to say to him once we're in the clear.

But he's done a Keyser Soze on me.

Poof! Just like that, he's gone!

Not even a whiff of his cologne to say he was ever here at all.

I stumble out into the courtyard, gasping for air as if I've been submerged.

Maybe I have been? In some kind of freakish undersea world of sleazy unreality?

I can still hardly believe any of it.

Sandy and Youngblood. And Stone.

Oh God, Stone!

I start shaking, really trembling hard, my teeth chattering in my head. And it's a head that's gone all light and swimming, whirling with shock.

I sat in a hidey-hole with the Director of Finance and he watched me masturbate. Have I lost my job? I certainly feel as if I might have lost my mind.

I spin around, looking up towards the first floor and that window where I saw him the other day. Is he still watching me?

But there's nobody there, and no sense of anyone hidden, just out of sight. The courtyard and the day itself look and feel perfectly normal. It's just me who's disjointed and out of step.

I sit down on one of the sets of steps that lead back into the building. It's sunny and the stone is warm beneath me and reassuring. I press my palm to it, trying to commune with its solidity and centre myself.

Did I imagine it all?

It seems not. There are smears of cellar dust on my skirt, and I blush because, as I shift my weight on the stone, I can feel that my knickers are sticky. I certainly masturbated, that's for sure, even if all the rest of it was illusory. I close my eyes and lean back, looking up towards the sun, which prints weird patterns on the inside of my eyelids. The heat of it reminds me of the delicate touch of Robert Stone's fingertips as he compelled me to close my eyes.

Yes, it was real all right. I can still feel his touch.

I breathe and breathe, trying to think. To face facts. What's done is done and I can't undo it, and I can't really think of anything else I could have done down there, in the circumstances.

If I'd said anything, leapt up, started babbling apologies, I'd be in an even worse mess now, embroiled in a hugely embarrassing situation that involved four people instead of just two. Not that Stone had looked in the slightest bit embarrassed.

No, he was clearly right at home, and comfortable, and enjoying himself. Maybe he watches people all the time down there? Maybe it's even *his* 'hide'? What if I've stumbled on the secret sexual perv of Borough Hall's arch peeper?

The fresh air isn't helping, is it?

Time to go back inside and face whatever music might already be playing.

But there is none.

I beat Sandy back to the office, even despite my little time-out in the courtyard. And, when she does reappear, I keep my head down and my nose firmly to the grindstone. In fact I do everything I can to avoid any kind of contact or confrontation with her, so that neither of us gets the chance to blush and give away our secret guilt.

But that doesn't stop me thinking.

Oh Sandy, you bad, bad girl! What would Nigel think if he knew you were banging William Youngblood on the side? The sudden feeling of power I experience is quite intoxicating, and I can't help but smile inside. I like feeling powerful! And it's the first time I've felt this way since I realised that I had to give up my London lifestyle, pull myself together and buckle down and work properly for a living.

Yes. Power. I've got it over Sandy now, even though she's senior to me. And in a way I've got it over Youngblood too, if I choose to use it.

But what about Stone? Do I have it over him? Well, probably not. Although there is a sort of balance between us. I shouldn't have been down in the cellar masturbating. But, equally, he shouldn't have been down there watching me either.

The nicest bit is that we both have it over Sandy and Youngblood, and it's shared. And the idea of sharing something so intimate yet so exciting with Stone makes my heart feel good just as it does my body.

We're in this together now, Clever Bobby, I think, drawing my secret bond with the Director of Finance close to me as the tedious working day draws to a close.

4 **Summoned to the Presence**

Come on, you bastard! Make a move! Do something!

Two days have passed, and nothing's happened. No response from Stone. Not a word. Not even a sighting. It's as if he's completely ignoring the fact I'm here in Borough Hall. Even ignoring my existence. As I said ... bastard!

What did you expect, woman? I ask myself, though, sipping at a cold cup of coffee and heaving an overly theatrical sigh.

'Anything wrong?' asks Sandy, appearing genuinely concerned. I realise that I've been mooching around the office like a lovesick fool. Or a lustsick one. I haven't even had the heart to attempt to bait her, or make low innuendos about her disappearances to the cellar. I haven't said anything to anyone else about it either, for fear of giving away my own less than savoury antics in the process.

'Fine, thanks,' I say brightly, then suddenly and inexplicably come over all confessional. 'Well ... sort of ... There's this bloke I was expecting to ring me, but he never did. And I thought we had a sort of "thing" ... you know?'

'Oh, they're so like that, aren't they?' she says, frowning. 'One minute they're all over you and the next, nothing.' In a swift, sharp, almost hacking movement, she places a big cross in what I know to be the 'loan declined' box on the application in front of her. Poor devils. 'I sometimes wonder why we bother with them at all. I think your friend Mel has got the right idea! At least women communicate with each other.'

This outburst takes me quite aback. What's going on

with Sandy then? Torn between two lovers, is she? And who's the one who's pissed her off so? Is it faithful but boring Nigel? Or the more exciting but forbidden and possibly unreliable Youngblood? I momentarily forget my own fretting over Stone.

'Er, yes, I suppose so,' I say, wondering how to phrase a possible enquiry into what's going on. 'But I thought you and Nigel were OK? He seems such a nice guy. You know? Steady and ... um ... devoted.'

'Oh, he's OK. I'm just having an off day. Nothing's wrong.' Sandy looks seriously alarmed, and it's obvious that she realises she's 'communicated' far too much to me. The next minute, she's piling a whole heap of work on my desk to distract me.

Fat chance of that. It's nice to know that I'm not the only one who's in a bit of a quandary over a bloke. She's not done one of her shifty little disappearing acts since the cellar incident, and I've not even seen the object of my obsession. Neither one of us is getting anywhere in the secret sexual thrills department.

And it seems as if it's going to stay that way until mid-afternoon, when all hell breaks loose in *my* sex thrills department.

It starts innocuously. Sandy picks up the phone, answers, then says, 'Yes. Right. I'll send her up.'

My heart begins to thud in my chest as if someone's beating my ribs with a hammer. I know exactly where 'up' is, and who's been summoned there.

And I'm right.

'Maria, can you go up and see Mr Stone?' My face must betray me, because she adds, quite kindly, 'Don't worry, it's nothing drastic. Probably just his usual "meet and greet". He usually has a little chat with new people a week or two after they've started. Just to see how they're getting on. Nice of him, really, isn't it?'

'Yes. Very nice.' I force the words out. I'm sure there'll

never be anything innocuous or 'nice' now between me and Robert Stone. Not after what happened in the cellar.

'Shouldn't you be on your way? Mrs Sheldon did say you had to go up now.'

I stare at Sandy, blinking, and I realise that I've been sitting here like a shop dummy for at least a minute, my mind a blank of pure emotional panic.

A few moments later I'm in the Ladies, tweaking my hair, preening, dashing in and out of the cubicle, my bladder playing nervous games with me. I'm torn between fear and longing, both emotions wreaking havoc.

It takes me around ten minutes to get my act together, and even then I'm trembling as I put my foot on the first of the deep stone steps that lead up to the first floor. I watch each step carefully, afraid that I'll trip on the patterned crimson carpet runner. Peons like me aren't even supposed to use the ceremonial staircase but I'm so disorientated I'm beyond caring. I experience an over-whelming desire to cop out and rush anywhere but where I ought to be headed. I toy with the idea of seeking out Mel, or even Greg in the IT department. I've got what I wanted, a summons to see Robert Stone, but now I'm completely freaking out at the thought of it.

'For God's sake, pull yourself together, Maria!' I mutter to myself as I reach the top of the stairs and round the corner on to the landing where the bigwigs' offices are. A passing secretary gives me a look as if I'm an escaped mental patient, but who cares? Only Stone's opinion of me matters now, and that's something I'm just about to discover.

I start to hyperventilate even as I face the outer door that leads to his PA's office, so I pause for a moment, hugging my middle, as if the pressure will stop my heart bouncing around.

Right. Let's go!

I knock and enter, and Mrs Sheldon, Stone's secretary, smiles cheerfully and says, 'Go right in, my dear!' I wonder if she has any idea about her boss's secret sexual proclivities. Which I assume he must have many of. I simply can't believe that 'watching' is the only one.

Breathing deeply, I march to the door to the inner sanctum, then hesitate. I feel like a high diver on the top board, a bungee jumper poised over a gorge, a skier at the top of an Olympic piste. I don't think I've ever been this nervous in my life. Not in examinations. Not at the dentist. And certainly not at a job interview. Even the one for this job didn't bother me, because at that point I hadn't yet met Stone.

I can feel Mrs Sheldon staring at my back, curious about my hesitation.

Is this a regular occurrence? I wonder. Does he have things going on with any number of female Borough employees? Or is it just me? Or just me at the moment? Who knows? What difference does it make? Now is now. I'm me. And just two days ago the man beyond that door watched me masturbate and gently closed my eyes.

Do it, Maria! Do it!

I grasp the handle, turn it and walk in, trying to hold everything together when it all wants to fly apart.

Stone is seated at his desk, the surface of which is strewn with piles of paper, reports, a personal organiser and even two empty coffee mugs. There's nothing immaculately godlike or omnipotent about him. He's just a busy, slightly harassed man in his shirtsleeves, who looks as if he's drowning in work and responsibilities. After all my fear and trepidation, I feel a sudden rush of sympathy.

The impression of a man under pressure is increased by the fact that at some stage he's run his hand through his hair, and that's made the natural curl more apparent and produced an endearingly dishevelled and boyish look. His shirt, too, looks crumpled and rumpled. It's a good one, a subtle pale blue in a fine weave, but he's a big man and obviously hard on his clothes, and it's nearing the end of a rough day.

To my surprise, he springs lightly to his feet. In my experience men of power don't always do this. They like to play games by remaining in their chairs and putting you in your place by not showing you any respect. But Stone, I sense, is beyond such silliness. He's too subtle to give up on old-fashioned good manners.

'Please sit down, Maria,' he says, his broad face alight with good humour as he shifts his weight from foot to foot in a way that's both nervy and unnerving. He gestures towards a rather plain, rather hard-looking wooden chair set in front of the vast acreage of his desk.

It's all so normal. I take the seat, and it's as hard as it looks and my bottom protests a little. Stone continues to smile genially, not a hint of suggestion or innuendo in his expression. I start to harbour the disquieting suspicion that I might have imagined the interlude in the basement after all.

Am I going bonkers?

'So, how are you liking Borough Hall?' he enquires, throwing himself down into his far more comfortable executive chair. It starts to spin a little and he steadies himself, his large fingertips braced against the surface of his desk. 'Do you think you'd like to stay here a while?'

Innocuous, and yet perhaps not? In London I bounced from job to job, not really applying myself to anything, not taking any real interest, because my social life had always taken precedence. Is he taunting me for being flighty and stupid? For wasting a good education and a reasonably good brain?

'Yes, it's fine. OK,' I say, thrown already by the fact that he seems to be totally immersed in the superficial, the normal. In bloody work, for God's sake!

'Only OK?' he queries, and I look at him sharply. Is that a challenge, a tease? It's so hard to tell. His expression is cordial, bland, but somewhere deep in those chocolate-brown eyes I can see a knowing light flickering.

He *is* playing with me. He has been all along. He's daring me to mention what happened down below. He knows he can go on as long as he likes, in perfect comfort, while I get more and more wired

'It's a just a job!' I say defiantly, knowing I've got to stir things up or I'll explode. I'll just lose it!

There's a long silence, while he regards me thought-fully. He isn't hostile. He isn't irritated. He doesn't even appear in the slightest bit surprised. A slight smile plays around his rather soft, almost tender mouth and he flips idly through sheaves of paper and files without even glancing at them.

'But you applied for it,' he says after another extended pause, 'and you took it.' He picks up his pen, balances it precariously between his two forefingers for a second or two. 'Perhaps we should have given the post to someone who'd take a little more pleasure in it?'

On the word 'pleasure' he drops the pen on to the top of his papers and watches it roll towards me.

'I'm sorry. I sounded a bit ungrateful there. I didn't mean to be,' I bluster. I have a wild, strange feeling in my chest. Everything's jittering. And down below I feel tense, tight, expectant. 'It's a good job. I like it. I'm glad to be here.'

'Well, that's a relief,' he says roundly, retrieving his pen, lining it up beside that ever-present zippered leather document case of his, which is also on the desk, set to one side. 'I thought I'd made a mistake with you, Maria.' He leans back in his seat, hugs his arms around himself for a second, then raises one hand, rubs the side his face, then studies his fingernails for a moment.

It's quite a performance, I realise. He appears to be the one who's fidgeting, but it's me who's thrown off balance by all those nervy little movements. It's part of a game and he's having enormous fun.

And I haven't the slightest idea what to say.

'I took a chance on you, you know,' he continues blandly. 'On paper, you were the least likely candidate. Over-qualified. Under-experienced in any way that's useful. You're too old for the job. Or too young.' He draws in a long breath and his deep chest lifts. 'If it had been up to friend Youngblood, you'd have been rejected out of hand.' His slight smile broadens. 'If I hadn't seen your potential, you wouldn't even have got an interview.'

Potential?

Potential for what?

'Yes, I fought for you, Maria,' he continues, and suddenly he's on his feet again, and around the front of the desk. He rests his backside on the edge of it, and places his large (size 11, at least) feet, shod in plain black Oxfords, on either side of my smaller ones, which are positioned neatly and tidily and primly together in front of me. He's deep in my personal space and I swear I can feel the heat of his thighs and shins against mine, through the cloth of his trousers. I don't know where to look, because inevitably, as has happened each and every time we've encountered each other, my maverick gaze is drawn directly to his groin.

'Thank you,' I say faintly, even though I've almost forgotten what I'm supposed to be grateful for.

'You are *so* welcome, Miss Lewis,' he says, and his deep voice is rich with excitement. I can hear it there, although it's a paradoxically calm brand of excitement. He's as keyed-up as I am, I can tell, but he's either a perfect actor or he just expresses the thrill in an entirely different way.

His over-bright eyes don't dart about any more now, and the nervy movements are all gone. He's as beautifully still as a graven image, and his hooded gaze holds mine without the slightest waver or blink as he looks down at me.

And then it's like receiving the first message from an alien intelligence.

On the surface, it's simple. It says 'hello, nice to meet you, we come in peace', but coded into some sophisticated harmonic frequency is a massive encyclopaedia of information. Everything about Stone, and his sexual tastes, and what it would like to be with him and service those tastes. And there's data about me too, passing to him, because the flow is bi-directional. He reads me, knows me, and knows things about me I barely understand myself yet.

But what I do know is that I'm most definitely 'Miss Lewis' now, and that everything's changed in my world. I feel slightly faint and I almost forget to breathe.

Suddenly, Stone tilts his head, ever so slightly, and lifts one hand, extending it between us.

I stare at it, taking in the strong, square fingers, nails trimmed and clean, but with – oh, how sweet! – a little ink smudge on the side of his thumb. We're in alien contact land again, and this is an artefact. What is its purpose? What am I supposed to do with it?

Then I understand.

Reaching up, I take the large, warm hand in both mine and bring it to my lips, pressing them against its back. I can feel the texture of his skin against my mouth, and the brush of the fine little hairs.

It's like the Mafia kiss of fealty. I'm pledging myself. But to what, my conscious mind isn't yet sure, even though the taste of Stone's firm flesh, when I touch my tongue to it, is exquisite.

I close my eyes, shuddering finely, and a second later

Stone's hand twists and then he's using a slight pressure to draw me to my feet, so I'm standing between his spread thighs. We're on a level now, but he still seems to loom over me.

I feel weak, and I recognise this as something that always happens in proximity to this man. My legs hardly seem capable of holding me upright, and it's only his strength, flowing from him to me through our linked hands, that keeps me from crumpling to the carpet. He gives my fingers a squeeze, and I'm forced to open my eyes. His are brilliant, shining, full of knowledge and mischief, and he glances quickly down at our joined hands as if he too feels the transfer of energy.

He unlinks our fingers, and I sway. He smiles slightly. Bastard!

Then he does something unexpected.

Sliding his right hand around the back of my head, he draws me towards him. And kisses me.

For some reason, it's the last thing I'd anticipated, and I gasp as our mouths meet. I feel his soft smile against my lips and the flex of his fingers in my hair as he holds me in the kiss. As he tilts his face to fit our mouths together better, his stubbly cheek momentarily rasps against my skin.

But it's all so gentle. His lips barely move, exerting only the lightest pressure, and there's no hint of tongue. At least not yet.

There's not really anything sexual about the kiss at all. And yet, in my body, it's all about sex.

I want. I want this man in a way I've never wanted a man before. I can feel my body preparing itself to receive him, and yet I'm not sure it's actually fucking I'm anticipating. That seems too simple, too obvious. Almost too commonplace for the mind and the imagination of the man who's kissing me. I have no way of knowing how I know this. I just do.

I feel a huge excitement building inside me. Whatever it is that I do want, I'm suddenly impatient for it. I try to coax him to kiss me harder, deeper, but he just laughs against my mouth. I sense him chiding me for my eagerness, but he indulges me by pressing his tongue delicately against the edges of my lips. The touch of it, the moistness, is incredibly potent, almost lewd, speaking to me of other moisture, other intrusions, other explorations. As I helplessly open my mouth to receive his quest, I experience a sudden flash vision. It seems unrelated to anything, but in another instant I realise it's crucial.

In my mind I see Stone writing. Writing with his left hand. He's a southpaw, and he's cradling my head with his right hand. So what's his other hand doing? What is he up to?

The question is quickly answered. As he continues to kiss me, more vigorously now, impressing his considerable will on me with the force of his tongue and his lips, I feel his hand – his strong, skilful *left* hand – settle on and curve around my hip. It's like a flaming brand through the woven cotton of my skirt.

Nerve-ends fire madly, and messages rush around my body so rapidly and powerfully I'm almost aware of them as sparkling lines of force. I give a little moan, just from the one touch. God knows what I'll be like when he really gets down to business!

And still he kisses. And still I kiss back. But now all the action is there in his left hand. He slides it slowly over my hip and thigh, each time lengthening the stroke. It's so exciting, even through my clothes, and I can feel dampness gathering in my knickers. No man has ever achieved so much with so little, and I realise all over again that this Robert Stone, this most unlikely of erotic obsession objects, is something of a phenomenon. Something remarkable. Something rare. And I feel like shouting with elation that he seems to have chosen me.

Until now I've hung almost limply in his hold, but now, with daring, I slide my arms around his broad, solid body. I half expect him to order me to unhand him, but he doesn't. I feel him smiling again, and I get a strong sense that he relishes my enthusiasm. The way he handles me seems to suggest precisely that.

He's moulding his fingers to the curve of my buttock now, exploring it, testing the resilience of the muscle. I'm glad now that I've kept up with a simple exercise regime in my flat, in front of a video, since I can no longer afford a personal trainer or a posh gym.

I can't help but wriggle and, as my movements grow more agitated, that seems to amuse him even more. He draws back a little and looks down into my eyes, his own dancing.

'Do you like that, Miss Lewis?' he enquires, giving me a slightly more intent squeeze, the tips of his fingers curving perilously close to my sex through my thin skirt.

My mouth is so dry, despite the lush liquidity of our kiss. 'Y–yes,' I stammer. 'Yes, I do like it,' I continue, when the darkness of his eyes seems to demand that I expand my answer.

'Good,' he says with satisfaction. 'And this?' With lightning swiftness, his hand whips down and up again. And his fingers are on my bare thigh, hot, hot, hot.

'Yes!' I squeak as his fingertips immediately begin to move. First they slide momentarily in beneath the leg elastic of my knickers. But then, and shockingly, he withdraws from there and almost roughly pulls my pants down from the waist until they're bunched around the tops of my thighs and my bottom's bare beneath my skirt.

'*Yes, Mr Stone,*' he prompts softly. There's no menace or even pomposity in it, but I'm still scared. Not so much of him, but more of the way my wayward body seems to be galvanised by the trappings of mock formality.

We're *Miss Lewis* and *Mr Stone* – and he's feeling up my bum.

His fingers flex and relax, flex and relax, palpating me. I feel totally eroticised, like an object or a doll for his amusement, and it's the most sexually thrilling thing that's ever happened to me. He starts to kiss me again, synchronising the kneading action of his fingers to the delicately moist slide of his large, invasive tongue.

I hug him tight as he handles me, glorying in the size and solidity of his body and the depth of his chest. He's a substantial man, so real and grounded, and yet, despite everything, I accept him as my fantasy. Until a few weeks ago, I hardly realised that I needed one, but now he's as essential as the breath of life.

He kisses and kisses. I hug and hug. He fondles my bottom comprehensively and at leisure. At the back of my mind is the fact that the door to his office is unlocked, and I wonder if he finds the very real possibility of discovery in a compromising situation a turn-on. I certainly do. Even as his fingers palpate me and slip into the crease of my bum with increasing regularity, I imagine intruders charging in and catching the action.

They arrive in a parade. Surprisingly, it's not Mrs Sheldon. She'd be the obvious one. And it's not even the Chief Exec or the Mayor, who can, theoretically, walk into any office at any time.

No, I imagine more familiar figures. Greg. Mel. Sandy and, ooh, William Youngblood. Tit for tat. In my mind the observed is now the observer.

For a moment, I imagine that cool creature watching warmly and avidly as Mr Stone concentrates on stroking my anus. He's found a hotspot and he's exploiting it. The caress is so naughty and rude and dirty and I want more and more and more of it. It's suddenly far more arousing to be fingered there than between my legs. I start panting and groaning and making little mewing noises. I desperately want to come and, as raw and stimulating as the touch of Stone's fingertip against my bottom is, I know I'll need something a tad more direct to send me over the top.

But I know I can't ask for it. Somehow, I know he won't permit that. So I take matters, and myself, into my own hand. Holding tight to his strong torso with one arm, I slip my hand – my right hand – down between us and into the wetness between my legs.

'Uh, uh, uh!' Mr Stone breaks the kiss and admonishes me, his smile wider this time, and more wolfish. It dawns on me that he actually wants me to transgress. It's part of the fun for him.

I still know that I shouldn't ask, but I do.

'But I need to come,' I say in a small voice, hand still between my legs.

'"I need to come, please, Mr Stone",' he corrects me, fingertip still rubbing, rubbing, harder now. He's almost rough, but boy, how I like it!

I repeat after him, like a Victorian child in an old-fashioned schoolroom drama, and he seems to consider my requirement, still working at me as I work at me too. Our respective fingers can't be more than an inch or two apart, both dancing in adjacent playgrounds.

'It'll cost you, Miss Lewis,' he whispers in my ear.

I continue diddling myself furiously, and he names his price.

Which does cause me to pause. And almost giggle. So, people do actually do that? It's sort of mildly hysterical, and clichéd, and at the same time deadly serious. And Mr Stone clearly understands all that, because he actually beams at me as I absorb what he's said. He's obviously thoroughly amused.

And it's that unfeigned delight of his that finally gets me off. His finger, my finger, that smile – it's all too much and I come like a runaway train, my hips jerking furiously against him. And I'm dimly aware that what I'm bumping against mainly is the splendid erection lodged in his dark, expensive trousers.

Oh, how I want some of that too! I think as my body clenches and clenches, and he holds me upright through the spasms. But at the back of my mind I begin to wonder if I'll get it.

In a little while, I find myself huddled in his arms as he leans against the desk, my belly still nestled against his remarkable hard-on. I reach for him, both because he's fabulous and because it might be a way of distracting him, but he gently but firmly takes hold of my hand and pulls it away from his cock.

'Naughty, naughty, Miss Lewis. Nobody touches that without my permission.' He plants a tiny kiss against the corner of my mouth, then pushes me upright. 'I think it's time for you to pay that price we negotiated.'

I don't remember me actually doing any negotiation, but I'm suddenly excited all over again. Especially by the glitter in his eyes.

So, how does this work? You hear about it on the telly, and read about it in celeb mags, and books, and what have you. So and so is into spanking, or a bit of S/M. But it's all talk, and it's not taken seriously. It's just a laugh, like something out of a *Carry On* flick or a bawdy 50s farce. It never actually dawns on you that people might really do this thing. And get off on it.

But for all his wicked little smile, and the fact that throughout this bizarre interlude he's clearly had his tongue very firmly in his cheek, it's patently obvious that Mr Stone means business.

And I just haven't a clue!

'You don't have a clue, do you?' he says, giving one of his characteristic head tilts, amusement writ large on his sturdy, slightly swarthy features while I nearly fall to the floor in shock. God, is the man a mind-reader?

He stands up straight and sort of spins us round, almost as if we we're dancing the tango. Then, almost before I've really worked out what's happened, he's sitting on the plain wooden chair that I sat on, what seems like millennia ago, holding my hand and staring at me with a challenging glint in his eye.

He exerts that gentle but inexorable pressure again, and I follow his direction. Before I know it, and hardly able to believe what's happened, I'm face down on his knee, studying the patterns in the carpet and trying to keep my balance whilst edging as close as I can to the fearsome erection that's digging into my belly.

How the fuck did I get myself into this one?

I can't help it. I start to laugh, and it's difficult to control myself. This is both the most hilarious and most erotic situation I've ever been in. And Robert Stone is the only man I could possibly imagine wanting to be in it with.

Talk about turning me on to new things!

5 The Director's Preference?

So, it looks like Mr Stone is going to spank me. All the signs point that way. I'm across his knee. I'm face down. He's fussing with my skirt and my knickers, and arranging them so that my bottom is completely naked and I'm nicely placed as his target.

My bottom. Again. A thought occurs.

Is this Mr Stone's big kink? Is he a bottom fetishist? At the expense of everything else? He certainly hasn't shown a massive amount of interest in other parts of me. He's kissed my lips, yes, and he seemed to enjoy that. But he hasn't paid even the slightest bit of attention to my breasts or my cunt. It was my bum he zeroed in on almost immediately, even while our lips were locked. Suddenly, I have to ask. Even though I sense that I might have to pay for it. It's not that I won't want to be with Mr Stone if all he's really interested in is my arse. It's just that I'd like to know the score, so I can get my head around the deal.

I leap an inch into the air as he places his palm on my bottom cheek, curving gently, almost tenderly around it. It's not quite a caress, but it has the quality of one. It's his hand saying, 'Hello, I'm your friend, even if it might not sometimes seem that way.'

This touch lasts several moments and, even though I can't see his face, I get the strangest idea that his eyes might be closed, that he's in some kind of fugue of delicious anticipation. I certainly am, even despite my need to ask questions. The notion of our unspoken communication becomes even more tangible.

But of course I'm an idiot, so I spoil it.

'Er ... can I ask a question?' Oops, that's not right, is it? 'Can I ask a question, please, Mr Stone?'

He takes a breath. He sighs, the sound barely audible. Is he cross? Or is he putting it on? Just a part of the drama.

'Yes, why not?' His finger and thumb flex against the muscle of my bottom cheek. It's not quite a pinch, but it's certainly the threat of one. 'Is it a personal question?'

'Sort of.'

'Hmm ...' My heart leaps. He does sound amused. This is fun. Even if it might turn out to be painful. 'Okay, fire away, Miss Lewis. But be aware that there might be consequences.' The finger and thumb tighten a little. 'Do you still want to ask?'

I nod, then launch myself into it. 'Er ... Mr Stone ... Are you ... Do you only ...' Oh hell, how to ask this? 'Mr Stone, are you a bottom fetishist? Do you only like girls' bums and not the rest of them?'

It sounds ridiculous spoken out loud, and Stone's low rumble of laughter tells me he thinks it's hilarious. I feel him shake his head despairingly. I watch in my mind as a smile lights his face and his eyes.

'I mean, I don't mind or anything,' I burble on, 'I just wanted to know.'

'A fair enough question,' he says at length, and then I'm jerking into the air again, as his square-tipped finger strays, rudely, and settles with delicious precision at the entrance to my vagina. It only stays there a second, but it's enough to give me my answer without him having to verbalise it.

Although he does.

'Don't worry, Miss Lewis, I like all a girl's "parts". I like them very much indeed.' He touches my sex again, a little more lingeringly this time. 'And I'm particularly taken with yours.' He hesitates, and I clench everything.

Suddenly I know exactly what's coming. 'But *this* is the bit that most interests me at the moment.'

On the word *this*, his large and shockingly hard hand comes down on my bum like a thunderclap and I feel as if I've just been electrocuted.

Life is suddenly a huge overload of sensations. My left bottom cheek seems to have burst into flames, and I hear a muffled groaning sound. There's the coppery taste of blood in my mouth. Through everything, I realise that knowing what was coming, I've bitten down on my lip to keep in the noise.

I also realise that I'm wriggling like fury, and that Mr Stone is laughing softly. He whacks me with another slap, and I'm biting my lip again.

The pain is astonishing! Like I never expected. If I'd thought about spanking at all, I'd imagined a sort of a tingle, a play tap. But this isn't a play tap and it's a damn sight more than a tingle. Only the thought of Mrs Sheldon on the other side of the door stops me from wailing out loud.

And yet, without being able to stop myself, I'm lifting my bottom to the blows, almost as if I'm asking my tormentor for more.

Which, with a low sound of satisfaction, he supplies.

Smack. Smack. Smack.

There are only about half a dozen in total, but by the time he's finished, it feels as if he's been beating me for half an hour and my flaming bottom has swollen to four times its normal size.

'Enough?' he enquires at length, his voice pleasant and conversational while his fingertips rest ominously on the fire he's created.

As if I had a say in it?

'Too much,' I reply through gritted teeth. Well, he asked, so I answered

He laughs again, but somehow it's not an unkind

reaction. Just the reverse. He sounds pleased with me, almost proud, and despite the throb, throb, throb in my bottom and – not exactly to my surprise – between my legs, I feel extraordinarily pleased with myself too.

It's mad, but the emotion is wonderful. I did something good! I 'performed' for Mr Stone and he's pleased with me.

This is the weirdest thing that's ever happened to me. The weirdest thing I could imagine. But I like it.

'Fair enough,' he says and, scooping an arm around my waist, he gets to his feet and sets me on mine. I find myself just standing there, like a living doll, while he smooths my knickers up over my sizzling bum and straightens and primps my skirt into place. I feel strangely protected and cherished, despite what he's done to me. I want to throw my arms around him and hug him. I also feel quite teary.

'Hey!' he says gently, and from his pocket he produces a white handkerchief. It's crumpled but perfectly clean and with it he blots my eyes, then dabs at my lip, where the blood is.

Confusing emotions grip me, and I fight for control. Grappling with them is far harder than being spanked but I avoid self-analysis. Instead I concentrate on Stone's face, broad and dark with stubble, and with such intensely gleaming brown eyes. Eyes that seem to be seeing everything that I'm trying to avoid. He tilts his head to one side, giving me a long, long look, then gently puts the handkerchief into my hand. He opens his mouth to say something, but at that moment the phone rings and, as he moves to his desk and lifts the receiver, I feel bereft, not knowing what it was he was about to communicate to me.

'Ah yes, of course, I'd quite forgotten,' he says crisply, all the time looking at me as I dab at my lip and more surreptitiously at my eyes. 'Tell him I'll be there in ten.

Thanks for reminding me.' He frowns as he settles the receiver down. 'All right now?' he asks in a gentler voice, his attention all on me again, whatever demand on his time the call referred to momentarily forgotten.

'Fine, thanks,' I mutter, hating the unknown caller. I don't know what I've been expecting, but what's just happened between us was so intimate that it feels like a massive, agonising wrench now that it's obviously over.

But, as I avoid his eyes, it suddenly dawns on me that our business isn't quite over. Glancing at his groin, I see that he's still quite unequivocally erect.

Naturally, he follows my roving eyes, and he shrugs expressively, making a swift flipping gesture with his long fingers, as if the state of his body is inconsequential.

'I could do something for you,' I say boldly, my hand already making for his crotch.

'That's kind of you, Maria,' he says, looking almost sad for a moment, 'but I'll deal with it myself.' He nods towards the door, at the end of the room, which I take it leads to a small executive washroom of some kind.

I'm 'Maria' now, and it *is* over.

'Right, I'd better be off,' I mumble, and start to back away.

Moving quickly, Stone anticipates me, and stops me in my tracks with the touch of his large, warm hand against my cheek. He doesn't speak, but his shining brown eyes impart volumes of information, and what might possibly be real emotion.

I nod. He nods. And he lets me go. At the door I turn, and he's still standing there, watching me, and, as I turn the door handle and scoot out, it's the brilliance of his eyes that stays with me, not the sight of that still impressive hard-on.

I nod to Mrs Sheldon, and wonder why she's looking at me curiously, until I remember that I'm still clutching Stone's white handkerchief.

'Bit of a nosebleed,' I babble. 'Mr Stone lent me his hankie.'

Mrs Sheldon expresses concern, but I bluff it out and exit swiftly by the outer door. I have to get out of here. I have to think. I have to try and work out what on earth's just happened to me. And what significance this event has for my future at the Hall.

But out in the corridor I don't find the escape I was hoping for. As I turn, I realise I'm not alone out there. Walking purposefully towards me is William Youngblood, and the expression on his face is intent and focused. He's clearly not going to sweep by me, ignoring me as an underling, this time. He looks a little fierce, but I'm instantly able to defuse any slight feelings of alarm.

I just imagine his bottom bobbing and tensing as he goes at it with Sandy!

I suppress a grin. He's such a self-consciously cool character, always an immaculate paragon of male chic in comparison to Stone's burly, more lived-in image. It's huge fun to know that he's a horny little monster underneath. Just like the rest of us, I think wryly, reflecting on the bizarre little sexfest without any actual sex that Stone and I have just shared.

Under other circumstances it might have been nice to linger and smirk knowingly at Youngblood, to see if I could put the wind up him about his exploits on the couch in the cellar. It would be enormously entertaining to set him wondering whether he and Sandy had been seen. After all, it's not really something he could confront me openly about, without giving himself away, is it?

But I'm still reeling from Stone after-effects, so I just flash Youngblood a tight smile and mutter 'Hi!' while trying to dive past without drawing too much attention to my pink face, my bright eyes, and the possibility that I might smell very strongly of freshly stirred arousal.

No such luck.

'Oh, good! Maria. Yes!' he says, all business, 'I'm glad I've caught you. I wonder if you could come and see me.'

Agh!

'What? Now?' I say, aware that I sound both lacking in graciousness, and lacking in the respect for authority that Youngblood is noted for demanding. Not the best way to get away from him unobtrusively.

Youngblood shoots a crisply perfect cuff and consults a notably fashionable watch. I think again, longingly, of Stone's cuddly late-afternoon rumpledness.

'No, I've got a meeting in a few minutes,' he says, still unperturbed and businesslike, which convinces me that he has no idea he was observed down in the basement. 'Why not pop up at eleven, tomorrow?' He gives me a reassuring smile, which actually makes him look remarkably fanciable. I suddenly wonder how I'd feel about him if there were no Stone in the world.

'Yes, OK, right,' I jabber, all confusion, wondering what the hell is the matter with me since I came to this place. 'It's a date.'

Twit! I chastise myself, as Youngblood really smiles now, obviously fancying himself mightily. Against all the odds, there is a bit of chemistry going on here, and the Human Resources Manager obviously likes the idea of it.

'Excellent!' he pronounces and, to my consternation, there's a silent, expectant little lull. I don't know what to say, and it seems he doesn't either, but that doesn't stop him checking me out.

And I him.

William Youngblood is a very handsome man and, as the seconds stretch out, he runs his hand over his head in an involuntary gesture. The hair department is where he really scores over Stone. And over most men. Because his is astounding! Smooth, a dazzling light gold, almost platinum, and always stringently well styled. It's very possible, I reflect, that he might bleach it but, curiously, that's much more exciting to me than if the colour were natural. And he certainly knows how to accentuate both his hair and his rather pale colouring. He always wears black, dark blue or charcoal grey.

'Right. OK. It's a date,' he mirrors back at me, his mouth curling in a smile that's far more than bigwig-to-pleb condescension. 'See you tomorrow, Maria.' And then he's away down the corridor purposefully, his stride quite rangy for a man who's comparatively short. I guess it must be a real irritation to him that Stone towers over him by a good seven or eight inches.

When he's gone, I wonder what the hell I'm doing because, basically, I'm meandering down the corridor in totally the wrong direction. It occurs to me to lurk in a doorway or something, in order to see Stone leave his office for his meeting. But I quickly squash the idea. It would spoil things somehow. We parted. And even though I would have loved more than anything in the world to stay, and perhaps pleasure Stone at least a fraction of the amount he pleasured me, there was a kind of finality to the leave-taking and I don't want to undermine its significance.

Not really sure where I'm going, and aware that I could get badly lost in this warren of a place, I walk to the far end of the corridor and unexpectedly find another smaller staircase, leading downwards.

On the ground floor, mercifully, I manage to reorientate myself physically, even if my mind and emotions are all over the place. Being a creature of habit, I nip into the Ladies and bolt myself into a cubicle.

I don't know what to do or what to think. The little run-in with Youngblood distracted me, but only for a moment. The instant I'm back in a private, secret place, my mind flies back to Stone's office, and what happened there.

Bloody hell, he spanked me! Far out!

Sliding down my knickers and sinking down on to the seat, I reach around and touch the cheek of my bottom, trying to commune with the spirit of Stone, which I imagine is still lingering there.

To my surprise it barely hurts at all now, and I wonder if this is the result of some special skill of his. Is there a way to spank that stings like all hell at the time but fades quickly afterwards? It's a fascinating prospect, and makes me speculate on how often Stone spanks women and just how many might have felt the impact of that beefy yet adept left hand of his. I feel a pang of jealousy, then, right on the back of it, a feeling that I don't have a right to be jealous. After all, it was only a few moments ago that I have to admit I'd found myself fancying Stone's arch rival!

But still, the notion of our esteemed Director of Finance being a championship spanker is a fascinating one. Who would ever have guessed, when I first followed Mel's suggestion and checked out the online ad for this job, that I'd be walking into such a nest of rampant eroticism? And pervy stuff at that?

I imagine him now, in his own little cloakroom, wanking quickly so he can go to his meeting or whatever without an embarrassing stiffy. I still can't help hoping that he's huge!

I mean, it shouldn't matter, but it does. In Stone's case it should matter less than usual, because he's obviously so blindingly great with his hands and the power of his imagination. But I still really, really want him to have a nice big penis. One that looks thick and heavy in the hand, whether it be his own hand, or mine. It's been longer than is good for me since I was in a relationship and have had chance to play with a man's equipment, but I'd really, really love it to be Stone's cock I get to fondle first after my dry spell.

Or maybe suck?

Oh God, yes! My mouth waters at the thought. I can almost feel the texture of him against my tongue. The firm flesh, the velvety, strangely tender feel of the stretched skin.

I must have him! I must! In my mouth and in my body! What started out as a mild, almost playful fancying when I first encountered this boss of mine has now turned itself into a full-fledged, full-blooded, full-on obsession. Robert Stone is the last man I should be suitably pursuing here in Borough Hall, but I'm beyond stopping myself now. He's got under my skin, and he's a constant itch I need to scratch. Even now, I realise I'm agonisingly turned on, just thinking and musing about him.

With a sigh, and almost in desperation, I begin to masturbate.

6 **Taken for a Ride**

It's been a weird day. I just want to get home as quickly as possible and watch television, eat chocolate and drink tea.

I want to do nice, normal things and stop my mind circling inexorably round and round Stone like a tiny insignificant moon circling a mighty planet. Alas, I get a phone call from Greg, saying he's going to a computer fair after work so he can't give me a lift.

I look forward to the gruelling experience of sitting on a crowded bus with only my dangerous liaison with the Director of Finance to occupy my mind.

Not that I don't want to think about Stone.

I *do*!

But thinking about him leads to speculating as to whether there are any future prospects with him, and, if not, how the hell I'm going to hang on to this job. Thinking about him also leads to rerunning and rerunning every astonishing, earthshaking, life-changing moment of what we did together. And that only leads to sticky knickers and the clenching, grinding ache of extreme frustration, as my body cries out for more and more and more of him.

I feel pretty grim by the time I reach the time clock, and of course I make a mess of things, passing my ID again and again in front of the sensor and getting a red error light at every single swipe.

'Fuck!' I growl, hating the bloody thing, wishing it was set low enough on the wall for me to kick the shit out of it.

For the dozenth time I try, and shout 'Fuck!', but then a hand reaches around from behind me, swipes the card and gets the green light on the very first attempt.

I'm shaking like a leaf, because for a second I thought that my saviour was Stone, back from his meeting and here to whisk me away to his home, or somewhere, and give me the damn good seeing-to that I know I want and need from him. But just as quickly I've realised that it's not him. The hand that's swiped for me might be capable and workmanlike, but it's far too small and feminine to be Robert Stone's mighty mitt.

'You have to be gentle with it, girlfriend,' says Mel as I turn around. She's standing there, obviously ready to go home herself. Whipping out her own ID she does another perfect first-time swipe.

'Yeah, I know,' I answer, 'but it's been a rough day and I can't be doing with the stupid bloody thing.'

'Ah well, love, that's why I'm here.' She's reaching into her pocket and she takes out a set of keys. 'Greg says you need a lift home tonight, and here I am, at your service, fair maiden!'

And she does look a bit like a knight or some sort of warrior. She's ditched her smart security-guard uniform and she's in civvies. Tough, utilitarian blue jeans, Docs and a biker jacket. Tucked under her arm she carries her helmet, which appears to have a design resembling a Valkyrie head-dress painted on it.

I'm gobsmacked.

'On your bike?' I say idiotically.

'Why not? It gets from A to B quite nicely,' she says with a grin.

I continue to gape at her. 'Don't I need a helmet or something? I can't just get on a bike like, this can I?' It's preposterous, but I already slightly like the idea of it. Maybe this is my big day for trying new things?

'Don't worry, I've got a spare lid in my bike box.

There's no need to worry.' She flashes me a big grin and darts forward, slipping her free arm through mine. 'Come on, Maria! Let's roll!'

And soon I'm walking arm in arm with a lesbian across an open car park. It's an interesting sensation and I wonder what Stone would think of it. I get a feeling it would make him grin. That he'd approve. That he'd encourage me to flirt with Mel – and more – then tell him all about it afterwards.

When we reach the small corner of the car park where there are stanchions to chain motorbikes to, I begin to have second thoughts. I've only ever seen Mel's Kawasaki from a distance. Close up, it's a bit of a monster. And it's very broad-looking. I glance down at my skirt, which is quite short, and even though the fabric has a bit of give in it, the stupid thing will be up around my crotch the instant I attempt to get astride.

Mel is smirking broadly. She obviously likes that idea very much. But I'm not so sure. Enough has happened already today, without getting into something with Mel. And I'm beginning to think that something will most definitely happen if I get astride this bike. Especially with my skirt up around my fanny!

'Don't worry,' she says, and with a shrug of obvious regret, she flips up a panel behind the bike seat, digs in and brings out a helmet and a pair of jeans and hands them both to me. 'I think these will fit. And preserve your modesty.'

The jeans are well-aged but freshly laundered, and the helmet isn't the fearsome full-face job that Mel is now shoving her head into, but a more girly-type thing with an open face, a peak and a strap. It's also bright pink, and looks like the sort of thing that some cool continental girl would wear while riding around Rome on the back of a Lambretta with Brad Pitt.

Oh well, in for a penny. 'Won't be a minute,' I say, and turn to make my way back to the Hall to change – only to have Mel catch me by the arm. She looks quite awesome now she's helmeted up, and I actually flinch.

'No need for that,' she says, her eyes glittering within the frame of the helmet. 'There's no one around. Change here!'

Er . . . Excuse me?

She's right. There isn't anyone in the vicinity.

Except *her*.

She shakes her head, the late-afternoon sun glinting on the shiny helmet. 'Don't worry. I'll turn my back. I won't look.'

But when she does so, I don't feel much better. She's got an imagination, hasn't she? And it'll be running wild, knowing I'm showing my knickers here in a public car park. And I'm not just flattering myself assuming that she fancies me because she's made it pretty obvious that she does.

I place the helmet on the wall beside the stanchion, and unfold the jeans. The logical way to proceed would be to wiggle them on under my skirt, then take that off. But suddenly all logic dissolves. I see a pair of brown eyes, a pair of laughing brown eyes, and they're daring me to live dangerously. I glance toward the distant facade of Borough Hall, but I know he can't possibly be observing me because his office overlooks the inner courtyard.

Yet still, as I unzip my skirt, and slide it down, baring my naked thighs and my skimpy knickers to the plain air and the cool, naughty breezes, it's Robert Stone for whom I'm putting on a show. I kick off my shoes and stand barefoot on the hard standing, then hesitate a moment, consciously posing.

And it's this very moment that Mel chooses to spin around for a peek!

'Very nice, girlfriend,' she purrs, not hiding her interest. Her green eyes look very dark and fierce all of a sudden.

'Mel! You said you wouldn't look!'

'Sorry! Sorry, sorry, sorry! I couldn't resist!' She whirls back again, but not before I've seen that there's not the slightest scrap of remorse in those eyes of hers.

I dismiss my silly fantasies about being watched by Stone and struggle into the jeans and back into my shoes as fast as possible. When Mel turns again, I'm buckling on the helmet, hoping that it doesn't completely squish the body out of my hair.

'Don't worry, it'll bounce back,' says Mel reassuringly, reaching out to arrange the blonde strands neatly where they stick out of the bottom of the helmet. Her touch is surprisingly light and impersonal – and pretty pointless because any minute now the wind will be blowing any exposed hair all over the place.

'I've never been on a bike before,' I choose this moment to admit. I haven't, and now I'm scared. It was just that there's been so much else going on that it's only now that I have a chance to think about what I've agreed to.

'Don't worry. It's a piece of cake. You don't have to worry about a thing. All you have to do is hang on and relax.' Pulling on a pair of gauntlets, she takes the handlebars, kicks up the stand, and then throws one long, jeans-clad leg across the heavy bike. Once she's straddling it, she gestures to me.

I'm shaking now, as I shove my bag and skirt into the bike box and flip down the lid. I look at Mel's strong back and her commanding hold on the handlebars. She's perfectly confident. Both in her own riding skills and in her ability to deal with a nervous bike virgin on her pillion seat.

'OK, get on. Grab me round the waist, throw your leg over the saddle, then settle down and put your feet on the passenger pegs.' I'm still hesitating. 'Don't worry, I can hold you.' She chuckles, the sound muffled as she flips down her smoky visor. 'I've had plenty of girls on the back of this baby, you know.'

Pondering the exact meaning of the word 'had' in this context, I obey her. I'm afraid that it'll all be horrifically unstable but, as I settle into place, a sense of security and a growing confidence in Mel is all I feel. That, and the rather alarming awareness of having my legs apart with a large, bulky and suddenly violently pulsating object between them.

The sensation of the revving bike is astonishing. Its vibrations are transmitted directly through my cunt as if the mighty Kawasaki is a giant sex toy, reawakening all the excitement there that Robert Stone initiated earlier. I begin to shake as I grab on even tighter to Mel's leather-encased torso, and it's not entirely through fear of the unknown. At this rate I'll be having an orgasm before we've got to the end of the street.

'OK, sweetheart, hang on tight!' shouts Mel over the cacophony and, after a last reassuring slap on my thigh, gives the throttle one last twist and pushes forward with her booted feet, and suddenly we're away and flying rapidly across the car park.

Out on the road, riding with Mel is a combination of pure exhilaration and abject terror. All jumbled up with thumping, thudding, thrumming sexual stimulation. It quickly dawns on me that no Magic Rabbit or clit tingler on earth has the horsepower of a high-powered motor-cycle. I cling on to Mel while her huge machine does the business between my legs.

I feel as if my hair's standing on end inside my helmet.

What would Stone think of this little escapade, I wonder? For a moment I imagine him as a big, burly biker, his solid body encased in black leather. There's nothing sleek or streamlined about him. He's all roughness. All earth. Beastly and primal. Automatically I hug Mel as if she's him, and she adjusts her position on the seat, pushing back against me.

Oh hell, what have I done now?

It's about this time I realise that we're not actually going home. In fact we're speeding in the opposite direction altogether, out of town, towards the ring road. I daren't squeeze Mel again, because she obviously thinks that means I want to cuddle her or something, so I just tap her lightly on the shoulder. Which she responds to immediately by pulling over, setting her booted feet firmly on the ground and turning off the engine.

'What's wrong, sweetheart? Are you scared?' she asks, flipping up her visor and swivelling in the saddle to look over her shoulder at me.

Her eyes flash, daring me to say, 'No, of course not', even though I am a bit scared. Especially as I'm still just perched on the bike, feet on the pegs, feeling precarious and unstable, Mel supporting the entire weight of the bike *and* me with her strong, jeans-clad thighs. But it's not so much the possibility of falling off it that's bothering me, it's more what *she* might be thinking, and what *I'm* feeling inside that's so unsettling and disquieting. 'No, not really. But I just wondered, where are we going?'

Mel smiles, what I can see of it inside the fearsome helmet. 'Don't worry, I'm not abducting you. I just thought you might fancy a bite to eat. And a trip to a real bikers' caff.' She pauses, still challenging me. 'Of course if you're not up for it, we can always turn around.'

Home would be safer. I don't really know Mel all that well, and me just going along with her like this might lead her to make assumptions. Assumptions I really don't know yet whether I'm averse to or in favour of. I've got far too much on my plate already at the moment with Robert Stone.

But the moment he's back in my mind, I know I have

to go with Mel. I know I *want* to! He's a watcher, an experimenter and a thrill-seeker himself, and to back away from anything right now would be letting him down.

And suddenly that's the last thing in the world I want to do.

'No, that's fine. I'm starving,' I say brightly, and my stomach grumbles as if to lend veracity to the statement. I am hungry, I realise. Today has been a weird, intense drain on my reserves and I have a feeling I'll need more energy ahead. 'Let's go!'

Mel nods. It's difficult to read the expression on her face accurately from within the confines of her helmet, at an angle, but her body language is energetic. And happy.

'Cool! Hang on then!' A second later the bike's thundering again and we shoot off into traffic, Mel slotting it expertly into the flow.

Ten minutes later we draw up outside the Blue Plate café. The bleak, sprawling car park is chock-a-block with all manner of commercial vehicles, ranging from little white builders' vans to giant big rigs. There's also a long, neatly aligned row of gleaming Big Bang motorcycles in all the colours of the rainbow standing in front of the low, shabby red-brick building.

Mel kills the engine, and I clamber off the bike, less than gracefully. My legs feel jellified, and all that vibration has had a real effect between them that I'm embarrassed to think about, given that I'm wearing somebody else's jeans. I watch as Mel secures the big Kawasaki alongside an equally humungous Honda, and have a horrible vision of her sniffing the crotch of these jeans later, when I've taken them off.

'What's the matter?' She's pulled off her helmet now, and she's fluffing out her short blonde hair again. It looks rough, and pretty and sort of boyish, but it's her eyes that seem to grab a hold of me. There's a distinctly Stone-like gleam of perception in them, as if she's done what he does. Which is read my horrible grubby mind.

'Nothing,' I mutter, 'I'm fine. Like I said, it's the first time I've ever ridden on a motorbike and it's made me feel a bit shaky.'

'Me too.' She grins and waggles her neatly groomed eyebrows at me, then sets her helmet on the seat of the bike.

I open my mouth to ask her what the hell she's talking about – even though I'm sure I know – but she shakes her head, then reaches across to unbuckle the strap of my helmet. She lifts it gently off my head, then ruffles my hair a little and smoothes it behind my ears in a strangely maternal gesture.

'Come on. Let's get some food inside you. You'll soon feel better!'

As we walk into the café, helmets under our arms, it's just like in a Western when the out-of-town gunslinger first enters the saloon. Classic metal still pounds out of the jukebox, but the level of conversation most definitely diminishes, and heads, almost exclusively male apart from the woman behind the counter, turn in our direction. Even the grease molecules in the air seem to hang motionless.

It's a cliché, but all eyes are on us.

A few of the bikers call out greetings to Mel, but most of the truckers seem more interested in me. I'm new. Unknown. Fresh meat. It doesn't seem to matter to them that theoretically I might be Mel's girlfriend. In fact they're probably hoping I am, in order to fuel their fantasies. It's a well-known fact that men love the thought of women getting it on. Another testosterone classic that's right at home in a macho establishment like the Blue Plate.

'Get us that table.' Mel gestures towards an empty

table by the window, and hands me her helmet. 'What do you want? I'll bring it.'

I haven't seen a menu. There doesn't even seem to be a board or anything with the dishes listed, but I guess that it's probably mostly just the high-cholesterol staples. It certainly smells that way, and the evocative odour of fried food makes my stomach rumble rebelliously again. My system is suddenly crying out for artery fur and calories by the million.

'I'll have what you're having,' I answer, then instantly think better of it the moment it's out of my mouth. Why not just ask her outright if she wants to go to bed with you, dummy! But it's too late now and Mel's smirking broadly, always several steps ahead of me.

I try to walk across the room without attracting too much attention, but it's a lost cause. I don't get any actual wolf whistles, but three or four interested bikers nearby say 'Hello, love!' when I shuffle into my seat and shove the helmets to one end of the reasonably clean but slightly sugar-strewn table.

And yet somehow it's all suddenly wildly exhilarating. The scrutiny of these men, the teasing presence of Mel, the strange idea that Stone is somehow with me, observing me, challenging me – everything combines to lift my spirits, goose me up, make feel daring. I smile back at the bikers who are smiling at me, and I lean back in my seat, flipping open the buttons of my jacket and running my fingers through my hair.

I'm preening. Displaying. Asking for trouble.

There, Stone, is that what you wanted? I imagine him sitting at a nearby table, that small, boyish, challenging smile on his broad face. Crazily, I feel my body rouse. Wanting. Wanting what? I'm not really sure, but I know I want something and I want it soon.

And as Mel walks towards the table, beaming broadly

and with a mug in each hand, I have an intimation of what it is I might soon be getting.

I've never really noticed before but, beneath her carapace of bravado and toughness, she really is a stunningly beautiful woman. She has the perfect oval face and cheekbones worthy of a Golden Age movie goddess, and, even in her chunky jeans and her leather jacket, it's easy to see she's got the body to match.

'Here!' she says, plonking down the mugs amongst the sugar. 'Nice cuppa tea. Just what you need after a long, stressful day.'

'Who says it was stressful?' I narrow my eyes at her, wondering what she's heard, or sensed. I could swear that what happened with Stone was secret between him and me, but you never know in Borough Hall. Every day I work there the place seems more preposterous.

'Oh, I could tell.' She shrugs out of her leather and places it on the back of her chair. And I'm transfixed!

Mel has on a plain, workmanlike white T-shirt, which makes it obvious that her breasts are just as spectacular as the rest of her. They're enviably high and rounded, and I don't know whether it's a lesbian thing, or some kind of gesture of libertarianism, or just because she doesn't need one, but it's flagrantly obvious that she isn't wearing a bra.

I have that feeling that my eyes are out on stalks again.

Mel catches my look, and laughs. Then shrugs. I can almost hear her weighing up whether to say something about the fact that I just ogled her nipples. But it seems she's a tactician, just like Stone, and she saves that for later.

'When I picked you up at the time clock, you looked as if you were just back from being abducted by aliens, love.' She blows on her tea, then takes a sip, her pink tongue scooting around her lips afterwards. 'Something happened today. And don't try to kid me that it didn't!' Without warning, she reaches out and gently touches my cheek for a second. 'You've got this look about you. Sort of a combination of shell-shocked and smug ... and a little bit glowing. And, much as I'd like to think it's the pleasure of *my* company that's lighting you up, I suspect it isn't.'

I get an overpowering urge to turn my face into the fleeting caress, but it's over before it's really started. Instead, I make a show of bristling in mock indignation.

'But I do enjoy your company, Mel!' I primp my hair again, sit up straight and then shrug out of my jacket too. I've got a bra on, and my breasts aren't nearly as perkily perfect as Mel's, but they're not bad and it seems like time to flaunt my assets. And bolster my confidence.

'Nice try, love, but you're not going to distract me,' says Mel with a smirk, clearly enjoying the view. 'Something *did* happen today, didn't it? My sex radar is binging! Now tell! Was it Stone?'

How the hell does she know? Does everyone in Borough Hall have psychic powers where sex is concerned?

'OK, yes, something did happen. And yes, it was with Stone.' For a breathing space, I take a swig of tea, and it's sensational. Hot, strong and reviving. Stone in a mug, I think, wondering if I'm going completely bonkers. 'But why do you ask? Has someone said something? I don't see how anyone could know.'

'Just a wild stab, love, don't worry,' replies Mel, reaching over and placing her hand over mine. 'There are no nasty rumours or anything. It was just the way you were looking at him the other morning. Like it was bolt-from-the-blue time, you know? And he was looking back at you and I could see all sorts of stuff going on in his mind. He's a very sexy guy, and you can just tell he thinks about it all the time.' I'm conscious of her hand on mine still, and it doesn't do a lot for my clarity of thought. I wouldn't have thought that she'd accuse any man of being sexy, considering how she's making it pretty obvious that she thinks *I'm* pretty sexy, but maybe she's a lot more complicated than I thought.

'*You* think Stone is sexy?'

'Yeah, I think Stone is sexy. I'd rather fuck you than him, but if I was alone on a desert island and it was a choice of him or a lifetime of masturbation, I think it'd be worth trying to adapt.'

There's a loud stage cough from just behind me, and I turn to see the woman from behind the counter. She's carrying a tray laden with two huge plates of double egg and chips, plus a mountain of bread and butter, and there's a wide eye-pop of a smile on her face.

'Thanks, Alice! Looks fab. As ever,' says Mel breezily. She removes her hand from mine without the slightest hint of self-consciousness, and sits back to allow Alice to set out our plates.

The food does indeed look fab. Mounds of chips, eggs crispy round the edges, with whitened yolks. Surprisingly, despite the bizarreness of the situation, my appetite is undiminished, and when Alice ambles off, still grinning, I plunge right in.

I gobble down chips, dipping them in egg, aware that even though she's eating too, Mel is watching and waiting.

'Oh, come on! Don't keep me in suspense,' she says at last, when nearly half my plateful is gone.

And so, in the midst of munching my way steadily through one of the greasiest but most delicious meals I've had in ages, and with no idea why I'm being so hair-raisingly frank with this gay woman I barely know, the whole bizarre 'thing' starts to spill out.

'Well, it started last week, sort of . . . I saw Stone again in the corridor, and he did that thing he does, you know?

He looked at me as if he knew what I was thinking and what I'd been doing.'

'What *had* you been doing?'

My face goes crimson. 'I'd been in the Ladies. Fantasising about him. And one thing led to another.'

Mel beams. 'You mean you were masturbating?'

'Will you keep your voice down!' I hiss. We're already the main focus of attention in here without Mel announcing my sexual habits to the rest of the diners.

'Well, were you?' she persists in a lower tone.

'Yes.'

'And what did he say? Did he ask you if that's what you'd been doing?'

'No, not in as many words. He just made a remark about me "coming down with something" and needing "a lie down".'

'So? What else? How did that lead to something happening today?'

I describe my visit to the basement, and my discovery there.

Mel laughs out loud, but I just can't be bothered to shush her any more. What difference would it make? Everyone seems to be watching us anyway.

'Hilarious! Sandy and the Blond Bombshell, who'd have thought it? But what have they got to do with you and Stone?'

'Everything,' I whisper. 'I was watching them, and it was sort of "exciting", if you know what I mean.' Mel rolls her eyes. Clearly she does. 'And suddenly, shazam! Stone was there! One minute I'm on my own in this little cubby-hole, watching Sandy and Youngblood bonking, and the next minute he's right there beside me, and *he's* watching *me*!'

Mel's fork stills half-way to her mouth.

'He wasn't interested in them. Just in me. He just sat

there, all hunkered down in this tiny little space, watching me while I . . . while I . . .'

Mel has the grace to only mime the word this time, and I nod.

'And by the time I'd finished, he'd just disappeared.'

'What do you mean, "disappeared"? Are you sure you didn't just imagine he was there? Or have an erotic dream or something?'

'No, it was all real. And I suppose that's why he sent for me today.'

'Good God, there's more?'

I reach for the tomato-shaped sauce bottle and splurge ketchup on to my plate, taking time out to gather myself for the next phase.

'Yeah, he sent for me to come up to his office . . .' I eat some more chips. Anything to calm my nerves. Mel doesn't actually say anything, but every last molecule of her seems to be screaming for me to get on with it.

'At first it was completely normal, as if nothing had happened. He asked me how I was settling in and all that bullshit, and it was all so mundane I was seriously convinced I *had* imagined being in the cellar with him . . . and then everything seemed to change somehow, and it was as if we were playing some kind of game. I don't really know how to describe it.'

I look away, stare out of the café window, and it's as if I'm seeing those intent brown eyes, and his face, and his body looming over me.

'One minute he's behind his desk, giving me the D of F meet-and-greet spiel . . . and the next, he's right there in front of me, and he takes a hold of me, and we're kissing.'

'Kissing?'

'Yes. And he's touching me.' I feel a desperate urge to wriggle in my seat. It's almost as if those seductive fingers are caressing me again. 'And then I was touching myself, too, and I wanted to come. And he said that if I did, it'd cost me ...'

Mel's completely given up on her food now. She puts down her knife and fork, just gaping at me. 'And did you?'

'Yes. Yes, I did ... and then he spanked me. And it hurt like hell. But it was the most erotic thing that's ever happened in my life.'

I close my eyes. Not because I'm embarrassed, even though I am. No, it's because behind my eyelids, I'm back in that office again, across Stone's knee, and it's just wonderful.

When I open them again, I discover that my plate is all but empty, and I can barely remember tasting the second half of my meal. 'And when it was all over, and I wanted to touch *him*, the phone rang and it was his PA telling him he had a meeting ... and that was it. We didn't really say anything, and I just left.'

By contrast, Mel's plate is still half-full, and she's wide-eyed, almost disbelieving. I'd have said she was the more sexually experienced of the two of us, but I've a feeling I might just have outstripped her.

'Fucking hell!' she says, pushing away her untouched food. 'I mean, I've heard mountains of anecdotal stuff about what goes on in that bloody Hall, especially about Stone, but this is the first time anyone's described a genuine, actual "close encounter". I thought it was all urban legend and now you tell me that you've been touched up and spanked by the Director of Finance *and* you've seen the Human Resources Manager banging Sex-less Sandy in the basement!' She takes a sip of tea, and grimaces because it's cold by now. 'God, I'm so jealous!'

'What, of Sandy and Youngblood?'

She scrunches up her face in disgust. 'Oh no, not those two nasty little shaggers. Bleugh!'

'Of me?' This isn't a desert island, is it?

'No, you twit, of *Stone*!' Her eyes look suddenly very, very green. Frighteningly bright. I knew she fancied me, but now she's got a hard, tough, almost martial look on her face. The expression, suddenly, of one who's not going to take no for an answer without a battle of wills.

And me, well I'm not so sure I want to say no. To tell the story is to relive the story, and I'm very, very aware that my knickers are damp and I very much need to come. It's a sharp, grinding, urgent sensation. It seems incongruous, in this setting and whilst eating, but I can't deny it.

I'm in a total muddle and I'm not sure whom I actually want right now, Stone or Mel.

She starts drumming her fingertips on the table, looking from side to side. She's really agitated. She takes in a deep breath, and huffs it out.

'If Stone was here right now, would you fuck him?'

Oh God, yes I would! Having relived his rude, possessive touch, and that heat of his large hand slapping against my backside, there's nothing I want more than to do anything, anything at all with him.

But he isn't here. And Mel is. And I know that when Mel poses the question I just know she's going to (have I become a mind-reader too?) I'll say yes, because it's Stone's will as well as mine.

I'll say yes, even thought I'm still really not sure what I'm saying yes to.

'Yes, of course I would!' I say with bravado. 'I think he's amazing!'

'Oh God, I *so* wish I was Stone!' She sounds so passionate, and there's a hunger in her eyes, and a strange touch of sadness that completely undermines me. I reach for her hand, feeling both bold and scared.

'But he's not the only one I fancy, you know.'

'Really?'

'Really.'

I experience one of those sudden moments of clarity when the world seems to flip somehow. It happened with Stone, and it's happened here, now, with Mel.

Suddenly I do know what to do. Sort of.

'I need to use the Ladies.' I'm already on my feet and moving towards the door succinctly marked WCs.

'Me too.' Mel's grin is so wide she almost looks as if she's going to burst with glee.

We almost run towards the loos, aware that we're being scrutinised with extreme interest, but no longer caring.

Once inside the surprisingly clean Ladies Room, I start to lose my nerve a bit. And I really do want to pee.

'I – I need to go first,' I stammer.

'Good, I'll help you.' Before I know what's what, Mel has strong-armed me into the cubicle and she's pulling at my clothes, working expertly at buttons and zips.

My excitement level ramps up and up, despite my suddenly renewed fears. This is so perverse! Kinkier even than been fooled about with by Stone.

In a few moments, I'm naked in the lavatory of a transport cafe, bursting to pee, and being ogled by a woman!

Mel wastes no time. She pulls me next to her, my bare skin against her clothed body, and her hand goes straight for my crotch as she pushes me up against the cubicle wall.

If I'd imagined girl-on-girl action as sweet and gentle and fluffy and goddess-worshipping, I'm totally and completely wrong. At least about Mel's style. She's rougher by far than even Stone is, squeezing me hard between my legs and really hammering at my clit. My bladder protests and so do I.

'I really do need to pee, Mel,' I whimper, rising on to my toes, trying to avoid the sensations in my abused bladder, and yet getting off on them furiously in a deep, dark way. I'm nearly fainting with it, and I throw my arms around Mel's cotton-clad shoulders for support.

'I know,' she purrs, and she doesn't let up. She twists her wrist for better purchase, massaging the pit of my belly with her thumb and using strong fingers between my legs.

It feels awful and fabulous, and Mel is relentless, despite the fact that I'm moaning and groaning and all over the place. I waft my hips about, but she stays on target, tormenting me. I get into it, really into it, and while I hang on to her with a kind of desperate headlock, I use my free hand to pull and tweak at my nipples.

In a sudden moment of clarity, I think, *Mr Stone would be so proud*, then in my mind he's right here in the cubicle, watching us. I see him rubbing the side of his stubbly face in delighted contemplation. He finds the sight of my humiliating pleasure so entertaining.

I start to pant. I'm nearly there. Everything clenches, ready to release.

'I'm going to pee! I'm going to pee!' I whine, forgetting to mention that I'm going to come too. That's a given.

With a strength I can barely credit in her, Mel hooks me round the waist, swings me round, and settles me on the pot. Then she hunkers down on her knees beside me and starts to rub again.

I can't help myself and I come and pee in one huge glorious rush and I don't quite know where the one ends and the other begins. I piss like a horse and all through it Mel still pounds on my clit. Her hand is drenched.

When I'm done, she grabs a handful of the rather industrial toilet roll and mops me up, while I just sit there, straddling the toilet, gasping for air.

I'm trying to remember every little bit of it, every nasty little nuance of sensation.

In case I have to tell a certain someone about it later.

* * *

Afterwards, Mel's needs are simple. I start to ask her what she wants, but she just grabs my hand and guides it into the open fly of her jeans and inside her knickers. It's as soggy as a swamp in there, and she just holds me against herself, jerks her hips once or twice and then climaxes quietly. It seems incongruous after all the fuss I've made, but her lips just move momentarily as if she's muttering a prayer, her eyelashes flutter, and that's it. I only know she's come because I can feel it against my fingers.

'Is that it then?' I ask as I wiggle back into my clothes.

Mel's outside washing her hands and then flipping at her hair. She seems virtually unconcerned. 'Yeah, girl-friend, I think that's it,' she answers lightly as I emerge from the cubicle, and cross to the basin. 'Let's get some more tea, eh? All that kerfuffle's made me thirsty again.'

Kerfuffle?

I follow her out into the café again, and even though I know we're under even more intense and probably sala-cious scrutiny than before, I barely notice it.

I feel confused. And a bit down.

I enjoyed that. I think. But I really don't think I'm an actual lesbian. I'd probably do it again, and do it with Mel, although I'm still not entirely sure I even like her very much. She's sexy and fun and empathetic, but I sense that she's a bit of a user where girls are concerned. Maybe she's just not met Ms Right yet? I know I'm certainly not the one, although I can't deny that I might say 'yes' to being Ms Now and Again sometimes.

'Hey! It might never happen!' says Mel, touching my hand, and I realise I've been in a fugue for God knows how long, 'Or maybe it has just happened?'

She gives me a long, perceptive look that's suddenly much more gentle.

'Do you regret it?' She nods towards the Ladies.

I think. Do I?

No. Not entirely. I don't regret the act, and I finally

decide that I do like Mel, even though I don't actually want to get into a big thing with her.

'No,' I say, 'I enjoyed it.' I grin, feeling better. 'It was a blast. But I don't think I'm a full-time lesbian, though. Not really.' I shrug and look for her reaction. 'Do you mind?'

'Of course not, baby. No sweat. But if you ever feel the need for a little walk on the distaff side now and again, come to me first, won't you?'

'Of course,' I answer, feeling the air clear suddenly between us. I lift my tea mug just as Mel gets the same idea, and we click them together, 'To the distaff side!'

'To the distaff side!'

But as I ride home on the bike with her, able this time to hold on to her in a companionable, comfortable way, I realise there is one little regret still niggling away at me.

It was wild, what Mel and I did together. That naughty little toilet game was a revelation.

But I just wish I'd saved it for Robert Stone.

7 Right Here, Right Now

I'm still pondering the next morning.

Mel and I went our separate ways once back at the house last night. She didn't push for more, and I probably wouldn't have acceded if she had. After my brief walk on the wild girls' side, I'm back in the even wilder groove of obsession with Robert Stone.

And hoping it's not long before I get a chance to feed it.

'Sorry about last night,' says Greg on the way to work, 'Bit of a last-minute thing.'

'No problem. Gave me a chance to ride pillion on a motorbike for the first time ever. *And* go for a fry-up in a bikers' café.' He flashes me a quick, surprised glance. 'It was fun,' I add in a massive understatement.

'Oh. Right.'

I can almost hear his thoughts and speculations. Which are typically male – 'Mel's a lesbian', 'she takes a pretty girl out for a meal', 'did they get it on?'

But I don't indulge him. I change the subject smartly to a news item on breakfast telly. Let him speculate. It'll do him good. When we enter the gloomy entrance where the time clock is, he swipes in quickly and dashes off with a slightly grumpy expression on his face, claiming a big day ahead.

I'm left fiddling ineptly with the login yet again, but almost before Greg has disappeared off up the stairs to the computer suite, the outer door swings open again, with quite a bump, and a tall figure strides towards me, his long coat flying.

'You! I want to see you!'

Stone's expression is hard and intense, unlike anything I've ever seen in him before. It's shocking, quite frightening but also thrilling. A big man angry is a force to be reckoned with, a force of nature.

My heart thuds hard.

He grabs my hand and I nearly swoon from the longed-for contact, the dark glitter in his eyes and the cloud of fragrance from his recently applied after-shave. His stocky jaw is freshly shaven, but already there's that faint veil of darkness there, the intimation of the vigorous whisker growth of later. I experience a clench of yearning to feel it rasping against my skin.

He's already pulling away towards the interior, taking me in his wake.

'But I haven't clocked in!'

His broad brow rumples. Dropping my hand impatiently, he grabs my ID, swipes a green light without even looking and then stuffs it back into my bag.

'Come on,' he growls as he collars me again. Then, without a moment to draw breath, I'm running behind him, almost scampering to keep up with his long, imperious stride.

He marches along one corridor, then another, then down some stone steps until we reach an emergency-exit door. Barely pausing in his progress, he whacks down the release and we burst out into a yard filled with large, lidded refuse bins. I realise we're in one of the many open wells in the Babel tower of a building. It's an L-shaped area and, as Stone drags me along, I can see a high, heavily locked gate at the far end. He manhandles me into a corner, between two of the bins, a natural blind spot for anyone looking down from the windows above. Well, at least, most of them. Theoretically, someone up on the third or fourth floor might be able to see us if they were into staring at rubbish bins first thing in the morning.

Stone backs me against a wall, following me in. He lets go of me but just looms over me, pinning me purely by the magnetic force of his presence. Casting a narrow sideways glance at me, he backs away again and begins to pace to and fro in front of me, like a hyperactive police interrogator with a perp in the box.

'Where were you going with the lesbian last night?' he demands suddenly, slapping his leather document case against his thigh. He spins, almost charges like a rhino right up to me, and stands glaring downwards, his face stern and fierce.

Or at least it seems fierce. For a moment I take him seriously, astounded that he knows I was with Mel, and even more amazed that he seems to be jealous. Then I catch the faintest hint of sparkle in his eyes, the hidden smile that his belligerently set mouth isn't revealing.

Oh my God, it's half-past eight in the morning and we're already playing.

'Where were you going with Melanie Harper yesterday evening, Miss Lewis?' he says, confirming everything with two little words.

Miss Lewis.

'How do you know I was with Mel last night?' I ask, craning my neck to look upwards and meet his excoriating scrutiny. I want to play, but I don't feel particularly meek with him somehow. I fancy some combat.

His eyes narrow. He's getting the measure of me. It's like chess and he's working out his strategy. The best way to get what he wants. And have some fun.

'I watched you leave,' he says silkily, his great head lifting, a smile on his face now. It's a smug, delicious, playful smile. Taunting, but also somehow benign.

My knees go weak, but my head comes up too.

'Were you stalking me, Mr Stone? Tut tut tut.'

If this were really an American cop show, he'd say something like 'Why, you little punk!' But this is Borough Hall and we're playing disciplinarian boss and floozy employee or something similar.

'Of course not, you silly little girl,' he hisses, and suddenly he's even closer, right up against me. Still not touching, but hovering just maybe about an inch or two from me, as huge and dark as fate. 'Why would I do that?'

Because you like touching me, and you want me, I say, but only with my eyes. His expression is so intense, so complex, almost beautiful on his solid, ordinary face. His lips give a tiny twitch – and that's complicated too. Maybe there is a bit of genuine jealousy in there? But there's laughter too and he's having a hard time keeping a lid on it.

I flinch when he spins away without warning, his dark overcoat billowing as if he's some kind of caped avenger. He looks at me over his shoulder – long, slow, considering, eyes hooded – then he's back in my face again.

He's putting on a performance and he's really having a ball.

Welcome to the Clever Bobby Stone Show, I think, having a hard time keeping my own lid intact.

His document case lands on the ground with a loud slap that makes me jump. With both hands on the wall, on either side of my head, he stares down at me, his face just an inch or two from mine. His cologne is like a truth serum, bending my senses, but the sweet minty smell of toothpaste is strangely touching. He might be a pervert and a power-tripper who's set his sights on me for God knows what kind of sex games, but he's also a real, human man with normal hopes and fears.

I suddenly want to kiss him, but the initiative isn't mine right now. I've even forgotten the question he just asked me.

'So, you and Mel, what happened?' Up close, his teeth are big and very, very white. All the better to eat you up, little girl. 'And please don't insult me by telling there wasn't anything.'

I wouldn't dream of it. Right now, I'd tell this man anything.

'She ... um ... took me for a ride on her bike. We went to a café and had a greasy fry-up. And we talked about some stuff.'

'Ah ... "some stuff",' he mocks, inclining so that his face is right against mine now. I can feel his breath hot on my skin, and the brush of his lips, and I'm in a movie now, not a cop show. It's the moment in the third *Alien* film when the beast shoves its fearsome features right up against Ripley's cheek – only without all the drool, and the armoured skull and the second articulated jaw.

But I'm in actual, physical contact with the most dangerous entity I've ever encountered.

Still leaning into me, still impressing himself upon me, he takes one hand from the wall and studies his finger-tips, which he rubs together to eradicate a trace of soot. Then he delicately smoothes my hair behind my ear.

'Would that "stuff" be me?' he whispers, his voice incredibly low. 'Did you tell your little lesbian friend about what I did to you?' The back of his hand moves over my face, and I feel his nails drift along the arc of my cheekbone. 'Did you share our secrets?' He presses his pelvis against me, and his penis is like a huge, hard knot against my belly.

I can't look away from him. I've heard the expression 'drowning in someone's eyes', and now I know exactly what it feels like. I wonder if he'll punish me again. Chastise me for betraying him, and do it right here in this less than fragrant bin yard with the possibility that some idle observer above us might get more of a show than they bargained for.

'Yes, Mister Stone, I did.' I bite my lip and those all-seeing, all-enveloping eyes record the action. There's still a bit of soreness there from where my teeth sank in when he made me come yesterday. The backs of his fingers trail downwards, and rest against my mouth. Instinctively I suck on his ring and index fingers, lost in a moment of sensuality, of submission. I'm not trying to be sleazy or provocative, I just want the taste of Stone on my tongue.

He laughs softly, and there's mintiness again, he's so close. He could almost kiss his own fingers now, and the thought of him doing that makes my body surge with longing.

Eyes glinting, unwavering, he watches me suck him. For such a nervy, volatile man, he's eerily still now, but in the depths of those eyes, the manic energy continues to move. He's thinking, assessing, imagining. No doubt wondering what my lips might feel like around his dick, which is still pushing, pushing, pushing against my abdomen.

When he finally speaks, it's not to condemn me for my indiscretion, or issue threats.

He simply says. 'I want you. Right here, right now.'

And then he dashes aside my hand, brings down his great head and he's kissing me, his tongue doing what his cock soon will below.

Dropping my bag to the ground beside me, I slide my arms around him, embracing his big, burly body, sneaking beneath his fine overcoat to get a better feel of him. I love that he's tall, solid and massive. He feels so reassuringly real in this fantasy situation.

He kisses me for several minutes, tongue exploring and tasting, while I remain passive, leaning on the wall, my arms around him, soaking in his heat and his presence through his clothes. Just the pressure and weight of him is making me hungry, making me wet.

When he pulls back, he says, 'I want you' again. Then he does that little head tilt thing of his, almost as if he's asking permission, and I just melt. He smiles as if he's totally aware of the effect.

I'm not passive any more. I hug tighter. I lift a hand up to bury my fingers in the crisp short curls at the back of his head. I grind my hips against him and kiss him as hard as I've ever kissed anyone in my life. He laughs softly but it seems as if it's a chimera laughing, a creature created from the pair of us, our mouths are so close and so melded.

But the time when kissing is enough is done now. Stone is all over me, his clever hands cruising over my body, first over my clothes, then under them. I feel him plucking at my knickers, but contact with the bare skin of my bottom makes him lose patience, and suddenly and thrillingly he rips hard at them, and the cotton tears, and then they're gone. I slump against the wall, almost losing my wits altogether.

God, I've always wanted a man to do that!

And then he's touching me, fingering me, caressing me down there with the precision of a surgeon or a master watchmaker. It's as if he knows my sweet spot without ever being told about it, and I start to groan and writhe even harder, swivelling and swirling about. He never loses contact or misses a beat.

When I come, quickly and lightly, he suppresses my cry with his tongue, and vaguely I wonder if he's concerned about anyone hearing us. Then I start to descend again and I realise he probably isn't. He seems to thrive on the very edge of being discovered, to relish the danger of exposure. I wonder if he even likes sex when it's all safe and easy in a bed.

A few moments later, he's gently stroking my face again, with his right hand, whilst with his left he's rummaging about in his own clothing now. Unzipping first, then digging urgently into his trousers to get his dick out.

I start to struggle, wanting to move, so I can see him, but he mutters 'Uh oh!' and gives me that naughty, crooked grin again.

'But I want to see you!' I protest boldly.

'All in good time,' he answers, his thumb under my chin, holding it so I can't look down, but only up, into his eyes, 'No time for art appreciation right now, Miss Lewis.'

I grin back at him, and suddenly we're both laughing.

Just like a man! He thinks his equipment is a goddamned work of art, the arrogant git!

But my skirt is rumpled up, almost around my waist, and my thighs and belly are bare. So I can certainly feel what I'm not allowed to see.

And it brings a lump to my throat.

He's huge!

I didn't think I was a size queen, but I'm suddenly so happy, so very, very happy that Mr Stone has a big one.

There's more rummaging and suddenly he reaches back, finds my hand and slips a condom packet into it.

'Make yourself useful, little girl,' he croons. 'Put that on me.'

I try to look downwards again, but his hold on my chin is unyielding.

'No, this is an initiative test. Do it without looking.'

I fumble around between us, ripping at the packet, my hands constantly bumping against the great, hot thing I'll soon be enrobing in latex. It's very distracting. I nearly drop the condom and he makes a little warning, hissing sound between his teeth. For heaven's sake, shape up, Maria, I chide myself, regaining control of my fingers and finally getting the condom into position.

He's so warm, so silky. It seems a shame to cover him

up, but I know I have to. Neither one of us has the slightest idea about each other's sexual history.

I roll, and roll, handling it like it's the hammer of God, yet made out of glass. All the time I'm looking up, into his face, and he snags his bottom lip between his teeth, his eyes like stars.

'Very good, Miss Lewis,' he murmurs when I'm done, then reaches down to check my work. I catch my breath as the idea and the feel of him handling himself make my sex flutter. Yesterday he must have brought himself off after our little scene, before he went to his meeting. I picture him in a toilet cubicle, working, working, working at this mighty thing bobbing and prodding between us.

Awesome! I offer up a tiny prayer that one day he'll allow me to see him do it.

'Now then, how are we going to make this happen?' he says almost conversationally, as he contemplates the logistics of a man who must be at least six foot four and a five foot five woman shagging against a wall. 'Do we need a box for you to stand on?'

I giggle. More from nerves and a jangling, head-scrambling desire than humour.

'Tut tut, this is no laughing matter,' he chides, even though he's actually grinning from ear to ear.

I stop laughing when his hand goes briefly between my legs again, dipping into my wetness, as if testing me. But it's a tender action too, as he caresses me briefly and lightly.

And then he's got me, lifting me beneath my thighs with those great mitts of his, and carefully positioning me. It's like some all-powerful external force lining up a space module for docking procedures.

But an omnipotent deity wouldn't say, 'I think I'm going to need a bit of co-operation here, Miss Lewis,' would it?

I wriggle. I reach down. I guide.

Then I throw my arms around his neck, and with a jerk of his strong hips, and one from mine too, we're connected.

And my eyes nearly pop out of my head, it feels so good! I expect him to start thrusting immediately, and feel almost fearful of it for a moment, but Stone being Stone, i.e. extremely contrary, he remains perfectly still with me speared upon his cock.

'So, what else did you do with Melanie then?' he asks, tilting his head again. We're more on a level now, and his gaze is almost too intense to bear.

'Nothing,' I gasp. I can't believe that he's asking me about Mel now, but I suppose that I should have expected it. That he'd interrogate me when I couldn't be more vulnerable.

'Liar.'

His brown eyes narrow. They look heavy-lidded and threatening. I feel myself quiver around him, so affected am I by his slightest mannerism or shift in expression.

'We ... um ... sort of played around a bit.'

'Really?' He's so arch, so knowing. I could almost imagine he had a spy camera or a peephole at the Blue Plate, and he knew everything anyway. 'And whereabouts did this "playing around" occur?'

Oh Christ, we're still in the cop show! Only no detective ever grilled his suspect quite like this. Maybe some of them should try it, though. There seems to be no way to avoid answering the question.

'At the café. In the cloakroom.'

'You mean in a toilet cubicle, don't you?' he persists, shaking his head a little. The slight movement transfers itself all the way through the great bulk of his body to his cock, and me, and I have to bite my lip again. 'You fooled around in a toilet, didn't you, Miss Lewis? Doesn't that seem a bit sleazy somehow?'

I nod. With vigour. To pay him back. And it works

because he's the one gnawing his lip now. He's a man who clearly has almost supernatural powers of self-control, but even so he's as excited as can be.

'Did she touch you? Here?' Leaning me harder against the wall, he frees his left hand and slithers it in between us, touching my clit. I start to wriggle, but he presses me firmly against the brickwork and the fingers of the hand that's holding me dig in a little.

'Answer me,' he commands, jigging his hips and at the same time letting his fingertip circle.

'Yes! Yes! She touched my clit and I wanted to pee. And it was awful ... but really exciting in this sick sort of way.'

'Go on.' His voice is barely more than breathing.

'I was desperate to go, but she just wouldn't stop fingering me. It was like pain and pleasure at the same time.' Stone's finger moves, just as Mel's did, but this time it's *all* pleasure. 'I told her I had to piss and she just sat me on the toilet and kept rubbing and rubbing and rubbing me until I came and I peed all over her hand at the same time.'

As it tumbles out, my sex flutters, reliving each dirty little detail. At first I look away, mortified, staring at bins, walls, the sky, anything but his face, but inevitably I can't keep this up for long, and I return to him, and to a pair of dark eyes that are also wells of light.

He looks amused but also strangely awestruck. And I'm so thrilled by that, I'd really like to kiss him again.

But before I can, his lips brush my temple, and I feel the faintest touch of his tongue.

'You mean you played pissing games with her before you've even played them with me?' He's enormous inside me, but he seems to swell yet more.

'Yes! Yes, I did! I'm sorry! Oh God!' I shriek as the tip of his finger flicks and circles with deadly purpose and I start to come again.

'Unwise, Miss Lewis, unwise,' he pronounces, but his efforts at being magisterial are undermined by the fact that he's gasping now, his big chest heaving against my breasts. He gives my clit one last flourish, then he's got both hands gripping and supporting my thighs again as he begins to thrust and thrust in earnest.

I lose it. I make hoarse sounds. I convulse around him, white fire collapsing at the juncture of our bodies. His hips are working, driving his wild, huge, beautiful cock into me, again and again, and I can feel his soft mouth open against the side of my face and his groans sweetly inarticulate against my skin.

There's a crazy, precarious few moments when he comes, and it seems as if his knees are going to buckle and we're going to end up in a tangled, humping heap amongst the rubbish that's spilled out of the bins. But then he makes a supreme effort of control and we stay upright, even though I can barely breathe when his entire weight bears down on me and jams me against the wall.

I fight for air, and immediately he makes space and lets me gently down on to my feet. His arms slide around me and he holds me, just holds me for several minutes. I can feel his chin against my hair, his chest heaving against me, and his cock – waning and still stickily clad in its condom – resting against my bare belly beneath my rucked-up skirt.

If I could stay this way forever, I probably would.

Eventually, we engage with life again, just as the Borough Hall clock begins to bong out the quarter hour. Stone looks over my shoulder at his watch.

'Shit! I've got a meeting!'

Releasing me, he steps back, divests himself of the condom, and zips up quickly. Flinging the used johnny into the nearest bin, he then swoops down and retrieves my ruined knickers, and shoots me an almost apologetic interrogatory glance, nodding towards the bin.

They're ripped beyond repair and I have neither sewing kit nor safety pins in my bag, so I shrug back at him. He tosses them in after the condom.

I feel lost and as deflated as his cock is. I've just had a sordid quickie, a knee-trembler, with my boss, but at the time it felt like so much more than that. I'm not promiscuous, but I've been with my share of men in my day, and never once have I felt the intensity and the sense of communion that I felt with Stone amongst the grime and the bins.

To my horror, my eyes fill with tears, and to avoid his scrutiny, and to fish for a tissue, I retrieve my bag. It's a wonder neither of us has stood on it and crushed my phone and anything else inside it in the mêlée.

But nothing escapes the eye of Clever Bobby.

'Hey, what's this? Tears again?' he says, his large hands cradling my shoulders. With a frown, he delicately touches my face, catching a salty drop at the corner of my eye. He stares at it for a moment, as if it's a jewel, then puts out his tongue and tastes it.

'Poor baby,' he murmurs, and an instant later he's cuddling me against him. He pats and strokes my hair, and whispers soft, soothing, fairly nonsensical words in my ear until I feel calm and happy again.

'What about your meeting?' I ask as he puts me from him again, with what seems like a distinct reluctance. And I think, as I pressed close just now, that I detected him hardening again.

'Fuck my meeting,' he says. His voice is superficially cheerful, but he purses his lips for a moment. And frowns. 'They'll wait.' But even so, he dodges down and picks up his document case again. Duty calls, even if all I want is for the two of us to run off for the day. To the park, maybe. Or the seaside. Or just to bed.

'Are you all right now?' he enquires, all seriousness, staring down at me. My heart sinks. I can sense him detaching from me emotionally, just as he so recently disengaged his body.

'I'm fine. Great.' I clutch my bag to me, mirroring the way he holds his case against his chest, and by unspoken agreement we make our way to the door back into the building. It's locked now, but Stone punches a code into the alarm pad and when it clicks open again, he ushers me inside. We walk in silence back the way we came, and when we reach the staircase where our ways must part, he stretches out a hand and strokes my cheek again, without even looking around to see if we're observed.

He gives me a long, odd look that seems strangely familiar. It's not exactly a frown this time, but even so, his large brow is furrowed.

'See you later!' The strange expression is gone as if it was never there, and he winks and turns to go. 'And if Allsopp asks where you've been, just say you've been—' He mimes *fucking Director Stone in the bin yard*, then flashes me his whitest, most boyish smile again. 'Oh, just say I waylaid you and asked you to run an errand.'

With that he flips his long fingers at me and sets off pounding up the stairs, taking them two at a time, without looking back.

And I'm standing here in the corridor, feeling lost and in trouble.

Stone is dangerous. Not so much for the risks he takes but for the effect he might be able to have on me if I let him. He wants to play sex games with me, that's a given, but now I think I've recognised that peculiar expression I saw on his face a few moments ago, and I'd better be careful, because it's one I've seen before.

It's the 'Shit! I'm in too deep. I'd better cool it' look.

8 Show and Tell

No questions are asked when I finally almost fall into the office.

In fact the morning proceeds perfectly normally. Despite the fact that I feel completely abnormal.

I've always been lucky with men. When I've seen the 'in too deep' look before, I've always been feeling as if I was in deeper than I wanted to be too. And, as a result, the relationship has usually ended naturally and amicably shortly afterwards.

But there's nothing natural, normal or usual about the relationship I'm in now. With Stone. If, indeed, I am in one with him.

Could it be that we're two people who are just playing games with each other? He's obviously a grand master at them, and I'm a newbie, but still. Best not to make too big a deal out of it emotionally, eh? Stone's in this purely for the sexual thrills, and so should I be. That way, when the games are played out, there just might be a possibility that I can get on with my life, and this job, without a disastrously messy disentanglement.

Which is all brilliant, in theory, but in fact I sit at my desk, going through my routine tasks on auto-pilot, unable to think on the deep levels about anything or anybody but Robert Stone.

Of course the fact that I now have no underwear on doesn't help matters either. I feel open and accessible down there in the way that my heart feels dangerously open and accessible to emotion. I feel a peculiar physical echo of Stone's penetration, but somehow it's far more than his flesh he put inside me.

But no. I'm not going to let this happen to me. I'm going to play safe, the way I've always done. It's so much less painful.

I'll take all the sex he offers but nothing more than that.

When Sandy offers to buy cakes for the office, on the strength of a smallish win in the works sweepstake, I jump at the chance of going out to buy them for her. I'm prepared to risk a bit of draughtiness around the nether regions, outside in the breezes, in order to clear my head and get out of Borough Hall for ten minutes.

It's a bright, sunny day, and as I walk down Wood Street, past the big stationery shop, the gas showroom, several newsagents and hairdressers, on my way towards the bakery shop, I feel my spirits lifting. People hurrying to wherever they're hurrying all appear reassuringly uncomplicated. All cheered up by the sunshine, thinking of no more than getting to the next shop, the next meeting or whatever.

I consider nipping down to Marks and Sparks and buying myself a pair of knickers to replace the ones now residing in the rubbish bin, but thinking of people meeting people – people who are *not* Stone! – has reminded me that I have a meeting pretty shortly myself.

With William Youngblood.

Yet another Borough Hall shagmeister, in his own way. As I carry my precious burden of cream cakes back into the cool, shadowy building, I wonder if Sandy would have bought him an eclair, or a vanilla slice, if she could have done so without raising any suspicions?

Or has she got other, even sweeter goodies she's planning to treat him to today?

The first person I encounter once I'm back inside is Mel.

Mel!

Oh God, I've hardly even thought about her today, despite what happened at the Blue Plate. After my run-in with Robert Stone in the bin yard, the thing that occurred between me and Mel seems like lifetimes ago.

She gives me an easy, knowing grin, and strangely, I suddenly feel almost at ease.

'Cakes?' she enquires, eyeing the boxes and running her tongue around her lips. It should look sexy, but somehow, it just looks like someone who loves cakes. 'Any going spare?'

'No. Not really, sorry. Sandy's a bit careful, even when she is treating the office.'

'No probs.'

We stand in front of each other, a bit stuck for words, but finally Mel says, 'Don't worry, kiddo, we're not engaged or anything.' She pauses, 'We can just be friends. If you like?' She tilts her blonde head to one side, and for a split second it reminds me of Stone.

Something must show on my face, because Mel frowns.

'Are you okay, Maria? About yesterday, I mean? I never meant to upset you or anything. I thought you were up for it. I really did.'

'I was.' I have to restrain myself from tensing up, hugging my boxes and squishing the cakes. 'It's not you. Not at all. It's something else.'

'Or someone,' Mel says sagely, shifting the sheaf of rolled-up posters she's carrying from one arm to the other. I still find myself a little dumbstruck, so she prompts me with just two words.

'Stone again?'

I nod.

'Want to talk?'

I do, but I can't.

'I'd love to, but I've got to get back with these.'

'We'll have coffee,' she says, patting me on the arm with her free hand. 'And that means just that. We'll have coffee and you can tell me all about it. Just let me know when's good for you.'

A moment later, I'm back in the office, dishing out the cakes, wishing I could rationalise my feelings for our esteemed Director of Finance as easily as I can the ones I have for Mel.

I go up in the lift when it's time for my meeting with William Youngblood. Usually I'd take the back stairs – exercise and all that – but I can't risk being followed up a staircase when I'm not wearing underwear. My skirt isn't particularly short, but I just daren't take a chance.

On the landing, I'm painfully aware that I have to pass the door to Stone's office before I get to Youngblood's. It's standing ajar, and my heart twists when I hear the sound of voices from the outer office where Mrs Sheldon sits.

It's Stone, of course, and though I can't make out the words, the low, intimate laughing tone makes me want to gasp for air. Mrs Sheldon laughs back at him, and I feel an alarming stab of jealousy. I can't believe there's anything going on there – she's a quiet, refined woman close to retiring age who seems the epitome of straightness – but who knows what kind of corrupting influence working day in day out with Stone can have on someone.

Enough! No envy! It's just sex, I tell myself, marching onward.

Even allowing for the venerable wooden panelling and the stone window surrounds, William Youngblood's office suite is light-years away from Stone's in sleek and minimal modernity. Even his PA looks like a high-tech Stepford clone.

'Go in!' she says, wasting as few words as possible. She's not exactly looking down her nose at me, but I can tell she thinks I'm a slapper.

Maybe I am? But I smile to myself as I pass her, wondering if she knows that her super-cool boss is the male equivalent.

'Hi, Maria! Nice to see you,' he says, rising to his feet as I enter.

Youngblood isn't tall, and he doesn't have the sheer physical presence of Stone, but in his own way he's a phenomenal piece of eye candy. He's lean, handsome, immaculately groomed, and his eyes are the most startling shade of blue. Couple this with the chiselled bone structure of a poster hunk and his unnaturally blond hair, and I can easily see how Sandy – and others – might succumb to him.

He flashes me a friendly smile, which quite takes me aback after his previous relative indifference to me, and then comes out from behind his desk, offering his hand for me to shake.

'Hello,' I say, a bit at a loss. For a moment, the vision of him shagging Sandy seems to blink out of existence, and I must admit I find myself impressed. I take his hand, and find mine shaken firmly and decisively. His skin is unexpectedly but not unpleasantly cool.

'Let's sit over here,' he says, visibly upping the wattage of an exceptionally effective smile. He gestures to a 'conversation area' at the far end of his office, by the window. It's all very chic and modern, and I wonder for a moment how he's swung all this brand new décor. Stone's office, though large, is filled with heavy, clunky furniture and fittings that have obviously been paying their way for many a year.

But as I come to sit down, I become aware of a huge problem.

Youngblood has ushered me to a low settee, and seems about to take an armchair opposite, facing me. If I don't take the most stringent care in the way I sit, I'm likely to flash him.

Oh thanks, Stone, you fuck! I think murderously, tucking my knees together tightly and perching on the edge of my seat.

'So, Maria, how are you liking life here at Borough Hall?' Youngblood enquires brightly, sitting back in his own seat with a studied, casual elegance. He does this so beautifully that I could almost imagine he practises, and to prevent myself being too taken in by his act, and to even things out a bit, I summon back the inner picture of him bonking Sandy.

There, that's better.

'It's fine. I'm really liking it,' I say, and I watch his mouth as he proceeds smoothly on about 'staff benefits', 'induction courses' and the 'social club'. It seems to be a pretty standard 'how are you settling in'-type spiel and half the time I'm barely listening, because I'm seeing him with his face between Sandy's legs and wondering what those rather lush, erotic lips would feel like against my sex. He doesn't seem to be aware that I'm zoning out all the time, because he's obviously fond of his own rather deep and mellifluous voice.

He turns his attention to my work colleagues, and in a spirit of impishness I remark how much I like Sandy and how 'generous' she's been to me. To his credit, Youngblood doesn't turn a single, perfectly-gelled blond hair.

'Yes, she's a nice woman, isn't she?' he observes as if Sandy is just another Borough employee and he barely knows her from Eve. Maybe he doesn't? Maybe he just shags anybody who crosses his path, on an ad hoc basis?

Must be a common trait here, I think a touch sourly, unable to stop myself glancing in the general direction of where Stone's office must be. It suddenly feels as if an errant breeze is sneaking right up my skirt.

I'm just trying to work out how to say something about Sandy that'll really get to him, when there's the faint sound of a contretemps from the office outside.

Raised voices. Youngblood's PA and a deeper tone, a very familiar one. The door doesn't actually bounce on its hinges or anything, but it does open rather fast and with some force, as Stone walks into the room, carrying a folder.

'He's with someone!' I hear Youngblood's PA say from outside, but it's half-hearted. She's already given up.

Stone doesn't even look at me at first, although every hair stands up on the back of my neck, and a seventh sense tells me he's totally aware of me.

'I need a minute, William,' he says, his voice all business, his attitude brusque and high-handed. 'These figures. They're not right. They don't reflect the latest reallocations.' He taps the documents in his folder with aggression.

The atmosphere in the room is suddenly electric, and that sense detector of mine is going off like crazy now. Youngblood's face is straight but I can almost taste his antipathy.

'I'm in the middle of something, Robert.' His voice is superficially calm, but I can see it's costing him dearly. There's the very slightest of nervous tics working at the edge of his tightened lips.

Stone 'appears' to notice me and gives me a bland smile. 'Oh, hello, Maria, how are you today?' His eyebrows lift, and suddenly nothing about him is bland at all, because that old demon I met this morning is back in his eyes again, 'You're looking well. You don't mind me appropriating William for a moment or two, do you?'

'No, of course not.' I prepare – very, very carefully – to get to my feet and leave, hotly aware of Stone's glance flicking narrowly towards the direction of my crotch. 'Shall I come back later?' I ask, pointedly addressing Youngblood.

But it's Stone, goddamn him, who answers.

'No need. This will just take two ticks,' he announces,

gesturing magnanimously towards me with a sheet of paper covered in figures. 'Just make yourself comfortable and you'll have him back in a minute.'

He places a distinct emphasis on the word 'comfortable', and it's hard to tell whether Youngblood is more perplexed about this, or about the fact that Stone seems to be treating this little encounter like an impromptu party at which he's the genial host. If I were in his place I'd want to smack Stone up the side of his head.

Youngblood's on his feet now, but I stay put. They launch into a heated discussion that seems to be about Youngblood overspending on staff training for the current fiscal year. Youngblood insists he's within budget. Stone insists Youngblood is using the wrong figures. Or something.

I'm not that interested. It's the two men themselves who have me mesmerised.

At around eleven in the morning, Youngblood looks as if he's just stepped out of the house. His dark suit and shirt appear to be freshly pressed and wrinkle-free, and, as I've already observed, he doesn't have a hair or anything else in the slightest bit out of place.

On the other hand, Stone is already looking pretty lived in. His blue shirt is obviously another expensive one, and the colour suits him, but it's slightly rumpled and the collar is pulled out of shape a bit as if he's been tugging at it. The perennial dark shadow of his beard is beginning to break through along his beefy jaw-line, and his hair has got that mussed-up look again as if he's run his fingers through it at least once.

He looks as if he's had a hard morning, and not just downstairs there in the bin yard.

But the greatest difference between the two of them is height, and I suspect this one issue is what drives Youngblood the most crazy.

He's not tall. I'm five foot five, and there's not a lot of

difference between us. Maybe three inches, not much more. Beside him, Stone looms like a towering giant. And when they speak, and argue, Youngblood always has to look upwards and be at a constant disadvantage.

'But these figures here.' Stone points to one of the documents, running his pinkie down a column for emphasis. 'How do you get those? They're nothing like the projections we agreed on.'

Youngblood frowns hard, looking puzzled. 'I don't know what you mean,' he says, sounding confused, really rattled. With a look of near rage on his elegant face, he strides away across the room towards his desk.

The very instant his back is turned, almost before he's begun to move, Stone is also in motion. With that peculiar nimbleness that seems out of place in one so solid, he darts towards my couch, and throws himself down beside me, making the cushions bounce and me almost fly up in the air. Giving me an almost satanic sideways glance and a flash of his white teeth, he spreads his documents out on the low coffee table in front of us, then leans back into the upholstery with a satisfied sigh. Winking slyly, he feigns the action of putting his arm along the back of the seat behind me, then shrugs and withdraws it, waggling his eyebrows at me again.

What the fuck is he playing at?

Youngblood is still at his desk, sifting through papers, and Stone nods towards him. He mouths something, but I don't get a real chance to decipher it, because at that moment, Youngblood spins and returns to us, his stride angry and determined. As he sets his documents alongside Stone's and gives the pair of us a long, slightly confused but decidedly suspicious look, I work out that my dear Director has secretly just called his colleague a stroppy little prick.

I feel both uncomfortable and excited, and I want get out of here just as much as I want to stay. I'm stuck in the middle of a titanic testosterone-fest, and given what I've seen of (and in Stone's case done with) each one of these men, I can't help but see the pair of them as sex objects.

I make a token protest.

'Are you sure you don't want me to come back later?'

Youngblood opens his mouth, but yet again, and to his obvious fury, Stone pre-empts him.

'No, no. I'll be gone in a minute. Just sit tight.' Turning towards me, he gives me a hooded, blatantly suggestive look, just out of Youngblood's eye-line.

If I wasn't here, I could quite imagine the Human Resources Manager launching himself across the table and attempting to kick the living shit out of his rival, but as I am here, I sense Youngblood making a superhuman effort to remain cool and unconcerned. He gives me a tight nod, and says, 'It's okay, Maria. We'll just be a moment.'

He applies himself to a close scrutiny of the two sets of documents, even though it's obvious he's still bristling with outrage at the situation he's been put in. Stone seems to be enjoying himself enormously, and proceeds to loll back in his seat even further, slowly twirling between his long fingers a pen he's taken from his shirt pocket.

I press my knees more tightly together and instanta-neously Stone registers the movement. He smirks at me sideways, having assured himself that Youngblood is still grappling with the figures, then nods very pointedly towards my thighs. He nods again, then looks towards Youngblood's bowed blond head, and nods in his direction.

What the hell is he up to now?

Stone repeats the action, then, slowly, and with great deliberation, he uncrosses his sturdy thighs, sits with them apart for a couple of seconds, then recrosses them with the other leg on top.

The penny drops and so does my jaw.

He wants me to do a *Basic Instinct*!

No way! I mouth, my eyes popping.

Coward, he mouths back, then slowly and seductively licks his lower lip.

But oh God, the seed is sown. It's too late. My head goes light and I'm in that weird, hypersexual parallel world I seem to inhabit any time Robert Stone is in the vicinity. I don't have any doubt that I'm going to accept his outrageous challenge.

'This is all wrong, Robert,' says Youngblood eventually, his smooth brow puckering, 'These aren't the figures I was given, I'm sure of it.'

'I can assure you they are,' Stone replies airily. He's slapping his pen into his palm now, even as he leans over to inspect the supposed discrepancy that Youngblood is pointing out. Then he drops the rollerball on the table with a clunk as he turns the page around.

As both men are leaning forward, studying the contentious document on the low table, I make my move.

I shuffle in my seat, hopefully in a way that's both discreet *and* noticeable. Then not too slowly, and not too quickly, I uncross my legs.

I'm not even sure that Youngblood will be able to see my crotch from his viewpoint, but with luck just the sight of my thighs will have the effect that Stone's after. Or a degree of it.

And now we're back in slo-mo land, as we often are when the bizarre things that have happened since I started here occur.

I'm sitting with my legs slightly parted, and that's tightened my skirt across my thighs, and lifted the fabric a little. And after what seems like a decade, Youngblood's perfectly groomed golden head tilts – and then he's looking straight up my skirt at what's underneath it.

Bingo!

And it's cartoon slow motion now. Youngblood's rather beautiful blue eyes bug and widen, and his mouth drops open. The pen he's been using to follow a line of figures on the paper jags sideways across the sheet like a black lightning bolt. He seems unable to look away for as much as three seconds – then involuntarily he looks up, away from the spectacle of my sex.

Our gazes glance off each other like a ricochet, but I'm unable to hide the fact that I know that he knows that I know – and on and on *ad infinitum*.

Enough already. As casually as I can, I recross my legs, concealing my pussy. Youngblood blinks furiously, stares at the document in front of him as if he's never seen it before, and almost but not quite puffs out his lips, as if he's been punched in the gut.

This has all taken but a few seconds and meantime, I realise, Stone has been giving a bravura performance of his own. I sneak a glance at him but he isn't looking at either Youngblood or me. He's frowning over the financial projections, his lips compressed as if he's irritated by the other man's sudden lapse of concentration.

But I know that inside he's laughing. I can feel it like a wave breaking over me. And right now, I really want him. I want him hard.

'What the devil is the matter with you, man?' Stone injects an impressive degree of professional tetchiness into his voice, and sits back again, full of exasperated body language.

'Nothing!' protests Youngblood, sounding slightly strangled, but a moment later, with an admirable degree of recovery, he shoots Stone a furious glance. 'Except that these figures are nonsense, Robert, and you know that.' He snatches up the paper. 'If you'll leave them with me,

I'll go through it all and get back to you!' With that he leaps to his feet, in an obvious attempt to regain some semblance of control of the situation and to get his hated nemesis out of his office as fast as possible.

Which will leave him and me alone. Oh God, what have I done? Will he say something? Has he got more self-possession than Stone's given him credit for? After all, he's a man at the top of his profession, and usually cool and poised.

And the unrepentant architect of this insane, overcooked situation is poised too. As if nothing untoward has happened, he gets to his feet, grabs his paperwork and starts to make for the door.

'I'll send you a copy through, William. No rush.'

Youngblood looks at him with murder in his eyes but again controls himself spectacularly well. I'm starting to find a new respect for him, dealing with this man who I know is some kind of monster, no matter how sexually delicious as well.

'Yes, do that, Robert,' Youngblood says crisply, 'and I'll get back to you by the end of the day.'

Stone nods curtly at his adversary, and then favours me with a far more benign expression. Benign, and undeniably salacious. I'm not looking at Youngblood now, but I can almost hear his eyes narrowing in suspicion.

'Maria,' murmurs Stone in what seems to be a leave-taking. But with his hand on the door-knob, he flings back an afterthought, 'Oh, you did manage to put away those files for me the other day, didn't you? Sorry to have put that on you, but there didn't seem to be anyone else free to do it.'

You bugger, you know I didn't!

'No problem. Yes, I put them away,' I lie.

'Excellent,' he says roundly, his eyes full of promises of the kind of evil retribution that would make my knickers damp if I had any on to get damp. 'See you later.'

And then he's gone.

And I'm left with Youngblood. Who also knows I've somehow lost my underwear.

We both stare at the door for a moment, as if, ironically, we both wish him back.

Then he turns to me. 'Sorry about that, Maria.'

Good grief, is he going to confront this thing head-on? That's bold.

But no.

'I'm afraid our good Director of Finance believes that his priorities override everybody else's. Where were we when we were so rudely interrupted?'

Uh oh, we're clearly going to play the 'pretend it never happened' game. I feel a bit disappointed in Youngblood. I thought I'd sensed an inkling of an almost Stone-like daring in him, but now it seems I was wrong. And, because Stone has imposed himself yet again on a situation, I now have absolutely no idea what Youngblood said to me before he arrived.

I just blather something about him asking me how I was settling in, and he seems to buy it.

'Yes, well, I think that seems to about cover it,' he says, all edginess. All his former polish and show of sang-froid has gone now, either from Stone's disruptive influence on his equilibrium or from the sight of what's hidden under my skirt. Either way, he seems anxious to conclude this interview as soon as possible. 'I'll let you get back now.'

His movements are tense and almost puppet-like as he escorts me to the door, but unexpectedly he grasps my hand in a quaintly formal handshake.

'Don't forget, Maria. Any problems and you can always come to me. Any time. My door is always open to you.'

This takes me aback, and on closer inspection, there's real intent in those exceptional blue eyes of his.

'Er ... thanks.' For a moment, I'm as flummoxed by

him as I am by Stone, and I really don't know what to call him. But before I can think, I say, 'Thanks, William.'

Triumph flashes across his face. Does he think he's scored a point somehow? Got one up on Stone?

It seems so, because I get a very definite feeling his confidence has come back up again.

'Yes. And especially if you have any trouble with Director Stone. He . . .' He's still holding my hand, I realise, and his fingers tighten. 'Well, let's say that he has a habit of exploiting members of staff sometimes. So if you feel he's assigning you duties that exceed your job description, do, please, come to me, and I'll intervene on your behalf.'

Exploiting? God, William, you don't know the half of it, I think. But then again, maybe he does know? Or at least have an inkling. This is all very, very interesting.

'Thanks,' I murmur, and he lets me go. I reach for the doorknob, grinning, and just longing to get out of his office and marshal my thoughts. But then, unexpectedly, his hand shoots out and rests on my arm.

'And Maria, if you ever . . . ever fancy a drink, say, or perhaps just a coffee sometime?'

He lets it hang, and suddenly, it dawns on me that he's half-way to asking me out. Good grief!

'Just think about it,' he says, looking far smoother now. 'No pressure. Nothing heavy. Just casual.'

And then, not quite sure what's happened, and how I got there, I'm out in the corridor, past his outer office, trying to work out who got the upper hand there.

I have to admire Youngblood's recovery. He's just come off a round of power games with Robert Stone, and been flashed by a junior employee, and he still has the presence of mind to ask me for a date.

Maybe Mr Stone has a worthy adversary here?

At the head of the stairs I hesitate, realising that

descending them sans underwear just isn't wise. But before I can backtrack, Stone himself is suddenly there beside me, almost out of nowhere. He's back in his jacket, his tie is straight, and it even looks as if he's combed his hair. He's on his way to one of his many meetings, but clearly he still has time to dally and manipulate me.

'That was fun,' he says in a low voice as we begin to descend the broad, main stone staircase at the heart of the Hall. Stone's large hand is lightly resting on my back.

'It was insane!' I shoot back, concentrating on my footing.

'Just the way I like it. Did Blondie say anything afterwards?'

'No. Except to watch out for you because you have a habit of exploiting people.'

Stone just laughs, then suddenly, he's darted ahead of me, and he's standing on the mini landing where the staircase turns the corner.

'Show me what you showed him,' he commands, his voice dangerously loud. In a panic I glance around, but there's nobody to be seen, for the moment.

'But—'

'Indulge me, Miss Lewis,' he purrs. 'There wasn't much opportunity for looking earlier. It's the least you can do to show me what you've just shown that little shit.'

I open my mouth to attempt a vain protest, but he forestalls me.

'One second.' He holds up a forefinger. 'Just one second.'

I can hardly breathe. He's unbelievable. He seems to operate totally outside any normal range of civilised behaviour – or even common sense sometimes – and yet he's irresistible and I'm compelled to do anything he tells me to.

As Stone swoops down, bending his great body at the waist, and cocking his head, his eyes gleaming, I gingerly set my foot on a higher step, and part my thighs.

His beautiful brown eyes widen, and he bites his lower lip. And utters a low, heartfelt, almost pained groan.

And then, almost in the same instant there are voices in the near distance.

I jump and skitter down the steps just as Stone straightens up and he catches me by the arm, preventing me from going head over heels all the way down to the ground floor.

'Whoah!'

His hold is sure and immediately I feel safe, in spite of everything. Still holding my arm, ever so lightly, he guides me downwards.

9 **Out to Lunch**

Two hours later and I'm in a queue, still feeling that guiding hand on my arm.

I've escaped for lunch and, after the frankly unbelievable events so far today, I've decided to treat myself to a posh sandwich and some delicious but over-priced coffee in Café Mario. Given the state of my bank balance and the progress of my loan repayments, I shouldn't. But what the hell, I don't care! I need a treat.

Or treats. I've got a couple of carrier bags dangling from my fingers, beneath my tray.

I've got a sandwich, a muffin and some orange juice in front of me, and the barista is just preparing my café latte. I dread to think how much this is going to cost me, but I've been so lost in my thoughts that it's too late to put some of the stuff back now.

The smiling waitress rings up my bill, names the amount and I wince, but before I can scrabble into a purse that I hope contains sufficient money, an arm reaches from behind me, proffering a twenty-pound note.

I close my eyes, and drag in a breath as my heart starts to thud. 'Thanks, but you don't have to,' I say, wondering how I could possibly think it might be anybody else. And – yet again – how he's tracked me down.

'I think I do,' Stone murmurs meaningfully as I turn towards him. I've no idea how long he's been here, whether he's been following me or it's a coincidence, or how he managed to get into Café Mario without my internal radar screaming. But here he is, standing right behind me, wallet out.

The girl behind the counter recognises authority when she encounters it and accepts the twenty, and as the barista hands me my coffee, Stone says, 'Get a table, Maria. I'll be with you in a minute.'

This is a popular lunchtime venue, but maybe he has special magical powers or something, because miraculously there's a primo table by the window looking out on to a busy pedestrian precinct. The sun's shining and people are meandering by with bags, or rushing back to work maybe, but suddenly nothing about them or the sunny space outside seems real.

I'm encapsulated in a parallel universe called Stoneworld. Looking down at my lunch I can't imagine ever having an appetite again. At least not one that isn't for, or inspired by, this man.

A few moments later, he slides his large body into the opposite seat, unloads his own lunch and sets his tray aside.

'So. Here we are again,' he says, obviously in high good humour.

I don't know what to say. Just seeing him in front of me like this has knocked the breath out of me. I must get a grip. But how can I when life is becoming increasingly surreal because of this man? Just what's happened this morning probably constitutes months', even years' worth of bizarre sexual happenings in most people's lives.

I just stare at him while he fusses with his paper napkin, critically inspects the filling of what looks like a pastrami and mustard sandwich, then takes a healthy bite.

'Aren't you going to eat your sandwich?' he enquires, still chewing.

My own ham on ciabatta looked yummy before he arrived, but now I don't want it.

'Come on, Maria, you need to keep your strength up!'

He reaches across, unfolds my napkin and tosses it in

the general direction of my lap, then picks up a cut section of sandwich and holds it up to my lips.

'What the hell are you doing?' I mutter, wanting to glance around to see who's looking, but instead succumbing, leaning forward and taking a bite.

What the hell am *I* doing?

I take the rest of the bread from him and return it to my plate.

'Just making sure that you get a sensible lunch.' He picks at the carton of salad he's bought, popping a couple of cherry tomatoes whole into his mouth, one after the other.

'I don't need you to nursemaid me,' I snap back, taking an angry sip of my juice.

Stone seems to look inward for a moment, and a sly, dreamy expression crosses his broad face. 'Now there's a thought.'

'Look, whatever it is you're thinking, stop thinking it!' My anger makes me bold. This man is my boss, or at least one of them, yet I suddenly feel I have to assert myself. At least here. I need a time-out with him for a while. Some semblance of normality.

His smile widens, and he slowly licks a trace of mustard off his fingertip. 'Yes. Of course. *Mistress.*' He places salacious emphasis on the totally unnecessary word.

'Stop it!'

To my horror, my voice has risen considerably in volume by now, and instead of me keeping a low profile, I've made people look at us. Which is just what I didn't want.

'I'm sorry, Maria,' he murmurs, in bogus contrition. I can tell he doesn't mean it because his eyes are twinkling like stars, 'but it's your fault. You seem to bring out the very devil in me.' He nods at my food. 'But I'll try to behave myself. Come on, eat your lunch.'

I try to eat, but it's difficult. I don't know where to look. If I look at Stone, he'll play havoc with me. If I look away, it seems sulky and brattish.

But he seems to let me off the hook. Chewing slowly, and pausing now and again to sip his black coffee, he grants me the breathing space I need by gazing relaxedly out of the windows, watching the lunchtime ebb and flow and indulging in just the casual people-watching session I'd promised myself.

For a second or two, I allow myself to people-watch him.

If I didn't know him his heavyset face would appear so very ordinary in semi-profile. If I'd never met him before and I saw him strolling through the shopping precinct, I might not give him a second glance, apart from his above average height.

Who would ever know that he's this crazy, sex-obsessed risk-taker who seems to have taken over my life and even my thoughts?

I look away. He's just too much. I don't know what to do.

The café has dark painted walls, dotted with antique prints of old Italy. It's a bit clichéd, but it has a good ambience, not too upmarket, not too trendy, just 'special' enough. It's mostly younger office workers. In fact Stone might well be one of the oldest people in here. Just as I wonder if I dare glance back at him, a young woman close by rises from her table, and makes her way to the back of the café, towards the door marked with the universal signs for 'WC'.

A second or two later, a young man from a nearby table follows.

And 'action!' An interior movie begins to play.

I imagine them scrabbling at each other's clothing in a cubicle, much the way Mel and I did back at the Blue

Plate. I imagine them up against the partition wall, banging away at each other, just the way Stone and I did down in the bin yard this morning.

'What's the matter? Fancying a quickie?'

My head snaps round to find Stone smirking at me. 'I'm up for it if you are,' he continues, his voice rather louder than it ought to be under the circumstances. Out of the corner of my eye, I see a blonde woman at an adjacent table lift her head in interest.

'Will you shut up!' I hiss, but he just hits me with that fabulous demon-boy grin again as he leans back in his seat and proceeds to twirl his unused teaspoon between his fingers like a conjurer doing tricks. The sight of those clever fingertips moving so deftly only makes things worse. I seem to feel their nimble dance between my legs.

'Why the indignation, Maria?' he says after a moment of this subtle psychological warfare. There is no way on earth I can believe he doesn't know the effect that he's having on me, manipulating the spoon like that. 'You told me yourself about your little exploit in a cubicle with Mel. So why can't you do the same with me? Well, allowing for different plumbing, of course.' He cocks one dark eyebrow at me, every bit of his body language a challenge.

'You're a greedy pig, M—'

I stop short. What the hell do I call him? I haven't the faintest idea. 'Robert' seems too intimate, even in spite of everything. The last thing I'd describe us as is friends. And if I call him 'Mr Stone', he might construe that as a signal that I'm willing to play games again. Which I'm not, right at this moment. Am I?

He waits, and I'm exquisitely aware that he knows my dilemma and is laughing inwardly at my attempts to resolve it.

'You're a greedy pig, *Stone*,' I repeat in the lowest possible voice I can use and still have him hear me. I'm only too acutely aware that the blonde woman nearby is probably straining every last bit of her auditory capacity in order to follow our conversation. 'You had your share this morning. I'm not letting you get to me again.'

'Oh, please, call me "Robert",' he says facetiously, pushing away his plate, 'we're friends, aren't we?'

'Look! I don't know what the fuck we are. But we certainly aren't friends, that's for sure.'

In a flash, he's leaning across the small table, almost in my face. 'Well, as far as I'm concerned, you're my friend, Maria,' he says, head tilted back a little, studying me narrowly, his brown eyes sensual and half-closed. 'When I was inside you, this morning, even then I still thought of you as my friend.' He runs his tongue along the edge of his teeth, almost like a wild beast anticipating its prey.

I can't believe him! I feel as if any second he's going to snake out a hand at eye's-blink speed and pull my mouth towards his.

But I can't back away. I'm paralysed.

For at least three or four seconds, he holds me, purely with the power of his eyes, then he snags his lip, shakes his head and lounges back in his seat, smiling arrogantly, almost nastily. The victor again.

'Fuck you!' I mouth, and proceed to stare grimly at my plate while I rip my innocent, unwanted sandwich into fragments.

The bastard!

He's the head of the department I work in. He's a great middle-aged ox of a man. He drives me insane. And yet I'd give anything now to be back in that yard with him, slammed up against the wall with his cock inside me as he pounds and pounds away.

But even as I think this, Stone reaches out and removes my plate of sandwich debris from in front of me. He replaces it with the muffin I chose, then, after a short pause, breaks a piece of that off and pops it into his own mouth, daring me to protest.

'This is crazy. What are you doing?' Almost unconsciously I mirror his action – and find that the muffin is fabulous, despite everything.

'Well, I thought I was having lunch with one of my staff. What's so strange about that?' Stone murmurs benignly, glancing briefly at the muffin again. I experience an urge to give it to him, as I give everything else, but mulishly I resist.

'No, I don't mean lunch. I mean ... I mean everything. Isn't it dangerous? The risks you take. Surely a man in your position has to be of, well, unimpeachable character or something like that?'

He just looks at me, smiling slightly, a picture of perfectly controlled mirth.

'Aren't you afraid of being caught?'

'Of course. But that's why I do it. It's my "pathology", as they say in the cop shows.' He just shrugs as if his dangerous behaviour is out of his own hands. As if he's a victim of his fate, and his own urges. 'If I play safe I might as well give up. Give in. Live half a life.'

For a moment, the mood seems sombre, and I sense something deep and almost sorrowful about this astonishing man, but then there's a sort of psychic flip and he dispels it without seeming to do anything at all.

He reaches over and takes another crumb of cake, then suddenly, still chewing, he's reaching around under the table and rummaging amongst my shopping, only to surface again with an M&S bag.

What else?

'Ah hah! What have we here?'

I half lunge across the table to whip it out of his hands. I wouldn't put it past him to extricate the contents and discuss them in full view of the entire clientele of Café

Mario. But he's too fast for me. He whisks the bag away to one side and, thankfully, confines himself to peering into it.

His broad brow puckers. 'Cotton and Lycra Midis. Five pack. White. Size 12–14.' He casts me a mocking glance. 'They're a bit serviceable, aren't they?'

'Yes, they are. Serviceable is what I want.' I consider another attempt to get the bag with my new knickers in out of his grasp, but I'm scared of what he might do if I don't succeed. 'I couldn't find any with Kevlar reinforcement. These are the nearest I could get.'

'Touché. And I'm sorry.' He cedes the bag to me at last, and reaches inside his jacket. Then from his wallet he peels off a couple more twenty-pound notes and places them in front of me. 'Just get yourself some nicer ones and I promise I won't rip them off next time.'

Part of me feels that I ought to act all outraged and tell him to keep his bloody money, and that I'm not a whore. But there's another part of me, the secret part, the part that's perfectly on Stone's wavelength, no matter how much I protest, that is thrilled and excited to be 'bought'. My fingers itch to take the notes and stuff them in my purse (God knows, I need the cash!) but I compromise by allowing them to sit on the table.

Stone moves in again, his voice soft. 'Well, if you're feeling a little too accessible at the moment, Miss Lewis, why don't you slip away and put on a pair of your deliciously serviceable knickers right now?' He nods in the direction of the cloakrooms.

My heart gives a series of heavy thuds, and that accessible place between my thighs flutters with longing.

I'm 'Miss Lewis' now, with no option to deny him.

My legs feel decidedly rubbery as I stumble into the Ladies and into a cubicle.

Will he follow?

Unlikely, because women are coming in and out of here all the time and with his eagle-eye he'll have noticed that. He's a risk-taker but he's not a total idiot.

I try to pee, but I'm so tense down there that it takes a minute. I know he'll be wondering and speculating and fantasising about what I might be doing in here, so, not to disappoint him, I give myself a little rub.

And another.

And another.

This is getting to be a habit, bringing myself off in toilets, thinking about Robert Stone. But I work myself to the logical conclusion in double-quick time, knowing he'll expect it.

The blonde woman comes in as I leave the cubicle but doesn't look at me in any way oddly, so I assume she didn't hear anything out in the café. As she takes the cubicle I left, I start to wash my hands.

Then stop again.

This isn't quite what he wants, is it?

Flashing back, I see my hand, cradled in his, held close to his face.

Drying my hands swiftly, I whip up my skirt and reach into my brand-new Cotton and Lycra Midis, white, size 12–14, and anoint the tips of my fingers with the stickiness there.

Panting like a boxer preparing to enter the ring, I walk swiftly down the little corridor and back into the café.

Only to find the seat I left occupied. By Greg.

Oh, what now?

As I approach, I catch snippets of conversation and to my relief it's about workstations and access restrictions and other stuff to do with the Borough's notoriously cantankerous, labyrinthine money-pit of a computer network. But when I approach the table, poor Greg's puppy-dog eyes nearly start out of his head. I've no idea who he thought was occupying the seat opposite Stone at our table, but I've a feeling he didn't expect it to be me.

He turns crimson, and stammers, 'Sorry, I didn't ... um ... I didn't realise I was sitting in your seat.' He continues to sit for a minute, as if stunned, then leaps to his feet. Stone, I notice, is already standing, and clearly playing at being Mr Look At My Impeccable Good Manners. Despite this, he offers no word of explanation for our being here together, and for my part, as I slide back into my chair, I can't think of anything to offer either.

'Care to join us, Greg?' Stone says expansively, gesturing to an extra chair at a nearby table.

'Er ... no ... but thanks, though.' Greg is still at sixes and sevens, his eyes skittering from me to Stone and back again, and bouncing off the money – that's still on the table – in the process. Lord alone knows what he thinks that's all about. I'm not even sure myself.

'I just came in for a takeaway,' he rushes on. 'Gotta get down to PC World and pick up some stuff.'

'That's a shame. Perhaps some other time?' Stone's back in his seat now, and we all know that Greg's been dismissed. A few moments later he's out of the café, but he glances back, frowning and tight-lipped, through the glass.

'Have you had him yet?' Stone enquires casually as Greg hurries away across the precinct.

'No, of course not. He's just a friend.' Which is probably not the best answer, given the bizarre theory he recently voiced on friendship.

'I think you should,' he continues, reaching out towards the M&S bag, as if to check its contents.

Instead, though, he grips my wrist and studies my hand for a moment. Then he draws it towards his face, exactly as I knew he would. When his sensitive nostrils detect my odour, they flare, and his large face creases in an almost cherubic, open-mouthed grin of sheer delight.

'Oh Maria, Maria,' he chuckles, 'you are *so* my kind of girl.' And like the kiss of a butterfly, he brushes his mouth against my fingers.

I feel as if I might faint, but the caress is over almost instantly. He releases me, and suddenly we're back on Greg again.

'He's young and he's obviously full of spunk and he clearly has a crush on you. I really think you should fuck him.'

I've had a few boyfriends in my time. Not all that many, and Stone doesn't qualify as a boyfriend anyway, but I can't imagine any of the men I've slept with before even beginning to countenance the idea of me being with another man. Under normal circumstances, men think it's the ultimate insult to their manhood.

Clearly Stone doesn't. But then again, he's far from a normal man.

His expression is bright, speculative, excited. He looks genuinely enthusiastic.

'But wouldn't it bother you?'

He's toying with his spoon again, and he gives me a curious, sneaky look as he twirls it over and over again between his fingers.

'No. I'd find it exciting.' He winks roguishly. 'Because now I've mentioned it, you'd be doing it for me, wouldn't you?'

And of course I would. Now. Since he caught me watching Sandy and Youngblood in the cellar, my entire sex life has been predicated by the need to please, amuse and entertain this man.

'But he might not want me.'

'Don't be obtuse, Maria.' His voice is sharp, almost annoyed. 'He's besotted with you, and you know it. It'd take only the slightest indication from you and he'd be slavering at your feet like a little pet doggie.'

The image takes me by storm, mutating fast. I see first

Greg, naked and crouched at my feet, then William Youngblood, then Stone himself. Men abasing themselves. It's not something I've considered before, but now I have, it stirs me. I doubt that Greg or Youngblood would be happy with the situation, but Stone is so perverse and omnivorous, I think he'd probably love it.

'What about other blokes? Youngblood, for instance?' I ask, not really interested in Youngblood, Greg or any other man any more, instead indulging in a fantasy of my foot, in a high-heeled shoe, on Stone's neck.

'Well, of course, our short, blond friend, obviously.' His tone is airy, unconcerned.

'He asked me out, you know.' Stone's eyes sharpen with interest. 'Well, sort of. He said if I ever fancied a drink or something any time.'

'You should go for it,' Stone recommends with genuine enthusiasm, 'Put him out of his misery, the randy little sod. He's probably still wanking over your exhibition, even as we speak.'

His mouth curves in that white, gleeful smile again.

'I already have done.'

10 **Crush**

The idea of a man wanking for you really gets a hold of your imagination.

And of other parts too.

I can't stop thinking about it. I haven't really stopped since lunchtime, in spite of everything else that's happened today. It's evening now and I'm back at my flat, but it still fills my mind.

After dropping his masturbation bombshell, Stone suddenly leapt to his feet, muttering and cursing about meetings, and being late. He seems to have the typical man of power's ability to switch from one persona to another with barely any transition time and no discernible regret. And as he left me high and dry, and well pissed off with him, he seemed unconcerned, already detached. He wasn't the smiling, irredeemable, game-playing pervert any longer but purely the coldly omnipotent Director of Finance.

Fuck him.

Oh, wouldn't I just love to!

Again.

When I went back down to the basement, finally to put those poxy files away, I hoped and prayed he'd somehow be down there, ready to dish out punishment for me not putting them away in the first place. And also perhaps masturbating while he waited for me.

But no such luck.

So I'm confined to just fantasising about him bringing himself off.

In my mind-picture, he's in his little bathroom, leaning

against a wall, his great head thrown back as he works furiously at his penis. He looks agonised, almost beautiful, and as he comes, he cries out, 'Oh God! Oh yes!' I hardly dare have him call my name, because that's more intimate, really, than anything we've done. But I wish he would. I replay the scene and he gasps, 'Maria!' and half-collapses where he stands.

As I daydream, my hand steals into my pyjama bottoms, but just as I'm about to touch myself, there's a soft knock on my door.

Who is it? A knock means it's someone from inside the building.

Mel?

Greg?

Mel roared off on her bike around half an hour ago, so it must be Greg. He was working late (or so he said) so I haven't seen him since Café Mario.

Hm ... Awkward.

Cautiously, I tweak my robe around me and open the door.

Greg stands there, but he's grinning shyly as if nothing's happened. He also has an acre-sized pizza box with him, from which divine smells are emanating, and a six-pack of strong continental lager.

Yum!

'Just wondering if you'd had your dinner yet?' He gives me the most winning look, and those huge, soulful eyes of his melt me. 'They were doing a super-size special at the place round the corner and it seems a shame to waste it.'

I'm already throwing back the door and ushering him in. 'I was going to open a tin of beans, but you've just made me an offer I can't refuse. Do you want to watch the telly or a DVD or something?'

A few minutes later we're watching the news like concerned citizens and scarfing down pizza as we view.

The beer is delicious too, but potent as rocket fuel, and it doesn't help my determination to play it cool and friendly and sensible and not do anything that might make things awkward.

I try very hard to not think about Stone. Or think about Greg in anything other than terms of him being a good mate. It's difficult, though. Stone pervades my thoughts now, as if he's coded into my genes. And Greg is undeniably a hottie.

He's young and pretty and he has a great body. And beneath that shaggy mop of light brown hair he has a brilliant mind, which is just as attractive to me as his physical attributes. Greg's technical genius is exciting in the same way that Stone's devious sexual intelligence is.

I don't know what Stone feels about me, not really. But it's as plain as the cute nose on his baby face and the soulful look in his puppy dog eyes that Greg has the mother of all crushes on me.

Which could make things very dodgy between us. Especially as I'm sitting here in some pretty flimsy pyjama bottoms, a vest and a very thin robe.

We eat in silence, not really watching a soporifically boring segment on EU trade talks.

'So, you and Stone? Are you ... er ... involved?'

I choke on a crumb of pizza crust and Greg has to slap my back.

'Sorry about that,' he apologises when I've got my breath back and I'm chugging a little beer to clear my throat. 'None of my business. I shouldn't have asked.'

'No, it's a fair question.' I put down my bottle, not really knowing how to answer. Stone and I are involved, but not in a way most people would class as involved. If I was involved with him in a conventional way, I should be eating pizza with him, not Greg.

'So?' he probes, obviously unable to fight his curiosity.

Or is it his jealousy? I glance at him and see the yearning in his face. I should lie to be kind, but I just can't.

'We've got a sort of "thing".'

He looks a bit crushed. 'Is it a "thing" thing ... or just a thing?'

What the hell does he want me to say? 'I don't know what you mean, Greg.'

He chews his pizza frantically, although I bet he's barely tasting it. 'I saw you.'

'Yes ... We were in Café Mario. So what?'

'No! I saw you down in the bin yard with him. I came back down to ask you if you wanted lunch and I saw him dragging you off.' He takes another bite, eating on auto. 'I followed you a bit, then I realised where you were going so I dashed upstairs and watched from the window.'

'Oh.'

Oh, indeed. Greg saw Stone fuck me, up against the wall. I should feel horrified and mortified. But instead I feel unbearably excited. I've never done it with an audience before, but the thought of it now, the thought of Greg's hungry eyes devouring my performance, and that of Stone, makes desire grind hard, deep in my belly. It's intense. Impossible to ignore. And I really, really want to do something about it.

I can't help hearing Stone's voice, saying 'You really should fuck him.' And I *would* like to fuck Greg. He's young and fresh and pretty, and on sneaking a sly sideways glance, I see that he's got a sizeable and impressive erection in his combats.

But would that be fair to him? I sense that Greg's feelings are far less subtle and devious than Stone's. With him it's 'boy meets girl', 'boy falls for girl' then 'boy fucks girl and she doesn't fuck anybody else'.

Greg shrugs and puts his plate aside. He's caught me

checking out his crotch. 'I can't help myself, Maria. I really like you. I think you're gorgeous. I should be jealous as hell and hate you for going with Stone.' He puffs out his lips, confused by his own reactions. 'But it was the hottest thing I've ever seen in my life!' Shrugging, he suddenly grins, all sweet and perplexed. 'At one stage I wasn't quite sure who I wanted to be. Stone or you!'

Holy hell! Suddenly, my lust increases exponentially. Stone and Greg. How sexy is that?

'Don't get me wrong!' he protests quickly, 'I'm not gay! It was just a thing.'

'Another thing, eh?' I observe and we both laugh.

Then he looks more serious. 'Look, I know you like him. Obviously. But you will be careful, won't you? He's got a dodgy reputation, you know? He ... he really does exploit people.'

Oh yes, oh, how I know that, I want to tell him. I know it and still I want to be exploited. But I also want to know more.

'What do you mean, Greg?'

'There have been women before who he's supposed to have been involved with. For a while, everybody would know there was something going on. Then suddenly this person he's supposed to have been banging ups and leaves.'

That's a shock. I know Stone is ruthless, but I hadn't thought he was actually callous enough to sack his discards.

'You mean he gave them the sack?'

'Oh no! There were two who went on to really great new jobs. Like a huge step up, you know? And another left to go back to college, and she got on to this really exclusive course. One you just wouldn't get a place on without some seriously heavyweight sponsorship.'

Yes, but it's still getting rid of a woman who's surplus to requirements.

Bastard!

'Like payoffs, then?'

'You could say that.' Greg's mouth twists. He looks angry, which is shocking in someone so easy-going. 'Men like him, with power and influence – they can get any woman they want. It's just not fair!'

I'm just about to say something palliative about cute men like him being able to get girls too, when my mobile rings. I consider ignoring it, but almost immediately know that I can't. My gut knows who it is, even though I've never told him the number.

'I'll just get this.' I snatch up the unit and make for my bedroom. 'Why don't you pick out a DVD to watch? There aren't many, but the ones I have got are good ones.' Then I dive out of the room before he can say anything.

'Good evening, Maria.'

The soft voice in my ear seems to fill my poky bedroom. How did he get this number? But there's no point in asking.

'Hi!' I say curtly, still angry with him, 'What do you want?'

'Just to chat. Are you alone?'

'No, I've got a guest. I can't talk long.'

'Aha! A guest!'

Uh oh, there's glee in his voice immediately, as if he knows it's another man, or at least he hopes so.

'Yes.' I'm pursing my lips. Even remotely, he has the power to make me want to spill out every thought in my mind and every sensation in my body. And because of him, my body's already feeling pretty sensational.

'Is it Melanie? Have I interrupted a little girl-on-girl action? If so I'm desperately sorry.'

Facetious pig! He's not sorry in the slightest. About anything. He just wants to know the sordid details.

'No, it's not Mel. And I don't see what business it is of yours who it is.' I can't think straight. It's like he's in the room with me. And it's a bedroom. It's almost as if he's reaching across, his big hand sliding my robe from my shoulders as he admires my nipples peaking beneath my thin cotton vest.

'Now, now, now. I think we both know it *is* my business, Maria.' So quiet, almost hesitant, and yet every word resonates and reaches out across the ether to control me. 'I guess it's a man then,' he goes on, and I can sense he's smiling. 'Don't tell me it's Blondie.' Despite everything, that makes me grin. 'If it is, I take my hat off to him. He's a fast worker!' There's another pause, then he comes back, 'Or did *you* contact *him*?'

'What if I did? You *told* me to!'

'It's not Youngblood, is it?'

How the hell does he know these things?

I shake my head, then I remember he can't actually see me. Even though I can as good as see him.

'No, it isn't.'

'Ah, well, it must be young Gregory then.'

So smug. I wish he was here so I could just slap him right in the mouth!

Then fuck the living daylights out of him.

'Yes, Greg's here. We're having a pizza and watching the telly. Nothing more than that. He is actually a bona fide neighbour of mine, you know.'

He just laughs.

I snap my phone closed, but it rings again immediately and I'm powerless not to answer.

'Go on! Fuck him! You know you want to!'

'Greg is a friend!'

More low laughter and I remember our conversation about friends who fuck.

'Fuck him, Maria, and then I can while away a boring, solitary evening imagining I'm there with you, watching you blow his mind.'

'Why don't you just watch the telly instead?' I suggest,

even while I'm getting hotter and hotter imagining myself on this bed with sweet, pretty Greg labouring industriously between my thighs while Robert Stone sits in the chair in the corner where my clothes are currently piled up. He's watching and he's masturbating. Slowly.

Suddenly, without warning, something else pops into my mind, and me being me, I just blurt it out.

'He saw us, you know. Greg, that is. Down in the bin yard. He was watching from one of the windows up above.'

Stone makes a low, heartfelt sound of appreciation and it suddenly dawns on me that he might *really* be masturbating. I gasp and my hand flies to my own crotch.

'Oh, my sweet, sweet girl, this is just getting better and better.'

There's a distinct lack of cadence in his voice, and I'm absolutely certain he's playing with himself now.

'You love that, don't you,' I say accusingly. 'You really get off on being watched, or in danger of being caught.'

'You know me so well,' he purrs, 'but you like it too, don't you? Don't tell me that it didn't give you a thrill when Greg told you he'd seen us. Admit it!'

It did. It still does. I close my eyes, re-imagining the scene, but this time with Greg watching avidly as Stone pounds away inside me. I clasp my hand to myself as the thought of it twists like a dark, sweet serpent inside me.

'OK! All right! Yes!' I almost shout into my mobile. 'I like it. It's a turn-on. Are you satisfied now?'

'Not yet, but I soon will be.' It's almost a whisper, barely audible, but latent with meaning. Desperation? Emotion?

His breath catches, once, twice, and it races through me like electricity. I'd do anything to have him with me now. Inside me. Pounding like before, his big body naked upon me as we struggle and strain against each other on this narrow, cheap bed.

There's a long pause, then he laughs, and the sound is bright, happy, relieved. He's just come, the bastard!

'You're disgusting!' I hiss, but it's half-hearted. I don't disapprove of what he's just done. No way. It's what I've been dreaming of half the day.

'I know,' he replies, utterly cheerful and unrepentant. 'Now it's your turn, Maria, my sweet. Go have some fun with your little computer nerd. I'll be with you in spirit. Watching. Now I know you like it.'

'Fuck off, Stone!'

'With pleasure,' I hear faintly just before I flip down the lid.

The room still seems filled with him. I throw the phone down on the bed. I don't know what to do. My first urge is to do what he's just done and masturbate. But that's precisely what he wants me to do. That, or to fuck Greg.

And somehow I'm not sure I want to do exactly what he tells me. He controls me far too much. I need to preserve at least a shred of autonomy.

Yet, staring at the door, it seems mean to cut off Greg's nose to spite Stone's face.

Back in front of the television, Greg is watching *Basic Instinct*.

Bugger! Did it have to be that? Reminding me of yet another instance of Stone manoeuvring me into doing something he wanted. Even though I know now that I wanted it too.

Poor Greg doesn't look as if he's enjoying the famous film very much though. He's still got the remains of a hard-on, but his handsome face is tense and cross, and a little sad.

'That was him, wasn't it?'

I sigh.

'If you mean Robert Stone, yes.' There seems no point in lying. He wouldn't believe me if I did.

'That fuck! I get an evening alone with you, and he has to muck it up!' Astonishingly, his large eyes are brilliant, almost swimming. 'I mean, I wasn't expecting anything. Just a chance to hang out, nothing more. And he just has to impose himself, hasn't he? He has to have everything . . . and I've got nothing!'

I suddenly feel even angrier at Stone. And so sorry for Greg.

More than sorry. He's a sweet man, and he's really cute. He deserves some fun, and I deserve some too. Why should I deny either of us what we need, just to get back at the pervert almighty, the Director of Finance.

I can always fuck Greg and tell Stone that I didn't fuck him.

Now *that* makes me smile.

'You've got a lot going for you, Greg,' I say gently, taking a seat on the sofa beside him and reaching over to take his almost empty beer bottle out of his hand. 'Forget Stone. He's not here, is he?' I touch his face and I can feel him shaking. 'You and me, we're here. We've got pizza, good beer, and a great movie. And that sad old fart's on his own at home. Just sod him!'

Greg blinks. Swallows. Looks gob-smacked. He's still trembling, and I know he's got to calm down a bit before he's any good to either of us. I snuggle up against him and place his arm around my shoulder. 'Come on, let's watch the movie and just see what happens, shall we?' I give him a little love-punch on the cheek and a grin that I hope reassures him.

'Er . . . OK,' he says, visibly brightening.

Greg restarts the DVD and we settle down. It's a great film and the music, the tone and the undeniable sexiness of it all quickly entrance us. As always happens, though, it's not the hero who gets my juices flowing but the heroine, the bad diva who seems to control every male character in the film.

She reminds me of Stone. She manipulates people with sex and charisma, which is exactly what he does.

I don't know who she reminds Greg of, but it's soon pretty obvious she's having an effect on him. One glimpse of her naked body and he's clearly hard again. I sit very still in the circle of his arm while he starts to wriggle, shifting himself about, then crossing his legs in an attempt to hide his erection.

After about a minute of this, I reach over, take hold of his knee and make him uncross his legs. 'Okay, so you've got a stiffy. It's nothing to be ashamed of. It's a sexy film.' With that, I grab his free hand and plonk it right in his crotch. 'Enjoy!'

I sound worldly-wise and all grown-up, but inside I'm both amazed and extremely impressed with myself. Being around Stone has changed me. Made me more powerful. Maybe I'm a latent bad diva too?

Greg flashes me a nervous, sideways smile, then suddenly relaxes. Grinning now, he gets into the spirit of things and cups his crotch. A few seconds later, he's kneading himself in a slow, easy rhythm – and it's very, very sexy.

Inevitably, when the heroine deliberately shows herself naked in her bedroom mirror, Greg gasps and starts to wiggle a bit again.

'Why don't you get it out?' I suggest, really wanting to see what his dick is like. I've not yet had a chance to get a good look at Stone's so I might as well see Greg's, mightn't I? 'We're all grown-ups here.'

Greg flashes me a sly sideways look. 'Hey, it's all me so far. What about you? What about a bit of quid pro quo?'

I feel a flutter of excitement down below. Oh God, yes, I want to do this. Both for myself and because, despite my desire to resist him, I know it would please Stone too.

'Fair enough.'

Lifting my bottom up off the couch, I slip my fingers beneath the elastic of my pyjama trousers and slide them down to my knees before I can even think about what I'm doing. Before I can wimp out.

Almost immediately, I feel myself moisten. This is so rude! I'm sitting beside a man I don't really know all that well, naked from the waist down, showing my pussy. I let out my breath, not realising I'd been holding it.

Greg laughs. 'Cool!' He shakes his head. 'Maria, you are something else! Really!' His eyes on my sex, he swallows, once, then twice, as if he's actually salivating at the sight of it. For the moment he seems to have forgotten Catherine Trammell.

'Right then. Your turn,' I say crisply, sounding a lot more matter-of-fact than I feel. The upholstery of the settee feels peculiar against my naked bottom and thighs. Really rude somehow. It's my turn to want to wriggle furiously, but I resist it. Even so, I experience this mad, powerful urge to sit down hard, and reach underneath myself and spread my buttocks so my anus is pressed against the rough cloth. I've no idea, really, where this compulsion is coming from, but the odds are that somewhere deep in my subconscious Robert Stone is at work.

Gamely, Greg unzips his combats and then scuffles around to push them and his boxer shorts down to his knees. His stiff cock springs up and bounces as he does so, and though he blushes furiously, he also laughs too.

'Down, boy!' he murmurs, gently pressing it down again and then allowing it to pop back up.

'Oh, no. Up, boy! Up!' I encourage, and we both giggle. It's like being back in school playing silly doctor-and-nurse games with your private parts before you even really know what they're for.

We both take ourselves in hand and return our attention to the film.

Pretty soon, we're at the famous interrogation scene

where the anti-heroine uncrosses and recrosses her legs, knowing that, because she's wearing no knickers, all the salivating cops will get an eyeful. I comprehend her power infintely better now after my own show this morning.

'Oh God, that is so hot!' sighs Greg, actually beginning to wank now. His hand slides slowly and carefully up and down his shaft. Which is a nice one – sturdy and of quite an impressive length for a fairly slightly built man. The tip is all shiny and red and sticky.

Which makes me want to swallow too. Because I'm the one that's salivating now.

Should I give him a blowjob?

I know he'd love it. What man doesn't? But again, I'm ever conscious of Stone, and what I have and haven't done with him. If I suck Greg off before I've sucked Stone off, it's putting two fingers up to my dark, kinky mentor, isn't it? Which is what I had in mind to do.

And yet still I feel I can't do it. Don't want to do it. I'm bound to him somehow, and that bond stops me dishing out gifts that he doesn't want me to give. He's told me to fuck Greg, but he hasn't given me a red light to blow him. And somehow I have to obey that restriction.

Suddenly, I realise that Greg's not watching the film, but staring at me.

'Hey! Quid pro quo, remember?'

Of course.

Realising this is my chance to get more skin area against the upholstery, I shift my position and spread my thighs. A little hitch and a hutch and my bottom cheeks are spread too, just as I wanted them to be. I'm not sure whether Greg's aware of this, but he doesn't miss the tiniest iota of the action when I slip my fingers into my sex and find my clit.

'That's better!' His eyes are wide. Hot. Excited. His hand moves faster on his cock, and I'm not the only one who's wriggling and bumping in their seat.

I'm furiously turned on, both in my head, and in my sex, which is all slippery. But I can't help laughing all the same. This is mad! I feel more than ever like a kid playing grubby little fiddling-about games. Greg frowns, as if he thinks that I'm mocking him, then he starts to laugh too, seeing the funny side.

'Are we in a race?' I pant.

'I – I don't know,' gasps Greg, still smirking as his eyes dart between the screen, my crotch and his own fist moving on his cock.

'Well, if we are, who wins?' I can feel my orgasm gathering, threatening, drawing closer. 'The first to finish or the one who holds out longest?'

'Fuck knows!' says Greg cheerfully, his hand stroking faster and faster, 'I don't really care. Do you?'

'Hell, no!' And I don't. This is all so naughty and daft and gross. It's the funniest thing that's happened to me in ages. Funny ha-ha that is, not funny bizarre, because Stone's the one who holds that particular prize.

As Stone pops into the forefront of my mind again, looming out of the shadows where he's been all along, I imagine him standing over us, watching. I bet he'd see the funny side of this too. But who would he be rooting for? Would it be me or would it be Greg?

'I think I need a tissue!' cries Greg suddenly. He's very red in the face now, and he's clearly very, very near. Pausing briefly in my own efforts, I fish beside the couch and pass the box to him.

Then watch in fascination as he tears one out and wraps it around the head of his cock like a little makeshift white hat.

'Do all blokes do that?' I ask, unable to stop myself tittering inanely. Greg's dick looks incredibly cute but so absurd.

'No idea!' He's biting his lip, his sweet, soulful eyes closing. He's really throwing himself into it with all he's got now, his lean thighs flexing and his closed hand zipping up and down his flesh.

It's a beautiful sight. And a privilege to see it, really. My own sex seems to lurch in silent tribute.

'Oh! Oh! Oh!' he yelps, the rapid motion stilling instantly as he just holds himself and comes. As I see the semen pulsing against the tissue, I come too. But it's quiet. Inner. Muted. I'm in the room, my sex fluttering and beating as I watch Greg come down and relax again.

But behind that image, there's Robert Stone, his clever smile sly and triumphant.

11 **Wuff! Wuff!**

It's nearly a week since I've seen Stone and I could kill him!

Not a word, not a peep out of him since that phone-call. Not even to ask if I've slept with Greg, or been out with William Youngblood yet. It's as if he doesn't give a shit about me. As if I was a temporary diversion, now forgotten. Moved on from.

Thank God things are OK with Greg after our little session watching *Basic Instinct*. I was scared stiff we'd be awkward, unable to look one another in the eye, our friendship completely screwed up. But not so. When we'd finished what you'd call our synchronised masturbation, we just watched the rest of the film and finished our beer and pizza, then Greg went home. We haven't discussed it since. But we haven't *not* discussed it either. Now and again we exchange glances in the car on the way to work, and have a little chuckle, but that's about the extent of it.

The only time there's any awkwardness between us is when Stone's name comes up in conversation. So I've tried to avoid that happening because it's obvious Greg hates him now.

Borough Hall seems dull. It's like the special electricity that I was feeling because I might run into Stone any minute has been drained out of the place. I'm almost considering starting to scan the local paper for another job, although with my pathetic to non-existent CV I suppose I ought to hang on to what I've got.

I'm so bored that I'm actually enjoying my work.

But my heart still lurches every time the blessed phone

rings. There's always hope, a tiny shoot of it, that it'll be Stone.

'Maria Lewis, Business Development,' I pipe cheerily.

'Robert Stone, Director of Finance,' purrs the longed-for voice, and every last nerve-end in my body goes 'bingo!'

For a moment, my jaw actually seems to lock while my ability to form coherent speech canters around in my brain like an unbroken pony. Finally, I say, 'Yes, Director, how can I help you?'

I meant it to come out sounding a cross between competent and sassy, but actually it's a breathy semi-squeak.

He laughs softly, and it's as if he's right here in the room with me, and he's touching me. I have to shuffle in my seat as if he's got his hands in my knickers and he's doing things to me, it's so real. And the fact that he teases out the sensation for several seconds without speaking again only intensifies the feeling. I'm almost ready to touch myself, right here in the office, with Sandy only a few feet away, when he finally deigns to reply.

'Did you watch the television last night, Miss Lewis?'

Uh oh.

'Er . . . yes. Yes, I did.'

The game's on, but I don't know what game it is yet. My brain's doing the cantering around thing again, searching frantically through the list of programmes I might have watched that have some special significance.

It doesn't take long though. Remembering, I start to shake. Remembering how I thought at the time, this is *so* him, it wouldn't surprise me at all if he's into this.

'So, do you fancy a little adventure?'

He's assuming I've watched the same programme. God, knowing him, he's probably read my mind again, and he knows I watched it.

'It' being a documentary about sex addicts, and people

who like to go out into woods and car parks and other public places and have sex while other people watch.

'Miss Lewis?' he prompts, ever so slightly sharply. And I realise that I've been sitting here, running through some bits of the programme in my head and thinking how absolutely bloody insane it is for a man in his position to be involved in anything like that.

But then that's the reason he probably likes it so much.

'Um ... Yes, OK,' I stammer, not giving myself time to think about the ramifications.

He likes taking crazy chances, running risks and living life on the edge of discovery and possibly disgrace. But do I?

I'm not entirely sure yet.

But what I am sure of is that I can't say no to him. I daren't risk it. I can't bear the thought of him discarding me because I'm not daring enough, and moving on to some other woman.

Oh shit, I've got it *so* bad!

'Excellent!' he pronounces, his voice almost boyishly happy. 'I'll pick you up at nine tonight.' He pauses and I sense the grin, the wicked, slow, devilish grin, in his voice. 'And wear something slutty.'

'How slutty?'

This time I forget to think, and when, a microsecond later, I do, I glance across at Sandy and see that her eyes are wide. She's no longer paying the slightest bit of attention to the applications she was supposedly so busy with that she didn't want any interruptions.

'Oh, I don't know,' Stone says, obviously enjoying himself. 'No underwear. Easy access. Use your initiative. Dazzle me!'

I'm not sure that anything can dazzle or amaze Robert Stone any more, so I just say, 'OK. Right. See you later,' and ring off.

If ever there was a pregnant silence anywhere, this is it. Sandy's still staring at me, with this 'Well?' look on her face.

I'm about to answer and then I think, hey, why should I? I'm not the only one with clandestine goings-on going on, am I? What about her and Youngblood in the cellar? She's never told me anything about that. Never explained her absences. She just goes on acting like Miss Goody Two Shoes Butter Wouldn't Melt.

So why should I explain what could have been a perfectly innocent (even if it isn't) phonecall?

I just stare back at her, smile blandly, then look back down studiously at my work again. But inside I feel a sense of deeply devilish manipulative glee that I know would make our Director of Finance proud of me.

Come nine o'clock, I'm standing outside the house where my flat is, wearing something slutty, as per instructions. I feel nervous and vulnerable and I'm thanking my lucky stars that both Mel and Greg are out tonight – because I look exactly like a prostitute plying her trade in a red-light district.

And I'm a bit cold too. Especially due to Stone's 'no underwear' stipulation. There's a nippy little wind blowing up and down the road, and as I scope back and forth, looking for his sleek black Mercedes, the breezes are reaching parts they really shouldn't reach.

I tug down my ultra-short denim skirt, a leftover from a 'Tarts and Vicars' party long ago, and wish I hadn't taken Stone's word quite so literally. Along with my abbreviated denim mini I'm wearing a pair of trashy white boots from the same fancy dress, and a neat, pink velour hoodie. Which would be great on a Saturday afternoon worn with jeans or tracksuit bottoms and a T-shirt, but feels disgustingly sleazy with nothing at all underneath it.

Around my throat is another part of the tart's costume, a little refinement I'm hoping Stone will appreciate. It's a pink leather studded collar. Which seems strangely apposite seeing that the activity we're about to indulge in is commonly known as 'dogging'.

Wuff! Wuff!

Ten minutes pass and with each one I feel more and more conspicuous. This isn't actually a red-light district, but anyone looking at me would swear that it'd become one. I'm thankful that it's a darkish night, and there's no streetlight shining anywhere near to attract the kerb-crawlers.

But the very second I've thought that, a dark, nondescript estate car slows to a halt beside me, and as the window winds down I feel physically sick. What the hell have I got myself into?

'How much for a blow job?' enquires a voice.

A laughing voice that's oh, so familiar.

'Fifty quid, guvnor. But to you, a hundred.'

'Get in, you cheeky bitch,' says Stone amiably, popping open the door.

Once I'm in, he pulls away from the kerb straight away, not giving me time to dither or change my mind. I can hardly believe that I'm here with him and we're on our way to God knows what. I certainly can't think of a thing to say, and it seems he doesn't even feel the need to speak or explain, because he just flashes me that sly, smug smile of his and then concentrates on his driving.

Which leaves me free to concentrate on him.

Tonight's Stone is a very different one from the expensively-dressed corporate man who prowls Borough Hall. This is dressed-down Stone, even though the aura is the same. That is, he looks just as irrationally and unexpectedly sexy in ancient denims, a shabby black jeans jacket and a black T-shirt as he does in his cool, well-cut suits. In fact, dressed like this, his big body looks even more solid and manly, and the testosterone inside the car feels so dense you could almost slice it.

But even if he looks scruffy, he still smells delicious, and that signature cologne of his seems unbearably condensed too. I hardly dare breath in, because if I'd been wearing knickers they'd be getting wet already.

Eventually, after God knows how many silent, nerve-jangling miles, I have to speak.

'What happened to the Merc?'

'It's at home,' he says, changing gear smoothly yet aggressively. 'It's not a good idea to use a flash car for these sorts of outings. You're likely to get remembered' – he flashes me a white grin in the darkness – 'and there's always the possibility you'll knacker up your paintwork.'

He seems about to say more when suddenly he frowns slightly and checks the rear-view mirror. His eyes flash to it once or twice, then he shrugs slightly and, when his shoulders drop, appears relaxed and unperturbed.

More miles. We seem to be escaping the county, not just the borough, but I suppose it's not a good idea to have outdoor sex in front of strangers in your own backyard. Especially if you're a local bigwig like Stone.

'The collar is a nice touch.'

It's so sudden that I nearly jump out of my skin.

'Yes, well, you did say "slutty" and it's the sluttiest thing I could find.'

'Mm . . . Initiative. I like that,' he says softly. And then, without warning, he reaches across, and with a nimble twist of his wrist, slips his hand up my skirt, touches my bush quickly, then whips it back just in time to change gear again.

'And I like that too,' he continues, accelerating sharply as if the grope has excited him.

Which I hope it has.

We're weaving at speed through country lanes now. Stone seems intent on the road, concentrating on his driving, but, as he speaks again, I realise that's not all that's on his mind.

'I like the idea that I can touch your cunt whenever I want to. I like to be able to play with you. Get you excited and wet. I like it that when I'm in the Hall, in a meeting or whatever, you're in the same building and I can imagine that I'm fingering your clit and you're wriggling and moaning, and that you need to come.'

I can hardly breathe again, imagining that situation, feeling as if his voice is his hand and he's actually doing just what he's describing. Masturbating me.

Yet his hands are on the wheel. Large, competent hands with immaculately clipped nails. Ordinary hands, yet capable of great beauty.

I let out my breath again and he glances at me, fleetingly.

'Exciting, isn't it?' My eyes dart to his mouth, where for a moment, he snags his lip between his teeth in that cute way that's becoming so familiar. 'I think about your cunt when I really shouldn't be thinking about it. Do you ever think about my cock?'

'Oh, all the time,' I shoot back lightly. It's a little bit of a lie, but not that far from the truth. 'Not that I've ever had a chance to actually *see* it properly,' I add, hinting heavily.

His smile broadens, all white and impish.

'Well, have a look now! What are you waiting for?'

'But you're driving! And you're driving fast!'

Immediately, the car decelerates.

My cue.

Reaching across, I flip open the button of his jeans, then fumble for the zip, my fingers shaking so hard I can't get hold of the tag.

He tut-tuts, reaches down, and guides me to the zip. I regain control of my motor skills and tug it downwards, then open his fly.

He's going commando tonight too, so, without much help from me, his penis springs out. The light inside the car isn't great, but it's enough to show me he's everything I imagined him to be.

Big, naturally. Bigger by far than Greg's dick, even in proportion to his much, much larger body. Lord, it's no wonder he stretched me when he was in me!

'You can touch it, you know. It won't bite,' he says cheerfully, as if it's the most normal thing in the world to be driving through the night with his cock poking up out of his jeans.

I let my fingers settle lightly upon him, shaping tentatively around the solid shaft. His skin there is stretched and hot, and exquisitely silky. Even if it wasn't a penis, it would still be a nice thing to hold.

Suddenly, I'm smiling like a Cheshire cat. How mad is this? Sitting here in a speeding car holding a man's dick in my hand.

I purse my lips tight, trying desperately not to laugh.

'What's so funny?' he enquires, although I can see he's smirking too. That's one of the things I'm beginning to really, really like about Stone. He doesn't take anything, especially himself, too seriously.

'This. It.' I nod at his stiffy. 'Me. You. It's all a bit mad, isn't it?'

'Indeed it is,' he concurs, then his breath catches and I realise that just my holding him is really having an effect on him. I watch – not his dick but his face – and see a tic working in his jaw as he exerts dominion over his own body and his responses.

'So,' he continues, calm again. Impressively so. 'What do you think? Better than young Gregory's?'

'What makes you think I've seen Greg's?'

'Didn't you do as you were told the other night?' His voice is silky again, arch and haughty. I flick a fingernail against his glans and his knuckles go white on the steering wheel.

'Have a care, Miss Lewis,' he murmurs, soft and low.

I consider bucking his authority. He's called me 'Miss Lewis', so we're playing now, and I should obey. But I could easily not do so. In theory. However, in fact, I find I just can't. It's like he's got me in his web of power just as surely as I've got his dick in my hand.

'So, did you fuck Greg?'

'No . . . no, I didn't.'

He's listening to me, and no doubt enjoying my hold on him, but once again his eyes flick to the rear-view.

'What's the matter? Are we being followed?'

'No!' he cuts back, ever so slightly sharply, 'and don't change the subject. Why didn't you fuck Greg?'

'I . . . um . . . I don't know. We sort of got doing other stuff instead.'

'Really? Other stuff. That sounds interesting. Please go on.'

That's got him, and he smiles, any thoughts of a possible 'tail' forgotten as I describe Greg and my little wanking game.

'Well, I suppose that'll do,' Stone concedes. I guess he's trying to sound world-weary and somewhat disappointed in me, but the stiff tenseness of his penis says otherwise. His penis says he's very, very pleased with me.

'Well, I think we'd better put this away for the time being,' he says all of a sudden, while at the same time swinging the car on to a track that leads into what looks like some fairly dense woodland. It's hard to tell in the dark, and I missed the sign, but I think we're heading towards a picnic area.

A classic dogging venue, so the documentary said.

I'm not quite sure how to deal with Stone's erection, but he quickly pulls the car to a halt on the track and with surprising deftness manages to stuff himself back into his jeans. Only a little grunt, as he zips up, reveals that it must be pretty uncomfortable.

We drive on a little further and come to an open area, a car park. There are several other vehicles parked up, and in the back of one of them, a people carrier, the interior light is on.

About fifteen men, and even a couple of women, are clustered avidly around it. Someone's even shining what looks like a mini floodlight into the tailgate for extra illumination of what's going on inside.

My God, these people think of everything!

'So, do you want to watch somebody else for a while? Or do you just want to get down to business?'

Oh, the finesse of the man!

'Actually, I need a pee before anything else,' I blurt out, realising all of a sudden that my bladder is full to bursting.

'There are some toilets over to your left.' He nods towards the dark, squat shape of a brick building at the edge of the parking area, and I throw open the car door, and step out, ready to scuttle towards it.

'Wait! You'll need me with you,' he calls in a low tone, getting out of the car and moving smartly to my side.

'I can manage on my own!'

'No doubt you can. But if you go in there alone it might be construed as an invitation. Now, come on.'

As he frog-marches me towards the toilet block, I do indeed notice a couple of men turn from the people carrier and look towards us. I can't see their eyes, but their body language is interested.

'I said that I can manage!' I protest once we're inside, and Stone has followed me to one of the cubicles – which doesn't have a door.

He says nothing, but even though it's almost pitch

black in here, I can see *his* eyes. And they're intent, glittering, implacable.

He wants to watch me pee. Obviously my little tale of playing piss games with Mel is in his mind.

My pelvis goes all tense as I crouch over the grubby pot, and for a moment I don't think I can go. Then I look again into Stone's eyes, and the heat there – and the slight nod he gives me – seems to open my urethra and my waters come gushing out.

The relief is delicious, almost orgasmic, and I let out a sigh.

'Good girl,' murmurs Stone, 'good girl.'

There's no paper, of course, but before I can scrabble for a tissue, Stone is crouching beside me, with one of his own. With utmost gentleness, almost a sense of decorum, he dabs at my pussy until I'm dry. He doesn't attempt to touch me, but when he's done, he lightly kisses me on the lips.

It's the most peculiar moment and, as we leave the little building, I feel strangely safe and cherished. What lies ahead is going to be wild, crude and blatantly exhibitionist, and yet with Stone beside me I know I won't be harmed.

We draw close to the people carrier and find a vantage point.

Inside, a naked woman is crouched on all fours with one kneeling man going at it from behind her while another is fucking her roughly in her mouth. A few of the men nearest to the action have their cocks out and are wanking furiously, and, even as we watch, one of them comes with a loud shout and his semen shoots out and spatters on the woman's bare bottom.

Bloody hell!

As the three bodies jerk and grunt, I feel myself getting wet. Do I want to be that woman? Do I want to be used that way, in two orifices? I'm not sure, but I think the man to the rear might actually be buggering her.

I realise that I'm holding Stone's hand, as a kind of talisman, and squeezing his fingers.

'Are you OK?' he whispers. 'We can go if you don't like it.'

I'm astonished. He really cares! He wants me, I know he does, but he's prepared to go without if I'm not happy.

'It's OK. I'm fine,' I whisper back, then reach beside me and lightly cradle his bulging crotch. 'Don't worry about me.'

OK, that's a lie. I like it when he worries about me. But still.

'You're a treasure, Miss Lewis.' His big hand closes over mine, keeping it in place.

I give him a little squeeze. 'I know, Mr Stone.'

The three figures in the back of the vehicle continue to hump and grind out expletives and go at each other. It's not a pretty sight, but it's erotic on a crude and basic level, and it's really getting to me. A little trickle of moisture slides down my bare thigh, and almost immediately Stone's fingers tighten over mine, as if aware of it. Has he smelt me? It's almost as if he's part bloodhound sometimes, his nose seems unnaturally sensitive.

Finally, the threesome in the back of the people carrier all seem to get their rocks off at more or less the same moment, and collapse in a sweaty, gasping heap on to the carpet there. Almost instantly, a sort of silent murmur passes through the assembled group of watchers and there's an air of expectancy.

What next?

Who next?

As if in answer Stone spins me towards him and begins to kiss me, really putting on a show. His tongue's in my mouth and his hands are everywhere. Before I know it my hoodie's unzipped and he's fondling my breasts with enthusiasm.

I can't help but respond. And put on my own show because the idea that the watchers are now watching me is astonishing.

I grind my pelvis against Stone. Kiss back as hard as I'm being kissed. It's all delicious and I really want him inside me.

But *just* him.

I don't mind playing the porn star for all these horny men, but I don't want them participating. I want to be fucked, and fucked hard, but just by Stone.

'Just you,' I gasp as his mouth travels, kissing my face and neck. 'I'll do anything, but only with you.'

'Don't worry.' His breath is like fire against my skin, his kiss wet and devouring. 'I've no plans to share you with anyone tonight.'

I don't have any time to ponder on the implications of the word 'tonight' because just at that moment, his hand slides up my skirt and he starts playing with me, quite roughly. My eyes are closed by now, but I'm well aware that the circle of watchers has re-formed – around us.

On another occasion, Stone would manipulate a woman with all the delicate accuracy of a microbiologist splicing cells, but tonight it's not precision that's called for. It's grosser, more visible actions that will entertain an audience. He fingers me fast and hard but it's just what I need. Within seconds, I'm climaxing as I cling to him.

And there's encouragement. Dimly, through my pleasure, I hear things like 'horny little slut', 'hot piece' and 'sexy little fucker' and the audience appreciation only makes me come the harder.

I don't particularly want to see them all, but I want to hear them. And have them see me.

As I come down from my orgasm, it's as if Stone has picked up my thoughts again.

'Trust me,' he says, and before I can tell him I do, he's pulled a soft black scarf from his pocket and tied it around my eyes.

Oh God, now I *have* to trust him! I've got no option.

Just as I'm wondering how on earth I'm going to stumble around out here, unable to see, something utterly thrilling happens.

Stone sweeps me up in his arms, lifting me up from the ground as if I'm virtually weightless.

I've never been carried by a man before, and it's so exciting, as he strides across the car park in the direction of God knows what, that my heart just thuds and thuds and thuds.

And in this, the least lyrical of all settings, it's deeply romantic.

In darkness I feel myself carried across the car park while our audience shuffles along in Stone's wake. He sets me down on what feels like a wooden picnic table, with my legs hanging over the side, thighs open. Swiftly, ruthlessly, he whips up my skirt and I sense eyes – those of at least a dozen men – zero in on my rudely exposed sex. It can be nothing less than the centre of attention now, especially if the enterprising bloke with the mini searchlight has it pointing right at me.

There's a mild commotion going on. Maybe some squabbling and jockeying for position. But I close my mind to it. The sense of being on show like this is one of the hottest things I've ever experienced, even with Stone. I feel so aroused that it's almost impossible to keep still. And as I start to wriggle slowly and enticingly against the gritty wood, whatever that dispute was is almost forgotten and my audience sets up a low baying of profane appreciation. There's still a bit of shoving going on, but I guess that's Stone pushing the over-keen ones away, protecting his prize.

Unable to stop myself, I reach down and touch myself between my legs. I need to come again. I need Stone. The baying becomes actual shouting. And stomping.

And then Stone is close, standing between my out-spread legs, his bulk pushing them wider. I hear his zip, then detect the minute movements of him putting on a condom, then, a second later, he lifts up my legs, man-handling me until my knees are over his broad shoulders, and the bulbous head of his cock is right up against me.

It's difficult to reach around him, in order to hug him and pull him closer, but gripping the slats of the table for purchase, I shove my crotch at his.

Contact! Oh God! He rams into me!

The crowd howls and so do I.

Oh God, I'd forgotten how big he is when he's inside. And he feels even bigger tonight. There's no finesse in the way he hammers himself into me, but I don't want any. I'm so close to coming that I don't really need any digital stimulation, but even so he spits out a command.

'Finger yourself, slut!'

His voice sounds strange, distorted, not like him at all. At least not like the clever, subtle Stone I'm used to.

I touch my clit, still scrabbling for a grip on the table with my other hand, but it's his hard, furious order that makes me come.

My body clutches at him, clenching and clenching and clenching as I heave myself around, whimpering and moaning. Somewhere up in the dark treetops, there's a detached, observing part of me watching all this and awarding points.

Ten out of ten, I think, my booted heels waving about, and very likely endangering the teeth of the closer watch-ers. I can almost feel their hot breath on my skin and the heat of them as they cluster around me like a bunch of over-sexed dogs around a bitch.

And still my lover labours away at me. A lesser man would have shot his load within seconds, but Stone is a greater man. He's determined to get good value from this fuck, and he even gets all artistic with a series of fancy swivels of his solid hips.

Which provokes me into new dramatic efforts too, even though I'm off my head and still half-climaxing. I thrust back at him as hard as he's thrusting at me. Equal and opposite forces in motion. If this goes on much longer it'll blow the top of my head off!

But finally, with a great lurch and a loud shout, Stone comes, flinging himself into me and over me. Bent in two, I manage to finger my clit again – and then I'm coming, coming with him, all the way.

12 **Uh oh! Busted!**

Sandy drops a file on the desk and I jump as if someone's let a gun off.

I wonder if I can actually get the sack if I'm fucking the Director of Finance? Would he be the one who makes these decisions? Or does it have to go to Committee or something? I wouldn't have thought so at my level, but this place is a palace of red tape.

Either way, I probably deserve to get the boot, seeing as how I've as good as fallen asleep at my desk at least twice today.

And that, unfortunately, is when I seem to be under surveillance. Sandy has had her beady eye on me since I walked in this morning, and especially so when the phone rings. I suppose she's waiting for me to say something incriminating. But the calls are all routine and not from Stone, and I'm too knackered for sexy banter even if he did ring.

I'm exhausted, sleep-deprived and too confused to think. But that doesn't stop me yearning for him.

I've got it bad. This thing we have might be kinky, and it might be dangerous, but it's real.

I just wish I knew what the hell he feels for me.

As a peace offering, I suggest I make coffee for Sandy. She eyes me suspiciously, as if she thinks I might pee in it or something, but accepts. I toss two spoons of Kenco into my mug, hoping the extra caffeine will wake me up, and, while I'm waiting for the ancient kettle to boil, a post delivery arrives, and Sandy graciously deigns to distribute it.

And there's an item of post for me.

Wincing at the strength of my coffee (and fearing for my stomach lining), I'm reluctant to open the ominous-looking brown circulation envelope with my name written in the last window in a very neat, small hand. Surely it's not my P45 already? I know I'm pretty useless in this job, but there are channels to be gone through before you're sacked.

Inside is another envelope. An ordinary white one marked 'Confidential'. And with 'Miss M Lewis' written on it in the same precise handwriting. My stomach flips inside me.

Sandy is still watching me (doesn't she have any work to do today?) so I slip the envelope into my drawer and put my head down and pretend to work.

It's not too long before she has to go out, and hands shaking, I retrieve my prize.

Maria, the note inside begins abruptly, in the same hand. *I hope that you're not too tired today. I should have suggested that you take the day off, but my mind was otherwise engaged. For my own part, I'm having a really crappy day, and would be delighted if you could pop up to my office at around 5 p.m. to give me something to look forward to.*

It's signed, without any kind of salutation, *Robert Stone*. But there's a PS.

Remember the thing I said I like to think about during the day? I'm thinking about it now.

What a bizarre little communication!

It's both distant and intimate, and not at all what I'd expect from him. Even the handwriting is a surprise. From a big man like Stone I'd imagine a big, bold, slashing script, not this diminutive, orderly, almost unassuming hand.

But that's Stone all over, I suppose. Always expect the unexpected.

I spend the day rereading the note at every available opportunity. Imagining him writing it. Imagining him imagining my cunt. Imagining him imagining me imagining him imagining my cunt.

And the more I think of him the more trouble I'm in.

At lunchtime I try to find Mel, or Greg, for a chance to take my mind off things by having a natter with someone a bit more fun than the work-drones in my office. But I can't find either of them. I'm especially uneasy about not seeing Greg. He left this morning before I did – without a word. If he can't give me a lift, he unfailingly lets me know.

But finally, after a day that must be at least as crappy as Stone's, 5 p.m. rolls around. I leave my stuff in the office, but I clock off so I don't get in even more trouble by goofing off in work time.

As I reach the landing where Stone's office is, I just catch sight of William Youngblood disappearing round the corner at the far end, and I get a really weird reaction. If I knew what hackles were, they'd be rising, but I can't for the life of me understand why. It's just some kind of prickle of awareness, but not in a good way. I can't explain it, but I suddenly know that man is trouble.

There's nobody in Stone's outer office. Mrs Sheldon's computer is covered up, and the coat-stand is empty.

So, Stone's here all on his own.

At the door, I hesitate, almost panting. I feel more nervous now than ever before, because of the dangerous feelings I'm experiencing. The last time I saw this guy, he'd just carried me bodily up to my flat, then deposited me on my bed fully clothed and virtually asleep. By the time he kissed me on the forehead, and threw a blanket over me, I simply could not keep my eyes open.

All this Prince Charming stuff scares me far more than being half-naked and fucked on a picnic table before an audience.

I knock.

'Come in.'

I study the shiny door.

'Come in!'

I grasp the handle, turn it and almost throw myself into the room.

Stone gets to his feet as I enter but doesn't come towards me, sweep me into his arms and kiss me as I've been half-imagining. He just cocks his great head on one side and studies me, his face strangely neutral.

I might be imagining things, but is he almost as confused as I am?

He looks as tired as me, at least. The slight bags under his eyes look really dark, and he's very stubbly indeed, more so than usual. What must have been a very sharp shirt at 8 a.m. is now rather crumpled, and he's rolled up his sleeves. His tie's all out of shape and tugged free of his opened collar.

Weary Stone. My heart turns over again.

'You look like shit!'

It's out before I can call it back, but Stone just laughs and suddenly looks ten years younger.

'Well, Maria, it would be nice to riposte and say that you look the same. But it would be a lie. Because you don't.' He shrugs and makes an expressive palms-up gesture with his large but beautiful hands. 'You look amazing. I just wish I had the energy to fuck you right now.'

Well, it looks like we're right back on track, with no mushy stuff. I don't know whether to be relieved or devastated.

I dither about, half-way across the room, not knowing whether to approach, stay where I am or retreat. We're obviously not game-playing right now, and we're way past the conventional 'subordinate summoned by boss' scenario where I pull up a chair and face him across the acres of his desk.

'Come here,' he says softly, the words injecting the energy into me to propel me across the room.

Stone whirls in his chair until it's at an angle to his desk, and shoves aside the pile of documents he's been working on. Then he pats the blotter.

He wants me to sit on the desk?

I perch. He grins up at me. Tired, slightly frazzled, very middle-aged, but still devastating.

'I should've told you to take the day off.' His hand settles on my thigh, and it feels warm but strangely asexual. 'It was the least I should have done after last night.' One long finger edges a little way up, towards my hem, and suddenly it stops feeling asexual. 'How do you feel? You were magnificent, you know.'

I tremble, yet I know it's the truth. I *felt* magnificent last night.

OK, so I was shagged blindfolded across a picnic table while a score of unknown men ogled me and wanked over me, but my chief memory – apart from the orgasms – was a sense of incredible power. I might have appeared to be subjugated but really, when it came down to it, I was in charge.

I wanted everything that happened, and I got it.

'You weren't so bad yourself,' I murmur, beginning to gasp as the wandering fingertip slips beneath my skirt and starts travelling ever upwards.

He shrugs modestly, even though it's obvious he actually thinks he's the fuck of the century.

'Are we wearing knickers today?' he enquires, although he's nearly in a position to find out for himself.

'Well, I am. I don't know about you,' I flash back, then scrabble at the blotter as he confirms my statement by brushing lightly at my gusset.

It's damp, of course. I've been thinking about him all day, but since I walked into this room my simmering hormones have boiled over.

He probes gently, pushing at the cloth, not going specifically for my clit or anything, but just greeting my sex as if it's a familiar friend.

Which it is by now, I think, taking a deep, deep breath.

'Why don't you take them off?' he suggests, his voice like silk. 'I need to touch you. I wasn't kidding when I said I think about your cunt all day.'

Fumbling, I start to obey him, but then suddenly there's the sound of the outer door opening, and some-body stomping across the room. As I wrench my knickers back into place there's a loud knock at the door and 'Stone! Are you in there?' rings out.

It's William Youngblood.

Stone's eyes flare for a moment, and I get the feeling he genuinely doesn't know what to do. But then he grins and, in a swift, unstoppable movement, draws me down and gently but firmly pushes me into the deep knee-well of his huge executive desk. It's a close fit as he slides his chair forward, but when he parts his knees there's a little more space for me.

'Enter!' he calls out imperiously, just as I realise that I'm looking directly at his dick.

Youngblood does enter and, judging by his tread, I imagine him almost stalking over to the desk. Cleverly Stone half-rises in his seat in acknowledgement, nearly giving me a thick ear with his knee in the process.

'Yes, William, how can I help you?' he says in a pleasant tone, pressing the inside of his thigh against my face.

Something lands on the desk with a soft impact. Phew, sweet William is in a feisty mood, flinging stuff at Stone like that.

'I want to go through these projections with you

again,' he announces. There's a strangely cocky note in his voice, as if he knows something Stone doesn't. It's quite unpleasant and, in spite of the intimacy and absurdity of my position, I feel a chill trickle down my spine.

Stone sighs. 'I believe we came to a conclusion on this last week, William. There's no more money for an expanded Staff Development Scheme. The Borough's coffers are finite, and you know that.'

'Bullshit! Everything's negotiable, Robert. You of all people should know that. Look again.'

'Very well. I'll take this home with me tonight and get back to you tomorrow.' He presses his leg against me again. Is that a prompt or something? I choose to interpret it as such, and reach up and place my hand over the nice fat bulge at his groin. He doesn't move a muscle in his chair, but inside his trousers his cock stirs thrillingly.

'No! Look now,' Youngblood insists, still with that almost gloating tone in his voice. 'Just read my summary.'

Stroppy little sod! How dare he be so rude and uppity with my lovely Stone? I decide to offer a little consolation, and cautiously reach for the tag of Stone's zip and give it an experimental tug. It moves smoothly and silently downwards.

'Fair enough.' Stone still sounds unperturbed – either by me or by Youngblood. 'Why don't you take a seat, William?'

I hear the drag of a chair across the carpet, then, astonishingly, two heavy thumps against the surface of the desk.

Good God, has Youngblood put his feet up on it? What the hell is going on? I can tell that Stone is as astonished as I am, but he's too cool a customer to show that to his antagonist. He makes no comment and I hear papers rustling.

Fuck you, Youngblood! I'm really cross now, and feel

compelled to put up a metaphorical two fingers to him. The zip comes down further and, slowly and painstakingly, so as to maintain silent running, I slide my fingers into Stone's fly and then in amongst the tail of his shirt and the jersey underwear beneath it.

Oh, you beautiful thing!

I can't see his dick all that well here under the desk, but now I know exactly what it looks like. Working with utmost delicacy, I begin gently to caress him.

Will he show anything on his face? Will he frown, pretending that the figures perplex him? Will he manage to conquer his laughter, knowing that he's being pleasured just feet from the unsuspecting Youngblood?

'It's all perfectly straightforward, Robert. Based on the figures you originally gave me, but which you've now conveniently denied all knowledge of,' sneers Blondie.

You git! I think, and extend my tongue to taste the head of Stone's cock.

He sighs and turns over a page with some emphasis. Oh, Clever Bobby! Covering up the effect I'm having on him with feigned exasperation. He tastes a bit foxy down below too. Which isn't surprising. It *is* the end of the day and a long time since his morning shower. To me, though, he's the most delicious thing on earth.

'But I told you there was likely to be some downsizing, William,' he says with another sigh (of pleasure?), 'which you accepted. Because we both know that all expenditure programmes, all across the Borough, are subject to review in light of our allocations from Central Government.'

I flick my tongue around and around, then I dive in, sucking him into my mouth like a lollipop.

'Look!' he continues, sounding harsher and crosser with Youngblood than I think he would be under normal circumstances. I begin to wonder if my efforts down here might actually be counter-productive in the war of nerves that's going on up top. But that doesn't stop me enjoying myself.

Yum!

'I can't concentrate on this now,' he says, his voice tight. 'I've had a long day. Let me take this home and go through it when I've had a meal and a shower. I'm sure we can meet on common ground somewhere.'

Youngblood laughs. And not a sarcastic laugh of defiance or anything. It's a real full-blooded laugh of rather nasty amusement. I pause, my tongue furled, really worried now.

'All right, Robert,' the Human Resources Manager says, his feet dropping to the floor as he gets up, 'but take a look at this first, and then think long and hard about that *common ground*.'

He laughs again, as if amused by the emphasis, and there's a faint plop, as something lands on top of the papers. A second later, I hear him stomp across the room, open the door and then leave without speaking another word.

What the hell is it?

I release Stone from between my lips and start to wriggle, pressing on his knees to make him let me out.

'Oh, no, you don't.'

He remains exactly where he is, and I feel his hands slide under the desk with me, guiding my face back towards his crotch and his still rampant penis.

'If this is what I think it might be, you'd better finish what you've started. I need it!'

There's a smile in his voice, but there's tension there too. Whatever gauntlet it is that Youngblood's thrown down, Stone is concerned about it. And that makes me burn with antagonism towards that blond bastard, and fret over what might be bugging my precious Mr Stone.

I part my lips again and take his cock between them.

I've never thought myself to be a particular virtuoso at blowjobs, but right now, I want to give the best performance possible so Stone will forget his troubles for the duration. I flick him delicately with my tongue, exploring the topography of his majestic dick, and my efforts are rewarded when his thighs relax, he slumps back in the chair and lets out a happy sigh.

I smile, as best I can, knowing I've found a sweet spot. Alternating with a suction to rival that of a brand-new Hoover, I stab and swirl and probe at this trigger zone again and again and again, until he's groaning and thrashing and squashing me with his knees while his fingers twist and flex against my scalp.

After a couple of minutes, in which he holds out against me valiantly, he shouts out a profanity and comes in my mouth with copious abundance.

I slump against his thigh with his taste on my lips, but even so I can't help wondering.

Just exactly what is it that William Youngblood threw down on Stone's desk?

It's actually a CDROM, or maybe a DVD, although it feels like a hot coal as I turn it over and over in my hands while I wait for Stone. He's told me to wait for him before I slip it on to the player, and he's busy getting us a sandwich and a drink.

Yes, amazingly, I'm at Stone's house. He brought me here with him after I climbed out from under his desk, having completed my blowjob duties.

Stone's living room is comfortable, subdued and elegant. I guess that, as a man living alone, he has a cleaner to keep it so neat and tidy, unless he has unknown and unexpected housework skills. Which, knowing him, I wouldn't entirely rule out.

The room does have a few homey touches, though. The coffee table is loaded with magazines. Car mags, financial journals, even *New Scientist*, *Private Eye* and the *Spectator*. So my boy is well read too. That doesn't surprise me.

Unable to settle, I get up and prowl the room. There are some elegant Japanese prints on the wall, and in the modular units, touchingly, a few trophies. Athletics. Rugby. Good God, *ballroom dancing*?

Are there no end to the surprises?

No, it seems, when I find his wedding photograph.

I see a young Stone. Thinner in the face, his hair longer, more curling and free of grey, and yet still essentially him, especially in the wide, white, happy grin. He's on top of the world, and beside him is the reason.

I frown. There's something about her. I feel a cold shudder ripple through me as I fight to work out what it is.

And then I twig it.

The late Mrs Stone and I could easily be sisters. Similar height. Similar build. Similar hair. Even our features bear an uncanny likeness.

Is this why he's singled me out from amongst all the many available women in Borough Hall? If it is, I might be in even more trouble than I thought I was.

Stone's tread sounds in the corridor. I replace the picture and scuttle back to the sofa.

'Here we are,' he says, placing a tray down on top of the magazines as I whip the CD out from underneath. 'Nothing fancy, just some sandwiches and water. Hope that's okay?'

'Fine. Thanks.'

I'm still a bit spooked from the wedding pic.

'Well, dig in!' He takes the CD from me and throws it to one side. 'We'll deal with that afterwards. Let's watch the news for now.'

Weirder and weirder.

Part of me thinks we should be investigating the CD. Part of me thinks – and wants – that we should be doing some mad, kinky sex thing. None of me could ever have imagined that we'd be here sitting watching the telly and scoffing sandwiches like a pair of platonic old friends.

Especially as I imagine I can still taste his semen on my tongue.

I take a few bites of chicken sandwich and a sip of water, then just goggle at the box, not really paying any attention at all to a segment on Middle Eastern peace talks. Stone appears to be following it closely (I imagine that he has some very erudite opinions on current affairs) but suddenly, out of the blue, he nods at my plate and my slightly mauled sandwich.

'What's wrong? Has something spoilt your appetite?' His pink tongue whips out and licks a dot of mayonnaise from his lower lip, but I know it's a different creamy white stuff that he's on about.

'Yes, but it's not your dick! It's that bloody disc!'

'OK, let's see what friend Youngblood has in store for us.' He sets aside his own plate, and I notice he hasn't eaten much either. My heart starts to thud when he slips the disc in the player.

'Shouldn't we play this on a computer?'

I don't know anything about the technicalities. I'm just stalling. I really don't want to see this.

'I think it'll be OK. This machine's handled everything I've thrown at it so far.'

A playlist comes up, with just two items.

Movie.

Slideshow.

I feel sick.

Stone zaps 'movie' with the remote.

It's exactly what I feared it would be. Which is me and Stone on the picnic table, bucking around, groaning and shagging. It's not exactly cinema quality, because the light is variable, but the shagger is unequivocally Stone, from his face, his voice and his general size. Being underneath, and blindfolded, I'm less recognisable. But anyone who actually knows me wouldn't be in any doubt.

I still feel slightly sick, but also – and horribly – aroused. Trying not to wriggle, I focus on the grainy, heaving image of a tall, heavyset man in black denims and a jeans jacket fucking a semi-naked blonde. I simply dare not look at the real man beside me.

The movie seems to go on forever. When it finishes, Stone immediately plays the slideshow, which is more of the same, only some clever technician has sharpened the images immeasurably, making it even more obvious who the perpetrators are.

Stone clicks the remote and the screen goes back to 'menu'.

'Oh fuck!'

His voice is soft, but he doesn't really sound all that troubled. When I finally dare glance at him, there's a little smile playing around his lips.

I don't know what to think. Or what to say. But I speak anyway.

'Do you think he was *there*?'

'Well, if he was, I never saw him.' Stone turns to me, and reaches out to touch my face. 'But then I never had eyes for anyone else but you, Miss Lewis.'

It's not a signal or anything this time. His expression is resigned, yet strangely affectionate.

'I never saw anybody filming, much less bloody Youngblood!'

Stone runs a gentle thumb along my jaw-line. 'Well, usually there's a tacit agreement amongst those who meet there that no filming's allowed. Or at least permission has to be asked. But if someone has a hidden camera – a very good one, obviously – there's nothing to stop them.'

Despite Stone's distracting caress, my mind is turning over and over and over now. Sorting through questions.

As he pulls me close, and I nestle automatically into his arms, I voice them and we come to conclusions together.

Youngblood could have been there, perhaps disguised. Or he could have paid someone to film for him. It might have been him following us to the dogging site, or someone following on his behalf. And it's not hard to find out the times and locations of meet-ups from web sites and chat boards.

'Looks like I've taken one too many risks, doesn't it?' Stone's hand moves over my hair, soothing and reassuring. 'I just wish I hadn't involved you in it.'

I draw back. Look into the deep pools of his eyes.

'Look, I know it's a fucking disaster but well ... I still wouldn't have missed it for the world!'

Stone gives me a light kiss on the lips. 'You're a jewel, Maria.'

He looks relaxed, unconcerned. Not in the slightest bit worried that his tenure as Borough Director of Finance might well be over.

'I bet he had technical help with this.' I nod in the direction of the screen, a horrible suspicion forming. I've a shrewd idea which clever geek put this disc together and obtained the hardware to record it.

Stone nods. 'There's no doubt about that. The silly sod's notorious for cocking up his workstation. I see the hand of your young admirer Gregory in all this. It's probably his way of getting back at me for fucking you.'

He's right. And I don't have to confirm it.

'What are we going to do? Do you think Youngblood's going to send a copy to the Finance Committee and get you sacked? Or maybe just hold it over you and gloat and use it as a lever to get his own way or something?'

'Do you know? Right now, I really don't care,' Stone whispers, kissing me again, soft as thistledown, on the cheek.

'Right now, all I really want is to fuck you.'

13 **A Cunning Plan**

Well, here I am in Stone's bedroom and it's nothing like I imagined it. It's an elegant restful place, furnished in blues and neutrals. There're no erotic lithographs on the walls, no mirror on the ceiling and no bondage accoutrements attached to the bed.

I slide naked between the sheets to wait for him. They were clearly laundered a few days ago, but there's a hint of his fragrance, and a delicious, cosy, slightly slept-in odour that's very sexy.

How much action has this bed seen? Have there been many women here since his wife? Or does he generally prefer his sex in out-of-the-way places nowadays, and maybe just wanks here on his own?

I hang out of the bed, and look under it. In search of a porn stash.

Then I sit up again, bringing with me a pile of magazines.

And there is some porn. Pretty classy stuff, though, *Penthouse*, *Playboy*. No *Readers' Wives Big Tits* or *Bonking Babes*. But amongst the stroke mags I find something totally unexpected.

Celebrity magazines. Just like the ones I read. I find a couple of recent issues, ones that I've got lying around my flat. And then – something a little older that I also have in my collection.

One with *me* in it! When I was temporarily a sort of C-list 'It' girl, living large and earning small to next to nothing in London.

'Ah, so you've found my deepest and most filthy secret then?'

Stone is standing in the doorway, hair wet, and wearing a thick dark-blue towelling robe. His feet are bare and his calves look muscular and slightly hairy.

'No, I think the ballroom dancing is the deepest, filthiest secret.'

He laughs, and comes and sits on the side of the bed. 'Well, a big chap like me has to find a way to be light on his feet somehow.'

Makes sense, and explains the very elegant and nimble way he moves sometimes.

I spread the page with my picture on it in front of him on the bed. As I do so, the sheet slips and exposes my bare breasts, but Stone studies only the printed image.

'Is this the reason I got the job?'

He stares at the article and my photo for a moment longer then looks up again. His broad face is open, perfectly candid, and his eyes hold mine unwaveringly.

'Yes, of course it is.'

He closes the magazine and puts it on the bedside table.

'I read these magazines because Stacy used to. It got to be a habit. A way of staying in touch with her somehow.' His eyes flick away for a second and he seems to go inside himself somewhere, to a thoughtful place. I shiver suddenly. Not from cold, but from his grief wafting over me like a breeze.

But then, suddenly, his attention is back on me again, as if Stacy has been returned to his palace of memories. 'Why did you leave London, Maria? What happened?'

'Well, I suppose it was when I saw those articles myself' – I glance quickly at the magazines again – 'that I realised just how shallow I'd become, and how stupid and pointless my life was.'

Which is true. I'd felt reduced by my moment of celebrity, rather than elevated. 'I was living beyond my means. Wasting my time. Not really enjoying myself at all. I just realised that I'd rather be out of the limelight ... and back where my roots are.'

He's still watching me, eyes level, perceiving everything that I only half understand myself.

'Well, when *I* saw the articles about you, I was just astounded by how much you looked like Stacy. Almost obsessed, really.' His expression is honest, unapologetic. 'And then, when your name appeared on the list of job applicants, I just had to see you, to see if it was the same person.'

It should seem a bit creepy, almost as if he's stalked me, but somehow it doesn't. He might be devious and manipulative, but he's not shifty or underhand about anything.

'But my CV was shit. I really shouldn't have got an interview at all.'

'No, you shouldn't.' He shrugs, then smiles, 'But sometimes I like to see people that Youngblood hasn't selected. Just to annoy him.'

'Oh yeah? Well, now look what annoying him has done!'

'It's not that. There's another reason why Blondie hates me. It's not just Borough Hall crap.'

'Why? Why does he hate you?' I ask boldly. It's my business now but I'm a nosy bitch anyway, especially where this man is concerned.

'Because he made a pass at me and I turned him down.'

Bloody hell!

'Er ... are you gay?' My mind's gone into overdrive. The images! The images! Then my pussy reminds me of certain patent facts. 'Or should I say, "are you bi?"'

'I'm not *not* bi, if that makes any sense.' He gives me another of those steady, challenging looks. And suddenly all the churning mind-pictures consolidate into one. Him and Youngblood going at it. Naked and sweaty, and all moaning and groaning. God, they'd make a fabulous couple! Youngblood, so cool and polished and urban with his pale skin and his slicked hair. Stone so different, kind of swarthy, a bit Mediterranean, big and beefy in comparison to Youngblood's shorter stature and slender build.

I wonder who the hell would be on top!

'But you turned him down?'

'Yes, it was a bad time.' Again, he seems to go inward, to that dark, melancholy place. 'He gave me a lift home from a staff social when my car had broken down.'

A frown puckers his brow, and I want to hug him close and comfort him, as if he's my kid who's skinned his knee. How bizarre is that?

'Under normal circumstances, I might have been tempted. But it was the anniversary of Stacy's death and I was feeling a bit fragile. I'd only gone to the social to stop myself from brooding.'

'I'm sorry.'

His big shoulders lift again in a shrug. 'Yes, it was all very, very messy. Very embarrassing. And William has never, ever forgiven me for it.'

I reach out and touch his arm, not really knowing what to say, but knowing I want to comfort him and help him forget pain and problems, both in the present and in the past.

Our eyes meet again and, as always, he reads my intent. Flashing me a smile, he stands, dims the bedside light a little, then shrugs off his robe.

Is he shy? What a bizarre thought! I catch only a fleeting glimpse of his naked body, but I don't think he has any reason to be ashamed of it. He's no steely-muscled young Adonis with a six-pack, but he isn't a doughy, slack-bodied slob either. Just a tall, rather solid middle-aged man in reasonable shape for somebody who sits at a desk most of the day.

When he pulls me closer, it's actually like being in bed with a huge, cuddly teddy bear. But a strong one. Strong in body and heart and mind and will. And all the time his eyes are scoping me, intense and brilliant. This close, they have an unnatural sheen to them that almost but not quite creeps me out. Until it dawns on me that he must wear contacts. I ask him and he says 'yes', with a little smirk.

'All the better to see you with, little girl.'

And suddenly he's not Daddy Bear at all, but the Big Bad Wolf about to lay waste to me.

'Come on. Let's get it on,' he murmurs, sliding his hand down my flank. I'm keen to, but something's still bothering me.

'I suppose just normal bed sex is a bit boring to you, isn't it?'

He makes a soft sound of feigned despair, shaking his greying head. 'There's nothing wrong with bed sex as long as it's with the right woman.'

I think of the photos, and of his wife.

'Am I the right woman?'

'Do you even have to ask?' With that he presses his large, warm body against me, and his large, even warmer cock tells me in no uncertain terms that, in this instance at least, I *am* the right woman.

The heat of him stirs me, as does the way he starts to kiss me and run his hands lightly over my body. But I'm still distracted. Thoughts of his wife and the magazine, and William Youngblood and the traitorous Greg, whirl around in my mind, short-circuiting my responses. I can feel myself getting a little bit wet, especially when Stone touches me there with his usual breathtaking precision, but still my blood's not boiling as it ought to.

He rears up over me, looking down into my eyes, his own glittering. And perceptive as always.

'Hey, where are you?' Resting on one elbow, he tucks my hair behind my ears, then tracks his fingertips over my face. 'I'm here. Come back to me. Stop worrying.'

Guilt washes over me. How stupid am I? We may not be doing anything forbidden or risky or kinky, but it's still pretty fabulous. Stone knows exactly how to use his fingers, his lips and his body, and, as I smile and start to really put my back into it, he employs all three, in leisurely succession, to give me pleasure.

And oh my God, the head is spectacular!

For someone with a big, broad tongue, he's capable of pinpoint accuracy and he roves and licks and dabs and sucks until I'm going crazy, beating him with my heels and pulling his hair. He knows exactly where my sweetest spot is without me having to tell him and, like the evil demon he is, he avoids any direct contact with it until I'm shouting profanities and imprecations about his parentage.

And then, and only then, when I swear I'm about to expire and Greg, Youngblood and every goddam person I've ever met is consigned to another galaxy, does Clever Bobby deliver the merciful *coup de grâce*.

I'm half passed out and still climaxing when he finally enters me, and I hug him and sob his name as he starts to thrust.

It's the middle of the night and I can't sleep. Maybe it's the strange bed? Maybe it's being in a strange shared bed? Maybe it's being in a strange shared bed with Robert Stone?

But I look down at him as he sleeps, and I know what it is.

I've fallen hard and, astonishingly, I want to protect him. Which is insane, because he's the most physically and psychologically powerful man I've ever met. But the thing is, he's been threatened, he's been attacked and he's turned me into a tigress, roaring to attack in return and defend him.

He looks relaxed in the moonlight, his broad face softer and younger, his mouth tender. I know that behind those closed eyes there's a brain that's sharp, devious, manipulative and perverted. And yet now, observing those dark, strangely luscious eyelashes resting on his cheekbones, it's the vulnerability I see there that touches my heart.

Goddamn Youngblood and goddamn Greg! I'll get the better of both of you for threatening and hurting my Bobby.

But first I have to come up with a cunning plan.

'So what do you want to do about it?'

I'm in Café Mario, having lunch, but not with Stone this time.

No, it's Mel facing me across the tuna salad and café latte, and genuine concern is writ large across her handsome features.

I've just told her everything. About Stone and me. About the dogging. About Youngblood and his fucking disc!

'I don't know, but I've got to do something! I feel responsible!'

Mel puts down her cup and reaches over to touch my hand. 'You're not responsible at all. Stone is a big boy. *He's* the one who's got himself into all this.' She looks fierce. 'And it's just a shame he has to take you down with him!'

I know she cares, and I know that in some ways she's right. But if I hadn't got Stone all steamed up, which I know I did, neither of us would be in the fix we're in now.

Although I'm probably in the worse fix, emotionally.

This morning, when he dropped me at my flat, Stone said casually that perhaps we'd better play it cool until we find out what Youngblood's plans are.

I agreed. Of course it makes sense. He's right. But there's still this gaping void inside me somehow.

I think I love him.

But I'll never tell him because I don't think it's what he wants. He loved his wife, and now he's not in the market for the mushy stuff. And I'm not in the market for the mushy stuff with a man who's not interested in it. Even though I would still like to go on having sex with him.

Being with Stone is mad. Dangerous, as I've found out to my cost. And scary. But being around him, and being touched by him, has made me feel more alive than I ever felt in London when my life was supposedly so glamorous.

Snap!

I jump, nearly spilling my coffee, when Mel clicks her fingers.

'Earth to Maria,' she says softly. 'You were miles away. Now, do you really want to do something about all this?'

Absolutely! I know Robert Stone will never love me the way I'm almost certain I love him – but that doesn't mean I'm not burning to get some payback for him! He's philosophical, resigned, almost unconcerned about what's happened – but I'm a woman and the instinct for revenge is hard-wired into my genes.

'Yes, I do. I want to get some dirt on Youngblood that's at least as dirty as the dirt he's got on Robert.'

'"Robert", is it? Oh dear, we have got it bad!'

'Don't be silly. Of course I haven't. I just like him, that's all. Now come on, you know everything about everybody in Hall. There must be a way we can get to Youngblood.'

'Well, what about the little nookie nest in the base-ment?' suggests Mel. 'That would be the easiest. I'm sure that between us we can coerce Greg into setting us up the same type of camera there that he supplied to Young-blood? We could get some footage of him banging Sandy.'

Good, but not quite right somehow. It needs to be more personal. More intimate. And although Sandy isn't my favourite work-mate, I don't want to drag her into this as well.

Mel sees my hesitation. Sighs. 'Get us some more coffee, will you? Let's use a bit of flexi-time here and think something out.' She hesitates, grinning. 'Actually, I'm getting an idea. It'll take some finagling and pulling in favours. But it might work.' Her smile broadens, and she gives me an outrageous wink. 'I *will* expect some recompense for helping you, though, you know. I'm not doing this for Clever Bobby or the good of my health!'

I know what she wants.

'You're on!' I wink back, feeling a flutter of excitement in spite of everything. 'How does egg and chips at the Blue Plate sound?'

'Delicious!' She licks her lips. 'Now let's concentrate. Here's what I've got in mind.'

The first step is getting Greg on board, and theoretically I've got a choice of either the sex card or the guilt card to achieve that.

In practice I'm so bloody furious with him that I could pull it off just from anger!

'Open up, you little shit! I know you're in there!' I shout, pounding on his door with my both my fists. I've just got home from work, on the back of Mel's bike because it's obvious Greg is still avoiding me.

A long silence. I thump again. I know he's in there, because I heard the television a while back and nobody's left the house since.

'Come on! Open up, you little wanker!'

Eventually the door opens a little way and Greg peers

through the crack. He looks genuinely terrified, and my confidence soars. I've got him!

'Is something wrong?' His voice sounds reedy and his face is white.

Feeling a sense of triumph that's almost sexual, I shove on the door and force him to step back into the room.

Scrub that, it *is* sexual! I've barely had to say anything, but I know – I can feel – that I've already got Greg right where I want him. Which is absolutely brilliant as my cunning plan depends almost entirely on gaining absolute power over a man.

'Why did you do it? How could you? I thought we were friends!'

Greg opens his mouth, then closes it again. His cute, boyish face is a portrait of utter guilt, and he appears to be dumbstruck.

As am I, momentarily, when I follow his eye-line and see what's pinned to his wall.

It's a life-size blow up of a photograph. Assembled from individual A4 sheets. It's grainy and the resolution is terrible, because of the enlargement, but it's quite clearly me on the wooden picnic table, being fucked by Stone. But even more shocking than the sight of myself in the middle of having an orgasm is the fact that every bit of Stone's face and body has been completely blacked out and it looks as if I'm being rogered by a shadow.

I'm almost on the point of losing my nerve, but then it dawns on me that I've just found conclusive evidence to validate my suspicions about Greg's involvement.

'I – I –' Greg seems to be finding his tongue, but with difficulty.

'You're jealous of Stone, aren't you?'

'Yes. Of course I am. You know that.' He stares at me hungrily, and I realise that I must be quite a sight. Eyes full of fire, body full of fury and – I realise – my nipples poking hard against the thin cotton of my T-shirt. I must be giving off tidal waves of pheromones.

'Don't you dare look at me, you little worm. You don't ever look at me again unless I give you permission. You don't get anything from me, ever again, unless you do what I want you to and put right what you've done wrong.'

He looks away, shamefaced, and shuffles his feet. I watch his fists clench, and realise that he's sporting a huge erection and he's obviously longing to clutch himself.

I've got him. I've got him just where I want him. But now's the time to keep my cool, and douse my temper. Now's the time to learn from Stone and wield dominance in a way that's quiet and subtle.

'Right,' I say softly, lowering myself on to the sofa, and lounging back, 'tell me everything. Every detail. Right from the beginning.'

It seems Youngblood has been cultivating Greg for quite a while in the hope of using his acknowledged technical wizardry to incriminate Stone in some way. But it wasn't until *I* came to work in the Hall that Greg really considered helping him. Until it became obvious I was heavily involved with Stone.

'Go on,' I prompt when Greg falters, even though inside I'm fighting my own guilt. It's inadvertent, but I have endangered the man I'm besotted with.

Then, the night of the dogging escapade, it all came together. Youngblood explained what he needed, and Greg had the technology.

'It was a bit pathetic really. He'd been following Stone about so he knew more or less where you were going. He just needed me to supply the camera. And do the tech stuff.'

A suspicion dawns.

'You mean you were there?' I nod to the gigantic image.

Greg blushes furiously. He's still standing there with a hard-on. I haven't given him permission to sit down yet, and it's as if he understands that he actually has to ask for it.

'Yeah, we both were.' For the first time, he grins, but only briefly and very nervously. 'It was hilarious. He had disguises for us. Hats. False moustaches and beards. Stupid really.'

But obviously effective enough on the night. I give him a long, stern look.

'We sort of hung back until the action started, then snuck forward when we were sure you wouldn't see us.'

And why would we see them? If Stone was half as into it, and me, as I was into him, all the men clustered around us were merely ciphers.

'I'm sorry,' says Greg when he's told all he can tell. 'I'm really sorry. I never wanted to do anything to hurt you. Not you. I'm crazy about you. And I don't really hate Stone all that much. I was only angry with him because you're obviously mad about him and not me.'

Suddenly I feel sorry too. Sorry for this muddle and for the fact that I've probably fallen for entirely the wrong man. In practical terms. With Greg, I could probably have a very nice, normal boyfriend/girlfriend relationship with a proper future. But with Stone? Well, that could never happen.

I feel myself weakening, but I control it. I've got to stay on top of things, and continue to hone my power.

'So, you care for me, but you help Youngblood damage me and someone I care about? How can you ever expect me to care about you as well?' I keep my tone steady, neutral, yet with the slightest hint of a tease. Inside I'm smiling, though. I've learnt this from a master.

'I'm sorry! I'm so sorry!' repeats Greg, almost in tears

now. And to my astonishment, he falls to his knees. 'Please forgive me!' Collapsing in a heap, he presses his face right to the carpet.

Exhilaration rushes through me. It's like the rush I get from chocolate or coffee. The wild singing thrill I get when Stone says 'Miss Lewis'. I could probably do anything I want with or to Greg right at this moment, and I'm seriously tempted to try it.

But instead I quietly and precisely outline Mel's ingenious plan for payback, and specifically the part I need Greg to play in it.

His big eyes widen as he listens, all attentive and docile and deliciously in my thrall.

Maybe I'll play with him, as his reward, if it all comes off. While Stone looks on.

14 Payback's a Bitch

'Youngblood.'

He sounds jaunty, full of himself. As if I'd caught him in the middle of relishing what he thinks of as his triumph. I glower at the phone that Mel's holding to my lips, and try not to let it show in my voice.

'Hello, William, it's Maria.'

I used to love drama back in school, so I suppose that's helping now. I mustn't show the slightest bit of hesitation, apprehension or nervousness. He's got to think that I either don't know about the disc or just don't care.

'Er . . . hello. How are you?'

Yes! The first-name thing has already thrown him a bit. 'I'm fine. And I've been thinking about your invitation. I'd like to accept. Are you free tonight?'

There's a pause, and I grin at Mel. I'd give her a thumbs-up, but I'm terrified of smudging the polish she's just applied to my fingernails.

'Yes. Yes, I am. Er . . . would you like to meet somewhere?'

I can almost hear the cogs of his brain whirling and trying to connect and work out what's going on. And what I might be up to.

'How about Waverley Grange? At eight? In the cocktail bar?'

More silence. That's really put him on the back foot.

Mel gives me the 'OK' sign, and I nod. She was so right about this.

'Yes. That's great.' He hesitates again, and I sense him gathering his nerve to ask questions.

'Yes, isn't it?' I purr at him, hoping I'm not piling it on too thick. 'That's a date, William. Looking forward to it. See you there.' I nod again to Mel, and she cuts the connection before he can respond, or pose any probing questions.

'You were brilliant!' She jumps up and starts doing some kind of Snoopy Dance. She looks a bit out of place in her work jeans and Doc Martens here in this passion palace of a hotel room, but I suddenly want to leap up too and kiss her for what's she's doing for me. Despite the fact that my toes are held apart by separators while the polish on my toenails dries too.

Mel has a sort of on/off thing going with the Assistant Manager here at the Waverley Grange, which is why we've managed to get this deluxe room for next to nothing.

'I hope I didn't sound too obvious,' I say as she comes back to sit beside me, lifting first one hand then the other, and blowing on my still tacky polish.

'You sounded incredibly sexy and confident. You sounded as if you expected Sweet William to grovel at your feet. Which is exactly what he will be doing before the night's out!'

Now I feel a shudder of apprehension.

'I'm not sure I can pull this off, Mel. Not if Saskia says he's used to being dominated by professionals.' The butterflies in my stomach are wearing Doc Martens too. 'He might just laugh at me and refuse to go along with it. I mean...' I pause, the image of Stone's cool, faintly amused face rising to the top of my imagination. 'I've never done any bondage or S/M or anything. The nearest thing I've ever experienced to it is ... is *Stone*. And then it's always been him who's running the power-trip on me. I'm not sure I can do it the other way round.'

Mel ceases her pacing and comes to kneel in front of me, taking hold of my forearms, carefully avoiding the polish.

'Look, you're a beautiful woman, Maria, and a strong one. You're a fighter. Why else would a man like Stone pursue you?'

'He didn't have to do much pursuing.'

'Bollocks,' she says dismissively, making me look at her. 'He recognises one of his own kind. Someone powerful.' I frown, even though I'm beginning to get her. 'He might play games. But that's only because *you* allow him to. *You* want him to. You choose to let him because it pleases you.' She releases my arms, and her hands settle on my thighs, which are naked, along with the rest of me, beneath the fluffy Waverley Grange bathrobe. 'Maria, love, you're just as much a game-player as he is. It's instinctive. Which means you can play games with William Youngblood. Easily. Because he's primed for it.'

Which is true. Mel's friend Saskia, the Assistant Manager here, just happens to be a dominant femme in her leisure hours, and she recognised a 'professional' colleague of hers, a call girl, whom William Youngblood has been known to meet here from time to time, for what you might call assignations. The Waverley is discreet (supposedly) and out of town – the perfect luxurious rendezvous for a bit of high-class kink.

In fact I'm surprised – and actually a bit miffed – that Stone's never brought *me* here. All I get is splinters in my bum from a picnic table in the middle of nowhere!

Yes, I see Mel's reasoning, but still I protest. More because her hands are slowly sliding up my thighs than anything else. 'Yeah, but he's used to pros and I'm just an amateur.'

'What's the difference? Really? You've got everything you need' – without warning, she parts my robe and bares my belly and my bush – 'right here.' Her eyes flick downwards then return to my face. 'He's seen it. And he wants it. The rest is just "basic instinct", love. He'll fall into line. Just play him the way Clever Bobby plays you. At least you've had a grandmaster to learn from.'

'But what about the actual ... um ... dominating?'

'Well, that's why we've been watching all those videos, silly!'

Over the last few nights I've been taking a crash video course in how to dominate a man. And it's been hilarious, mostly. Most of the tapes have been contrived and a bit silly, inducing uncontrollable giggles rather than any kind of arousal. But one or two of them, especially a very good documentary ... Well, they got to me. I'm not sure whether I was identifying with the dominants, who had men grovelling – literally crawling on their bellies – or the submissives, who were rendered exquisitely helpless, not so much by physical force as by tone of voice and aura. Either way, I ended up masturbating once or twice.

'You can do it, love,' repeats Mel, gently slipping her fingers into my sex and beginning to stroke me. 'You'll be amazing, all you have to do is relax.'

Her touch is light, clever and just right. Informed by the knowledge and perfection of touch that only someone else with the same anatomy can achieve. I close my eyes and slump back, succumbing to her. And for the moment, really wanting her. Yet at the same time I know that this is the least I can do when she's helping me so much.

But as I come, it's not her who's in my mind. It's the man for whom I've embarked on this mad endeavour.

Youngblood's waiting at the bar when I enter the cocktail lounge. I'm ten minutes late. It's part of my strategy to undermine his self-confidence as quickly as possible.

He looks sensational.

Under other circumstances, and in another life, I'd melt at the sight of that lean face and the blond hair and the really, really good black clothes. But this is this life, and

I've got a job to do. The lady's not for melting. At least not in that way.

I might cream my knickers but my will has turned to steel. Faltering is not an option.

'Good evening, William,' I murmur as I reach him.

Oh yeah! I've got him already! His handsome face is a picture of confusion. For one thing, it's plain he wasn't expecting this much confidence. For another, I know I look as sensational as he does.

A little body-skimming black dress, left over from my London days. Heels, ditto. Sleek hair and make-up, courtesy of Mel, who's a bit of an artiste despite her own predilection towards mannishness. The belt of vodka I just had as Dutch courage has probably given me a bit of colour in my cheeks, but as far as Youngblood's concerned that's arousal, not booze.

'Er . . . Hello, Maria. You're looking very lovely tonight,' he says, slipping off his stool and on to his feet, then pulling out a stool for me. His blue eyes are very brilliant and they're skittering about all over the place, checking out my lips, my breasts, my thighs, my heels – and most of all a nice little refinement that Mel's friend Saskia has lent me.

I'm wearing a collar again. But not my tacky pink Tarts and Vicars thing this time. No, this is far more classy, and the real deal for the job. It's narrow black kid leather, studded with tiny Swarovski crystals. Not really a piece of fashion jewellery, in fact pretty peculiar to most eyes, but, judging by the sudden colour that's risen in Youngblood's cheeks, he fully understands its significance.

I take my seat, crossing my legs, reminding him of what he saw back in his office.

'Thank you,' I reply. No simpering. No false modesty. I *do* look incredibly hot. 'I'll have one of those, please.' I point to his drink – a mineral water – to set a precedent of me calling the shots.

He gives me a tight little smile, then turns to try and attract the barman's attention.

I feel as if a slow fuse is starting to burn. And a huge rush is building. I almost want to gasp at the intensity of it, but I school myself to stay calm. I've got to stay super-cool and totally in command.

I've already got Sweet William off balance. He knows I flashed him deliberately in his office, but because he pretended it didn't happen, it's too late now to call me on it. He also has no idea whether I know about the disc and the recording of Stone and me on the picnic table. And he's been thrown completely off kilter by the collar. As a man who's dabbled in the scene, he's wondering whether it's a signal or whether it's entirely innocent on my part because I don't really have the first idea about submission and dominance games at all.

He's trying to calculate so many variables at once that it's no wonder his hand shakes slightly as he signals to the barman. He glances at me nervously and I favour him with a slow, amused smile.

When I receive my iced water, I take a sip, nod my thanks but say nothing. I don't have to. I don't want to. Let him stew.

'I'm so glad you rang me. I was hoping you would.'

He still can't really look me in the eye, and he keeps sneaking little peeks towards my crotch, almost as if he can't help himself.

I quell him with an admonishing glance, and his colour comes up even more. 'Did you think I wouldn't bother?' I say coolly.

'I . . . I wasn't sure.' He grabs a quick drink, his Adam's apple bobbing. 'I thought you might be otherwise involved.'

'With Robert Stone?' No need to be coy here. Let's crank up the odds.

'Yes, actually. He has this habit of pouncing on new

female employees. Especially the beautiful ones.' It's an attempt to flirt. He's game, I'll give him that.

After a few beats, I respond. 'And you think I'd allow myself to be pounced on?'

'Er . . .' His knuckles are white where he's clutching his glass. I hope he doesn't shatter it. 'No, not really. You strike me as a woman who knows her own mind. But he is your boss, and I thought . . .'

'He's my boss in the Hall. As are you.' I lock my eyes with his, compelling him not to look away. 'But outside the Hall, William, I do what I want. If I were to see Robert, that would be my choice. Just like seeing you tonight is my choice too.'

The use of Stone's first name has completely flustered him. He drinks quickly from his glass, replaces it on the counter, drinks again. I can see he's absolutely desperate to know what I know but, despite his supposed sophistication, he has no idea how to ask.

I feel sorry for him. I want to take control of him and put him out of his misery. It's the strangest emotion. Like having a child or a pet that you know you've got to be firm with because you actually care about them.

And I do feel a peculiar fondness for William all of a sudden. He thought he was so clever, but he's really out of his depth. He might think he's got the better of Stone, but he just doesn't have that inner core of strength.

But I've got it. I don't smile at the knowledge, but in my mind I see Clever Bobby's boyish grin. He's known all along.

'What's the matter, William?' I ask, not giving him time to answer me. 'You seem nervous. A bit out of sorts. Would you like to go somewhere a little more private? Where we can talk more freely? Relax a bit?'

Those rather beautiful blue eyes widen at the emphasis I place on the word 'relax'. It's as if he's forgotten all about Stone and the disc and everything. And simply can't believe his own luck.

And he's already on his feet, like an eager puppy bouncing on his leash, ready to go.

'Of course. Let's go to my place. It's not far. I've got my car. What about you? Did you take a taxi?'

'Why go anywhere? I have a room here.' I stay in my seat, sipping a little water.

Youngblood looks thunderstruck.

'You're staying *here*? Isn't it a bit expensive?'

'Expensive for a Borough Hall drone, you mean?'

He simply cannot speak.

'Don't worry. The Assistant Manager here is a friend of mine.' Only a semi-fib. I would like to get to know Madam Saskia better. 'She gives me a very favourable rate.'

And that throws another element into the mix. He has a very expressive face and I can see him trying to work out if I'm as bisexual as he is.

God, this is fun!

I slip from my seat and walk towards the foyer and the lifts. I don't look back because I know he'll follow.

Stone would see right through all this. He'd know it was some kind of payback, but he'd probably play along just for the hell of it. William Youngblood, however, is more susceptible. He's so hard-wired to obey a dominant female that it almost seems as if his higher faculties – and his suspicions – just aren't functioning any more. The puppy image is dead right. He's responding like Pavlov's dog to the stimulus of a take-charge woman. It happened with Sandy in the basement, where she was clearly the one calling the shots, and it obviously happens with Saskia's professional friend too.

I feel so hot for this that I'd give anything to touch myself. But I've got to be patient and take my time. And close the trap.

In the lift, William surprises me. He tries to move in and put his arm around me, but I step back and press him away from me with my evening bag.

'Not yet.'

He retreats immediately.

Is this too easy?

The room is far too chintzy for my taste, but the voluminous draperies and furbelows of the brass-framed bed are ideal for hiding the necessary technology. William had just the one camera for his sting operation, but I've got multiple concealed webcams for mine. If it all works. Greg reckons he tested everything thoroughly when he set it all up earlier, so I suppose I've just got to believe him.

'Why don't you get us something from the mini bar?' I suggest, heading for the bathroom and not looking back at him, not explaining.

Inside, I do a few deep-breathing exercises. I'm starting to enjoy myself – a lot! – but it's still scary stuff. Taking the opportunity to pee, I squat down on the loo and at the same time flip open my phone and send a single-word text.

Action!

It's as much down to Greg's webtech wizardry now as it is to me and my fledgling dominatrix skills.

Back in the bedroom, Youngblood has opened a split of champagne and looks quite pleased with himself.

Time to nip that in the bud.

'Champagne?' I inject a note of mockery and faint displeasure into my voice and his pale, handsome face falls.

'It's all right, I'll pay.'

'You most certainly will.' I take the glass and retreat away from him, taking a seat in one of the overstuffed bedroom chairs. Sigh, yet more chintz.

'Sit down, William.' I nod to the bed and he subsides a little awkwardly on to it, still clutching his glass and sipping from it nervously. I set mine aside on the dressing table, even though I'd quite like to swig down the contents in one for extra courage. 'Why don't you make yourself comfortable?' I uncross and recross my legs in a way that's guaranteed to make him far from comfortable, given our history.

'Look, about Stone—' he begins as he shrugs off his jacket.

'Forget Stone. He's not here. You are.'

And yet, as Sweet William begins to shed his clothing, I know that Stone *is* with me. In spirit. He would love this. Not so much for the subjugation of his rival, but just for the game itself. It's so very much his thing.

'Aren't you going to undress?' He's down to his trousers now, and I'm enjoying the sight of his smooth and lightly muscular chest. He has lovely skin, and there's not a hair in sight on his pecs and his abdomen. A wax job, obviously.

With a cool glance his way, I unclasp my watch and place it on the dressing table.

The thing is, he's still not quite sure what we're here for, that's obvious. He's still trying to work out whether the collar is just jewellery. Or something else.

Time to set the record straight.

'Take the rest off,' I instruct. He's still hesitating. 'Or leave. Your choice.'

He swallows, his fingers frozen on his belt. I can almost see his brain working, weighing the options. Maybe he's even sensed the trap now? But still, the compulsion, the hunger is too great. His dick's already in control of his grey matter. In quick succession he heels off his shoes, peels off his socks, drops and steps out of his trousers. Said dick is already very much in evidence, pushing a tent in his black jersey underpants. He falters again, but when I narrow my eyes, he whips down his underwear too.

Very nice! I have a much better view than I did that day in the basement at the Hall. His penis is nicely lengthy, slender and quite elegant in shape. Not quite the colossus that Stone's is, but nothing to be ashamed of, all the same. He starts to fondle himself as soon as he's naked.

'For heaven's sake show some self control,' I admonish and his hand drops away as if his dick's suddenly on fire.

But it isn't just Sweet William's dick that's blazing.

Down below, I'm tingling, getting wet. I need to move this along, not because I want some incriminating dirt on this man. But for myself, because I'm turned on. I want to come.

'Lie down on the bed,' I say, softly but with backbone.

He obeys instantly, settling back against the deep, soft mattress, his body tense and his erection a stiff red pole at his groin. For two pins I'd just peel off my panties, get my leg over and envelop him, but there are a few rounds yet to go in this game. So I manage to contain myself.

The champagne is cool and dry and creamy. I sip slowly, teasing out the tension while William watches me with eyes wide and blue.

'How did you know?' he asks suddenly.

To snap at him would be too obvious, so I ignore the question, rise to my feet and cross the room. Looking down at his beautiful rampant body, I favour him with a smile. 'What? Do you think all I'm into is being banged in public car parks and picnic areas?'

He flies up into a sitting position, his mouth opening to protest, but before he can get a word out I land a ringing slap against his pale, sculpted cheek.

'I said lie down and I meant it.' I keep my voice low, but throw every bit of myself into it, every bit of my will, everything I've learnt, everything I want. William subsides, his lips still parted, a look of fear and wondrous hunger in his eyes.

Not giving him time to do anything but feel, I reach beneath the puffy, flounced pillows, pull out my little clutch of borrowed 'props' and spread them out beside him on the duvet cover.

His eyes widen in real alarm, and he drops out of his role.

'Do you know what you're doing?'

'Don't be impertinent.' I manage a sensationally good impression of icy displeasure and the fantasy is restored. I'm really getting into this now. Any status this man might have had with me has disappeared into thin air. He's just a pretty face. A body. An erection. All for my pleasure. And not his.

He's half propped up on his arms, but when I take his hands he just drops back against the duvet and allows me to push them over his head. I take the first prop, a pair of padded wrist cuffs on a longish chain, a chain that I slip quickly through the rails of the brass bedhead.

Working as deftly as I can, and not, I think, revealing the fact that I've never used anything like this before, I fasten William into the cuffs. In a couple of seconds he's secured to the bedhead, but there's sufficient play in the chain for him to roll over on to his front if I need him to. And I'm looking forward to needing him to.

'Good boy,' I murmur when he's settled, and I give him a treat. My breasts in his face. I lean over and allow him my cleavage, enjoying his warm breath against my skin as he strains up, trying to kiss as much of it as he can reach.

It would be nice to push down the front of my dress, and my bra, and let him mouth and suck on my nipples, but I think that would be far too much of an indulgence at this stage. This is supposed to be a punishment scenario, after all. He mustn't like it *too* much!

What would be totally delicious now would be to have Stone here. And have him make free with me, touch me, fuck me, have me. Do anything he wanted while William looked on, frustrated.

But would that undermine my authority? Would Stone kowtow to being simply my instrument of pleasure, and not the master of it? Who knows? Maybe I should have let him in on this. Although I've a feeling he wouldn't approve and, when he does find out, I'll be the one in trouble for being the rashest kind of fool.

I sit up and tweak the deep neckline of my dress, as if William's efforts have misaligned it.

There's still a bit of defiance in his eyes. And suspicion. He's not a fool, even if his rampant dick is trying to make him one. It keeps getting the better of him, but he keeps fighting back.

Suddenly he laughs and it's quite alarming.

'This is a sting, isn't it? I should have bloody well known. Where's the camera? That fuck Stone's set me up, hasn't he?'

Words of anger rise to my lips, but with a huge effort I bite them back and school my face into mocking impassivity.

'I'm very disappointed in you, William.' I keep my voice soft. I mustn't lose my nerve. 'And I'm insulted that you'd attribute your own tactics ... childish and despicable tactics, I might add ... either to me or to a fine man like the Director of Finance.'

I trail the backs of my fingers up his still rampant cock, from root to tip, to distract him.

And it works.

'I – I'm sorry,' he stammers.

'"I'm sorry, mistress",' I prompt, trying to remember from the videos how this all goes.

'I'm sorry, mistress.'

His voice sounds so small now, so meek, and the yearning look is back in his brilliant blue eyes. His pupils are hugely dilated. He's either forgotten his suspicions or he's so longing for what I can give him that he just doesn't care any more.

'So you should be, William. So you should be.' Delicately, I finger the tip of his penis, smoothing the clear pre-come over the stretched red skin. He's dribbling quite freely all of a sudden.

'I think you should be punished, don't you?' I observe, all casual as I play with his seeping organ.

He nods, clearly beyond speech now.

My fingers are wet and sticky, and I consider licking them, then decide against it in favour of something a bit more devilish. I press them against William's lips instead.

He resists for a second, but I push and his mouth opens, he yields, and he cleans his own moisture off my fingertips, suckling like a baby. When he's done I wipe them dry against the hot skin of his chest.

I'd better get down to it, I suppose. The actual punishment, that is. I'm still a bit doubtful about it. The only practical experience I have is from being on the receiving end.

It seems like a hundred years since I was across Stone's knee in his office, but it's really not all that long ago. I try to summon an impression of his confidence, his calm and his exquisite sensitivity to the finer points of punishing another human being.

I've decided not to put William across my knee. He's only a slight man, but he's still too big for a beginner like me to handle and continue to appear accomplished. I need to seem as if I've done this dozens and dozens of times before.

Help me, Stone! I cry silently. Guide me through this. Give me power. Give me wisdom.

I was going to make my little 'slave' roll over, but suddenly, as if by divine providence, I change my mind.

Thank you, Clever Bobby.

I pick up the so-called 'instrument'.

It's a small black leather strap, carefully shaped. A hand-crafted flogger. Saskia says it's easy to use for a beginner dominant, and I'm glad of that. I don't want to hurt William in the wrong way.

It's substantial, though, and his eyes flare with fear as I toy with it, hefting its weight.

'What's wrong? Are you afraid?' I purr, running the black leather lightly up and down his cock. As he stirs and wriggles I suddenly get a contrary urge.

To really hurt him.

I get a momentary, almost visceral desire to lash his penis with the flogger and make him scream. The rush is incredible, quite frightening, and it takes my breath away.

Fucking hell! I must be the worst kind of sadist! But then it dawns on me. The sudden need to really hurt him has nothing to do with sexual play at all. It's just me wanting to hurt him because he's threatened my beloved.

Right. Now. Let's get back into the role.

I know I'm likely to be slightly clumsy, and I don't want any distractions in the form of complaints and protestations.

Abandoning the flogger for a moment, I pick up a black scarf, much like the one Stone covered my eyes with the other night. It doesn't quite do it for me somehow, though. I need something more diabolical. Something Stone himself might come up with.

And then I have it.

I hop off the bed, then, with William's eyes tracking me both nervously and hopefully, I step out of my knickers as gracefully as I can while at the same time not flashing my bush at him.

Oh boy, am I fragrant! More aroused, obviously, than I realised. My black lace thong is wet and sticky and odoriferous. Perfect for my purpose.

I wad the flimsy thing into a ball, then, grasping William by his narrow, elegant nose, I force him to open his mouth so I can press my underwear into it.

He starts to protest, but he can't do anything about it when I secure the thong in place with the black scarf.

'There, that's better, isn't it?' I murmur in a gentle 'Mommy' voice. It seems more natural, easier, more do-able than trying to maintain a high-concept 'mistress' role.

He nods.

Goody! It's working.

'Now, it's time for your treatment, William. You've got to learn not to do evil and underhanded things. And there's only one way you'll remember what you've learnt, isn't there?'

He nods again, and almost looks as if he's going to cry.

'Right, here we go. Be brave. For me.'

I kick off my shoes, climb back onto the bed, and get into a comfy kneeling pose, looming over William and his erection.

Slap!

I bring the flogger down briskly on his pale, bare thigh and he lurches up off the bed, grunting uncouthly behind the fabric in his mouth. As the point of impact reddens, he squirms and jiggles about. I slap him again, on the other thigh, and he jerks again.

'Now, now, now, William. You must keep still and be a good boy.' I lean over him again, kissing him softly just where his lips are distorted by the gag while I trail the flogger over his belly and his rigid dick.

His gloriously blue eyes are full of tears.

So soon?

I expected defiance, grit, resistance – and he's fallen apart like a cheap watch after just two strokes.

Poor baby. He's so confused. Just when I'm seeing things much more clearly.

I've been bad cop. Now I've got to be good cop.

'It's all such a muddle, isn't it?' I croon, pressing his face into my cleavage again. He can't kiss me now, but he rubs his cheeks gratefully against the slopes of my breasts.

'You were angry. Jealous. All mixed up. Weren't you? You're envious of Robert, yet you want him. You wanted to hurt him even though you'd like to be with him. And you'd like him to want to be with you too. Am I right?'

He nods his head against me.

'And you want me too, don't you? And that makes you even more jealous of Robert. Because he's had me.'

I sit up a little and look down at his face. He really is quite beautiful in his own way. Far more handsome in a classical sense than Stone is. And yet he's still a boy, while Stone is a man.

'Relax, William.' I kiss his cheek, his jaw and his brow. 'Take your medicine and you'll soon feel better and calmer.'

I strike him hard on the thigh again, doubling up on an existing red mark. Tears trickle down his smooth pale cheek and his stoppered mouth works.

I slap him again and again, working up and down his long, well-shaped thighs, evening up the colour. In between every slap, I grant him a caress. A kiss against his throat, or his chest, or his belly. A gentle touch feathering lightly along his cock. I have to be careful though. His erection is so ferocious that it could be made of red marble.

Eventually, I need a break. And I know he does. I retire back to the chintz armchair and take a sip from my champagne. I seem to have been working on William for hours, but the delicious wine is still lively.

The room is quiet, apart from his sobs. He's closed his eyes now, and seems to have sunk into a silent inner world.

So it's quite a shock when my phone rings.

I could ignore it, but it might be Greg or Mel reporting a problem. Or wanting to know how long to keep the link open. I'd better answer it.

But when I prise the little unit from my bag and read the LCD, I realise I should have expected to see this identity. I don't know how or why, but the man has spooky powers far beyond my comprehension.

The little greenish screen bears a single word.

Stone.

15 Mentor

'What are you doing, Maria?'

I'm in the bathroom. I need privacy for this, even though William barely noticed either the phone or my leaving the bedroom.

'Maria?' he prompts into my continued silence. And there's a note in his voice that tells me he probably knows exactly what I'm up to.

'I'm . . . I'm out.'

He makes a tiny sound of impatience.

'I know that. So am I. But what are you *doing*?'

'Sorting something out.'

He sighs and somehow it's the sexist thing I've ever heard. I don't know why.

'You don't have to do this for me, you know,' he murmurs into the phone. It's not an admonishment. It's far too gentle for that. 'I can take care of myself, my sweet, you know that, don't you? But I'd never forgive myself if anything happened to you. Or if anyone hurt you.' My heart turns a somersault. 'Now please tell me you're safe. And you're OK.'

I don't know what the distinction between the two is, and I don't think of trying to evade him any longer.

'How did you know?'

'Because "playing it cool" was driving me insane. I needed to be with you. So I called at your house. And when you didn't answer, I rang young Gregory's bell instead.' He pauses delicately, and despite having had the breath knocked out of me by what he said about needing to be with me, I feel a plume of anger too.

Did he really think I'd turn to Greg for sex at a time like this? For technical assistance, yes ... but sexual healing? Oh no, no, no!

Then suddenly, guilt replaces anger when I think of Mel's hands on me. God, I am so fickle! Such a faithless slut!

But he's talking again, his voice flowing through my veins like honey over a spoon. 'And I'm afraid he'd never stand up under interrogation, my love. I knew from his face that something was afoot. And he was telling me everything almost before I'd even asked.'

Another man who's susceptible to Stone's wiles. I remember Greg's confused words about seeing Stone and me in the bin yard. Faced with a man he may or may not fancy, even if he'd never admit it, I can quite see how Greg would sing like a bird.

I start to fantasise, filling my head with pictures of man-on-man action, but Stone's voice cuts through them, low and intense.

'Are you OK? Tell me you're all right!'

I'm fine. I'm more than all right. Especially now that Stone has rung and allowed me to hear the real emotion in his voice.

'Don't worry, everything's OK. In fact, I'm having fun.' I pause, and smile, knowing he'll hear it in my voice. 'Does that bother you?'

'Of course it doesn't, you sexy bitch!' he growls, letting me hear the laughter – and the desire – in his voice. 'I just wish I could be there to see it.'

'Then come here. See it!'

I don't even have to think. I certainly don't stop to consider William's feelings. I want Stone here as soon as possible.

'I'll be up in two minutes.'

'Two minutes?'

'Yes, I'm downstairs in the cocktail bar. You didn't think I'd allow you to do this on your own, do you?'

'You arrogant fuck! And it's Room 17, in case you don't already know.' I laugh as I click the phone shut.

I pee. Wash my hands. Smooth my hair. Dab on more lip-gloss. Shaking as I go.

If I was turned on before, I'm up in flames now.

I try to imagine the effect of this on William, but I can barely begin to. My heart is thudding as I return to the bedroom, and almost as soon as I set foot in the room there's a soft knock at the door.

William's eyes flare and he starts to struggle, but I quickly cross to his side and give him a swift, calming kiss.

'Don't worry. It'll be all right. You'll see.' I can see him desperately wanting to pull at his bonds, but I give him a stern look and he subsides, still frowning.

Stone knocks again.

Hold your horses, Clever Bobby! All in good time!

I open the door and here he is. Tall. Broad. Like music to my eyes. And he seems to be doing William's 'Man In Black' thing tonight too. Black jeans. Fine black sweater. Boxy black leather jacket.

'Can I come in?' He cocks his greying head on one side while those naughty dark-chocolate eyes of his rove devouringly up and down my body.

My first urge is to pull him in and devour him back where he stands. What is it? A day or two since I was with him? And I've missed him like fury. But a thought occurs, and I hold up a hand to halt him.

'One second.'

He looks puzzled but shrugs his great shoulders and just leans against the door-jamb to wait, almost filling the entire space.

I dash for my phone, ignoring William's even more

frantic thrashing and protesting on the bed. He can't quite see Stone from his position, but he's certainly heard his voice.

'Cut! It's a wrap! And I mean it, Greg. We're done here now.'

Greg protests. Obviously he's been watching the feed, even though I said I preferred that he didn't. I guess that Mel has too because I can hear her complaining in the background. It really doesn't surprise me that they've been watching, though. In fact, I expected it. It just adds an extra layer to the fun.

'I mean it. Turn it off! Or I'll have to come round there and deal with you too.'

'I wish you would,' he says with feeling.

I just bid him goodnight and snap the phone shut. Maybe he'll turn it off, and maybe he won't – but the thought of dealing with young Gregory too makes me smile.

And all the time, Stone is watching me, his eyes unwavering, his expression complex.

'Are you all right?' He reaches out and touches my face most tenderly. 'I've been worried. I nearly got pulled for speeding getting here.'

I want to melt. I want to collapse at his feet. He's everything to me now. Teacher. Lover. Mentor. Without him, I would never have been able to deal with William at all. No amount of watching videos can match the sight of power itself in action.

But now I have to show him I'm his equal.

I give him the same cool admonishing smile that worked so well with his arch rival and his lips part in amazement. He straightens up, squares his shoulders, almost stands to attention. It's an impressive sight.

Without a word, I turn and walk back into the room, confident he'll follow. I suppress a smile when I hear him lock the door behind him.

William is wrenching so hard at his bonds now that I fear he might hurt himself.

'Be still,' I command him quietly and he obeys instantly, even though his eyes are still fiery. 'If you don't calm down, I shall be forced to give you something that'll make you.'

He blinks furiously, his glance darting frantically between me and Stone.

I turn and find Stone taking in the scene, a slight smile on his face. He barely seems to be paying any attention to William, just a helluva lot to me.

'What are *you* smiling about? Just sit down and shut up.' I nod towards the chintzy chair. 'Unless you want the same?'

His face straightens and he sits down as instructed. There's still mirth in his eyes but there's not a lot I can do about that.

I catch up the black flogger and toy with it as a prop to hide my nervousness, then take up my station halfway between the two men. William, nude and vulnerable on the bed, and Stone, a looming dark-clad figure who seems to own the fussy, upholstered chair and make it seem like his rightful throne.

Well, fuck you, Clever Bobby! I'm in charge now.

'You two. You're hopeless. Two grown men playing power games with all the finesse of a pair of snot-nosed brats in a playground.' I slap the flogger lightly in my palm and nearly lose my thread. The damn thing hurts! 'He's got something on you.' I nod at William, who glowers. 'Now you've got something on him.' I nod at Stone, who's half hugging himself and tapping his lower lip with his fingertips. He looks as if he's barely restraining himself from shaking his head in pure amazement.

'And now you've both got something on me.' I'm warming to my theme now, buoyed up by the admiration that my mentor just can't hide. 'But, quite frankly, I don't give a shit about that. All I want is for the two of you to play nice and co-operate with each other.' I allow myself a sly, sexy grin, and shudder with inner pleasure when Stone bites his lip as if I've just slid my hand into his jeans. 'It's kiss-and-make up time, boys. Are you going to make that happen for me?'

'Anything, Miss Lewis,' he breathes. 'Anything for you.'

And he means it. 'Miss Lewis' isn't the signal of his power this time, but of his submission to my will. My heart sings and I look towards William, who is nodding now, clearly resigned to his fate.

'Good!' I say crisply, then stride into the bathroom without looking at either of them, and return with one of the thick, luxuriously fluffy bathrobes.

Time to release my prisoner and give him a chance to negotiate on more equal terms. Aware of Stone's intense scrutiny, I undo William's gag and prise my knickers from out of his mouth. When it's revealed what they are, I hear Stone gasp, and I turn and give him my sternest stare. He shakes his head in awe.

William says nothing, but just meekly allows me to unfasten his cuffs. Then, with grateful haste, he struggles into the robe and hides his still rampant cock.

'Now then, you two. I'm going to take a long, scented bath, and when I've done, I want you to be friends again.' I look from one to the other, accepting their adoration. 'At least.'

With that, I sweep from the room, head up, heart racing, and just amazed that I can turn my back on two such handsome, desirable men when I'm so desperate for one of them to fuck me!

I'm a bit conflicted. I leave the door ajar so I can hear, and start the bath running furiously so I can't. But as I begin to peel off my clothes, then carefully cleanse away my face makeup but not my eyes and lips, I find myself drifting towards the bedroom time and time again.

The men are talking in low tones, although occasionally one of them raises his voice slightly. They're not kissing and making up yet. William actually has a slightly deeper voice than Stone, which is odd given their differing builds. But Stone has a soft yet powerful resonance about him – a strong centre that his rival seems to lack.

I fling in a variety of the complimentary bath oils and suddenly the room smells a bit like a Turkish brothel. I have to let some water out and top it up again to make the fragrance more tolerable.

By the time this has finished and I've settled beneath the bubbles, things have gone ominously quiet in the bedroom.

They've either killed each other or they're making out.

Giving myself the quickest ever sluice between my legs and under my arms, I climb quietly out of the bath again and slip into another of the robes. With a bottle of the high-end moisturiser supplied by the Waverley clutched in my hand, I pad towards the open door, then rub some on my face and neck as I creep forward to peek through the gap into the room beyond.

Holy Christ, they *are* kissing and making up! And it's the hottest thing I've ever seen in my life, William and Sandy in the cellar and me and Stone on the picnic table notwithstanding!

Stone's on top, very much the man, still clothed and oh so dark and massive compared to William's towelling-clad golden slenderness. Their mouths are clamped together, and I can see from the way Stone's jaw is working that his tongue is half-way down his partner's throat. He has one hand at the nape of William's neck, controlling the kiss, while the other is buried somewhere beneath his robe. William is writhing, his heels dragging at the duvet.

Delicious! Delicious! Delicious!

I can't stay away from this. Millimetre by millimetre, I nudge open the bathroom door and slide through. Stone gives me a narrow, hooded, conspiratorial look out of the corner of his eye, but William is totally gone. Completely out of it. I could have crashed the door back on its hinges and shouted 'Banzai!' for all he'd notice. I slink to the bedroom chair and make myself comfortable. Well, as comfortable as I can be with lust clenching and twisting in my belly.

As if for my benefit, Stone flips open William's robe so I can see his hand roving all over that smooth pale skin, caressing his thighs, his flanks, and again and again his rampant slippery erection. William grows more frantic with every touch, rearing up against Stone's hand, wriggling and enticing like the most shameless of sluts. He's whimpering in his throat too, although the sound is still muffled by Stone's marauding mouth.

I'm so wet I'm scared that I'll soak right through the robe I'm wearing and make a damp patch on the chintzy chair seat.

And I'm still not close enough.

As if led by fate and the typhoon of heat that is my rapacious lover, I pad towards the bed and stretch out beside them, at the edge so as to give them the maximum amount of space for their gymnastics. As I slide my hand inside my own robe, I'm still convinced that William hasn't noticed.

The acme of consideration, Stone adjusts his position to give me a better view of the action, bless him. His hand looks like a great big paw around William's slender dick, but all the same he seems to be handling him with all the delicacy he exhibits when he touches me. He isn't just cynically wanking him off, he's caressing him. Using his undoubted skills to give William pleasure. And the way William's moving and moaning says he's hitting all the marks.

William is pliant, accepting, submissive. He's reactive, not proactive, letting Stone do all the work while he just lies back and allows things to happen to him.

Selfish Blondie!

I touch myself, but I'm imagining how I might touch Stone and pleasure him to even up the score. With my free hand I splay my fingers across his back, enjoying the play of his muscles beneath the fine cotton weave of his black sweater. He glances sideways at me and gives me a swift wink.

A moment later, his mouth begins to rove, kissing William's taut throat, his collar-bone, and his pecs. When he starts to lick and suck on the blond man's tiny brown coin-shaped nipples, he induces more gasping and writhing. William reaches back, grasping the bedhead, arching upwards to press his pale flesh against Stone's rosy mouth.

I stroke Stone's head as he sips and laps at William's chest, loving the feel of the crisp curliness of his grey-flecked hair. I want to be a part of this. I want to help and share the burden of bringing our prey off. The sooner that happens, the sooner Stone can have his reward too.

Stone looks up at me, his long tongue still rudely circling William's teat. There's communication between us, silent and multilayered, and I sense that he's immediately got my drift. He releases William's cock and gestures me forward. Hunkering down, I take the glans into my mouth.

'Oh God! Holy fucking Christ!' shouts William, his whole body stiffening and his penis lurching with the motion. I can't see too well, because of where my face is, and the presence of Stone's massive body next to me, but I can just imagine William looking down and seeing two mouths, two lovers, at work on him. I wrap my fingers around him and start sucking him like a lollipop.

I'm afraid I'm nowhere near as subtle and circumspect

as Stone might have been. I'm in a hurry. Even though William tastes deliciously gamey – no doubt from being aroused and seeping for a long, long time – I don't want to linger over the dish. Because I'm famished to move on to the next course. The main course.

As I lift my head to adjust my position for a better angle, I see that Stone is alternating licks and sucks and little bites now. He has one large hand flat on William's abdomen, and fingers splayed, and his other arm is cradling William's shoulders.

I put my head down and apply myself diligently to my task.

It doesn't take too long, because I use every trick I know. Pointed tongue flicking around the head, and into the love-eye. Suction. Really hard suction, just on the head. Alternating both while I finger his perineum.

After a couple of minutes, he actually screams. Screams just like a woman. And as his hips buck, he fills my mouth with spunk.

For several long, thudding heartbeats, we all remain like a frozen tableau, still locked in place, two mouths on one body. Then we gradually unwind and disengage. I let William's subsiding cock slip out of my mouth and settle against his body all wet and flaccid. And Stone straightens up, looks down at his would-be nemesis almost fondly, and then places swift kisses on his lips and his tightly closed eyes.

William doesn't seem to want to see the aftermath of what's happened to him, but Stone's smile is broad and white with satisfaction.

Job well done, it seems.

But then he gives me a narrow, sultry look, and hitches himself around the bed, moving William bodily aside as if he's a doll that's served its purpose.

As he now looms over me, he waggles his eyebrows and looks pointedly at my semen-coated lips.

Before I can protest, he's having a taste, his tongue in my mouth.

He kisses me hard, lapping and sipping and savouring William's essence.

'Mm ... Yummy,' he murmurs, his lips still only inches from mine as he lifts his head. He goes up in my estimation yet again. It takes a pretty liberated man who's sure of his own masculinity to admit to liking the taste of another man's spunk.

And not only liking it. When I reach down to fondle the bulge in his jeans he's like iron.

'Mm ... Yummy,' I echo, giving him a squeeze.

He prises away my fingers. 'Be careful there, wench. I'm so desperate to fuck you that I might pop off any second. Come on, give me a hand to get my clothes off!'

Gladly!

As he peels his sweater off over his head, I tug off his socks, then attack the belt of his jeans. It's big and heavy, and for a moment I wonder how it would have performed across William's bottom, but then I forget that as I unship it and unfasten the jeans themselves. He's commando underneath them, and a second later they're off, half draped across our companion's motionless legs.

And I'm fondling Stone's cock.

He's rampant, and far more solid and chunky than the man I've just sucked. The big, fat head seems almost to smile as if it's glad to see me.

I'm certainly glad to see it.

'Uh oh,' chides Stone, unwinding my fingers, 'remember what I said?' He pushes me back against the mattress and folds the wings of my bathrobe away from my body. Then pressing the full length of him against the full length of me, he starts to kiss again.

Oh, and it's so lovely! Naked kissing. There's nothing quite like it. I'm hugging my big cuddly teddy-bear again and he's hugging me. He presses his sumptuous penis against the inside of my thigh, but makes no particular move to enter me. Which isn't a problem because I just like feeling him there.

I suddenly feel ineffably warm and safe and comfortable – in spite of the fact that I'm on a bed with *two* men.

Stone kisses me for a while, his hands rambling over my body in a leisurely fashion, sliding here, exploring there, until eventually he gets impatient with the robe, and he manhandles me in a friendly way until that's off too. He flings that in the general direction of William, and we get a grunt of protest that makes me realise that our companion has come back to life again, and is enjoying the show. I sneak a glance and find him lying on his side, head propped on his hand while with the other hand, he fondles himself tentatively.

He gives me a strange, shy little smile and suddenly all my antipathy towards him vanishes. I smile back then return my full attention to Stone.

Who seems to have decided to give William a master class. A virtuoso performance in how to pleasure a woman.

The kisses and touches grow more focused. More elaborate. He tries daring combinations of fingers, lips and skin. I cry out and writhe as he very delicately abrades my nipples with his warm, stubbly cheeks. Over and over, again and again, alternating with flicks and sucks and kisses. Down below, I'm going crazy for some action and I drag his big hand between my thighs and move it encouragingly.

I'm half surprised that William hasn't rolled closer to oblige me, but there seems to be an invisible barrier between his side of the bed and ours.

Then Stone's on the move again, rearranging my body to suit his explorations. He seems intent on kissing every inch of me. Which is something I'd always thought was just a cliché out of romantic novels, but now realise isn't that at all. Some of the bits he kisses aren't ones I'm even sure I *want* kissing, but they induce an alarming degree of pleasure – and a lot of thrashing about – when vigorously tongued by Stone.

For those bits I keep my eyes very firmly closed. I don't want to risk meeting William's gaze while I'm going ballistic with Stone's nose between my bottom cheeks!

Eventually, when Stone seems to have ticked all the boxes on the checklist of where he wants to lick and probe and finger, he pulls me up on to my hands and knees and then moves in behind me.

I feel his cock nudge at my bum, and for a moment I really do panic. Do I really want him to bugger me? Here and now? With an audience?

But he lays his great body over me and whispers sweet, reassuring nothings in my ear.

'Not just yet.'

'Maybe another time.'

'When we're alone.'

His voice is so gentle and so intimate that I almost want to say 'Go ahead! Do it anyway!' But then the moment is gone. He rolls on the condom that William's just handed to him and presses himself into the usual channel.

I fall forward against the pillows, feeling infinitely slutty. I waggle my bottom against him, and reach back with one hand to clasp his sturdy thigh and encourage his endeavours, while with the other I keep my face out of the bed-linen and stop myself from smothering. Stone is a big, big man and he goes at me with some force.

But he's not selfish.

He reaches under me, still fondling me, still taking care of the business of my pleasure as well as his. My heart turns over even as my body clamps down on him in hard, wrenching, extended orgasm.

I love him. There's no two ways about it. I'm lost.

* * *

And afterwards, I'm knackered. Completely exhausted.

I lie spooned against Stone like a wrung-out rag, just basking in his heat and his presence. I could lie here forever like this, and I drift off to sleep until the bed bounces a little when William gets up. He pads away to the bathroom, and it's just Stone and me at last. He doesn't make a move, though, just hugs me a little closer to his belly, his chest and his thighs. I detect a bit of a twitch in his cock, but it's half-hearted, as if both he and it are as sleepy as I am.

Drifting, I listen to the small sounds. A shower running. William coming back into the room, gathering his clothes. Eventually he coughs softly and both Stone and I are compelled to rouse ourselves and take notice.

Our friend the Human Resources Manager looks as if nothing's happened. He's poised, elegant, restored to confidence again. There's no indication, or at least very little, of the submissive dewy-eyed victim of not so long ago.

Stone sits up in bed and gives William a long considering look. William answers with a small, shy smile and I see the confidence isn't quite as full-on as he'd have us believe.

'I'm off now.' He hesitates, and the smile widens. 'It's been . . .' He rolls his eyes. 'It's been indescribable.'

'It has indeed,' murmurs Stone, and he grasps the edge of the sheet he's pulled over us, almost as if he's going to get up and go over and give William a goodbye kiss.

Ah, how sweet. And hot.

But I'm thwarted in my desire to see a touching homoerotic leave-taking. William as good as runs for the door before Stone gets a chance to unveil himself. 'I'll . . . I'll see you around the Hall.' He opens the door, and seems just about to dash for it when he hesitates one more time. 'Goodnight, Maria.' It's barely more than a whisper. 'Goodnight, Robert.'

And then he's gone and the door snicks quietly shut behind him.

'So, are you two going to keep the peace now?'

I turn to face Stone, tweaking at the sheet to keep it under my armpits. Bizarrely, I feel a bit shy now. It doesn't make sense, but I can't bring myself to sit up brazenly and exhibit myself.

Stone gives me a fond little smile, as if he understands and finds my irrational bashfulness endearing. 'Oh, we'll probably be at each other's throats like a pair of pit-bulls within a week.' He gives his big, bear-like shrug. 'But at least we have a way to mediate our differences now.' His eyelid droops in a sexy wink, and he settles back again, scratching at his furry chest and then reaching out, hooking an arm around me and pulling me back tight up against his body, re-spooning us.

'What?' I protest. 'After all I've gone through to sort things out between you? You really are the most ungrateful pair of sods.'

'We're men. We're just naturally stupid,' he pronounces equably, 'but don't worry, I'll always let you watch.' He hitches his pelvis about a bit, as if to draw my attention to the slightly perky nature of his dick.

'I should bloody well think so!'

'But you've got to let me watch when you fuck him.'

'That's fair,' I concede, essaying a little pressure in a critical direction.

We rub against each other lightly for a moment or two. Nothing serious. Nothing heavy. Just a bit like two animals sharing one basket.

We seem to be drifting into sex again, but suddenly, out of the blue, I'm swamped by melancholy. Even though Stone's cock is definitely thickening now, ready for action, I have to ask a question that might well have the power to deflate it again.

'So, will you give me a good reference?'

Epilogue

I'm staring at the door again. That big old looming great door that leads to his office.

Somewhere in my innards I start to quiver. I suppose it's the sensation you get when you're just about to take a parachute jump. Overweight butterflies in the stomach. Adrenalin rush. Heart in the mouth. Only in this case the promised high is so much better value. It usually lasts much longer and the chances of breaking your neck in the process are zero to nil.

'Do go in, Miss Lewis,' says Mrs Sheldon, giving me one of her warm, motherly smiles. 'He's always glad to see you.'

She still hasn't the faintest idea what's really going on, poor old dear, but I can see she thinks there's romance in the air.

Actually, she's not a million miles off-beam there, but it's not the hearts and flowers and tender protestations kind.

I march purposefully into the office, letting the door swing closed behind me with a firm thump. He looks up, his eyes bright, searching and assessing.

My breath catches, although I don't let him see that. Every time is like the first time with this man. I'm sure anyone who didn't know me – or him – would wonder what I see in this stocky, unremarkable, middle-aged servant of the Borough. His hair is peppered with grey and he's in his shirt-sleeves, with his tie slightly askew. He's nothing special. Not my type. Mr Average.

Wrong! Wrong! Wrong!

'Good afternoon, Maria. What can I do for you? Won't you take a seat?'

He points to the hard chair in front of the desk.

No way! Not today.

I stride up to the desk and toss a manila folder down in front of him.

'It's about this performance review, Mr Stone,' I announce, all crisp and businesslike. 'I've read it carefully, and I feel that it's unfairly biased.' I pause, lock eyes with him unwaveringly. 'I feel that we need to address some of the issues in it rather urgently.'

Don't you dare laugh, you bastard!

But he doesn't. He wouldn't dream of it. No more than I would if the positions were reversed. This might be fun, but it has to be taken seriously.

Stone flips open the folder and reads the single sheet of paper with a perfectly straight face. Actually, all it says on it is 'Robert Stone is a horny fuck' but for the purpose of the exercise it's supposed to be a ten-page performance review.

'Which issues would those be?'

His eyes don't waver either. They're large and brown and lustrous. He's still challenging me slightly, as he sometimes does. Testing my nerve. I'm not yet out of the novice stage in all this, despite a truly stunning debut, and he enjoys trying to push me and raise my game.

Hang tough, Maria. Don't falter. He's only trying it on.

'Your attitude, for one. I find you insolent. And sexist. You're a dinosaur, Mr Stone, and I feel you're in need of some refresher work in Modern Gender Issues.'

It's all ludicrous bullshit, of course, but I'm pretty pleased with the way I'm thinking on my feet.

He sighs, but it's in mock regret, not impatience, and I know I've got him.

'Yes, I fear that you're right, Miss Lewis.' His expression is bland, pensive, no longer challenging. But his eyes are

No deflation. Not even the slightest hesitation in the fondling.

'Why would you need a reference? You're not thinking of leaving the Hall, are you?' His breath is warm against my neck.

'Well, no. I don't want to. But that's what happens, isn't it? You have a thing with someone, and when you want to get rid of them, you give them a fabulous reference and they get a better job.' I can't breathe. I can't think for the sound of me shooting myself in the foot.

His hands are still moving. His penis is still hard. He doesn't even seem tense.

'What makes you think I'd want to get rid of you?'

Thud. Thud. Thud. It's my heart. Can Stone feel the vibration through my back?

'I bet you always say that.'

'Well, yes, I do.' His lips shape into a kiss against the side of my throat. 'But usually I don't actually mean it.'

There's a long silence, and something starts to flutter inside me that's got nothing to do with sex, despite the fact that my back and buttocks are skin to skin with the chest and groin of a glorious, rampant man.

'But you'll get bored with me.'

'Well, we'll just have to find ways to keep things interesting, won't we?' His cock nudges a little more insistently at the crack of my bottom, as if dropping a big hint. 'Shouldn't be a problem with an imaginative girl like you, Miss Lewis.'

I know what he wants, and I think I know what he's saying. So I push back against him, gyrating my rear end with all the subtlety of a Triple-X porn-flick strumpet.

After all, if you can't have unnatural sex with the man you love, who can you have it with?

Especially when he just might love you back.

happy. Oh, so happy. 'How would you suggest we tackle this?'

I walk around to his side of the desk and move right up to him, forcing him to push back his big executive chair a little. When I glance down, I really have to work hard to tame my smile.

He's got a huge erection tenting in his dark suit trousers. I give him a narrow dismissive look as if I find the sight disgusting, but really it makes me clench inside. With longing.

'Well?'

His expression is genuinely puzzled. I'd like to smile, but I don't. I'm trying something new.

'I'd like to sit down if you don't mind.' I keep my voice cool, reasonable. There's no need to shout or get aggressive at times like these. If you do, it only shows that you're losing it.

He surrenders his seat and I take it, loving the body-warmth and the scent of him that lingers on the upholstery. Standing respectfully aside, he waits for his next cue.

'Show me your dick,' I say in a perfectly normal voice.

His face remains straight, but his eyes are on fire. After just a half a second's hesitation, his hands go to his belt, and as they do I reach up, push lightly on his mid-section and force him back so he's sitting on the desk. Thus positioned, he goes to work, his large hands deft and nimble on buckle and zip. A second later, he's on show, his penis glorious. It pokes out of his fly like a big, juicy reddish club, and I feel as if I need to sit on my hands to stop me from reaching out and touching it.

Or touching something else.

'No underwear?' I query, keeping my tone neutral. The question itself should be condemnation enough.

'Er . . . no.'

Ah hah! Hesitation! Gotcha!

'Isn't that somewhat inappropriate for a man in your position?'

'Yes, I suppose so,' he concedes, flexing his long, square-tipped fingers as he too feels that burning compulsion to touch.

'"Suppose" has nothing to do with it,' I say crisply, rising to my feet, my skirt brushing the tip of his cock and making him dig his teeth into his soft, red lower lip. 'What if you were in a meeting with the Mayor and you got an erection? With no underpants to blunt the impact, so to speak?' I press myself against him, face on a level because he's still perched on the edge of the desk. 'He might become uncontrollably aroused and have to have you.'

Stone's still gnawing at his lip, but it's with mirth now. Given that our Mayor is a seventy-two-year-old Methodist lay preacher, my scenario is pretty ridiculous. Even so, I doubt that anyone could resist my Clever Bobby if he really put his mind to seducing them, regardless of their status, their sex or any number of strictly followed codes of moral nicety.

I'm certainly having a hard time of it now.

So I give up trying.

I press a kiss to those soft red lips, and curl my fingers around that hard red penis. As if released from some unspoken bond, he makes a low sound in his throat, reaches for me and pulls me closer.

There'll be a time and a place to play the cruel diva and really put it to him. And a whole future full of opportunities to punish my lover for his impudence.

But for now I'm entertaining Mr Stone.

Also by Portia Da Costa:

The 'Accidental' trilogy

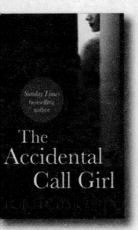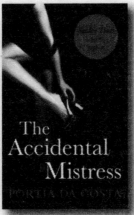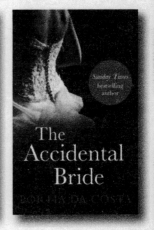

Read on for an extract from

THE ACCIDENTAL CALL GIRL

1

Meeting Mr Smith

He looked like a god, the man sitting at the end of the bar did. Really. The glow from the down-lighter just above him made his blond hair look like a halo, and it was the most breath-taking effect. Lizzie just couldn't stop staring.

Oops, oh no, he suddenly looked her way. Unable to face his sharp eyes, she focused on her glass. It contained tonic, a bit dull really, but safe. She'd done some mad things in her time, both under the influence and sober, and she was alone now, and squarely in the 'mad things' zone. She'd felt like a fish out of water at the birthday party she was supposed to be at in the Waverley Grange Hotel's function room with her house-mates Brent and Shelley and a few other friends. It was for a vaguely posh girl who she didn't really know that well; someone in her year at uni, who she couldn't actually remember being all that pally with at the time. Surrounded by women who seemed to be looking at her and wondering why she was there, and men giving her the eye with a view to chatting her up, Lizzie had snuck out of the party and wandered into the bar, drawn by its strangely unsettling yet latent with 'something' atmosphere.

To look again or not to look again, that was the question. She wanted to. The man was so very hot, although not her usual type. Whatever *that* was. Slowly, slowly, she turned her head a few centimetres, straining her eyes in order to see the god, or angel guy, out of their corners.

Fuck! Damn! He wasn't looking now. He was chatting to the barman, favouring him with a killer smile, almost as if he fancied *him*, not any of the women at the bar. Was he gay? It didn't really matter, though, did it? She was only supposed to be enjoying the view, after all, and he really was a sight for sore eyes.

With his attention momentarily distracted, she grabbed a feast of him.

Not young, definitely. Possibly forty, maybe a bit more? Dark gold-blond, curling hair, thick and a bit longer than one would have expected for his age, but not straggling. Gorgeous face, even though his features, in analysis, could almost have been called average. Put together, however, there was something extra, something indefinable about him that induced a 'wow'. Perhaps it was his eyes? They were very bright, and very piercing. Yes, it *was* the eyes, probably. Even from a distance, Lizzie could tell they were a clear, beautiful, almost jewel-like blue.

Or maybe it was his mouth too? His lips were mobile, and they had a plush, almost sumptuous look to them that could have looked ambiguous on a man, but somehow not on him. The smile he gave the lucky barman was almost sunny, and when he suddenly snagged his lower lip between his teeth, something went 'Oof!' in Lizzie's mid-section. And lower down too.

What's his body like?

Hard to tell, with the curve of the bar, and other people

sitting between them, but if his general demeanour and the elegant shape of his hand as he lifted his glass to his lips were anything to go by, he was lean and fit. But, that could be wishful thinking, she admitted. He might actually be some podgy middle-aged guy who just happened to have a fallen angel's face and a very well-cut suit.

Just enjoy the bits you can see, you fool. That's all you'll ever get to look at. You're not here on the pull.

With that, as if he'd heard her thoughts, Fallen Angel snapped his head around and looked directly at her. No pretence, no hesitation, he stared her down, his eyes frank and intent, his velvet lips curved in a tricky, subtle quirk of a smile. As if showcasing himself, he shifted slightly on his stool, and she was able to see a little more of him.

She'd been exactly right. He *was* lean and fit, and the sleek way his clothes hung on him clearly suggested how he might look when those clothes were flung haphazardly on the floor.

The temptation to look away was like a living force, as if she were staring at the sun and its brilliance was a fatal peril. But Lizzie resisted the craven urge, and held his gaze. She didn't yield a smile. She just tried to eyeball him as challengingly as he was doing her, and her reward was more of that sun on the lips and in the eyes, and a little nod of acknowledgement.

'For you, miss.'

The voice from just inches away nearly made her fall off her stool. She actually teetered a bit, cursing inside as she dragged her attention from the blue-eyed devil-angel at the end of the bar to the rather toothsome young barman standing right in front of her.

'Er . . . yes, thanks. But I didn't order anything.'

There was no need to ask who'd sent the drink that had

been placed before her, in a plain low glass, set on a white napkin. It was about an inch and a half of clear fluid, no ice, no lemon, no nothing. Just what she realised *he* was drinking.

She stared at it as the barman retreated, smiling to himself. He must go through this dance about a million times every evening in a busy, softly lit bar like this. With its faintly recherché ambience it was the ideal venue for advances and retreats, games of 'Do you dare?' over glasses of fluids various.

What the hell was that stuff? Lighter fluid? Drain cleaner? A poisoned chalice?

She put it to her lips and took a hit, catching her breath. It was neat gin, not the vodka she'd half expected. It seemed a weird drink for a man, but perhaps he was a weird man? Taking a very cautious sip this time, she placed the glass back carefully and turned towards him.

Of course, he was watching, and he did a thing with his sandy eyebrows that seemed to ask if she liked his gift. Lizzie wasn't sure that she did, but she nodded at him, took up the glass again and toasted him.

The dazzling grin gained yet more wattage, and he matched the toast. Then, with another elegant piece of body language, a tilt of the head, and a lift of the shoulders, he indicated she should join him. More blatantly, he patted an empty stool beside him.

Here, Rover! Just like an alpha dog, he was summoning a bitch to his side.

Up yours!

Before she could stop herself, or even really think what she was doing, Lizzie mirrored his little pantomime.

Here, Fido! Come!

There was an infinitesimal pause. The man's exceptional eyes widened, and she saw surprise and admiration. Then he slid gracefully off his stool, caught up his drink and headed her way.

Oh God, now what have I done?

She'd come in here, away from the party, primarily to avoid getting hit on, and now what had she done? Invited a man she'd never set eyes on before to hit on her. What should her strategy be? Yes or no? Run or stay? Encourage or play it cool? The choices whirled in her head for what seemed like far longer than it took for a man with a long, smooth, confident stride to reach her.

In the end, she smiled. What woman wouldn't? Up close, he was what she could only inadequately describe as a stunner. All the things that had got her hot from a distance were turned up by a degree of about a thousand in proximity.

'Hello . . . I'll join you then, shall I?' He hitched himself easily onto the stool at her side, his long legs making the action easy, effortless and elegant.

'Hi,' she answered, trying to breathe deeply without appearing to.

Don't let him see that he's already made you into a crazy woman. Just play it cool, Lizzie, for God's sake.

She waited for some gambit or other, but he just smiled at her, his eyes steady, yet also full of amusement, in fact downright merriment. He was having a whale of a time already, and she realised she was too, dangerous as he seemed. This wasn't the kind of man she could handle in the way she usually handled men.

'Thank you for the drink,' she blurted out, unable to take the pressure of his smile and his gently mocking eyes. 'It wasn't what I expected, to be honest.' She glanced at his identical glass. 'It doesn't seem like a man's drink . . . neat gin. Not really.'

Still not speaking, he reached for his glass, and nodded that she take up hers. They clinked them together, and he took a long swallow from his. Lizzie watched the slow undulation of his throat. He was wearing a three-piece suit, a very good one in an expensive shade of washed-out grey-blue. His shirt was light blue and open at the neck.

The little triangle of exposed flesh at his throat seemed to invite the tongue. What would his skin taste like? Not as sharp as gin, no doubt, but just as much of a challenge and ten times as heady.

'Well, I am a man, as you can see.' He set down his glass again, and turned more to face her, doing that showcasing, 'look at the goods' thing again. 'But I'm happy to give you more proof, if you like?'

Lizzie took a quick sip of her own drink, to steady herself. The silvery, balsamic taste braced her up.

'That won't be necessary.' She paused, feeling the gin sizzle in her blood. 'Not right here at least.'

He shook his head and laughed softly, the light from above dancing on his curls, turning soft ash-blond into molten gold. 'That's what I like. Straight to the point. Now we're talking.' Reaching into his jacket pocket, he drew out a black leather wallet and peeled out a banknote, a fifty by the look of it, and dropped it beside his glass as he slipped off the stool again. Reaching for her arm, he said, 'Let's go up to my room. I hate wasting time.'

Oh bloody hell! Oh, bloody, bloody hell! He's either as direct as a very direct thing and he's dead set on a quickie . . . or . . .

Good grief, does he think I'm an escort?

The thought plummeted into the space between them like a great Acme anvil. It was possible. Definitely possible. And it would explain the 'eyes across a bar, nodding and buying drinks' dance. Lizzie had already twigged that the Lawns bar was a place likely to be rife with that sort of thing, and it wasn't as if she didn't *know* anything about escorting. One of her dearest friends had been one, if only part time and not lately, and Brent would most certainly be alarmed that she'd fallen so naively into this pickle of all pickles. She imagined telling him about this afterwards, perhaps making a big comical thing out of her near escape, and hopefully raising some of the old, wickedly droll humour that fate and loss had knocked out of her beloved house-mate.

Trying to think as fast as she could, Lizzie balked, staying put on the stool. Escort or casual pick-up, she still needed a moment to catch her breath and stall long enough to decide whether or not to do something completely mental. 'I think I'd rather like to finish my drink. Seems a shame to waste good gin.'

If her companion was vexed, or impatient, he didn't show it. In a beautiful roll of the shoulders, he shrugged and slipped back onto his stool. 'Quite right. It *is* good gin. Cheers!' He toasted her again.

What am I going to do? What the hell am I going to do? This is dangerous.

It was. It was very dangerous. But in a flash of dazzling honesty, she knew that the gin wasn't the only thing that was too good to waste. The only question was, if he *did* think she was a call girl, did she tell him the truth now, or play along for a bit? She'd never done anything like this before, but, suddenly, she wanted to. She really wanted to. Perhaps because the only man she knew from the wretched party she'd left, other than Brent and some other friends from the pub, was a guy she'd dated once and who'd called her uptight and frigid when she'd rebuffed a grope that'd come too soon.

No use looking like a pin-up and behaving like a dried-up nun, he'd said nastily when she'd told him to clear off.

But this man, well, there wasn't an atom in her body that wanted to rebuff *him*!

What would it be like to dance on the edge? Play a game? Have an adventure that was about as far from her daily humdrum routine of office temping as it was possible to get?

What would it be like to have this jaw-droppingly stunning man, who was so unlike her usual type? She usually went for guys her own age, and Fallen Angel here certainly wasn't that. She was twenty-four and, up close, she could see her estimate of mid-forties was probably accurate. A perfectly seasoned, well-kept, prime specimen of mid-forties man, but still with at least twenty more years of life under his belt than she had.

And if she explained his mistake, he might well just smile that glorious smile at her, shake her hand, and walk away. Goodnight, Vienna.

'Cheers!' she answered.

He didn't speak but his eyes gleamed a response.

I bet you know what to do with a woman, you devil, paid for or otherwise.

Yes, she'd put any amount of money, earned on one's back or by any other means, that when Fallen Angel was with an escort, it was no hardship to be that working girl.

And she couldn't keep calling him Fallen Angel!

On the spur of the moment, she made a decision. This was a game, and she needed a handle. A name, an avatar that she could hide behind and discard when she needed to.

Looking her companion directly in the eye, and trying

not to melt, she set down her glass, held out her hand and said, 'I'm Bettie. Bettie with an "ie". What's your name, Gin-Drinking Man?'

Apparently ignoring the offered handshake, he just laughed, a free, happy, hugely amused, proper laugh. 'Yes, obviously, you *are* Bettie.' Looking her up and down, his laser-blue eyes seemed to catalogue her every asset; her black hair with its full fringe, her pale skin, her lips tinted with vivid bombshell red, her pretty decent but unfashionable figure in a fitted dress with an angora cardigan over it. When she went out, especially to a party, she liked to riff on her superficial resemblance to Bettie Page, the notorious glamour model of the 1950s. And being an Elizabeth, Bettie was a natural alternate name too.

Having subjected her to his inspection, he did reach for her hand then, grip it, and give it a firm shake with both of his clasped around it. 'Delighted to meet you, Bettie. I'm John Smith.'

It was Lizzie's turn to laugh out loud, and 'John' grinned at her. 'Of course you are, John. How could you possibly be anyone else?' The classic punter's name. Even she knew that.

He rocked on the stool, giving his blond head another little shake, still holding on to her. 'But it's my name, Bettie. Cross my heart . . . Honestly.'

The way he held her hand was firm and no nonsense, yet there was a tricky quality to the way his fingertip lay across her wrist, touching the pulse point. She could almost imagine he was monitoring her somehow, but the moment she thought that, he released her.

'OK, I believe you, Mr John Smith. Now may I finish my drink?'

'Of course.' He gave her the glittering smile again, laced

with a sultry edge. 'Forgive me, I'm being a graceless boor. No woman should be rushed . . .' There was a pause, which might have included the rider, *even a prostitute*. 'But once I know I'm going to get a treat, I'm like a kid, Bettie. When I want something, I tend to want it now.'

So do I.

Lizzie tossed back the remainder of her gin, amazed that her throat didn't rebel at its silvery ferociousness. But she didn't cough, and she set the glass down with a purposeful 'clop' on the counter, and slid off her stool.

'There, all finished. Shall we go?'

John simply beamed, settled lightly on his feet and took her elbow, steering her from the crowded bar and into the foyer quite quickly, but not fast enough to make anyone think they were hurrying.

The lift cab was small, and felt smaller, filled by her new friend's presence. Standing, he was medium tall, but not towering or hulking, and his body was every bit as good as her preliminary inspection in the bar had promised. As was his suit. It looked breathtakingly high end, making her wonder why, if he was looking for an escort, he didn't just put in a call to an exclusive agency for a breath-takingly high-end woman to go with it? Rather than pick up an unknown quantity, on spec, in a hotel bar. Leaning against the lift's wall, though, he eyed her up too as the doors slid closed, looking satisfied enough with his random choice. Was he trying to estimate her price?

'So, do we do the "elevator" scene?' he suggested, making no move towards her, except with his bright blue eyes.

Oh yeah, in all those scenes in films and sexy stories, it always happened. The hot couple slammed together in the lift like ravenous dogs and kissed the hell out of each other.

'I don't know. You're in charge.'

'I most certainly am,' he said roundly, 'but let's pretend and savour the anticipation, shall we? The uncertainty. Even though I do know that you're the surest of sure things.'

Bingo! He does think I'm an escort.

Confirming her suspicions like that, his words should have sounded crass and crude, but instead they were provocative, exciting her. Especially the bit about him being 'in charge'. Brent had always said it was the whore who was really in charge during a booking, because he or she could just dump the money, say 'No way!' and walk out. But somehow Lizzie didn't think it'd be that way with Mr John Smith, regardless of whether or not he believed she was a call girl.

This is so dangerous.

But she could no sooner have turned back now than ceased to breathe.

'And anyway, here we are.' As he doors sprang open again, he ushered her out, his fingertips just touching her back. It was a light contact, but seemed powerful out of all proportion, and Lizzie found herself almost trotting as they hurried along the short corridor to John's room.

As he let her in, she smiled. She'd not really taken much note of their surroundings as they'd walked, but the room itself was notable. Spacious, but strangely old-fashioned in some ways, almost kitsch. The linens were in chintz, with warm red notes, and the carpet was the colour of vin rouge. It was a bizarre look, compared to the spare lines and neutrals of most modern hotels, but, then, the Waverley Grange Hotel *was* a strange place, both exclusive and with a frisky, whispered reputation. Lizzie had been to functions here before, but had never seen the accommodation, although she'd heard about the legendary chintz-clad love-nests of the Waverley from Brent's taller tales.

'Quite something, isn't it?' John grinned, indicating the deliciously blowsy décor with an open hand.

'Well, *I* like it.' Perhaps it was best to let him think she'd been in rooms like this before; seen clients and fucked them under or on top of the fluffy chintz duvets.

'So do I . . . it's refreshingly retro. I like old-fashioned things.' His blue eyes flicked to her 'Bettie' hair, her pencil skirt and her angora.

Lizzie realised she was hanging back, barely through the doorway. Now *that* wasn't confidence; she'd better shape up. She sashayed forward to the bed, and sat down on it, trying to project sangfroid. 'That's good to know.' Her own voice sounded odd to her, and she could hardly hear it over the pounding of her heart and the rush of blood in her veins.

John paused by the wardrobe, slipping off his jacket and putting it on a hanger. So normal, so everyday. 'Aren't you going to phone your agency? That's what girls usually do about now. They always slip off to the bathroom and I hear them muttering.'

Oops, she was giving herself away. He'd suss her out any moment, if he hadn't already. 'I'm . . . I'm an independent.' She flashed through her brain, trying to remember things Brent had told her, and stuff from *Secret Diary of a Call Girl* on the telly. 'But I think I will call someone, if you don't mind.' Springing up again, she headed for the other door in the room. It had to lead to the bathroom.

'Of course . . . but aren't you forgetting something?'

Oh God, yes, the money!

'Three hundred.' It was a wild guess; it sounded right.

Sandy eyebrows quirked. 'Very reasonable. I was happy to pay five, at least.'

'That's my basic,' she said, still thinking, thinking. 'If you find you want something fancier, we can renegotiate.'

Why the hell had she said that? Why? Why? Why? What if he wanted something kinky? Something nasty? He didn't look that way, but who knew?

'Fancy, eh? I'll give it some thought. But in the meantime, let's start with the basic.' Reaching into his jacket pocket, he slipped out the black wallet again, and peeled off fifties. 'There,' he said, placing the notes on the top of the sideboard.

Lizzie scooped them up as she passed, heading for the bathroom, but John stayed her with a hand on her arm, light but implacable.

'Do you kiss? I know some girls don't.'

She looked at his mouth, especially his beautiful lower lip, so velvety yet determined.

'Yes, I kiss.'

'Well, then, I'll kiss you when you come back. Now make your call.'

2

Something Fancy

Well, well, then, 'Bettie Page', what on earth did I do to receive a gift like you? A beautiful, feisty, retro girl who's suddenly appeared to me like an angel from 1950s heaven?

John Smith considered having another drink from the mini bar, but, after a moment, he decided he didn't need one. He was intoxicated enough already, after the barely more than a mouthful of gin he'd drunk downstairs. Far more excited than he'd been by a woman in a long time, and certainly more turned on than he'd ever been with an escort before. Not that he'd been with a professional woman in a while. Not that he'd been with a lot of them anyway.

It was interesting, though, to pretend to Bettie that he had.

Sinking into one of the big chintz armchairs, he took a breath and centred himself, marshalling his feelings. Yes, this was a crazy situation, but he was having fun, so why deny it? And she was too, this unusual young woman with her vintage style and her emotions all over her face. That challenging smile was unmistakeable.

'Bettie, eh?'

Not her real name, he was sure, but perhaps near to it.

She looked the part for Bettie Page, though. She had the same combination of innocence, yet overflowing sensuality. Naughtiness. Yes, that was perfect for her. But *how* naughty? As an escort she probably took most things, everything, in her stride. Surely she wouldn't balk at his favoured activities? And yet, despite her profession, there was that strangely untouched quality to her, just like the legendary Bettie. A sweet freshness. A wholesomeness, idiotic as that sounded.

How long had she been in the game, he wondered. What if she was new to this? She was certainly far younger than his usual preference. His choice was normally for sleek, groomed, experienced women in their thirties, courtesans rather than call girls, ladies of the world. There might be a good deal of pleasure, though, in giving something to *her* in return for her services, something more than simply the money. Satisfaction, something new . . . a little adventure, more than just the job.

Now there was the real trick, the deeper game. And with any luck, a working girl who styled herself as 'Bettie' and who was prepared to take a client on the fly, after barely five minutes' chat, was bold enough to play it.

Suddenly he wasn't as bored with life and business as he'd been half an hour ago. Suddenly, his gathering unease about the paths he'd chosen, the insidious phantoms of loss and guilt, and the horrid, circling feeling that his life was ultimately empty, all slipped away from him. Suddenly he felt as if he were a young man again, full of dreams. A player; excited, hopeful, potent.

When he touched his cock it was as hard as stone, risen and eager.

'Come on, Bettie,' he whispered to himself, smiling as his

heart rose too, with anticipation. 'Hurry up, because if you don't, I'll come in there and get you.'

When Lizzie emerged from the bathroom the first thing she saw was another small pile of banknotes on the dresser.

'Just in case I have a hankering for "fancy",' said John amiably. He was lounging on the bed, still fully dressed, although his shoes were lying on their sides on the carpet where he'd obviously kicked them off.

'Oh, right . . . OK.'

Fancy? What did fancy mean? A bit of bondage? Spanking? Nothing too weird, she hoped. But it might mean they needed 'accessories' and she had none. You don't take plastic spanking paddles and fluffy handcuffs to the posher kind of birthday party, which was what she was supposed to be at.

'I don't have any toys with me. Just these.' The words came out on a breath she hadn't realised she was holding, and louder than she'd meant to. She opened her palm to reveal the couple of condoms she'd had stashed in the bottom of her bag. 'I wasn't originally planning to work tonight, but the event I was at was a bit tedious, so I thought I'd take a chance in the bar . . . you know, waste not, want not.'

What the hell am I babbling about?

John grinned from his position of comfort and relaxation. A tricky grin, as sunny as before, but with an edge. He was in charge, and he knew it. Maybe that was the 'fancy'?

Something slow and snaky and honeyed rolled in her belly. A delicious sensation, scary but making her blood tingle. His blue eyes narrowed as if he were monitoring her physical responses remotely, and the surge of desire swelled again, and grew.

She'd played jokey little dominance and submission games with a couple of her boyfriends. Just a bit of fun, something to spice things up. But it had never quite lived up to her expectations. Never delivered. Mainly because they'd always wanted her to play the dominatrix for them, wear some cheap black vinyl tat and call them 'naughty boys'. It'd been a laugh, she supposed, but it hadn't done much for her, and when one had hinted at turning the tables, she'd said goodnight and goodbye to the relationship. He'd been a nice enough guy, but somehow, in a way she couldn't define, not 'good' enough to be her master and make her bow down.

But golden John Smith, a gin-drinking man of forty-something, with laughter lines and a look of beautiful world-weariness . . . well, he *was* 'good' enough. Her belly trembled and silky fluid pooled in her sex, shocking and quick.

Now was the moment to stop being a fake, if she could. Maybe explain, and then perhaps even go on with a new game? And yet she could barely speak. He wasn't speaking either, just looking at her with those eyes that seemed to see all. With a little tilt of his head, he told her not to explain or question or break the spell.

But just when she thought she might break down and scream from the tension, he did speak.

'Toys aren't always necessary, Bettie. You of all people should know that.'

Had she blown it? Maybe . . . maybe not. Schooling herself not to falter, she shrugged and moved towards him. When she reached the bed, she dropped her rather inadequate stash of condoms on the side table and said, 'Of course . . . you're so right. And I love to improvise, don't you?'

Slowly, he sat up, and swivelled around, letting his legs swing down and his feet settle on the floor. 'Good girl . . .

good girl . . .' He reached out and laid a hand on her hip, fingers curving, just touching the slope of her bottom cheek. The touch became a squeeze, the tips of his four fingers digging into her flesh, not cruelly but with assertion, owning her.

With his other hand, he drew her nearer, right in between his spread thighs. She was looking down at him but it was as if he were looking down at her, from a great and dominant height. Her heart tripped again, knowing he could give her what she wanted.

But what was *his* price? Could she afford to pay?

He squeezed her bottom harder, as if assessing the resilience of her flesh, his fingertips closer to her pussy now, pushing the cloth of her skirt into the edge of her cleft. With a will of its own, her body started moving, rocking, pushing against his hold. Her sex was heavy, agitated, in need of some attention, and yet they'd barely done anything thus far. She lifted her hands to put them on his shoulders and draw the two of them closer.

'Uh oh.' The slightest tilt of the head, and a narrowing of his eyes was all the command she needed. She let her hands drop . . . while his free hand rose to her breast, fingers grazing her nipple. Her bra was underwired, but not padded so there was little to dull his touch. With finger and thumb, he took hold of her nipple and pinched it lightly through her clothing, smiling when she let out a gasp, sensation shooting from the contact to her swollen folds, and her clit.

Squeeze. Pinch. Squeeze. Pinch. Nothing like the sex she was used to, but wonderful. Odd. Infinitely arousing. The wetness between her labia welled again, slippery and almost alarming, saturating the thin strip of cloth between her legs.

'I'm going to make you come,' said John in a strangely normal voice, 'and I mean a real one, no faking. I think you can do it for me. You seem like an honest girl, and I think you like the way I'm touching you . . . even if it *is* business.'

Lizzie swallowed. For a moment there she'd forgotten she was supposed to be a professional. She'd just been a lucky girl with a really hot man who probably wouldn't have to do all that much to get her off.

'Will you be honest for me?' His blue eyes were like the whole world, and unable to get away from. 'Will you give me what I want? What I've paid for?'

'Yes, I think I can do that. Shouldn't be too difficult.'

Finger and thumb closed hard on her nipple. It really hurt and she let out a moan from the pain and from other sensations. 'Honesty, remember?' His tongue, soft and pink slid along his lower lip and she had to hold in a moan at the sight of that too.

She nodded, unable to speak, the pressure on the tip of her breast consuming her. How could this be happening? It hurt but it was next to nothing really.

Then he released her. 'Take off your cardigan and your dress, nothing else.'

Shaking, but hoping he couldn't detect the fine tremors, Lizzie shucked off her cardigan and dropped it on the floor beside her, then she reached behind her, for her zip.

'Let me.' John turned her like a big doll, whizzed the zip down, and then turned her back again, leaving her to slip the dress off. He put out a hand, though, to steady her, as she stepped out of it.

She hadn't really been planning to seduce anyone tonight, so she hadn't put on her fanciest underwear, just a nice but fairly unfussy set, a plain white bra and panties with a little edge of rosy pink lace.

'Nice. Prim. I like it,' said John with a pleased smile. Lizzie almost fainted when he hitched himself a little sideways on the bed, reached down and casually adjusted himself in his trousers. As his hand slid away, she could see he was huge, madly erect.

Oh, yummy.

He laughed out loud. He'd seen her checking him out. 'Not too bad, eh?' He shrugged, still with that golden but vaguely unnerving grin. 'I guess you see all shapes and sizes.'

'True,' she replied, wanting to reach out and touch the not too bad item, but knowing instinctively it was forbidden to do so for the moment. 'And most of them are rather small . . . but you seem to be OK, though, from where I'm standing.'

'Cheeky minx. I should punish you for that.' He laid a hand on her thigh, just above the top of her hold-up stocking. He didn't slap her, though perversely she'd hoped he might, just so she could see what one felt like from him. 'Maybe I will in a bit.' He stroked her skin, just at the edge of her panties, then drew back.

'You're very beautiful, you know,' he went on, leaning back on his elbows for a moment. 'I expect you're very popular. Are you? Do you do well?'

'Not too badly.' It seemed a bland enough answer, not an exact lie. She had the occasional boyfriend, nothing special. She wasn't promiscuous, but she had sex now and again.

John nodded. She wasn't sure what he meant by it, but she didn't stop to worry. The way he was lying showed off that gorgeous erection. 'Do you actually, really like your job, then?' He glanced down to where she was looking, unashamed.

'Yes, I do. And I often come too. The things you see on the telly. Documentaries and stuff . . . They all try to tell people that we don't enjoy it. But some of us do.' It seemed safer to cover herself. If she didn't have a real orgasm soon, she might go mad. He'd barely touched her but her clit was aching, aching, aching.

'Show me, then. Pull down the top of your bra. Show me your tits. They look very nice but I'd like to see a bit more of them.'

Peeling down her straps, Lizzie pushed the cups of her bra down too, easing each breast out and letting it settle on the bunched fabric of the cup. It looked rude and naughty, as if she were presenting two juicy fruits to him on a tray, and it made her just nicely sized breasts look bigger, more opulent.

'Lovely. Now play with your nipples. Make them really come up for me.'

Tentatively, Lizzie cupped herself, first one breast, then the other. 'I thought you were going to make me come? I'm doing all the work here.' A shudder ran down her spine; her nipples were already acutely sensitive, dark and perky.

'Shush. You talk too much. Just do as you're told.' The words were soft, almost friendly, but she listened for an undertone, even if there wasn't one there.

Closing her eyes, she went about her task, wondering what he was thinking. Touching her breasts made her want to touch herself elsewhere too. It always did. It was putting electricity into a system and getting an overload in a different location. Her clit felt enormous, charged, desperate. As she ran her thumbs across her nipples, tantalising herself, she wanted to pant with excitement.

And all because this strange man was looking at her. She could feel the weight of his blue stare, even if she couldn't see him. Were his lips parted just as hers were? Was he hungering just as she did? Did he want a taste of her?

Swaying her hips, she slid a hand down from her breast to her belly, skirting the edge of her knickers, ready to dive inside.

'No, not there. I'll deal with that.'

Lizzie's eyes snapped open. John was watching her closely, as she'd expected, his gaze hooded. Gosh, his eyelashes were long. She suddenly noticed them, so surprisingly dark compared to his wheat-gold hair.

In a swift, shocking move, he sat up again and grasped the errant hand, then its mate, pushing them behind her, and then hooking both of them together behind her back. Her wrists were narrow and easily contained by his bigger hand. He was right up against her now, his breath hot on her breasts.

Bondage. Was this one of his fancy things? Her heart thrilled. Her pussy quivered. Yes. Yes. Yes. He held her firmly, his arm around her, securing her. She tried not to tremble but it was difficult to avoid it. Difficult to stop herself pressing her body as close to his as she could and trying to get off by rubbing her crotch against whatever part of him she could reach.

'Keep still. Keep very still. No movement unless I say so.' Inclining forward, he put out his tongue and licked her nipple, long, slowly and lasciviously, once, twice, three times.

'Oh God . . . oh God . . .'

His mouth was hot and his tongue nimble, flexible. He furled it to a point and dabbed at the very point of her, then lashed hard, flicking the bud. Lizzie imagined she was floating, buoyed up by the simple, focused pleasure, yet tethered by the weight of lust between her thighs.

'Hush . . . be quiet.' The words flowed over the skin of her breast. 'Try not to make any noises. Contain everything inside you.'

It was hard, so hard . . . and impossible when he took her nipple between his teeth and tugged on it hard. The pressure was oh so measured, but threatening, and his tongue still worked, right on the very tip.

Forbidden noises came out of her mouth. Her pelvis wafted in a dance proscribed. A tear formed at the corner of her eye. He dabbed and dabbed at her imprisoned nipple with his tongue, and when she looked down on him, she could see a demon looking back up at her, laughter dark and merry in his eyes.

He thinks he's getting the better of me. He thinks he's getting to a woman who's supposedly anaesthetised to pleasure, and making her excited.

Hard suction pulled at her nipple and her hips undulated in reply.

I don't know who the hell this woman is, but the bastard's making me crazy!

Lizzie had never believed that a woman could get off just from having her breasts played with. And maybe that still was so . . . But with her tit in John Smith's mouth she was only a hair's breadth from it. Maybe if she jerked her hips hard enough, it'd happen. Maybe she'd climax from sheer momentum.

'Stop that,' he ordered quietly, then with his free palm, he reached around and slapped her hard on the buttock, right next to her immobilised hands. It was like a thunderclap through the cotton of her panties.

'Ow!'

The pain was fierce and sudden, with strange powers. Her

skin burnt, but in her cleft, her clit pulsed and leapt. Had she come? She couldn't even tell, the signals were so mixed.

'What's the matter, little escort girl? Are you getting off?' He mouthed her nipple again, licking, sucking. Her clit jerked again, tightening.

'Could be,' she gasped, surprised she could still be so bold when her senses were whirling, 'I'm not sure.'

'Well, let's make certain then, eh?' Manhandling her, he turned her a little between his thighs. 'Arms around my shoulders. Hold on tight.'

'But . . .'

'This is what I've paid you for, Bettie' His blue eyes flashed. 'My pleasure is your compliance. That's the name of the game.'

She put her hands on him, obeying. The muscles of his neck and shoulders felt strong, unyielding, through the fine cotton of his shirt and the silk of his waistcoat lining, and this close, a wave of his cologne rose up, filling her head like an exotic potion, lime and spices, underscored by just a whiff of a foxier scent, fresh sweat. He was as excited as she, for all his apparent tranquillity, and that made her dizzier than ever. This was all mad, like no sex she'd ever really had before, although right here, right now, she was hard pressed to remember anything she'd done with other men.

'Oh Bettie, Bettie, you're really rather delightful,' he crooned, pushing a hand into her knickers from the front, making her pitch over, pressing her face against the side of his. His hair smelt good too, but fainter and with a greener note. He was a pot-pourri of delicious male odours.

'Oh, oh, God.' Burrowing in with determined fingers, he'd found her clit, and he took possession of it in a hard little rub. Her sex gathered itself, heat massing in her belly she was so ready from all the forays and tantalising gambits he'd put her through.

'If you have an orgasm before I give you permission, I'll slap your bottom, Bettie.' His voice was low, barely more than a breath. 'And if you come again . . . I'll slap you again.'

'But why punish me? If you want me to come?' She could barely speak, but something compelled her to. Maybe just the act of forming words gave her some control. Over herself at least.

'Because it's my will to do it, Bettie. Because I want you to come, and spanking your bottom makes me hard.' He twisted his neck, and pressed a kiss against her throat, a long, indecent licking kiss, messy and animal. 'Surely you understand how we men sometimes are?'

'Yes . . . yes, of course I do . . . Men are perverts,' she panted, bearing down on his relentless fingertip that was rocking now. 'At least the fun ones mostly are, in my experience.'

'Oh brava! Bravissima! That's my girl . . .' Latching his mouth on to her earlobe in a wicked nip, he circled his finger, working her clit like a bearing, rolling and pushing.

As his teeth closed tighter, just for an instant, he overcame her. She shouted, something incoherent, orgasming hard in sharp, intense waves, her flesh rippling.

The waves were still rolling when he slapped again, with his fully open hand, right across her bottom cheek.

'Ow! Oh God!'

John nuzzled her neck, still making magic with his finger, and torment with his hand, more and more slaps. Her body was a maelstrom, her nerves not sure what was happening, pain and pleasure whipping together in a froth. She gripped him hard, holding on, dimly aware that she might be hurting him too with her vice-like hold.

'Oh please . . . time out,' she begged after what could have been moments, or much longer.

The slaps stopped, and he curved his whole hand around her crotch, the gesture vaguely protective . . . or perhaps possessive?

'Not used to coming when you're "on duty"?' His voice was silky and provocative, but good-humoured. 'It's nice to know I managed to make you lose it. Seems that I've not lost my touch.' He pressed a kiss to her neck, snaking his arm around her back, supporting her.

Lizzie blinked, feeling odd, unsorted. She hadn't expected to feel quite this much with him. It had all started as a lark, a bit of fun, testing herself to see if she could get away with her pretence. She still didn't know if she'd achieved that, and she wasn't sure John Smith would give her a straight answer if she found a way to ask him.

Either way, he'd touched her more than just physically. He'd put heat in her bottom, and confusion in her soul.

For a few moments, she just let herself be held, trying not to think. She was half draped across the body of a man she barely knew, with several hundred pounds of his money in her bag and on the dresser. His hand was still tucked inside her panties, cradling her pussy, wet with her silk.

'You're very wet down there, sweetheart,' he said, as if he'd read her thoughts again. He sounded pleased with himself, which, she supposed he should be if he really believed she was an escort and he'd got her as dripping wet as this. 'And real, too . . . not out of a tube.' He dabbled in her pond.

'It's not unknown, John. I told you that . . . Some of us enjoy our profession very much. We make the most of our more attractive clients.'

'Flatterer,' he said, but she detected a pleased note in his voice. He was a man and only human. They all liked to be praised for their prowess. His hand closed a little tighter on her sex, finger flexing. 'Do you think you could oblige this attractive client with a fuck now? Nothing fancy this time. Just a bit of doggy style, if you don't mind.'

In spite of everything, Lizzie laughed out loud. He was a sexy, possibly very devious character, but she also sensed he was a bit of a caution too, a man with whom one could have good fun without sex ever being involved.

'I'd be glad to,' she replied, impetuously kissing him on the cheek, wondering if that was right for her role. Straightening up, she moved onto the bed, feeling his hand slide out of her underwear. 'Like this?' She went up on her knees on the mattress, close to the edge, reaching around to tug at her knickers and make way for him.

'Delightful . . . Hold that thought. I'll be right with you.'

Over her shoulder, Lizzie watched him boldly, eager to see if his cock was as good as it had felt through his clothes.

Swiftly, John unbuttoned his washed-slate-blue waistcoat, and then his trousers, but he didn't remove them. Instead, he fished amongst his shirt-tails and his linen, pushing them aside and freeing his cock without undressing.

He was a good size, hard and high, ruddy with defined, vigorous veining. He frisked himself two or three times, as if he doubted his erection, but Lizzie had no such doubts. He looked as solid as if he'd been carved from tropical wood.

'OK for you?' Jiggling himself again, he challenged her with a lift of his dark blond eyebrows.

'Very fair. Very fair indeed.' She wiggled her bottom enticingly. 'Much better than I usually get.'

'Glad to hear it.' He reached for a condom, and in a few quick, deft movements enrobed himself. A latex coating didn't diminish the temptation.

Taking hold of her hips, he moved her closer to the edge of the bed in a brisk, businesslike fashion, then peeled off her panties, tugging them off over her shoes and tossing them away.

'Very fair. Very fair indeed,' he teased, running his hands greedily over her buttocks and making the slight tingle from where he'd spanked her flare and surge. 'I'd like to spank you again, but not tonight.' Reaching between her legs, he played with her labia and her clit, reawakening sensations there too. 'I just want to be in you for the moment, but another time, well, I'd like to get fancier then, if you're amenable.'

'I . . . I think that could be arranged,' she answered, panting. He was touching her just the way she loved. How could he do that? If he kept on, she'd be agreeing to madness. Wanting to say more, she could only let out a moan and rock her body to entice him.

'Good, very good.' With some kind of magician-like twist of the wrist, he thrust a finger inside her, as if testing her condition. 'I'll pay extra, of course. I don't like to mark women, but you never know. I'll recompense you for any income lost, don't worry.'

What was he talking about? She could barely think. He was pumping her now. Not touching her clit, just thrusting his finger in and out of her in a smooth, relentless rhythm. And when her sensitive flesh seemed about to flutter into glorious orgasm, he pushed in a second finger too, beside the first. As she wriggled and rode them, she felt his cock brushing her thigh.

'Are you ready for me?' The redundant question was like a breeze sighing in her ear, so soft as he leant over her, clothing and rubber-clad erection pressed against her.

'What do you think?' she said on a hard gasp, almost coming, her entire body sizzling with sensation.

'Ready, willing and able, it seems.' He buried his face in her hair, and nuzzled her almost fondly. 'You're a remarkable woman, Bettie.'

And then she was empty, trembling, waiting . . . but not for long. Blunt and hot, his penis found her entrance, nudging, pushing, entering as he clasped her hip hard for purchase and seemed to fling himself at her in a ruthless shove.

'Oof!' His momentum knocked the breath out of her, sending her pitching forward, the side of her face hitting the mattress, her heart thrilling to the sheer primitive power of him. She felt him brace himself with a hand set beside her, while the fingers of his other hand tightened on her body like a vice, securing his grip. His thrusts were so powerful she had to hold on herself, grabbing hunks of the bedding to stop herself sliding.

'Hell. Yes!' His voice was fierce, ferocious, not like him. Where were his playful amused tones now? He sounded like a wild beast, voracious and alpha. He fucked like one too, pounding away at her. 'God, you're so tight . . . so *tight*!' There was surprise in the wildness too.

Squirming against the mattress, riding it as John rode her, Lizzie realised something. Of course, he had no idea he was taking a road with her that not too many men had travelled. She'd had sex, yes, and boyfriends. And enjoyed them immensely. But not all that many of them, throughout her years as a woman. Fewer than many of her friends, and hundreds fewer than an experienced escort.

But such thoughts dissolved. Who could think, being possessed like this? How could a man of nice but normal dimensions feel like a gigantic force of nature inside her, knocking against nerve-endings she couldn't remember ever being knocked before, stroking against exquisitely sensitive spots and making her gasp and howl, yes, howl!

Pleasure bloomed, red, white heat inside her, bathing her sex, her belly, making her clit sing. Her mouth was open against the duvet; good God, she was drooling too. Her hips jerked, as if trying to hammer back against John Smith as hard as he was hammering into her.

'Yes . . . that's good . . . oh . . .' His voice degraded again, foul, mindless blasphemy pouring from those beautiful lips as he ploughed her. Blue, filthy words that soared like a holy litany. 'Yes, oh God . . . now touch yourself, you gorgeous slut . . . rub your clit while I fuck you. I want you to be coming when I do. I want to feel it around me, your cunt, grabbing my dick.'

She barely needed the stimulus; the words alone set up the reality. The ripple of her flesh against his became hard, deep, grabbing clenches, the waves of pleasure so high and keen she could see white splodges in front of her eyes, as if she were swooning under him, even as she rubbed her clit with her fingers.

As she went limp, almost losing consciousness, a weird cry almost split the room. It was high, odd, broken, almost a sob as John's hips jerked like some ancient pneumatic device of both flesh and iron, pumping his seed into the thin rubber membrane lodged inside her.

He collapsed on her. She was collapsed already. It seemed as if the high wind that had swept the room had suddenly died. Her lover, both John and *a* John lay upon her, substantial, but not a heavy man really. His weight, though, seemed real, in a state of dreams.

After a minute, or perhaps two or three, he levered himself off her, standing. She felt the brush of his fingers sliding down her flank in a soft caress, then came his voice.

'Sorry about calling you a "slut" . . . and the other stuff. I expect you've heard a lot worse in this line of work, but still . . . You know us men, we talk a lot of bloody filthy nonsense when we're getting our ends away. You don't mind, do you?'

'No . . . not at all. I rather like it, actually.' Rolling onto her side, then her back, she discovered him knotting the condom, then tossing it into the nearby waste bin. His cock was deflating, naturally, but still had a certain majesty about it, even as he tucked it away and sorted out his shirt-tails and his zip.

'God, you look gorgeous like that.' His blue eyes blazed, as if his spirit might be willing again even if his flesh was currently shagged out. 'I'd love to have you again, but I think I've been a bit of pig and I'll be *hors de combat* for a little while now.'

You do say some quaint things, John Smith . . . But I like it. I like you.

'Perhaps we could go again? When you've had a rest?' She glanced across at the second pile of notes on the dresser. It looked quite a lot. 'I'm not sure you've had full value for your money.'

John's eyes narrowed, amused, and he gave her an odd, boyish little grin.

'Oh, I think I've had plenty. You . . . you've been very good, beautiful Bettie. Just what I needed.' He sat down beside her, having swooped to pick up her panties, then pressed the little cotton bundle into her hands. 'I haven't been sleeping too well lately, love. But I think I'll sleep tonight now. Thank you.'

A lump came to Lizzie's throat. This wasn't sexual game playing, just honest words, honest thanks. He seemed younger suddenly, perhaps a little vulnerable. She wanted to stay, not for sex, but to just hug him, and hold him.

'Are you OK?'

'Yes, I'm fine,' he said, touching her cheek. 'But it's time for you to go. I've had what I've paid for, and more, sweet girl. I'd think I'd like to sleep now, and you should be home to your bed too. You don't have any more appointments tonight, do you?'

'No . . . nothing else.' Something very strange twisted in her mid-section. Yes, she should go now. Before she did or said something very silly. 'I'm done for the night.' She got up, wriggled into her knickers as gracefully as she could, then accepted her other things from John's hands. He'd picked them up for her. 'I'll just need a moment in your bathroom, then I'll leave you to your sleep.'

She skittered away, sensing him reaching for her. Not sure she could cope with his touch again, at least not in gentleness.

John stared at the door to the bathroom, smiling to himself, but perplexed.

You haven't been working very long, have you, beautiful Bettie?

How new was she to the game, he wondered. She didn't have that gloss, that slightly authoritative edge that he could always detect in an experienced escort. She was a sensual, lovely woman, and she seemed unafraid, but her responses were raw, unfiltered, as if she'd not yet learned to wear a mask and keep a bit of herself back. The working girls he'd been with had always been flatteringly responsive, accomplished, a massage to his ego. But there'd always been a tiny trickle of an edge that told him he was really just a job to them, even if they did genuinely seem to enjoy themselves.

But Bettie seemed completely unfettered by all that. She was full throttle. There was no way she could have fabricated her enjoyment of the sex; there was no way she could have faked the unprocessed excitement she'd exhibited, the response when he'd spanked her luscious bottom.

She loved it, and maybe that was the explanation. Most whores encountered clients who wanted to take the punishment, not dish it out. Maybe she wasn't all that experienced in being on the receiving end of BDSM? But she was a natural, and he needed a natural right now. Someone fresh, and vigorous, and enthusiastic. Unschooled, but with a deep, innate understanding of the mysteries.

He *had* to see her again. And see her soon.

Also by Portia Da Costa:

The Accidental Call Girl

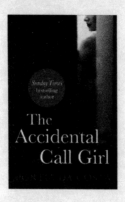

It's the ultimate fantasy:
When Lizzie meets an attractive older man in the bar of a luxury hotel, he mistakes her for a high class call girl on the look-out for a wealthy client.

With a man she can't resist...
Lizzie finds herself following him to his hotel room for an unforgettable night where she learns the pleasures of submitting to the hands of a master. But what will happen when John discovers that Lizzie is far more than she seems...?

A sexy, thrilling erotic romance for every woman who has ever had a "Pretty Woman" fantasy.
Part One of the 'Accidental' Trilogy.

BLACK
LACE

Also by Portia Da Costa:

The Accidental Mistress

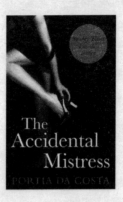

Seduced by a billionaire...

After being mistaken for a high-class call girl when they first met, Lizzie now enjoys a fiery relationship with John, her gorgeous and incredibly rich older man. Devoted, romantic and devilishly kinky, John knows exactly how to satisfy her every need.

But John has a dark side – and a past he won't talk about. He might welcome Lizzie in his bed – and out of it – but will she ever be anything more than a rich man's mistress?

Part Two of the 'Accidental' Trilogy.

BLACK
LACE

Also by Portia Da Costa:

The Accidental Bride

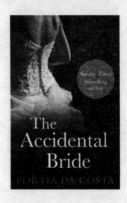

Marrying a billionaire?

It's every girl's fantasy but ever since meeting brooding sexy tycoon, John Smith, Lizzie has never been entirely sure of his true feelings for her.

   Has he proposed marriage because he truly loves her or just to keep her in his bed?

Part Three of the 'Accidental' Trilogy.

BLACK
LACE

Still can't get enough of Portia Da Costa?

Read on for a sneak peek at

THE GIFT

Chapter 1

'Fuck! Fuck! Fuck!'

Throwing himself on the bed, Jay gritted his teeth and rode the pain.

When the hell was this going to get easier? It had been over a year now. Well over a year of feeling as if someone was driving red-hot spikes into his joints and bones whenever he overdid it. Months and months of fighting the fight against taking weapons-grade painkillers. Surely one of these days he'd be able to run again without ending up feeling as if he'd been put through an industrial grinder?

Pulling his 'worst' leg up to his chest, he tensed and released, tensed and released, longing for the almost supernatural ministrations of his masseur, yet knowing such luxuries were off the menu for the time being.

One of the many prices to be paid for mixing business with the irrational pursuit of an adolescent dream.

Heaving himself upright again, he glanced around. It was an old-fashioned room, a little too fussy and chintzy for his taste, but immaculate. The Waverley Grange was a deeply weird hotel, but it was in the area and he'd wanted to stay here and find out what all the fuss was about. He'd

never seen his father quite as pissed off as he'd been last
year over this place.

The old man had had the Waverley in his sights, only to
be denied by an unexpected management buyout. At one
time, this would have pleased Jay mightily. He'd been at
odds with his father for so long. But in recent years, they'd
come to an accommodation, and begun to work together at
last. And now, the Waverley was ideally situated for Jay's
current mission of fact-finding and general reconnoitring
of the area. Not to mention the fact that the cable porn on
offer was first class, the hottest and most explicit he'd ever
seen. He'd never expected such a degree of sophisticated
cosmopolitan perversion in a provincial country house hotel,
but it seemed to be a speciality of the Waverley.

No wonder the old man had been niggled at losing out.
The thought of porn, sex and women made Jay frown. Back
to that bloody conundrum again. He shuddered as if
someone had stamped snow on his grave.

*I am so screwed up. I haven't a fucking clue what I want. Or
with whom.*

And yet here he was. Chasing a fantasy. Probably a
figment of his imagination. But one that made sex, and his
dick, come alive again, despite its confused and fragmentary
nature.

He reached for his wallet. There was a secret treasure in
it, something only he knew about, a little clipping from a
magazine, with a photo. The tiny scrap of paper was a
bridge between the present and the past. And an unlikely
fantasy that unscrewed his screwed-up libido.

*You stupid prick! Mooning over her like a moronic teenager!
Is this what getting mangled in an Aston Martin has reduced
you to? Weaving sick masturbation fantasies over an idealised*

memory, but struggling to get it up with a real live sexy woman?

Recent memories of humiliation and disappointment surged up in his throat like bile, but with a supreme effort he banished them, and returned to the panacea of dreams where he was in control, where his body was unfaltering and always obeyed him.

With reverence, he unfolded the clipping. He'd found it by chance in a local magazine, amongst his father's background materials, and the thought that he might just as easily never have flipped those pages made his blood run cold. Now, he traced his fingertip lightly over the gentle heart-shaped features and the mass of wild red hair of the smiling woman in the picture. She looked just the same as she'd looked fifteen years ago, if you didn't count the scrapes and bruises and the terrified, thunderstruck and numbed expression she'd had then.

You were a very very sick young puppy, man.

But he could still remember the slight weight of her body as he'd carried her, the scent of her fresh, girlish perfume, and the sweetly yielding softness of her lips, in that one brief kiss.

Kiss it better.

He'd meant it as a comfort while they'd been waiting for the ambulance, but shame washed through him even now, remembering how horny he'd felt, even while he was doing his saintly, rescuing knight act. He'd felt as bad, if not worse than he would have done if he'd been the bastard who'd knocked her to the ground.

He lay back on the bed again, holding up the little magazine clipping like a religious icon as his dick hardened spontaneously in his sweaty jogging pants.

Local café owner gets Fresh Food award.

'Alexandra . . . Alexandra . . .' he rasped, savouring the printed name on his tongue, his damaged voice rougher than ever because he was tired.

His bitter laugh rent the air. She'd probably tell him to take a running jump. She had every reason to. The twists and tangles of life's ironies were unlikely sometimes, but this juxtaposition of circumstances beggared belief.

'You'll probably never fuck me in a million years now, Alexandra, and yet you're the only woman I seem to be able to get it up for now. How about watching me toss myself off instead?' He shook his head. Fatigue and pain were making him demented. He was convinced the face in the picture had winked and smiled at him.

'OK then, a wank it is.'

He pressed a kiss on her image, and placed it carefully on the bedside table. Then, not without a groan and a profanity, he hitched his aching body around until he was sitting propped up against the pillows, with a perfect view of her smile, her amazing hair and those sweet curvaceous breasts in a pure white T-shirt.

He drew in a deep breath and then let it out as a sigh. He slid his hand into his joggers and took a hold of his penis. Fingers tightening around himself, he sank into a familiar fantasy.

Princess.

That was what he called her in these secret private moments. Because she did look like a perfect fairytale princess with her long red curls and her huge green eyes. And her hands that handled his cock as if she loved it.

Slowly, slowly she worked him, her imaginary hand cool and light, moving the skin of his organ seductively over the hard core within. She teased and she twisted ever so lightly, almost threateningly. Mm, just the way he liked a woman to touch him. Her fingertips rode him delicately, cajoling and coaxing one moment, ruthlessly pumping and pulling him the next.

Oh, God, yes! Princess!

But no, not Princess any more. Now she had a name and it was time to get used to it.

'Alexandra.'

Closing his eyes, he slid down on the bed. He didn't need the little picture any more, because now his mind showed him the product of fifteen years of visualisation, speculation and obsession.

In his fantasy, Alexandra Jackson peeled her pristine white T-shirt off over her head to reveal her adorable breasts beneath. His imagination dressed her in a lace bra, just the sort he liked to see on a woman. It was white and sheer, showing nipples like sweet dark berries through the mesh. As she wiggled out of what he speculated were a pair of skinny jeans, she revealed a tiny matching G-string beneath, a scrap which only enhanced the view of her pussy rather than impeding it.

No ballet dancer, no athlete could have been more graceful than Alexandra as she climbed astride him and, using her slender skilled fingers, guided him into her, pushing the fragment of lace aside. In his rational mind, he knew it was still his own hand that pleasured him, but since when had his rational mind had anything to do with this relationship? He'd had fifteen years to develop its verisimilitude.

Oh Lord, but you're tight! And so hot. So embracing.

In his mind, her expression was everything seductive. Her lips were sweet and soft and full, curving into a slow, greedy and deliciously lascivious smile. She was pure sex but at the same time fresh and tender.

Yet despite his lurid imagination, while fucking him she remained an enigma. And it was that sense of mystery, and the tight caress of her sweet, hot and totally illusory pussy that tipped him over.

White-hot pleasure poured down his spine, up from his balls and jetted from his penis. Dimly registering that he'd have a cleaning-up job to do when he was finished, he surrendered himself to bliss and blind sensation. He was a victim of his orgasm, a willing slave to it.

It took him a while to come down. He lingered in a floating hinterland between consciousness and sleep, not quite aroused, but skirting it, his mind awash with vague scenarios. Fairytale princess fucking. Perverse scenes from the Waverley's high-class porn channel. Fond memories of kinky experimentation, and the sexual adventures he'd indulged in prior to the day he'd woken up in traction and with his entire head swathed in bandages.

Finally he sat up, clearing his mind of fantasy in order to focus on reality.

It was time to take a shower, trim his beard, make himself as presentable as was possible nowadays. This afternoon he was heading for the Little Teapot Café.

Chapter 2

The back of her neck was prickling again.

Sandy Jackson spun around on her heel, and sure enough there he was, the man from the Teapot. The scarred husky-voiced stranger with militaristic shaven head and the roguish little goatee beard. The one who'd been scrutinising her so unremittingly that afternoon over his tea and scones. She wasn't sure what he was doing here tonight, but he was definitely the same one who'd never taken his eyes off her once. Even when her back was turned, according to Kat.

He wasn't watching her now. Or at least, if he was, his reflexes were like lightning. Right now, he was chatting to a handsome middle-aged woman, his stern expression mellowed by an attentive sexy smile, his dark eyes twinkling and flatteringly focused on his companion.

Git! I thought you were my stalker.

Irrationally jealous, Sandy turned her back on the aggravating man and inched away towards the edge of the room. She felt like a fish out of water at this Chamber of Commerce pre-Christmas soirée. She'd only come in the hopes of picking up some news about the supposed development of the old Bradbury's supermarket site. If the

surprisingly reliable rumour mill was to be believed, and
Forbes Enterprises was going to make it over into a new
open-all-day food pub, it might well mean the end of the
Little Teapot Café.

Forbes Enterprises. More gits!

Plastering on a smile, she fabricated a few bits of semi-
auto small talk with one or two fellow guests. Blah, blah,
blah, not long to Christmas now, eh? Blah, blah, wasn't this
place splendid? Blah-diddy-blah, did you know it has a
rather risqué reputation?

A waiter appeared at her elbow with a tray of hors
d'oeuvres and, still on automatic, she took one.

Mm, not bad. Something tomato-flavoured, a bit like a
large cheese straw. Before the lad could get away, she
grabbed a second one, a miniature tartlet filled with what
tasted like minced prawn in herb mayonnaise. Again, not
bad at all. She hoped that Kat, her cook, was taking notice
of all this stuff. It was always nice to try out a few new
flavours and more imaginative goodies in the Teapot now
and again, instead of concentrating on basic confectionery
and then simple grills and fries at lunchtime. If they could
grow their reputation for irresistibly moreish snacks, it
might help them survive the onslaught of that bloody fun
pub.

Her neck did the prickle thing again and, before she
could stop herself, she looked round again, searching for
Mr Hard-Case Stalker with the sexy goatee beard.

And there he was of course, but this time he didn't
bother to hide the fact he was looking at her. In fact, he
nodded slightly, tipped his glass, and favoured her with an
enigmatic half-smile.

Sandy flashed him a vague semi-smile of her own in

return, although she tried not to make it too encouraging. For some reason – she couldn't work out why exactly – she wasn't all that sure she wanted to talk to him. He looked like a brutally attractive serial killer, and there was something about him that scared her and made her nerves twang. He was probably perfectly nice when you actually got to know him, but looking at him now was like having him walk straight through her soul.

Not my type. Not at all. Too battered. Too macho. Probably far too complicated.

The wine in her glass was indifferent, but she sipped at it anyway. It wasn't strong enough to act as an anaesthetic, but she had to do something to take her mind off 'The Man'.

And her feet. Why in God's name had she let Kat persuade her into wearing these stupid heels? They looked fabulous and did wonders for her legs. But they were seriously killing her and it demanded an Oscar-winning performance just trying not to show it. Sweat popped out at her hairline as she smiled brightly at one of the Teapot's patrons, wishing someone would turn the central heating down. If she needed to make a quick getaway, she certainly couldn't run for it tonight.

A psychic sideswipe made her almost spill her dreary wine.

Getaway?

A powerful fist seemed to clutch her innards.

What, after all this time? Why think of such ancient history all of a sudden?

A memory both sharp and fuzzy zipped through her mind, bringing with it cold fear and the warm fleeting image of a face. A smooth young male face, almost angelically handsome. Long, thick, rather shaggy dark hair. A soft voice and soft lips on hers, her saviour whispering, 'Kiss it better.'

But as soon as the impression appeared, it began to fade again, leaving her shaking her head and, back in the present, glancing around.

Shrugging off the last of her disorientation, she focused on her surroundings.

This was the first time she'd ever been to the Waverley Grange Hotel and, probably like most people here, she was curious about its rumoured reputation. The place was supposed to be a den of rampant sexual iniquity beneath its sleek veneer of luxury and old-world charm, and some of the prints on the wall of the Lawns Bar certainly seemed to confirm the provocative whisperings.

Sandy fanned herself with her fingers. God, it was hot in here. And that was even before you got near the saucy artwork.

In front of her was a stylised photograph of a naked couple tangled up in a complex mandala of limbs, sweat and sensuality. Sandy sincerely hoped the rather prim Mayor's wife didn't catch sight of it, because its blazing frankness made her own blood stir and pulse. The man's hand was between the woman's legs and, even though the resolution was indistinct, she could almost feel those ghostly fingers touching her. They seemed to move in the cleft of her pussy, stroking and paddling and playing. She almost whirled around again, imagining the man from the café just behind her. Or maybe someone else, someone impossible, from a dream.

The sensation made her giddy, and the claustrophobic crush of real bodies around her made her heart trip.

Excusing herself, she slid away between two other art connoisseurs who'd been attracted to the photograph. Someone wasn't using quite a strong enough deodorant, and she wrinkled her nose as she moved on in search of fresher air.

Next to a window, she found another art photograph on the wall. It showed a handsome man with long dark hair also standing beside a window, in dramatic shadows. He was gazing out into the middle distance with a pensive expression on his face and, like the couple in the previous shot, he was stark naked.

Not my type either. But you do look familiar.

Narrowing her eyes, Sandy leaned close, and then chuckled, recognising the rather sexy owner/manager of the hotel, to whom she'd been introduced a short while earlier.

'So, is he your type?'

Sandy rocked – literally – on her silly heels. She knew exactly who was standing beside her, and the deep and strangely raw voice really seemed to fit him. She'd only heard it briefly in the Teapot because Kat had served him, but it was unmistakeable, never to be forgotten.

Schooling herself to stay calm, she turned slowly towards the hard man with the beard, who'd been watching her and who was now only a couple of feet away.

'Not really.' She dared to look up at him. His eyes were sharp and intelligent, dark grey and glinting with a strange disquieting light. Shaken, she returned her attention to the man in the photo – the rather glamorous Signor Guidetti. 'But I do believe that's our esteemed host, the hotel manager.'

'Indeed it is.'

For several seconds, they stared at the image in silence, then, as one, they scanned the room, looking for the hotel's suave, slightly flashy Italian proprietor.

'So, why isn't he your type?'

Put on the spot, Sandy frowned. What business was it of his? Yet still the ghost from her past resurfaced.

'He's too groomed. Too slick. Too perfect.'

Unlike you.

She suppressed a flinch. Up close, her tough-looking man was tougher than ever. Tall, he towered above her, his shoulders broad and his lean yet muscular limbs strong looking beneath a rather beautiful lightweight suit in midnight grey. His buzz-cut hair was dark and looked velvety against his fine nobly shaped skull. He had the look of a Roman emperor, civilised yet savage.

But it was his face most of all that made her swallow. She was both intrigued by it and also faintly frightened. His features were even, sculpted and masculine, and just as imperial as his cropped hair. But the network of fine white and pink scars that traced the planes of his high cheekbones, his mouth and jawline, framed by his crisp dark beard, spoke eloquently of pain and suffering.

'Unlike me.'

The fierce damaged face softened in a smile as he echoed her thoughts, and Sandy almost gasped. Once again, a fleeting sense of memory almost rocked her.

'There's nothing wrong with looking as if you've lived a bit,' she countered, regaining her wits. For all his scars, the tall man had charisma. And his strong body was affecting her, making hers quicken irrationally. Was he scarred all over? Were the clean hard lines of his limbs marked and battered? It suddenly seemed important to find out.

'Well, that's good to know.' His low laugh was as rough as his speaking voice, but Sandy felt it reach out and touch her like a phantom hand. Hormonal reactions fired throughout her body and she experienced a tingling all over her skin, as if her awareness of him was creating a subtle field. She'd been warm before, but now she was burning up.

'Care for another drink?'

Her companion nodded at her glass, which Sandy suddenly saw was empty. She couldn't remember drinking the wine, but obviously she'd been nervously swigging away without realising it. Another drink would slip down well, and soothe her parched throat, even if it was a tepid and uninspiring vintage.

'Yeah, great! I'd love one, thanks.'

She held out the empty and, as the tall mysterious man took it from her, their fingers briefly touched. Electricity seemed to arc between them, ramping up the tingling sensation. She suppressed a gasp as his dark eyes widened. He'd felt it too.

'Be right back. Don't go away.'

The urge to defy him, and run like the wind, welled up in her, and if her shoes hadn't been so bloody ridiculous she might have succumbed to it. Something about his broad dark-clad back as he walked away from her was deeply unsettling. Threatening. Everything about him made her senses leap and prickle and, if she was going to cope with that, she needed some air first. If he was sufficiently interested, he'd follow her outside, wouldn't he?

It was a while since she'd experienced spontaneous desire like this, and to feel it for a scarred and troubling stranger was just as unsettling as he was. But she couldn't ignore it or shut it off, hey presto. It was there, palpable nagging lust, low in her groin like a heavy and not entirely uncomfortable weight.

I should go. I should really get out of here.

Where was Kat? They'd shared a taxi here. She'd have to tell her friend she was leaving.

She's probably getting it on somewhere with Greg.

A sudden, sharp image of herself getting it on only heightened the spiralling sexual mayhem. She swayed as images rushed in again, but not the usual fairly soft-focus ones of her mysterious rescuing prince from years ago, or the occasional movie star or actor. No, this time the scarred and bearded stranger who'd just left her was centre stage. And he was touching her in a way that no imagined or remembered lover ever had. Doing things her cook had described getting up to with her sexually adventurous boyfriend, who worked here at the Waverley part-time.

Swiftly, she moved away from the photo of Signor Guidetti and walked purposefully in the direction of the exit to the hotel's reception area. Her feet screamed blue murder but she ignored the gathering pain.

'Leaving so soon?' enquired a voice in her ear as she attempted to sidestep a chattering knot of guests that barred her way.

Her mystery man of scars was holding out a glass to her. The wine in it was effervescing, and an exquisite pale gold. She had a feeling it wasn't from the general vat of industrial Chardonnay that everyone else was slurping. It looked as if the stranger had brought her a glass of Champagne.

'Thanks.' She took it from him, careful to avoid touching his fingers this time. She didn't want to spill a fine vintage all over him. 'And no, I wasn't leaving. I just thought I'd slide outside and get some air.'

It's December, Sandy. He'll think you're nuts!

Grey eyes like brushed steel narrowed infinitesimally, as if he didn't believe her story, and their controlling expression compelled her to turn back towards the centre of the room.

'And you were confident I'd follow and find you then?' He clinked his glass to hers, and then took a sip of his wine. 'Mm . . . that's better. Drink up!'

Sandy sipped, and then sighed spontaneously. Oh, what a pleasure! The Champagne was superb, dry and crisp yet almost buttery, the very essence of French glamour in a glass.

'Thanks,' she said again, with much more fervour, 'this is delicious. Thank you very much.'

'You can thank me properly by telling me your name.'

The steely eyes challenged her. Sandy felt her stomach flip. If names were exchanged, the game was on in earnest. She couldn't just walk away, because it wasn't just a casual but disquieting moment any more.

'I'm Alexandra Jackson. It's a pleasure to meet you.' She shuffled the strap of her bag on her shoulder, swapped hands with her glass, and then held out her right one to him. He swapped his glass to his other hand far more smoothly than she'd managed to, then offered a large tanned right hand that seemed to dwarf her slender paler one. There were even crooked white scars across the backs of his knuckles.

'I'm Jay Bentley. And the pleasure is all mine.' There was a wealth of meaning in the low gravelly words, and Sandy stifled a gasp as, between her legs, her sex fluttered.

'Er . . . is that a capital "J" or like the bird?' she burbled, saying the first thing that came into her head to cover her confusion.

'Jay' laughed, his sharp eyes narrowing. 'Either. Or both. I've never thought about it. You choose.'

Surely you know your own name?

'Like the bird then.'

' "Jay" it is then, Alexandra.' Reaching forward, he finally took her hand.

His skin was warm and smooth and dry, and Sandy was instantly aware that her own palm was sticky with nervous perspiration. She tried to snatch it back, but Jay held on, staring directly into her eyes as if engaging her in a contest.

'It's "Sandy" . . . my friends call me "Sandy".'

'So I'm your friend then, am I, Sandy?' He tilted his closely cropped head on one side, still holding her hand, still pouring a stream of electricity into her body that found its way unerringly to her groin. 'I had a feeling that you didn't really like me all that much.'

Blood burned in Sandy's face. He was right in a way. She'd found him intimidating, worrying. She still did. And much more so now.

'I . . . Well, I don't really know you yet.' She almost threw the glorious Champagne down her throat, insulting its magnificent quality.

'And yet you want me as a friend?'

Again that raw sexy laugh that seemed to play across tender sensitive areas. The man was starting to goad her, provoke her. Did she like him? She still wasn't sure. Especially as there was the possibility he was stalking her.

But you want him, Sandy, don't you? Boy, how you want him.

'You know what I mean. Don't be perverse!'

His grin looked almost boyish all of a sudden, and lights danced in those North Sea-grey eyes.

'Me, perverse?' He took a long swallow of wine, his strong throat undulating against the open collar of his dark shirt, then paused, licking a droplet off his lips. 'Well, not in that way.' He finished his drink in another deep swallow. 'I'm a plain and simple man, Sandy. I just see what I want and go after it.'

'Like me?'

What on earth was she thinking? What had she said? It could be pure coincidence he was here. But then again, what was a perfect stranger who she'd first set eyes on this afternoon doing at a Chamber of Commerce Christmas party? She'd lay odds on the fact that he'd gate-crashed and, if he had, was it specifically to meet her?

His laugh pealed out, a rough sexy sound that drew the attention of folk nearby, mostly the women. The way they looked at him suggested that his scars and his fierce appearance didn't reduce his attractiveness one bit. In fact, their hungry glances told Sandy that the way he looked made him infinitely more desirable, rather like a glamorous pirate or some other ruthless sexy scoundrel.

'You're very direct. But then, so am I. As a rule.' Long, dark and splendidly thick eyelashes flickered down for an instant.

'I'm staying here at the hotel for a few days. Would you like to come up and see my room, Sandy Jackson?'

'No.' Yes! 'Of course not.'

She cursed a blue streak inside, feeling her face colour with a furious revealing blush. Hell, she didn't know this man from Adam but suddenly she did want to go up to his room with him. It was insane, it was dangerous and it was downright sluttish, but there was something about his strange, scarred but still handsome face, and his large powerful body that spoke directly to her own body, making it want him.

'Why not?'

'Because I don't know you. I'm not sure I even like you. And I certainly don't sleep with perfect strangers just minutes after I've met them.'

Jay shifted his weight between his feet, his eyes on her. She didn't know how he was doing it but she couldn't seem to move a muscle.

Her eyes moved though. She couldn't stop skittering all up and down him, noting his white taunting smile, his uncompromising haircut and the long muscular lines of his limbs beneath his good suit.

She also noted, with a thud of her heart, that he was starting to get the makings of an erection.

Looking up again, her face crimson, she found his eyes upon her. Dropping her gaze again, she focused on her glass, twirling its pointless emptiness in her fingers.

'More Champagne?'

He was laughing at her, the beast, laughing his arrogant sex maniac's head off.

'No . . . no thank you. I think I'll get some air now. It's been nice meeting you, Jay. I'll see you around. Presumably . . .'

Still clutching her glass, she spun and darted for the door, cursing the stupid shoes that meant she couldn't walk as fast as she wanted to. A second later, Jay was at her side. 'Good idea. That air you mentioned . . . It's too warm in here. I'll join you.' Reaching out confidently, he plucked the empty Champagne glass out of her fingers, and deposited it and his own on a passing waiter's tray. 'Let's go that way.' With his hand beneath her elbow, he began to guide her towards a set of patio doors that led out to the Waverley's gardens.

Disorientated, and fighting both Jay and her shoes, Sandy stumbled, only to be caught around the waist and held upright, almost off her feet, as if she weighed nothing. A piercing sense of déjà vu swept through her, and she teetered dangerously. Not pausing to give her time to protest, Jay gathered her up in his arms and began to carry her towards the doors to the garden.

'Get off! Let me down! It's just my shoes!' she hissed in his ear, but his grip only tightened and his smile became infuriatingly arch and he-man.

'All the more reason for me to carry you. Don't make a fuss, woman.'

Sandy's brain sent messages to her hands and arms to beat at Jay and to her body to wriggle in order to get loose. Her little evening bag swung on its chain from her shoulder as he walked and she felt like catching hold of it and using it to batter him around the head with. Yet somehow the nerve impulses got sidetracked, swept away by the raw power not only of him but of a deep persistent memory.

Transported across time, she relaxed, became pliant and curled her arms around his neck. She was suddenly living in the world of fifteen years ago, being rescued and carried to safety by her perfect knight. A beautiful Prince Charming figure, barely out of his teens, a scruffy backpacker, large and wonderful in his strength and kindness, with the face of an angel and long dark hair that tumbled to his shoulders. She even seemed to smell again his distinctive odour of male sweat and some musky incense-like cologne.

The expressions of astonishment and interest all around her seemed to come through a thick filter. The cocktail party was a million miles away, apart from one grinning wag who stepped forward to open the door for them. All that really existed was the warm haven of protective arms, keeping her safe and comforting her after trauma.

The crisp winter air of the Waverley's formal gardens rudely awakened her though, reminding her that she was a grown woman. She hadn't just been mugged, and this was most definitely not the romantic Bohemian prince of her dreams whose large hand was curved evocatively around her thigh. Instead, it was a rude and overconfident man who might well have an unhealthy fixation on her. And one who'd just seen fit to make a complete exhibition of her in front of many of Kissley's worthies and quite a few of her friends and acquaintances!

'What the hell do you think you're doing? I was going to get my wrap first,' she lied. 'It's the middle of winter and I'm wearing a strappy dress!'

Wriggling like fury achieved nothing, and she was about to escalate to thumping and punching when Jay stopped in front of a bench in a deep, hedged alcove, and set her gently down on it. Shrugging off his jacket, he swirled it around her shoulders, and then, sinking to his knees on the turf, he pulled off first one of her offending shoes, then the other.

'Your feet were hurting and I carried you,' he said, giving her a look as if she were an airhead. 'God knows why you women wear these stupid things.' He tossed the borrowed slingbacks away with obvious male disdain.

'If you must know, they're not mine and I was persuaded to wear them because they look good with this dress.' It should have come out assertively, but the sweet relief of being out of the horrible shoes was warping her mind. All she could do was lean back on the bench, wiggling her liberated toes and trying to get her bearings.

'Hobnail boots would look good with that dress as long as you're wearing it.'

Sandy's eyes had closed in bliss because her toes were hurting less, but now they snapped open.

Perfect knight-type compliments too?

She opened her mouth, but couldn't think of a single appropriately gracious remark. Jay's eyes were glinting with a strange, vaguely confused intensity. He wanted her, that was obvious, but there was more than desire there. Something indefinable and enigmatic and possibly not even connected to sex at all.

'Let me give you a foot massage.'

His rough voice was soft and low and, before she could answer, he took her right foot in both his hands, cradling it as if it were fashioned out of porcelain. Then he began to massage, delicately and yet with assertion, and what had been bliss became sublime, almost breathtaking pleasure. The sensation of his cool hands on her skin was like having an orgasm right there in her foot, and unable to stop herself she made a noise that told him so.

'Good?'

'Oh God, yes.'

What the hell am I doing?

She tried to wrest her toes from his grip, but he held on firmly. The pressure of his hands was unyielding without hurting her abused foot.

'Hush . . . hush . . . Why are you struggling? You like this, don't you?'

His fingers began to move again, pressing, circling, releasing tension and unwinding knots.

What is this? Reflexology?

Never one for alternative therapies, Sandy suddenly found herself an instant convert. His sensitive kneading of her metatarsals was having effects in most unexpected places.

Her sex. It was as if he was touching her sex. Stroking. Pressing. Fondling. Exploring. The impending orgasm was no longer confined to her foot.

'No,' she murmured, closing her eyes again, her face flaming. She tried to struggle again, but it was half-hearted, merely token.

'Yes,' he asserted, fingers still moving and circling.

Sandy slid down in the seat, her thighs parting. It was like being hypnotised by touch, mesmerised by sensation. All her negative reactions to him were dissipating like mist in the moonlight, leaving only a woman's yearning for his strength and his mystery.

He was intent on her foot, studying it closely as he worked. Sandy felt drugged and dreamy, her body loose now, and fluid. Her sex was soft, open and ready, and she could feel silky arousal drench the crotch of her panties.

It's a fantasy . . . just a fantasy . . . It's not real.

And it seemed that way as she shifted her hips on the bench, bunching her dress beneath her as Jay continued to caress her foot. Drenched in euphoria, she stared down at him, loving the dark fuzz of his hair as it clung to his scalp, and the focused expression on his austere face. There seemed to be nothing sexual in his expression, but in her gut she knew he knew precisely what he was doing. The foot massage was a deliberate assault, a careful strategy for seduction.

And God, was it ever working. Her pussy felt wide and

pouched. Surely he could smell her arousal? He was close to it, and her dress was thin and silky, and her knickers even less substantial.

As if he'd heard her thoughts, he looked up at her, and with one last squeeze of her toes he abandoned her foot and ran his long fingers deliberately up her calf, to her knee. He cupped his hand around the back of it, the very tips of his fingers on the underside of her thigh, then he gripped harder, shifting her leg a little to the side on the bench, making space. Edging forward a little, he grew closer, ever closer to the heart of the matter.

Seemingly satisfied with his position, he slid his hands down flat, one on each of her thighs, and began to edge the silk hem of her dress up her freshly waxed legs. The dress was dark green, slightly iridescent with flashes of emerald, and it seemed to fluoresce in the twilight as if reacting to a magnetic field, or just the presence of Jay.

Looking directly into her eyes, he slid the edge of the silk up to her crotch, right up to the level of her panties. His expression was more complex than ever. Hot and hungry, but with drifting shadows in the dark-grey depths of his eyes. He seemed to want her, but not like a normal man. There was a strange reverence in his face, as if he too couldn't quite believe what was happening.

Then, with a gasp, he pushed her silk skirt further, in a bunch, exposing her knickers.

Sandy felt weak, yet somehow also strong. Suddenly it was as if she were some kind of erotic goddess, exhibiting herself for his pleasure, and she sagged against the hard back of the seat, her body loose and boneless. Wanton.

Let whatever might happen now happen. She no longer cared about propriety or what was sensible. She no longer cared that she barely knew this unusual scarred man. All that mattered was the way he looked at her, and the way that made her feel.

And she could smell herself now. A gust of warm, musky arousal seemed to float up from her crotch, from the saturated gusset of her fine panties. They were thin and lacy, not her usual style at all, and tiny curlicues of red pubic hair escaped the confines of the elastic at the edges. She supposed she should have trimmed or waxed there too, but there just hadn't been time. Life running a small café on the edge of viability was always busy, and she was a practical girl, not a finicky fashion victim.

Two long, square yet tapered fingertips settled against the lace, flexing, pressing ever so lightly. The touch barely registered, yet at the same time it was the most profound sexual contact she'd ever experienced.

He'd been watching, watching what he was doing, and suddenly he looked up again, a raw question in his eyes.

Do you want this? he seemed to say. *Only say stop, and I will.*

Not needing to think once, let alone twice, she nodded.

His grey eyes widened. His entire face almost seemed to glow. Suddenly he looked divinely beautiful to her, beard and scars and all, and whatever was going to happen was right. Was good.

His flexible fingers hooked into the waistband of her knickers, and he raised his other hand to the job, tweaking the silk and lace down with both hands. Deftly, he teased the garment down over her thighs, and instinctively she lifted her bottom to help him take them off her.

As he tossed aside her pants, he let out a hiss of air, as if he'd been poleaxed, sideswiped simply by the sight of her fragrant ruddy-haired pussy. Before she could analyse his reaction, and this unexpected expression of awe, he dipped forward and pressed a kiss to her pubic floss.

It seemed perfectly natural to cradle his skull in her hands, and she gasped with delight at the sensation of touching his scalp. It was like suede, heated suede, as if he was running a temperature.

He kissed the surface of her pubic hair, nothing more, lightly nuzzling her and uttering rough male purrs of wonder and delight. She opened her legs wider to him, loving the strong shape of his head beneath her fingertips, and as he pressed deeper she felt him murmur something against her, a word, low and fervent.

What had he said? She could barely tell ... but it sounded like 'Princess'.

Also by Portia Da Costa:

The Gift

It's going to get hot and steamy...

Sandy Jackson still dreams of the sexy stranger who came to
her rescue years before.

And when she meets Jay Bentley again she doesn't recognise
him. Horrifically wounded in a car crash, Jay has both physical
and psychological scars and is more Beast than Prince Charming.

But he has not forgotten their earlier encounter either...
And all he wants this Christmas is Sandy in his bed...

BLACK
LACE

Also by Portia Da Costa:

In Too Deep

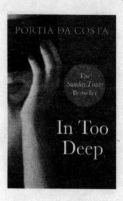

I just want a taste of you. Or a touch. My fantasies about you plague my every waking hour. My only comfort is imagining that similar fantasies might obsess you too.

When young librarian Gwendolynne Price finds increasingly erotic love notes to her in the suggestion box at work, she finds them both shocking and liberating.

But who is her mystery admirer and how long will he be content to just admire her from afar...?

The *Sunday Times* bestseller. *In Too Deep* is a dark sensual romance to fuel your fantasies

BLACK LACE

Also by Portia Da Costa:

The Stranger

Once she had got over the initial shock of the young man's nudity, Claudia allowed herself to breathe properly again...

When Claudia finds a sexy stranger near her home she discovers that he has lost his memory along with his clothes.

Having turned her back on relationships since the death of her husband, Claudia finds herself scandalising her friends by inviting the stranger into her home and into her bed...

BLACK
LACE

Coming soon from Portia Da Costa:

The Devil Inside

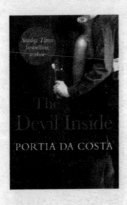

Just what the doctor ordered...

Alexa Lavelle is engaged to a man who doesn't truly excite her.
But on holiday in Barbados she experiences a mind blowing
sexual awakening courtesy of a sexy doctor and the devilishly
handsome Drew Kendrick.

Back in London Alexa is determined to keep her newfound
passions alive, especially after she runs into the enigmatic
Drew...

BLACK
LACE

Also available from Black Lace:

Fallen

by Justine Elyot

A lady of pleasure...

In the backstreets of London in 1865, James Stratton makes his living writing saucy stories for anonymous clients. But then he receives an enquiry of a far more personal nature.

Lady Augusta Heathcote is blind and has lived a very sheltered life, overseen by her watchful companion Mrs Shaw. But Augusta has a yearning to experience the intimate pleasures of dominance and submission and she makes James an offer he finds impossible to refuse...

BLACK
LACE

The Delicious Torment

by Alison Tyler

With every affair of the heart there are twists and turns.
Boundaries to overcome. Safe words to spill...

In a penthouse apartment overlooking Sunset Boulevard,
a dark affair entwined in a dominant-submissive relationship
blossoms.

Based on the author's personal diaries, *The Delicious Torment*
is a coming-of-age story fuelled by love, lust and longing.

BLACK
LACE